Serenity Heights

(a novel)

Other books by Bill Zaferos:

Poison Pen (a novel)

Serenity Heights

(a novel)

Bill Zaferos

Milwaukee, Wisconsin

Copyright © 2022 by Bill Zaferos
All rights reserved.

This is a work of fiction. This novel's story and characters are fictitious. Certain long-standing institutions, agencies, and public offices are mentioned, but the characters involved are wholly imaginary.

Published by
Three Towers Press
The fiction imprint of HenschelHAUS Publishing, Inc.
Milwaukee, Wisconsin
www.HenschelHAUSbooks.com

ISBN: 978159598-891-1
E-ISBN: 978159598-892-8
LCCN: 2022936327

Printed in the United States of America

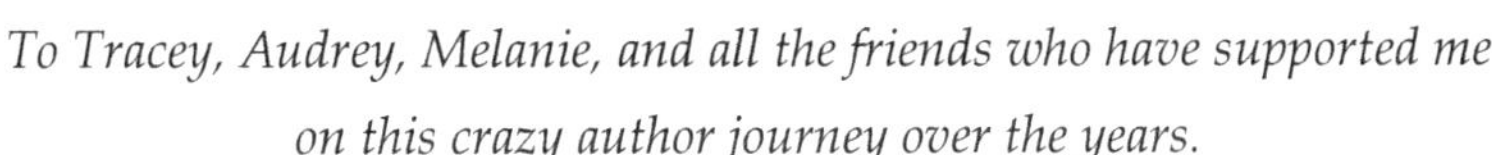

To Tracey, Audrey, Melanie, and all the friends who have supported me on this crazy author journey over the years.

Special thanks to Don, who used his literary skills to help make sense of it all.

And a big thank you to Jerry, whose keen eye and tremendous editing skills made this mess readable.

I love you all.

— 1 —

NIGHT SHIFT IN DEERHEAD, MINNESOTA

As a self-proclaimed rock-and-roll legend, "Rockin' Donnie" Derringer always thought he would die in a cheap, sleazy, rent-by-the-hour roadside motel room surrounded by empty liquor bottles, dope and a woman — no, two women — he didn't know or remember having met.

He thought it sounded romantic, even kind of cool for a has-been hotshot disc jockey. And if that was to be his inglorious fate, he was headed in the right direction.

It would be the perfect way for a frustrated memoirist, erstwhile comedian and sometime radio "personality" to skid into the afterlife.

As it was, Donnie was dying a slow death working the night shift as a disc jockey at a tiny, dingy low-wattage radio station in Deerhead, Minnesota with an audience that could be measured in the dozens. KYJL, "The Rock of Deerhead," was traditionally last in the overall ratings, to the extent that ratings even mattered in a podunk town like Deerhead. The radio station was the kind of place where old radio personalities like Rockin' Donnie crawled off to die in towns where death was a welcome relief from the boredom of small-town life.

The station's format was a tired mishmash of '70s rock: REO Speedwagon. Bob Seger. Rush. The dreadful poseur John Mellencamp, and the like. Occasionally Donnie would sneak a tasty obscure nugget like "Silver Tightrope" by Armageddon, "Born Late '58" by Mott the Hoople or even Buddy Guy's great blues song, "The First Time I Met the Blues" onto the night airwaves. Sometimes Hound Dog Taylor's "Gimme Back My Wig" would challenge his sleepless listeners.

Rockin' Donnie Derringer was *The Man*, a music connoisseur who knew more than you.

And he had better taste in music than you.

So there.

But whenever KYJL station management found out about his straying from the hackneyed "classic rock" format — and they often didn't find out because even they weren't listening to the overnight shift — he'd get the usual threats that his days were numbered if he didn't toe the line and stick to The Who and the Stones and Yes. He usually ignored the station management's warnings because he knew he had them over a barrel. Even the most eager young go-getter wouldn't spend a week working an 11 p.m. to 7 a.m. shift in a dumpy town in northern Minnesota.

So, here's "In the City" by the Jam, good people of the night. Or maybe some of The Residents' one-minute ode "Moisture" to freak out the stoners. Better yet, some Lightnin' Hopkins. Go ahead. Fire me, boss man. It would almost be a relief, he thought. But they never canned him because he always, or usually, anyway, showed up for work relatively sober, if a bit hungover or stoned, and ready to rock the night.

Mostly, he hated the music he was forced to play. He had grown sick of most of it by the time he was 30, and at 60, he had long since had enough of Aerosmith and their ilk. There were some artists — The Who, Bruce Springsteen, Janis (did she really need her last name to identify her?), Patti Smith, Dylan, Tom Waits, Jesse Malin, The Clash, any blues — that he could actually listen to all night if he had a drink and a joint. But except for Springsteen, and only "Born to Run," "Thunder Road," or "Dancing in the Dark," everything else was off limits at KYJL.

Management certainly wouldn't want night owls in Deerhead listening to the Sex Pistols or Public Image Limited. It would be too much of a shock to their small-town musical sensibilities.

Donnie tried to tune out the awful noise he was forced to play while he was pulling the graveyard shift. But it was nearly impossible to block out songs like the syrupy orchestral version of The Moody

Blues' "Nights in White Satin" after the 200th time. "Gathering gloom," indeed.

At least it wasn't Beyonce. But that was cold comfort when he was forced to play James Taylor or Fleetwood Mac until his ears bled.

He often relived his glory days as many people his advanced age have a tendency to do. At 60, most of his stories were the products of his broken drug- or alcohol-infused mind, and even by his own admission, his adventures had likely been embellished.

There was the concert, for example, where he introduced Rod Stewart and the Faces — this was long before Rod sold out and did songs like "Tonight's the Night" and "Do Ya Think I'm Sexy?" of course — and actually partied with Rod and the band after the show. That he could remember anything from that night actually cast doubt on whether he'd really been there.

The thoughts of those good-rockin' times were useless to him now. But they were his memories, and although the memories were fond, they also tortured him. They were reminders of what was and what he could have continued to be if he'd only stuck to some semblance of personal discipline.

Donnie felt like the worst kind of has-been: He used to be somebody. That was the worst thing he could think about himself. That the once popular character he had created for himself, "Rockin' Donnie" Derringer, no longer existed in the public mind beyond his small, restless listenership in Deerhead.

Rockin' Donnie Derringer was now working the 11 p.m. to 7 a.m. weeknight shift in Deerhead, Minnesota.

Unbelievable.

Donnie sometimes wondered what had happened. But the answers, if he cared to face them, were as clear as the gin and joints and coke that got him fired countless times from stations in larger markets. He always seemed to be on be verge of some great career breakthrough that instead left him just plain broke.

Sure, he'd had a sort of personal career pinnacle during a gig at some of the lesser AM stations in Chicago and Minneapolis, but that last gig in the Twin Cities came to a grinding halt when he had an on-air breakdown after he refused to go along with a format change to talk radio.

But when he was "somebody," or at least in his mind the radio version of somebody, he'd had his moments when he got to introduce some of the big acts like The Replacements at concerts and play "real" music during his show.

He always loved to party, although these days most of his partying took place alone in front of his TV or laptop. But there was nothing like blowing the roof off with the real gods of rock and roll. Smoking a joint with Bowie. Snorting coke backstage with Keith. Hanging with rock stars made him feel like a star himself.

Except he wasn't.

In fact, he was simply a purveyor of their music. Nothing more. He wasn't a superstar, he was a personality, not even a "celebrity," and by the time he realized the difference he had drunk and partied himself out of a dozen jobs. When he showed up for work that fateful morning in Minneapolis, still loaded and high from the previous night's festivities with some unknown regional band and horrified about the impending new talk radio format, Donnie had bolted himself in the booth and blasted The Replacements' Gary's Got a Boner four consecutive times while manically screeching the chorus during the morning drive-time shift.

"Boner!"

Funny!

But that was that.

It was Donnie's first breakdown, but deep down he knew it probably wouldn't be his last. He was a mess. But left untreated, he proceeded with his party-boy lifestyle until the money ran out and Deerhead was the only place he could get a job.

The breakdown came just before the Minneapolis station's metamorphosis into a talk radio blow hole. He had wanted to sign off by playing Hendrix's Woodstock performance of "The Star-Spangled Banner" and burn the station down on the way out, but they had already gotten rid of the station's massive record library in anticipation of the format change. Donnie sometimes brought forbidden music of his own to the station, and "Gary's Got a Boner" was all he could find.

He made do with his exit song and awaited the sharp axe of management's fury.

Donnie should have gotten help right then and there, but he continued his unhinged lifestyle unabated even as he lost job after job.

But yes, during his fabled younger days, he had had that snobby cult following on his Minneapolis show. He introduced listeners to acts like Lene Lovich, The Ramones, and a young Elvis Costello when the other stations were playing Peter Frampton's "Show Me the Way." He even got away with slipping in some Dead Kennedys or X onto the air once in a while.

Donnie loved X's song, "I Must Not Think Bad Thoughts." It was kind of a personal anthem.

But he did think bad thoughts. And he acted on them.

Rockin' Donnie had enjoyed a long leash in the early days of his career as a jock. But through excess partying and an inflated sense of himself, he choked on it. He simply went too far too many times. He was in love with his own wild-man persona. Station management, after a time, was not.

Rockin' Donnie wasn't a bad guy. Sometimes he did nice things for people, even when he himself did not benefit. He could be a loyal, if not always dependable, friend who helped many of his pals out of jams. He held their hair while they puked up that night's potables. He bailed them out of jail. He gave them money. He even let some of them stay with him when they were too rattled from dope or pills to spend time at home alone.

Donnie often talked his pals out of destructive acts, which was ironic given his own propensity for breaking the china and overturning the tables. Once, when a buddy suffering from a recent breakup had called him late one night to drunkenly say he was going to blow his brains out, Donnie, in a pot-infused stupor of his own, drove to the guy's house and spent hours talking calmly to him before he was able to relieve his broken-hearted comrade of the gun.

Donnie also had a certain roguish charm that attracted some women who thought his rugged, weathered looks and wicked sense of humor were entertaining enough for hot, but brief relationships.

However, his permanent relations had been broken for years. For myriad reasons he had lost touch with his daughter, who wanted nothing to do with a "rockin'" absentee father. His former wife, Sandy, gave up on him while he traversed the country with various bands he always thought were "the next big thing" but were instead regional one -hit wonders.

Eventually, the "Rockin' Donnie" persona he created became bigger than himself, and he always thought he had to live up to the hard-partying, rocking image of a drug and alcohol-fueled rock star.

His rockin' reputation always preceded him wherever he went, and he always thought he had enough of an image that smaller stations would hire him for his "star" power after the larger ones gave up on him. After getting dismissed time after time, it became painfully obvious that he could only get work in new markets, markets that got smaller and smaller as he wore out his welcome in larger cities. Wherever he went, though, radio became more corporatized and formats became more rigid, and Donnie's freedom to rock with a diverse playlist became even more limited than when local ownership controlled the stations.

So, he found himself trying to conform to corporate standards as he tried to hold down jobs at dinky joints where station ownership didn't care that much about on-air content as long as everyone stayed true to the format and the station was making money.

The limited playlists made Donnie bored. Such tedium was dangerous for a man who sought action and it often led to perverse on-air buffoonery. He was once fired from a station when he did his radio show without pants, asked his listeners to guess the length of his penis and dared his callers to see if they could make him erect.

That one left him jobless again and he had to contact old radio pals to see if they could help him find work.

After being repeatedly turned down for new gigs, he contacted a friend of a friend who knew a guy named "Hooter" Hurd. Hurd had a job opening for the overnight shift at his station, and after a cursory phone interview Hurd hired Donnie to DJ at KYJL, "The Rock," in Deerhead. Hurd liked to joke that KYJL stood for KY Jelly.

Get it?

As it turned out, Donnie realized "The Rock" was probably his last career stop. Even though he had always liked to tempt station management to can him, and although he still wasn't ready to admit his wild man days were over, he tried hard to be good. Since he had pissed away most of his savings and retirement on alcohol, drugs, and women during the course of his sordid career, he couldn't afford to stop working.

He needed this miserable Deerhead gig and he knew it.

Deerhead. His destiny was in a shithole town.

That in itself was torture. He was in a cage and there was no way out except to play crummy, worn-out music, smoke cigarettes outside the station all night long while playing Journey "double shots" and wait for his first opportunity to go home and light a doobie.

He felt like he was finished with life. He'd gotten married, had a kid, divorced and never found another woman to put up with his shit except for Liz, his occasional lover in Deerhead. So, he had done everything life expected of him. He'd spawned, kept the species going. Had a career, of sorts. What else was there except to enjoy a joint, some rotgut liquor and watch MLB.TV and NHL hockey or re-runs of The *Rockford Files* while heading into some kind of career glide pattern leading toward life's ultimate end?

He had begun as an angry young man. Now he was just a bitter old man.

Deerhead wasn't nearly as bad as Donnie thought. It had a certain wholesome, small-town charm. Peaceful. At night you could hear the frogs croaking and the cars roaring down the Interstate a few miles away. He thought he could grow to be content in Deerhead, and although contentment was a long way from happiness, it was the best he thought he could do at this sad stage of his twisted life.

Donnie initially could not see Deerhead's appeal. You don't criticize a mouse for not being an elephant, but Deerhead was not exactly NYC. Or Jersey City, for that matter.

Still, he made do in Deerhead. After all, his lifestyle was portable. He could smoke dope, drink brown liquor or gin, depending on his mood, and watch TV anywhere. He didn't need to live in San Francisco to do that.

Still, for Donnie, working at KYJL was an awful fate. In order to keep his sanity during those dark nights at KYJL, he took calls during his radio show on the decades-old dirty, boxy, five-lines-and-a-hold-button, no-caller-ID phone.

Mostly the calls were requests for shopworn "classics" like Queen's "Bohemian Rhapsody" or Kansas' "Carry On, Wayward Son." But he didn't always care how crappy his callers' musical tastes were. He simply wanted some sort of human connection at the lonely hours of three and four a.m. He took solace in the fact that his callers were probably lonesome misfits themselves, kindred dead souls.

He thought it was his duty to indulge them, and he talked to them all. Sometimes he even ran into them at wedding gigs where he was the jock. These people were fellow spirits in the night even if their musical preferences sucked.

Donnie and his listener cronies usually talked about music while a record was playing. They exchanged anecdotes about their crazy days. They talked about sports or how dull life was in Deerhead. They sounded as desperate for company as he was himself.

Most of them were bored insomniacs, and he got to know them by their nicknames. "Sleepy John" or "Mad Max" or "Charlie the Tuna" and "Rude Boy." He knew them all to the extent anyone can know anybody from late-night phone conversations. They were his telephone buddies, and in some strange way the empty night brought them together.

During those frequent periods when there were no phone calls, Rockin' Donnie mused about writing his memoir. Donnie thought about writing about his life a lot, although like most things in his life he did little to act on the impulse. He wasn't sure who would be interested in the adventures of a washed-up disc jockey, anyway, but it he thought it might be good therapy. Writing about his life could help him come to terms with how he ended up chasing dreams and hitting brick walls he himself had built.

Maybe writing would help him understand why he had consistently torpedoed his own career.

And his own life.

Writing, he thought, might help him explain to himself how he went from partying with Jerry Garcia to rifling tequila shots with guys with names like "Stiv" and "Snake" at Milt's Town Club Inn in downtown Deerhead on Saturday nights.

But one night, a night when he had actually jotted down a few notes for the memoir and none of his erstwhile late-night friends had called, his train of thought was rudely interrupted by the ringing phone as God-help-him Stevie Wonder's "Superstition" was playing. Thinking it might be "Hazy Dave" or one of the other creatures of the night, he picked up under the impression he would soon be discussing whether Jeff Beck or Jimi Hendrix was the better axman.

"Yeah, what?" he said, with the indifferent tone of an operator at the Department of Motor Vehicles.

"Hey there, Mr. DJ, this is Jerry Most, and I have a request," said a man on the other end who clearly was under the influence of some psychotropic drug that made him sound chipper even in the wee hours.

"Who?"

"Jerry Most, famous former host of the smash-hit TV show *Die Trying*," he said. "The host you like to toast. Or was it 'roast'? Anyhoo, don't you remember my show? It had boffo ratings. One guy even fought baboons before a record audience on national television!"

"Jer Bear, I don't watch much prime-time TV, or any TV show that doesn't involve a ball, a puck, or Jim Rockford. And why are you calling me in the middle of the night? What's your request? Maybe some Fleetwood Mac, post-Bob Welch and Peter Green? I'm sure some of that musical pablum would be right up your alley."

"No, my friend, my request is for you to appear on my new cable TV talk show and podcast, *Losers on Parade*," Jerry Most said. "While my small staff tracked you down, I myself have no other way of knowing your specific whereabouts, where you live and all, Deertail or something I heard. I thought I'd call you during the latter part of your graveyard shift at KYJL. The 'Voice of Rock' or something, isn't it?"

"Maybe it's my pot-confused brain, Jerry Most, if that is indeed your real name and identity, but I can't figure out how you found me. I'm not exactly at the high point of my career right now and I live in an obscure little village of the damned."

"Look, Rockin' Donnie, I may not be as prominent as I once was when *Die Trying* was ruling the airwaves, but I still have a loyal and highly effective, if tiny, staff," Jerry Most said. "They could find five of the FBI's ten most-wanted while drunk. Finding you wasn't as hard as you might think, even in Deerhoof."

"Thank you for tracking me down, Jer. It's always nice to talk to a famous game-show host, even if I don't know who the hell he is. But seriously, whatever you're peddling, I'm not interested."

"Too bad, my late-night zombie friend," Jerry said. "*Die Trying* was a great show even if nobody really died trying. Haw haw haw."

"Yeah, well, look Jer," he said, "'Superstition' is almost over, so I gotta run. You know, slide on "Stairway to Heaven" to stimulate my intellectually moribund audience."

"Oh, but wait. Don't go. I want to pitch my idea to you."

"Listen, Mr. Formerly Famous, the last time I was involved in a proposition it got me a night in jail. I'm kind of over-quota for propositions, lifetime. Why don't you just request a depressing song to bring you down a bit from your current manic state? There are a few I can recommend. Clapton's awful "Tears in Heaven" could make anyone suicidal. Or homicidal. Whatever."

"I don't want to be either," said Jerry Most. "Seriously, I really do want you on my new local access cable show and podcast, *Losers on Parade*. I'm trying to hunt down hotshot has-beens like you for the entertainment of hundreds, if not thousands. It makes for compelling TV and if all goes well maybe I can get a network deal again. You can tell your whole miserable life story to a national audience and get a little stipend. I'm sure it will provide some dough for you to indulge your drug and alcohol habits.

"You can confront your demons, not to mention the women you've burned, in front of a studio audience as I ask the tough questions to make you spill your guts. Maybe we can even dredge up some of your old cronies and gal friends. You can talk about the good old days with them. It's sort of a *This is Your Life* format for your miserable existence. Sounds like fun, no?"

The conversation had already gone longer than Donnie had intended. In the background, Robert Plant was whining the last few words of "Stairway." *"... she's buy-yi-ying..."*

"Um, no, Jerry Most, I'm not interested. Look, I gotta go. Don't want dead air in Deerhead. The locals might think the end of the world had finally arrived."

"Put on another record, Slick. We have business to discuss."

"Slick?"

"Yeah, throw on 'Layla.' That takes forever, or at least it seems to."

Since Layla was not at his fingertips, and since Donnie detested Clapton anyway, he grabbed another magnum opus, "I'm Your

Captain/Closer to Home" by the great Mark Farner and Grand Funk Railroad.

"OK, Jer, you've got about six minutes till the song ends. Or my patience."

"It'll take only three. I want you to come on my show and talk about your life. Your story will show how creeps like you eventually get their comeuppance. Even the sins of a low-life small-time, late-night, long-forgotten disc jockey would make for a great show."

"Why me? Why not just leave me alone with my records, my booze, pot, and misery?"

"Because you used to be somebody," Most said. "I'm guessing you're a bit depressed about your awful situation. I want to make you somebody again on our small cable TV station. A podcast too! I know how it is. I was a hot commodity once myself before my ugly divorce from the lovely Pinky Lee, and we could create a mutually beneficial relationship that gets me back on a network and gets you a job in a bigger market. Everybody loves hearing a loser talk about his life. It makes people feel better about their own horrible situations. It's a known fact that schadenfreude sells. Come on, really, it'll be fun."

"I'm sure it would be a blast, Jer," Donnie said. "I'll be happy to give you the grim details of this tale of self-made personal and career tragedy. If the price is right. I ain't cheap in spite of my circumstances. Or maybe because of them, I don't know."

"Oh yes, you'll be compensated with fabulous prizes," the former *Die Trying* emcee said. "I think. Here's how we get started: You just start writing down some memories, Slick, and give them to my staff when you arrive the day before the show. We'll have rounded up the usual suspects from your past by then and we'll have a nice trip down your tormented memory lane. The memoir will help my staff to develop questions for the interview I'll conduct live on cable access and the podcast. I'll get back to you later with more details."

"Yeah, okay, Jer Bear. Can't wait to hear from you. Ya know, I have kept a personal journal over the years and I've always thought about starting a memoir. When you take a look at my pot-riddled missive, I'm sure you can make me a star again," Donnie said acidly. "I'll grab my journal, light a joint, and start crapping out my chronicles as soon as I get home in the morning."

Donnie had no intention of sending his makeshift memoir to Jerry Most, assuming he bothered to write it in the first place, but he played along for the fun of it. Then upon further review, Donnie thought this proposal may actually lead to something. After all, Jerry Most used to be somebody, too, but he probably still had connections that would end Donnie's torpor in Deerhead.

"Yeah, sure, Jer, I'll do it," Donnie finally conceded.

"That's the spirit, Slick," Jerry said. "I, or my staff anyway, can't wait to read about your misadventures, be they real or the figments of your unglued imagination. Either way, I'll get you some great publicity and maybe even a new job in a larger market, say Poughkeepsie or Bemidji. Plus, I think we can get you a new fridge or microwave. Of course, that depends on my staff's ability to swindle would-be sponsors out of their merchandise."

"Thanks, Jer Bear," Donnie replied. "I'm a renter so appliances aren't really fabulous prizes I can actually appreciate. A tasty bale of pot would be among my needs, though. How 'bout it? That would make my decision easier. Plus, a little late-career advancement would be a welcome escape from this dump. But, hey, Grand Funk is getting closer to their home, so I gotta go. Dead air in a dead-end burg like Deerhead leads to job insecurity, even at this hour."

"Terrific!" Jerry said with mock enthusiasm. "I'll be in touch."

Jerry hung up, and once Donnie thought about Jerry's offer to vomit his life's misdeeds on television, even local access cable television and a podcast, seemed dangerous to what was left of his fragile ego.

On the other hand, how could things get any worse?

It was a question that was often answered in awful ways for Donnie.

— 2 —

THE RISE AND FALL AND RISE OF JERRY MOST

When Jerry Most was the host of *Die Trying,* a network game show in which contestants performed ridiculously inane and dangerous death-defying acts for cash and prizes, he was at the pinnacle of his career.

But he abandoned the show after granting the ill-fated wish of a death-by-baboon attack on a depressed small-town jerk who wrote poison pen letters for a living. As it turned out, the baboons were drunk and high from eating burned-down joints and drinking the last bits of vodka left in bottles left by under-age drinkers. The primates were so hammered they were completely unable to sustain a barrage and the sad-sack contestant escaped death, as did all of the show's contestants — and Jerry hit a slump.

Jerry Most, known for a cruel, acerbic wit he inflicted on contestants as well as his wives, tried to become Mr. Nice Guy with a new show about redemption called *Try Living,* a saccharine and mawkish human interest show. After initial success based largely on Most's popularity as host of *Die Trying,* the show was cancelled after a brief run and Most began to drift.

He went for several years without a TV show, but he lived off the riches he had gained as a game show host.

Before long, the nice-guy shtick faded as further career opportunities disappeared and he began to act like the bitter, mean-spirited jerk he had been all along. Being nice was just too hard for Jerry Most.

His return to form had cost him his third marriage to the beautiful but deranged Pinky Lee. It also cost him most of his riches in a nasty divorce.

After years of Most's typical verbal abuse, Pinky Lee had had enough. She had left him several times and always returned within days. But when Most, who was eternally jealous and suspicious, told her she was too homely and fat to have an affair so she had better get used to living with him, she took off for good.

Pinky Lee, who was actually quite attractive, was unable to conjure a rejoinder more creative than "Fuck you, jerk. I'm leaving," and walked out of Jerry Most's life forever. Or so Most hoped. After spectacular failures at marriage, Most had finally come to the realization that he was not designed for successful relationships.

His highly publicized split resulted in the loss of a good chunk of Most's fortune and his suburban New York — New Jersey, actually — mansion. Most was living in a two-bedroom condo a few miles from the mansion he owned with Pinky Lee. He could no longer afford to engage in a lavish lifestyle, but that fact did not deter him from spending like he still had it.

His fortune dwindling, Most decided to stage a comeback. He had enough money to hire a small staff and rent studio time on a local cable access channel in New Jersey. He would use the cable station and YouTube to grab the attention of network execs or thousands of followers. He set up a podcast. Most had used his caustic wit on a few too many network executives, so a national show was not an option for him. Not yet, anyway.

Jerry Most decided his fortunes lay in the creation of a new show where his dickish tendencies would be an asset. After several gin martinis one night, Jerry dreamed up a show called *Losers on Parade*, a show about has-beens whose famous lives had crashed into anonymous meaninglessness. He could be a jerk on television again as he viciously poked fun at his once-famous guests before a small studio audience.

In return, his broken guests would receive a small appearance fee as well as fabulous prizes like the refrigerator he had promised to Donnie if he appeared on the show.

It was only cable access and a podcast, and he decided to distribute it as a podcast as well. He thought a couple of raucous shows and a podcast would once again gather interest from the networks. He longed to be a national big-shot again, and he hoped the new show would be a ticket back to the Big Time.

Most made a mental list of guests who had fallen on hard times and would be willing to suffer public humiliation at his hands for cash, prizes and a chance to return to the spotlight.

Jerry was a music snob. He preferred jazz to rock-and-roll. He thought Miles Davis's "Kind of Blue" was the apex of human musical creation, and he had no use for most rock bands with the exception of The Who, Bruce Springsteen, and maybe The Clash. Even those artists were seldom heard in Jerry's home.

Anything from John Coltrane to Sun Ra was OK by Jerry Most.

Nonetheless, Most had heard about Rockin' Donnie Derringer's on-air meltdown and the "Gary's Got a Boner" incident, and he decided to listen to the song at some point. He thought Donnie would be a perfect first guest for *Losers on Parade*.

He directed his trusted and enthusiastic intern, Haley, to find Donnie so the erstwhile rock and roll legend would appear on the first show.

What would Donnie have to lose? Most thought. He had already done a sterling job of demeaning himself throughout his own rocky career. Most figured he could offer to find Derringer a new and better gig than the one he had wherever he was, and he knew Donnie would take the bait.

Haley doggedly searched for Rockin' Donnie Derringer and found him in Deerhead.

Jerry Most had his first target for *Losers on Parade*. Rockin' Donnie Derringer would help Jerry Most make his big comeback.

Jerry Most stood to gain on the back of Donnie's suffering.

Excellent!

— 3 —

DONNIE STARTS THE MEMOIR

Donnie sometimes thought he had a good story to tell. The story of a rock and roll legend like Donnie would mean a lot of book sales. His memoir would be a best-seller!

Right?

When Donnie was of a mind to write, which wasn't all that often, he always wrote in the dark. He usually penned his thoughts on late weekend nights when he didn't have a shift and his on-again-off-again sweetheart, Liz, wasn't around for a little action. The darkened living room and the yellow glow of his desk light, mixed with a little dope, some cigarettes, a little cheap scotch and good music — really good music — could sometimes inspire him to commit his story to a thick but largely empty leather-bound journal.

He had tried his hand at memoir-writing hundreds of times but usually wound up with scraps of thoughts. "How to handle Marie, the discovery in the laundry room, and the tragic breakup," said one, referring to an old girlfriend, Marie, a woman with whom he had been obsessed since he was young radio personality and whose heart he had broken.

"Was my childhood all that weird?" said another.

"What if my parents were spouse-swapping when I was a kid?" one entry said.

And so on.

As much as Donnie thought about his life, he had previously had no inclination to get his thoughts written in organized form because there was always something to distract him on TV. Maybe it was an old black-and-white crime film noir on TV. Or he would watch *Casablanca* for the umpteenth time. Or maybe there was an infomercial about a product that ended foot pain forever.

So many diversions.

He had no idea anyone else would really be interested in his story until Jerry called. His sordid tale wasn't really too distinct from the story of any other kid who grew up in a houseful of neurotics and alcoholics in a neighborhood where kids threw rocks at passing cars for entertainment while the parents threw key parties.

But the story was important to him in spite of his aversion from writing it. It might help to explain to himself how he became a drunk. A stoner. A serial womanizer. A loser.

How he lost Marie, the love of his life.

A lot of his life was really too painful to review, let alone commit to a written documentation of his beginning, middle and probably end. Most of it was just goofy, even fun to write about in a *Twilight Zone* kind of way. Harkening back to Marie's departure from his life, though, was excruciating and he didn't know if he had the courage to write about her.

But he would drive off that bridge when he came to it.

Before Jerry Most called, Donnie could have spent his days and nights avoiding composition of his chronicles.

He could have just watched TV or mellowed out with a joint. But for whatever reason he became a man on a mission. His new muse was Jerry Most, the biggest asshole in the world, and in some ways, he was grateful to Jerry for that. It was just the kick in the pants he needed.

Donnie was indifferent to whether anyone read or would even see his autobiographical missive. But he needed to write, and in the spirit of "writing what you know," Donnie began to get his life on paper before it reached some ignominious end.

Maybe, he thought, if he got published, his wild, self-destructive behavior would serve as a cautionary tale for those who might follow in his ill-fated footsteps. Maybe he could even make some much-needed cash from book sales, assuming any publisher was brave enough to publish his story.

Donnie got home at one morning about 7:30 a.m., after his graveyard shift at KYJL. He wanted to go to bed, but he was somehow energized by the thought of his writing project. It would break up his otherwise drab existence and maybe bring back some amusing memories.

Or some awful ones.

Inspired by Jerry Most, Donnie gathered his courage and his thoughts, opened his journal, picked up a chewed-on ballpoint pen, and began cranking out content.

Either way, he was prepared that morning to become the rock-and-roll version of Proust.

Donnie walked into to his filthy kitchen and made himself a peanut butter sandwich, a staple of his diet, to accompany some cheap Scotch and a joint so that he could think straight while he penned his life story.

Even the title on the memoir was overblown and prosaic, but he used it as a placeholder until a more drug-infused wave of creativity allowed him to capture a better idea.

Donnie decided to begin the account of his strange life in the recent past. He would get to recounting his barbaric childhood and early adulthood in a later entry, after he had conjured a few long-ago recollections. For starters, Donnie thought in this journal entry he'd write about his decision to try stand-up comedy because the memory was still thick and sore in his memory.

Could it also appear on a YouTube channel?

Donnie began like this:

DRUNK IN PUBLIC:
THE ADDLED MEMORIES OF AN OLD ROCK 'N' ROLLA

By "Rockin' Donnie" Derringer

It's hard to know where to start, how to describe how I went from a poor and highly dysfunctional beginning to a moneyed wild man middle and a dreadful ending in a dead-end town.

My life has been, if anything, abnormal, manic and fraught with peril. A tragi-comedy filled with self-made jams I had created for myself and from which I usually escaped unscathed.

Rather than go back to the beginning, you know, the old "I was born in a shotgun shack on the edge of town" cliché, perhaps a guided trip through the recent past will serve to explain how I wound up in Deerhead, a place I hated but where I was stuck.

First, I am a radio personality. A sometime celebrity. A disc jockey. I love music. Good music, and I am a snob about it.

I make no apologies about that.

I also think I'm very funny. Although some people think my comedy stylings are in poor, usually puerile taste. The radio offered me a stage for my spontaneous on-air antics, but deep down I wanted to be a comedian. I thought the stage would propel me to new career heights, heights such as the ones when I was a top-drawer, highly popular jester who drew great ratings for the stations where I worked.

But that career course came crashing down like a crystal chandelier in an earthquake after a few stunts went awry. The greased pig at the children's hospital, for example, delighted the youngsters but infuriated the medical professionals who wound up stepping in the beast's fecal matter in the sterile hallways.

Yeah, I've always been a laugh riot.

So, I'll begin with my career denouement in Deerhead, a puny town without so much as an offramp from the Interstate, where I eventually wound up on my life's gnarled journey after years of radio stardom.

My life in Deerhead was so dreadfully dull that I thought it would be the perfect place to experiment with stand-up comedy as an outlet. Since any on-air shenanigans at KYJL in Deerhead were verboten, I figured I could create some merriment on stage at a local comedy club.

I needed an outlet, and stand-up comedy would be just the ticket for the train to recovering my lost career. The comedy club would be the first stop.

Yes, Deerhead has a comedy club. And a main street cluttered with dive bars and broken glass from long-ago shuttered local businesses.

The comedy club, Laffs!, was a gathering place for those who did not want to be pounced upon by a local drunk looking for free liquor or worse yet be accosted by a hooker shimmying up and offering her services for the cost of two or three shots of high-end tequila.

Laffs! was a class joint. At least by Deerhead standards.

I didn't think it would be too tough to generate laughter from a bunch of bored rubes by tossing them some of the material I had developed over decades of debauchery, self-indulgence and regret.

After years of thinking about stand-up, I decided that Deerhead's brain-dead and inebriated denizens would be the perfect audience.

The results were, uh, less than enthusiastic.

I was always an "established" personality locally wherever I went, even working the night shift in Deerhead. But since I worked in radio no one really knew what I looked like except those who might have seen me when I gigged at weddings or appeared at local auto and boat shows at the local Veterans Memorial Civic Centers. Every city and town in America has some sort of public facility named for veterans. Honoring veterans is a fine and worthy notion, of course, but the naming idea always helped get political support to get the project built.

After all, who is against honoring veterans?

But I digress.

The idea of stand-up comedy always appealed to me, but until Deerhead I never had the balls to try it. I was driven by sheer boredom and the weed I smoked to stave off the torpor of small-town living.

I finally screwed up my courage for the stage by realizing that as a radio guy, no one knew me by sight, just by voice.

That meant I could be more or less anonymous on stage. My delicate ego would not be savaged by drunks because I would go under a different nom de guerre. The character I created, Mort Spiker, would be the victim if he bombed onstage, not Donnie Derringer.

I figured I would bring up all of the "A" material I had developed during years of considering the course of a peculiarly outlandish existence.

The audience would be in stitches!

As it finally turned out, my first and last attempt at stand-up comedy was fitting for my life, which was to say it was a disaster. I'd never had the testicles to try stand-up before in spite of the fact that I thought I was hilarious. But my life was so boring in Deerhead that I thought maybe a little something different would awaken the creative juices in me and make me feel more than half-dead.

Or half-alive, whatever the case may be.

It was open mic night at Laffs!, and I was Mort Spiker.

I told no one I knew in Deerhead, even my townie sweetheart Liz, that I was going to pull this stunt. For once I was a little nervous. The radio booth offered cover, but on the stage you're naked. Unlike most of the capers I'd ever involved myself in, I was highly insecure about exposing myself to further embarrassment by taking a stab at trying out my comedy stylings before a live audience of mean drunks.

I wrote a few jokes I'd been thinking of for years one late, dope-fueled night. I was always at my creative best while I was stoned. Or so I thought anyway. I memorized my monologue as best as my drug-infused brain would allow over the next couple of days. I was usually pretty good on my feet, so I wasn't worried about forgetting a line or two.

I could always improvise, I told myself. I always did on my radio shows, although those riffs often got me into trouble.

As it turned out I lacked the confidence to drive the jokes home. Or tell good ones, as finely aged though they might have been. The audience turned out to be tougher than my old man, a quick-fisted drunk who was easily offended. I hated the idea of being heckled, a hazard which is de rigueur for stand-ups, especially amateurs like me, an unfunny dilettante engaged in a one-off.

Too bad.

That night at Laffs! I nervously gathered my thoughts as I waited backstage to be introduced. Facing a live audience couldn't be worse than disarming my violent old man with a joke or two, right? At least I wouldn't get slugged if I died up there before indifferent drunks besotted with watered-down drinks.

And then...

"Ladies and Germs, please welcome the funniest man in the Zip Code, Mort Spiker!" shouted the emcee, a fat, slick-pated little man in blue jeans, red Converse All-Star high tops and a black "Foreigner" T-shirt that I hoped he was wearing for ironic effect.

As I heard my intro I promptly stumbled unintentionally as I walked on stage.

It would be one of the few outright laughs I received that night. But I strode onstage as if my stumble was intentional, grabbed the mic with artificial swagger and launched into my material.

"Good evening, everybody. I'm Mort Spiker and I have a few things to get off my chest if you'll allow me. How ya doin'?"

The sound of clinking glasses and soft conversation was all that could be heard.

"Hey, pay attention!" I called out as I began my monologue. "This is important! Get ready for some real hilarity."

Oops. I probably over-sold it a bit.

In this spirit I began.

"Did you ever wonder why comedians ask how the audience is doing? What are the poor slobs supposed to do? Say they feel awful? Filled with angst? That they need a Xanax? Some shots of Jack Daniels and a bullet in the brain? They're in a dumpy comedy club that sells cheap drinks, for pity's sake. How are they supposed to feel? Let's just go under the assumption that you guys are fine, just fine.

"Am I right?"

A few muffled chuckles rolled through the sparse group.

My stuff already wasn't working, but I trudged on.

"Seriously, ya know I've been looking for a job, but I never get past one interview question. I'm 60, see, so when they ask me where I see myself in 20 years I say, 'In the grave,' and that pretty much ends the conversation."

Nothing. Internally I was dying. At this moment the grace didn't sound too bad. Please laugh, I thought, this is a lifetime of material.

My next jest didn't help.

I paused and said: "Hey, everybody, look! Here comes the future! Wait! Here it is! Now it's the present and, oh shit. It's gone. Now it's just part of our lonely and futile past. Damn."

The sound of a loud belch penetrated the silence. OK, maybe that joke was too metaphysical for a bunch of small-town inebriates. Not a great start, but again I pressed on.

"I saw a mime on a street corner who was handing out fake dollar bills with nothing but zeroes on them. Instead of 'In God We Trust,' the bill said, 'Spend This On Anything.' The pantomimist gave me one, so I went out and bought a bunch of nothing."

No reaction. That one must have been over their heads. Let's bring in an animal joke. Everybody loves dogs, right?

"People must think dogs have low self-esteem," I said, then pausing and waiting for a laugh. I received no reaction. "I mean, why are they always reassuring them. 'Who's a good boy? You are! You're a good boy.' Let's face it, they're only good boys because you feed them. If you didn't fill their dish with some kind of kibble laced with garbage-like heavy metals, they'd tear your throat out as you slept on the sofa in front of the TV. Yeah. Who's a good boy, my ass."

"You're an idiot," shouted a gravel-voiced wit from the audience over the sound of clinking glasses and general conversation. It was probably the guy who belched. "Even your dog probably hates you, jerk."

I ignored him. No use battling with a heckler, and I had never had a dog in my adult life. Carrying on and trying desperately to relate to the bumpkins I said:

"When someone is choking why do people always say, 'Are you OK?' What is the victim supposed to say, 'Oh, of course, I enjoy having a chunk of tenderloin jammed against my trachea. Tell me more about your Florida time-share.'"

"I hope you choke on a chicken bone, dickhead," called out my foil.

I tugged at my collar like a worn-down Rodney Dangerfield.

"Wow, no respect here. No respect. No respect."

No respect indeed. But if I was going to be a comic I would have to put up with this kind of abuse. Heck, I lived through my nightmarish childhood. I felt like I was dying now, but I had spent a lifetime coming up with my material and I had to test it.

"Speaking of dying, I'd hate to be autopsied. After I die, of course. But think of it, you're dead, you're bloated and naked, not looking your best. But then some fiend is cutting out your sclerotic liver while making fun of the size of your cock. It's just not right."

Thick silence.

"Am I right?" I pleaded to the dark room.

Still looking for a connection with the boozed-up audience I asked again, "Am I right?"

The response was less than enthusiastic.

"No, you're not right. You're an asshole," was an anonymous woman's tip from the back of the dim room. "I hope someone cuts off your pencil prick while you're still alive."

I again paid no mind to my invisible tormentor. She was no match for Mort Spiker. Neither was the Neanderthal hounding me.

I decided a little self-deprecating humor might assuage the savage, if sparse, audience.

"I tried out for a professional baseball team when I was younger. I wasn't too bad but when you try out, they give everybody numbers on their uniforms, and the higher the number, the less likely you were to make the team. So, they gave me pi, because it's infinite."

The oppressive silence was pierced only when Mr. Gravel Voice said simply and cleverly, "Fuck you! You're not funny. I'd love to shove a pie up your ass!"

It was hard on the ego, but this was Mort Spiker taking the abuse, not the delicate ego of Donnie Derringer. I figured if I could survive my violent boozehound parents, who will later play a starring role in this memoir, I could endure a few liquored-up critics. I mean, this was priceless material, after all.

Wasn't it?

"Can you imagine the life of a kid who only wants two front teeth for Christmas? What the hell happened to him? Why are his teeth missing? Was it child abuse? And why would anyone want to say, 'Sister Susie sittin' on a thistle' in the first place? There's something dark about a kid missing teeth and begging to get them back for the holidays."

"You should sit yourself down on a thistle, moron," shouted the lout.

I fought an internal "fuck you" reflex and continued.

"I think it's a good thing Michelangelo wasn't afraid of heights," I said with a straight-faced delivery. "What if he had said, 'Fuck you, I'm not going up on that rickety scaffold!? Go find some freak with a can of Dutch Boy if you want someone to paint this ceiling.'"

I paused for laughter that never came.

Then it got worse.

"I have a friend who got testicular cancer, and I thought to myself, 'How the hell did you let that happen?' If there's anything a guy knows, it's the condition of his yarbles.

"Am I right?"

"No, you're a jerk-off! Cancer isn't funny," shouted an irate woman in an "I'm with Stupid" T-shirt and cut off, tattered jeans.

"I suppose you're right," I said with mock sensitivity. "Cancer isn't as funny as, say bunions or leprosy."

My audience found all of this in poor taste – of course it was – and a few boos rolled out of the dark. But I was on a roll. I was Mort Spiker.

Tonight Show, here I come!

I quickly changed subjects.

"Anybody out there like the old *Star Trek*?"

Dead silence. Jeez, I thought everybody loved the original *Star Trek*.

"What's the difference between a Klingon and a Romulan? They both look the same, and some of them were even played by the same actors. Couldn't the writers have come up with another type of alien being to attack the *Enterprise*? Maybe lobster people or something."

"You're a cling-on on my ass, shithead!"

"No Trekkies in the audience?" I asked.

A few people walked out and those who remained were determined to take apart ol' Mort. Still I bravely carried on.

"I went to a family-style restaurant but I didn't like it much. Everybody was drunk and arguing. Yeah. Family-style. Reminded me of home.

"That's like the guy I saw on TV, a used car dealer who said he treats you like family. Does that mean he slaps you across the face cuz he doesn't like the smart-ass look you gave him when he tried to sell you a 'pre-owned' Pinto?"

Again, this was not the audience for anything more clever than knock-knock jokes. Maybe my stuff was too opaque. Maybe it just wasn't any good. The family stuff probably hit home, though.

Just then the same voice rose again from a darkened corner.

"Your mother should have aborted you, jerk. Get off the stage. I want some laughs, not this bullshit. No wonder your old man slapped you around. You yourself should get cancer and die. I bet you'd think that was funny, too, you insensitive dickhead."

"Dad? Is that you again?" I asked pointedly, hoping to quell the discussion.

A few uncomfortable titters rippled through the audience as the tension built.

"Hey! Leave my mother out of this," I said. "If she had aborted me there would be no one here to make you face the facts of your failed life. Plus, she's on stage next and you can take a shot at her then."

The repartee was apparently just too much for these mouth-breathers. Mort's ego was disposable to me but it was, like mine, delicate and I couldn't get used to hecklers after all. I wasn't prepared for this. It was an open-mic, for God's sake. The few comebacks I had were stolen from the great Rodney Dangerfield.

I unloaded on the guy.

"Where ya from, pal?"

"Cedar City. What's it to you?"

Cedar City made Deerhead look like Tokyo. A perfect target for ridicule.

"Ooooo! Cedar City? You're a city slicker! Is Cedar City even a city? I guess your anger is rooted in your own life mistakes. Married your high school sweetie after your first lay and you got her knocked up and now you have to sleep next to the cow for the rest of your life while your snot-nosed kids snoop around the house and steal your pornos and your pot. Say, what's it like to have a sex life that consists of skin magazines and Mazola?

"'Fuck you!"

"What a wit! Maybe later you'll call me a dickhead or shithead. Methinks your imagination is a bit stilted. I know you are but what am I?"

A few people laughed out loud but the loudmouth had other, more homicidal intentions.

As the hick rushed the stage, I made a hasty exit out the back-stage door and headed to my car. I drove home miserable. Maybe I just wasn't cut out for stand-up, after all. A lifetime of material had bombed.

That was that for my comedy career.

An act of utter futility.

There you have it. "Rockin' Donnie Derringer," or in this case, "Mort Spiker," an erstwhile comedian and the alter-ego of a late-night jock who washed up on shore of an island that turned out to be desolate.

But that more or less ended the idea of being a comic. I had had enough abuse as a kid. Abuse was free and plentiful everywhere. I didn't need to subject myself to it at some open mic in a shithole town.

Donnie finally called it quits after a few hours of memoir-writing during that first sitting. He wrote in hopes he could use his dimmed star power to pen a bestseller and make something out of his once-promising life as an entertainer. But the gin bottle was almost empty, he had polished off a joint, and the sun was up. Like Dracula, it was time to return to the bed that was his coffin before the sun shone on his leathery puss. It was mid-Saturday morning and he had to be ready for Saturday night, a time when he should be out tying one on.

He needed some deep sleep, but he slept fitfully as he tried to recount any other incidents that could be added to his missive. After dozing on and off throughout the day, Donnie finally awoke for good around 4 p.m.

Just in time for cocktail hour!

— 4 —

ANOTHER PAINFUL STROLL DOWN MEMORY LANE

Donnie made himself some eggs and peanut butter on white bread toast, then fixed himself a gin martini, very dry. As he ate, he decided to spend a little more time on his memoir while his creative juices were still flowing and the memories of his childhood were clear. A thick breakfast doobie to accompany the martini would give him a boost as he recounted more of his twisted life.

He finished breakfast, threw his dirty dish in the kitchen sink and shuffled to the living room, where his journal was waiting atop a makeshift desk. He pulled up a folding chair, picked up his journal and a pen. He took a breath and began to write. This time he rambled, but he knew he could get his story out if he just kept writing. He could organize it later.

The result of that session was this:

> In order to put my tangled life in context, I have some 'splainin' to do.
>
> This account might help the reader, and the author, understand how the highs and lows of my life resulted in penance in Deerhead, Minnesota.
>
> At the height of my career there were concerts. There were pre-show parties. There were after-show parties. There were drugs and alcohol. And women. Lots of women.
>
> It was a lot of fun up to a point although the hangovers were so savage that only a little morning hair-of-the-dog could cure them.

It was as a result of all that strange behavior that I wound up in Deerhead, Minnesota, working the overnight shift because it was the only work I could get after a highly checkered past.

My adult life can best be explained by my childhood, a background that was weird, yet funny. It was filled with love and hate, hugs and abuse. Milk and cookies, liquor and pills.

The family situation was enough to confuse any kid, especially a kid with a budding mental health problem exacerbated by the creepy, bizarre environment he inhabited.

It's too easy to start with family life. Doesn't everybody use family life to describe their neuroses? To a certain extent, everyone in America thinks their family life was dysfunctional in some ways and was the cause of their raging madness. But I had been thrust by birth into a uniquely screwed-up scene. My family was nuts. The whole neighborhood was crazy. That didn't make me unusual in the typical screwed up American Dream sense. The whole country's a mess, after all.

But somehow, the tale of what I had become, whatever that was, has become a point of interest for Jerry Most, a former big-time game show host. He'll never see this journal — he'll have to do his own research if I actually appear on his dreadful cable TV show and podcast.

Here goes.

When I was a kid, I had terrible asthma and allergies. We even kept adrenalin in the fridge in case I had a bad attack and I had to give myself a life-saving shot. To their credit, my otherwise oblivious parents did everything they could to find a cure or the medicine that would effectively treat my seemingly hopeless condition.

Of course, it might have helped if my father had given up his four-pack-a-day unfiltered Phillip Morris Commander cigarette habit and thereby eliminated the blue haze of smoke that hung heavily in the living room like a San Francisco fog. Getting rid of the mangy two cats who lived in the basement might have helped, too.

But they once took me to a chiropractor in a futile and desperate search for a cure. After taking chest X-rays and conducting other tests, the quack determined that my problem was rooted in my irregular bowel movements.

Even at the age of six, I believed that was a load of crap, so to speak.

I was also very frail. In fourth grade, I weighed in at 45 lbs. When I left for college at age 18, I was a hefty 118 lbs. The culprit, I now know as an overweight adult mass of goo, was my mother's cooking.

We didn't have a lot of money, so Mom made do with whatever came in a can. She would serve bizarre casseroles consisting of peas, creamed corn, white rice, and whatever else she could cram into the pot. On Fridays, she would make the casseroles with tuna, the reasons for which escape me, because we were not Catholic and compelled to avoid eating meat on Fridays. The old man referred to this repast as "tuna asshole."

The dog always sat next to my chair, knowing that I would drop some of Mama's mash onto the floor in the name of a clean plate. Sometimes, even the hound walked away from the wretched concoctions.

Still, Mama and Daddy insisted that I eat everything on my plate because I was so skinny, apparently unaware that the food was inedible, even to the dog. If I didn't eat every stinking morsel, they would make me sit at the table until I accomplished the amazing act of swallowing the rest of the cold slop on my plate.

Since we lived in a small house and I could see the TV from my kitchen table perch, I usually waited them out with the patience of U.S. Grant at Vicksburg. I could sit there all night without eating another bite while watching Shindig, Hullabaloo, Get Smart, Mission Impossible or other classic shows that represented 1960s television fare.

Eventually they would give up and send me to bed. For me, being hungry was better than being sick to my stomach after eating the garbage I had been served. I would fall asleep listening to them argue about everything from what to watch on TV to mom's concerns about Dad's voluminous drinking.

As for the neighborhood, my earliest hazy recollection was one of my next-door neighbor Dick, working on a beat-up Ford Mustang in his gravel driveway. Dick was always working on the car because it never seemed to work. Now Dick, Dick was strange by any standards. He said he was clairvoyant, and he would often lie on the sidewalk, sometimes even in the street, predicting the imminent flyover by an airliner or the drive-by of a dark blue Mercedes. The fact that the Mercedes never materialized or that we were in the flight path of a local airport seemed not to diminish Dick's conviction that he could indeed predict the immediate future.

But Dick wasn't a clairvoyant. Dick was just a nut job, and that description wasn't unlike the rest of the characters in my neighborhood.

Dick's family tree was also filled with some twisted branches, much like the rest of the neighborhood cast of characters.

One of the two mutant sons Dick had sired, a kid they called Blinky although his real name was Ernest, was a real little shit. He loved to torment people in general with his imaginative mischief, but his father was his favorite target. Blinky's hair always seemed to be dirty, and his nose was constantly running. He ran around in blue jeans and a dirty, torn white T-shirt. He was often in bare feet since the calluses on his feet were impervious to anything but the glass from broken beer bottles which were part of the neighborhood landscape.

One day, Dick's head was deeply embedded under the hood of the Mustang. He was swearing and beating on some stubborn unseen auto part with a monkey wrench. He was not in the mood for another car breakdown. He had to get to his job at the carpet store, and the car wasn't cooperating. Again.

Meanwhile, Blinky, the little bastard, snuck into the driver's seat of the junker. Catching his dad defenseless while his head and upper torso were submerged, Blinky laid it on the car horn. Dick, startled and pissed off by the blaring noise, threw up his head and smacked it on the hood of the Mustang.

"Goddammit!" Dick screamed, issuing a blood-curdling noise that is probably still circling the planet.

Blinky, knowing the prank put his life in serious danger, threw open the car door and ran cackling down the street as Dick pursued him with the wrench.

"Come here, you little fucker, I'm going to brain you," Dick yelled futilely as he waved the wrench and ran wheezing after an elusive Blinky. Blinky ran like a cockroach and Dick lost pursuit after Blinky cut through the Smith's yard toward the next block. He'd be back by dinner, but by then Dick would be selling orange shags on second shift at World O' Carpets.

As dumb as Dick seemed, and as devious as Blinky was, they were only two components of a much larger tableau of neighborhood dysfunction.

So many memories. Like the time Mr. Wagner chased his son (and my friend) Wayne down the street with a butcher knife and drunken homicidal intentions.

Then, of course, there was the spectacular fire at the paint warehouse down the street. Huge colorful flames licked the night sky as the joint burned down to its skeletal remains and burning paint cans dropped to the ground.

Oooh! Aaah!

From then on, my friends Markie and Jonathan, two known vandals and petty thieves but otherwise fun, wise-cracking guys, became mysteriously quiet and would cast each other knowing glances after the authorities determined the fire was the work of arsonists. The code of silence and lack of evidence pointing to the pair meant no criminal charges.

Omerta.

We all thought it was funny when Dickie Shuster would walk around the neighborhood wearing his mother's panties, bra and a nightie. But we were scared when Dickie's father Elmore came out of the house during a drunken rage, armed with a pistol, and threatened to shoot anyone he saw.

When the SWAT team finally subdued and disarmed Elmore, all the neighborhood kids, who had been watching from a safe distance through their bedroom windows, thought it was the coolest thing since *Hawaii Five-O.*

Still, in our neighborhood everybody thought all of that was normal behavior — fathers chasing sons with butcher knives, kids egging cars and stealing Christmas lights right off of houses while the family was inside watching *A Charlie Brown Christmas*, mothers drinking themselves blind and block parties that wound up in street fights. It was all part of ordinary life.

Of course, strange begets odd and the kids in our neighborhood stretched the boundaries of even that definition of irregular behavior.

There was Eddie, an older kid known to be trouble who invited me and my friend Steven into his bedroom to show us his comic books. When Steve and I walked into his room, Eddie closed the door behind him and pulled out a knife. He then invited us to unzip our pants and show him our nine-year-old penises.

Since a knife was involved, and since Eddie was speaking in dark tones, we did as Eddie said, opened our pants and displayed our pre-adolescent wankers. Then, as though some powerful realization of the immorality of his act had just side-swiped him, he ordered us to zip up and get the hell out of the house.

"You two are perverts!" Eddie screamed at us. "You're fucking sick!"

We exited with great haste, although our race to the back door was rather clumsy as Steve tripped over a kitchen chair leg and I fell on top of him.

There was plenty of entertainment for the kids in the neighborhood, and some of the ideas popped up as we sat on the little bridge over a polluted creek in which we all played and caught frogs, crawfish and other aquatic wildlife while absorbing various water-borne pathogens and carcinogens.

During one bridge-sitting brainstorming session, Otto, Blinky's brother and a contemporary of mine, decided to steal a pair of his father Dick's blue jeans and a flannel work shirt, connecting them with his mother's yarn. He stuffed the apparel with newspapers and fashioned a head by cutting two round pieces out of Naugahyde upholstery that his father had intended to use to patch a hole in the family sofa, but never did.

One night, Otto dragged his lifeless Frankenstein monster to the bridge where three or four of us were hanging around and passing the time by throwing mudballs at passing semi-trailers. There was no moon that night, but a street lamp provided just enough dim light for passing drivers to see Otto's dummy lying in the middle of the road as they drove over it.

We watched from a nearby fox hole we had dug just a little way away down the road from the bridge and prepared for hilarity.

Sure enough, the first car to drive by ran over the dummy and the driver locked up his brakes with a satisfying screech. He ran back to the victim only to find that it was Otto's dummy. The driver, an angry male, picked up the homemade mannequin and threw it into the ditch.

"You little bastards are sick," he bellowed as we crouched in the fox hole and stifled laughter.

Comical!

The act was repeated several times before one woman picked up the dummy, threw it in her car and said she was calling the cops.

Thusly ended that night's entertainment. It was late, and it was a school night. We disbursed, headed home and each of us awoke that night giggling about our prank.

For me, school was relatively easy at first.

After slogging through a relatively easy series of A's in elementary school and junior high, my academic success came to a screeching halt when I simultaneously hit algebra and discovered girls. My academic record would never be the same. I had other priorities and I knew as long as I managed a weak 3.0 GPA I would get into some college or university, preferably one with low academic standards for admission and where the ability to fog a mirror was the only prerequisite for entering the realm of state higher education.

I could fog a mirror.

Teachers always told my parents who, when they bothered to show up for parent-teacher conferences, that I didn't apply myself, that I was distracted by baseball and girls and music and hanging with other dead-end freaks.

After the requisite post-conference parent-pupil debrief and the beating that followed, I would straighten up for a few weeks before returning to my usual indifferent academic form.

I quickly developed a defense mechanism in my sense of humor.

In high school, where I was a budding smart-ass, any teacher, or any person, who screwed with me would suffer the results.

One incident involved a theme I had written in Mr. Gosikowski's English class in which I was assigned to write under the topic: "If you could be anyone at any time in history, who would it be?"

Naturally, as a maniacal fan of the greatest rock and roll band in the world, The Who, I wrote that I would choose to be brilliant guitarist Pete Townshend playing with the band at Woodstock.

It was then that I discovered teachers talked about their students while smoking in the teachers' lounge. My Townshend dispatch apparently had become the subject of talk between Mr. Gosikowski and my priggish English Literature teacher Mrs. Peters.

A few days later in Mrs. Peters' class we were dissecting *The Great Gatsby* beyond all recognition. While I was supremely bored and daydreaming about classmate Nancy Glass' perfect legs, Mrs. Peters broke my erotic train of thought by calling on me to discuss the use of various colors in the book and their literary significance. (Really!)

"Mr. Derringer," she said sharply, "perhaps you could discuss the meaning of calling one of the characters Daisy, or perhaps you're daydreaming about being Pete Townshend at Woodstock."

I considered that a low blow, so I returned serve with a reply that probably could have sent me to juvenile court under current standards of criminal behavior.

"No, Mrs. Peters," I said innocently. "I was daydreaming about what it would be like to run up to you and strangle the life out of you."

Stunned, she looked at poor Michael Stencil, who was giggling uncontrollably, and asked him to discuss the significance of Daisy.

Mrs. Peters didn't call on me very often after that, and she usually blanched when I raised my hand to comment on the proceedings in class.

At home, things weren't much better. My dad had a wicked temper worsened by an alcohol problem that could turn Mother Teresa into a shrieking banshee. In addition to getting screamed at for not changing the TV channel on his immediate command — this was when remotes were outrageously expensive and out of reach for the family budget — you always ran the risk of getting clobbered for the smallest infraction in family life.

The key to survival in our family was to make sure the tyrant was mad at someone else. As a result, my sisters and I would rat each other out for each other's misdeeds so someone else took the beating. Josef Stalin would have been proud of our family's tradition of generating suspicion and tension amongst family members.

The old man had such a bad temper that sometimes it was hard not to laugh.

During dinner one night when I was about five years old, he was in such a rotten mood that no one at the table was allowed to speak. The silence created such stress as to create pressure laughter.

I snickered. Then I began to violently shake with strained giggles.

"Hey, dummy, what's so funny over there? Knock it off or I'll come over there and I'll really give you something to chortle about. What's so goddamned funny, laughing boy?"

Of course, I couldn't say that his sullen countenance was the source of my amusement. He'd bash me in the skull with a fork, so I had to come up with another reason.

"Um, I was thinking about clowns," I muttered.

"Then stop thinking about clowns, you idiot," he said in a voice that in itself expressed violent behavior was about to ensue.

For my own safety, I clammed up and picked at my canned green beans, overcooked and limp as a wet dish rag.

Yes, indeed, my father had increasingly odd ways of expressing his inner rage.

He once stuck a fork in a full carton of milk parked on the dinner table and screamed at Mama because she asked him to mow the lawn. As the homogenized moo juice leaked all over the Formica-topped dining room table and dribbled to the floor, he stood straight up, turned on his heel, and marched out the back door, heading toward the car where he drove to his final destination for the evening, Ma 'n' Pa's Tap.

Another time he decided to make Sunday dinner, a meal that was to include his own special recipe for potato pancakes. We were all excited to taste the wondrous pancakes. To a kid, pancakes always sounded good even if they were made of potatoes. Our eager anticipation of culinary excellence quickly turned to terror.

Daddy, whom I also called "Dad" or "Pa" depending on what I thought he liked best at any given moment, was happy, whistling and drinking as he sliced the potatoes and added his key ingredients. The problem was that instead of using baking powder, which Mama didn't stock, he used baking soda. The results were, of course, an epicurean disaster, but he served them to us anyway.

As we tried to choke down the would-be gourmet flapjacks while he seethed, I tried to lighten things up by commenting on how good they tasted.

"'Shut the hell up, you fucking little liar," he spouted, waving his butter knife menacingly.

He then proceeded to violently berate Mama for her lack of shopping skills and for failing to keep baking powder in the house. After all, it was her fault the pancakes tasted like toothpaste. In his mind she was at fault for a crummy dinner because she made him use baking soda.

Yummy! Just like in a restaurant!

Of course, the meal was awful and I managed to drop a few pieces on the floor, but the dog was having none of it. She took a sniff, gave it a lick, and walked away indignantly, as though she herself was insulted by the offer.

Dinner ended with the usual parental arguing, with dad sitting in his chair and drinking Muscatel until he passed out, snoring.

Like Dick and his Mustang, the old man was always fixing the TV. He figured he could use his minimal skills at television repair to fix the vertical or horizontal hold. He could even determine which vacuum tube needed replacement.

Handy!

But invariably he would need a tool of some kind while his head was entombed in the back of the TV/stereo counsel. That's when the trouble started. "Donnie!" he would say in a shout muffled by the wood that surrounded his head. "Donnie! Get me a goddamned screwdriver! Right now!"

He was never specific about the type of screwdriver he needed, but having been dispatched to the basement tool panel, in a panic I would try to guess which one would do the job. If I guessed wrong, I would suffer the consequences. I'd fetch one, hurry back upstairs and hand him a screwdriver.

"That's a Phillips-head screwdriver, dummy!" he would yell, then he would grab the tool and rap me on the back of the hand with a whack.

Ouch!

Eventually, he would go downstairs and find one himself because everybody else in the house was just too damned stupid.

Sorry, Pa!

It wasn't long after that that I decided I couldn't take my home life any longer. Running away was not an option; where would a skinny asthmatic kid go? So, I had another idea, one of the first of what would be a series of very bad ideas that popped into my head.

Speaking of popping, it was always a treat to give the old man a bare-back rub. He would lie face-down on the carpet and demand that anyone nearby should give him a back rub. When it was my turn as juvenile masseuse he would moan gloriously while I dug into his trapezius with all the strength of my emaciated forearms. Sometimes he would ask me to walk on his back, which tested my balance abilities like a gymnast on the balance beam.

Still, and it nauseates me to even think about it, and maybe I should spare any reader of this missive the sickening idea of this act, he would ask that the pimples on his acned back be burst. It's something that haunts me to this day and still triggers a gag reflex.

Yuck!

I also had the benefit of my booze-soaked father's astute observations on life's quirks. The monologues stick with me to this day. During one alcoholic haze he told me that if I really loved someone, I had to hurt them, because then they'd appreciate it more when you were nice to them. He used our dog as an example. Calling the sleeping canine to his side as Pa roosted in his easy chair, the dog happily came to see him. Then, with one big thwack, Pa hit the hound in the snout and sent her to bed. A few minutes later, he called the dog back in a syrupy voice and the confused animal returned. He patted her on the head and said, "Good dog. Who's a good dog?"

As the hound wagged her tail and he stroked her fur, he said, "See how glad she is that I'm being nice to her? See how it works?"

He then instructed me to conduct my relationships with women in the same way.

Helpful!

Dad did have a sense of humor, in a sense. One day he came home chortling, a relief to those of us who suffered when he was in his usual foul mood, because he said he had done something funny.

Really funny.

His story was so side-splittingly humorous that he couldn't wait to tell Mama. She was cooking some chicken-and-green-bean atrocity as he walked in, still amused.

"You gotta hear this," he said, his voice shaking with laughter. From the other room we kids were listening.

"I was at a red light and I was picking my nose," he said. "Just then these two pretty young girls pulled up next to me and laughed at me for probing my proboscis, so I dig out a big green booger and flicked it on their passenger window."

He paused for another gale of laughter, then continued after he caught his breath.

"They were gagging! Gagging as they pulled away on green. I thought they were gonna puke. I could not stop laughing and I almost ran the next red."

Oh, Dad. What a card!

My father also fancied himself a political expert. He once told me, "Always remember, if you shoot a guy, he's dead. But if you hold a gun to his head, he'll do anything you want."

Thanks for the tip.

And there was this mob-like encomium to political and personal conduct: "Punish your enemies and reward your friends. But always have something on your friends that could destroy them, too."

Appreciate the advice, Don Corleone.

Needless to say, such twisted counsel did much to screw up my young mind, and unfortunately, I may have applied some of his guidance in my behavior in future years. Not that I ever engaged in the physical violent behavior he exhibited toward the dog. Thankfully, though, I managed to come to the conclusion that if I wanted to be a good person I should do exactly the opposite of the old man. I never fully recovered from his teachings, though. They always hung in my mind like a vestigial neuron group machine-gunning away inside my brain.

Armed with all the heavily intoxicated life lessons he could dispense before he passed out, clad only in his underwear, I carried on.

OK, so maybe lots of other people grew up in that sort of insanity, but I had an especially hard time dealing with all of it.

I was about ten years old when first the idea of killing myself became a plausible alternative to living in the oppressive gulag that was my house. My grandparents had given me a red, beginner's bow and arrow set for my birthday, and I loved to go target shooting, sometimes even with the old man when he was sober enough to hit the targets and not the trees behind them instead.

Suicidal ideation, a term with which I would be more familiar as an adult, came one day when I was being screamed at in stereo by both of my parents. I retreated to my room and picked up one of the red target arrows from the little red quiver, sat on my bed and tried to jam the long dart straight into my heart. The arrow had a blunt tip since it was meant for hay-stuffed targets, not human flesh, and it did little but bruise my solar plexus. It didn't even puncture the skin.

But afterward I was frightened by what I had just attempted. I also knew something was very wrong with my psyche but at ten years old I had no idea what to do, so I normalized my behavior.

Everybody thinks about suicide.

Right?

As for the old man, it was always best to stay out of his hair, so of course humor became my best defense. I could usually defuse a situation by making my antagonist — be it my drunken father or a schoolyard bully or my sometimes-testy mother — laugh at the situation. Once, when Mama was chasing me around the house with a belt threatening to whip me for some long-forgotten infraction, I grabbed the belt as she wildly swung it at me and I tugged it out of her hand.

Having wrested the leather weapon from Mama, I folded it in two and began slapping it menacingly against my own hand as I smiled and said: "OK, now we talk."

"You think you can get out of trouble by making people laugh," Mama said, as she fought to keep a smile from cracking across her face.

"Well, so far so good," I replied.

The pursuit having ended, she just walked away chuckling.

On another occasion, I had committed an unacceptable act that caused Mama to bring out the belt again. This time I changed tactics. As she was looking for the belt I went to my dresser and stuffed as much underwear as I could down the back of my pants.

I lay in bed on my stomach waiting for the punishment I would probably not even feel.

She walked in the room with the belt and began flogging me on the ass.

"Ouch, Mama, that hurts, that hurts," I screamed, stifling sniggers as she continued to whip my padded butt.

"That'll teach you a lesson, you little brat," she said, huffing and puffing from her efforts to punish me severely.

When she had completed meting out justice, I reached back and pulled the underwear stuffing out of my pants and threw them at her.

"Nice job, Mama," I said. "I'll never do that again, whatever it was."

She stared at me and sputtered out a laugh.

"Jesus, kid, I really don't get you," she said, breaking into outright guffaws and leaving the room.

After that she didn't bother with the belt or any other type of punishment. Instead she would give me the words that struck terror in the hearts of every kid in our neighborhood: "Wait till your father gets home," she would warn.

The old man, well, the old man was a tougher audience, but I usually tried find a way to get through to that booze-wracked brain with some kind of witty *bon mot*.

Once, when I was due for a clobbering due to a mysterious hole in the house's back-porch screen door, I almost spared myself some bruising with this line: "Wait! Wait! I have a question: What would have happened if the Romans had released Jesus instead of Barabbas?"

The old man paused for a second, then considered my query and then said: "I'll give you Barabbas, you destructive, disrespectful little smart-mouth shit."

And then the beating proceeded. Unlike Mama, who did not possess the old man's physical strength, he did not need a belt to express his overwhelming inner rage. His fists were enough to knock out Tyson and the blows always left black marks on both body and psyche.

He never did fix that door, and the hole remained long after I made my escape for college.

Since every other kid in the neighborhood was suffering from some sort of alcohol-fueled wounds — belt buckles on the back was a favorite of angry fathers in those parts — it seemed perfectly normal for kids to be beaten by their fathers.

When a guy chases his kid down the block with a butcher knife and homicidal intentions, all of this was normal, no?

No part of the American experience was without its own terror for me. On July 4, in a year when I had just turned six years old, the old man took the family to a fireworks display at a park across town. My sisters and I were excited to see our first explosions in the sky.

Of course, even that night went awry. As we watched the star-spangled sky, the cinders falling from one shell that exploded like a giant willow tree traveled downward in brilliant, tiny spirals onto the blanket of the family in front of us. The still-smoldering debris ignited the family bedspread — this was in the days before federal regulations prevented blankets from being flammable — and flames began to shoot upward toward the low-hanging trees branches and set the mom's hair afire. She ran around screaming wildly until the dad captured her and doused the flames with the still-smoking coverlet by throwing it over her head like a hunter netting quarry.

And the rockets' red glare ...

We left immediately and thereafter watched fireworks from the top of a nearby bridge. None of us wanted to be anywhere near them again.

What constituted family life, then, was a carnival of warped experiences and chaos.

Leaving home for Lincoln and Smith College, a tiny diploma mill in rural Indiana, was a real reprieve. I felt like I had been paroled. Finally, I was out of the iron grip of my autocratic father. I could do anything I wanted to do.

And I did. From then on.

What fun!

My dictatorial old man at first refused to give me his permission to go to L&S when I announced my intentions to him and Mama. My Pa, my Daddy, whatever I was calling him at the time, was a martinet till the end, and he told me I needed his permission to cross the street. My doormat mother simply nodded her head and fetched him another drink.

But since I had already secured a student loan (which was used to buy stereo equipment, pot and an aquarium and eventually became delinquent), paid tuition and got dorm housing, off I went for some of the best times of my life at Lincoln and Smith College in Lincoln, Indiana.

When my parental tormentors finally dumped me off at my dorm, I thought I saw Daddy shed a tear. But for me it was like that Beatles song, "You Never Give Your Money," when they sang about the magic feeling with nowhere to go.

Although I joined a local radio station in my junior year and never graduated, those days in school were the apogee of my life. Considering my high school grades, it was a miracle I was even accepted for admission at any institution of higher learning, but I was officially a college student and I loved it.

Compared with my life growing up, little Lincoln, Indiana was paradise in spite of its natural small-town limitations. It was there that I learned I could get away with just about anything if my apologetic expressions of shame after the fact were charming enough. It was during those academically futile years that my "Rockin' Donnie" persona emerged. There were few women I wouldn't sleep with and little else that I wouldn't smoke, snort or drink in the name of a good time.

And a good time was had indeed. At least by me.

Or so it seemed.

For example, at my request a few of my friends dangled me from a third-floor apartment window while I screamed out my love for then-Second Lady Joan Mondale who was attending a theater opening across the street. For some reason my inverted antic did not attract the attention of Mrs. Mondale, and more importantly, the Secret Service.

When my then-girlfriend Toni discovered it was me who was swinging upside down by my ankles at the hands of my pals, she demanded that they pull me back in. As they yanked me into the living room, Toni scolded me.

"Are you trying to get killed, you idiot?" she screamed.

"'Um, well, I'm not sure,'" I replied in an answer that gave away a true self-destructive streak that had only just begun.

Fun!

I drank what was available and smoked a lot of pot that was always purported to be Colombian but was probably just ditch weed from some rural area of the state. I never did magic mushrooms or acid. Mushrooms and acid Kool-Aid were plentiful at parties, but I never wanted to see shit that wasn't there. Reality was scary enough without imagining paisley bats swooping down and nesting in your disheveled hair while you fought off giant spiders and other phantom vermin.

No, siree.

Studies were secondary to partying, of course. Although I enjoyed some of my classes and I loved political science studies — Soviet foreign policy was my favorite class — my chronic inattention to course work delivered me to academic probation, a status I would suffer twice until it was mutually decided with school administration that college wasn't for me and I left for good.

While still living in a ratty apartment near the Lincoln and Smith campus, I soon joined a small "underground" radio station in a nameless nearby city that played all the cool stuff that the local Top 40 commercial stations weren't playing. Talking Heads. Wall of Voodoo. Jonathan Richman and the Modern Lovers. Even the Fabulous Poodles.

I was a real hipster, a minor celebrity among students who won contests on my show with prizes like concert tickets, albums and gift certificates to the local food co-op. Some of my more outrageous and offensive acts — I once had a friend buy a beat-up dining room set for me to smash up as the high point of a beer bash — became legend in my little coterie of followers.

Oh, and how I smashed that table into splinters.

I fancied myself as a real Keith Moon-type party guy. Moon was The Who's amazing drummer, and when Moonie died, I commemorated his passing by drunkenly smashing a telephone with a baseball bat. "Here's to the greatest drummer who ever lived," I screamed as I wielded the Willie Stargell Louisville Slugger that had been with me since childhood.

Moon's drug-and-alcohol lifestyle, combined with what was surely severe mental illness, should have served as a warning to me, a self-styled wild man whose own mental health was crashing.

But Moonie's death didn't do anything but make me worse as I tried to top some of his nutty feats. I was carrying on Moon's destructive work, so to speak. Someone had to, and I was Moon's self-appointed Chosen One.

I hope I made Moonie proud as he plucked out strings of angel harps in Heaven.

I loved my new-found notoriety, the feeling of having "fans" who loved my "show" and inviting me to their house parties expecting — with no false hopes — that I'd do something crazy, maybe break the ceiling light fixture with my head while high jumping and hitting the ceiling like Pete Townshend during Roger Daltrey's scream in "Won't Get Fooled Again."

If you needed a party-starter, I was always happy to oblige.

My radio persona was slowly overcoming my own sense of identity. I was, without knowing it then, becoming "Rockin' Donnie." I wasn't Donald Derringer, mediocre college dropout who had a penchant for locally grown pot, the juniper berry and crazy antics. I was a big-shot, I was rockin' and I could do anything I wanted.

Top o' the world, Mama!

Screw you, Dad!

Look at me, Marie!! (More on Marie later.)

Donnie closed the journal and called it quits for the night.

— 5 —

DONNIE CRACKS UP -- AGAIN

Several years earlier, before Deerhead, Donnie had landed in the loon hatch for the first time after his on-air "Gary's Got a Boner" breakdown and subsequent dismissal from yet another station. It was a very brief stay at Hope Towers, nicknamed by its staff as "Hopeless Towers," and Donnie signed himself out after an overnight stay when it occurred to him that they were going to try to fix him by drugging him up and wasting his time in idiotic talk sessions with psychology majors who flunked out of med school and couldn't be psychiatrists.

That first hospitalization, though, surprised none of his friends and associates. Anyone close to him had witnessed helplessly over the years as he drank, smoked weed, snorted coke and took the occasional Ex. He ran through relationships with women like Hugh Hefner at an orgy.

Donnie had been stuck in Deerhead for the better part of a year when the second disintegration came and he was finally forced to get help. He had called people threatening suicide before. It was part of his wish to portray the down-on-his-luck misunderstood genius routine. He thought it was a kind of artsy, Jim Morrison thing to do, except Donnie produced no art. Just irritation and anger from those who were still in his life.

The trigger incident that sent him to Deerhead's crazy house had started out innocently enough.

He was, that Saturday evening, in a misty mood after his journalistic trip down Memory Lane, and he was quietly bemoaning his lot in life as a nobody in a nobody town. Since he didn't have a shift at "The Rock" that night he went to the local sports bar, Bubba's Home Plate, to catch a ball game and maybe drink a martini or twelve in a moody solitude.

The problem was, he had taken a few lorazepams to take the edge off before he got to Bubba's. When he arrived, he plunked himself down at the greasy bar and ordered a martini. Gin. Very dry. Shaken not stirred.

Classy.

Bubba indifferently and mechanically scooped up some ice and dumped cut-rate rail gin into a glass. He picked up the sticky dry vermouth bottle and poured a drop into the icy liquid. Then he poured a stream of liquid from a jar. He covered the glass with his hand and shook it. Then he poured the drink into a highball glass, stuck a wrinkled olive in it and walked to Donnie's perch.

"Here," Bubba grunted. "Enjoy, my bedraggled friend."

Donnie took a sip, smacked his lips loudly and exhaled dramatically.

"Hey, Bubba, how do you make these potables so dry and delicious?" Donnie said with fake cheeriness.

Bubba turned around and stared at Donnie.

"Piss, my friend," Bubba deadpanned. "Just a few drops of pee."

Bubba held up a beaker of something that looked like, dear God no, actual urine.

"Don't worry, it's not human, although in a pinch..." Bubba quickly explained, having anticipated the question. "I get it from a horse doctor in town. He tests the ponies for diabetes and he gives me the leftovers. It won't hurtcha. I think he sterilizes it or something. Don't ask questions when you don't wanna know the answers. Just enjoy!"

Donnie gagged a little as he took the second gulp of his equine-enhanced libation, and he then proceeded to drink three pee-laden martinis in succession with the enthusiasm of a skid-row drunk. They weren't bad, horse pee or no.

He quickly felt a buzz and the dizzying effects of the meds kicking in when his hazy quietude was broken by a thick-set shaggy drunk in greasy blue jeans and an AC/DC concert T-shirt that barely covered his bulging gut.

"Hey, aren't you that disc jockey? Rockin' Ronnie or somethin'?"

Donnie ignored him and pretended to be mesmerized by a Twins-Mariners game on the TV, a Quasar no less, behind the bar. Twins up 3-2 in the fourth inning.

The guy stared at Donnie like a chimpanzee examining a handful of its own excrement. He kept up the questioning. He apparently thought he was in the presence of a local celeb since anyone in Deerhead who used a microphone for a living was automatically a star.

"No really, it's you! Rockin' Ronnie!"

"Rockin' Donnie, if you must know. Donnie, not Ronnie," Donnie grumbled.

"Love yer show, man," said AC/DC Man. "It really rocks. I listen to it all the time when I'm partying into the night. I seen you at that car show at the civic center a few months ago. You look different than your voice sounds on the radio. I always thought you'd be younger."

"Yeah, well, I appreciate your support, but I must say your choice of music leaves something to be desired," Rockin' Donnie said. "I can't believe people like you haven't been sick of crap like AC/DC for decades. I mean, how many times can you listen to shit like Twisted Sister or Rush? Can I make some recommendations that might challenge that tiny brain of yours? Maybe some Pat Metheny. If that's too jazzy for you, you might try 'My Morning Jacket.' In your case, maybe even Otis Redding's 'Try a Little Tenderness' is a little complicated for you. You know. The tension, the build-up and then Otis blasts into the song.

"Of course, I've always had a soft spot for The Replacements. But it's a little painful to listen to them these days. Brings back some bad memories."

"Hey, what's wrong with Twisted Sister? They rock! You gotta fight for your right to par-tay!" said AC/DC Man.

"Yeah, well, that was the Beastie Boys who wanted their freedom to par-tay. But to put it in terms you can understand, your music sucks ass."

Why was Donnie engaging this moron? It had to be the meds, the martinis and his deep-seated resentment of his self-earned lot in life. He stared straight at the ballgame. Bases loaded for Seattle. Two outs.

"Hey, fuck you, Mr. Hot Shot DJ," said AC/DC Man. "What makes you such a music know-it-all? You're a fucking snob."

"Well, it all starts with a modicum of intelligence, an element that obviously skipped you in your family's in-bred gene pool."

"You calling me stupid?"

"No, my dear mutant of a friend, I'm calling you an idiot. Anybody who thinks that garbage is music doesn't have the brain of a..."

It was just about then that Donnie turned his head and saw AC/DC Man swing the pool cue by the thin end. The fat end hit Rockin' Donnie square on the bridge of his nose. He went down from his barstool like a sack of potatoes off a runaway truck, and then the kicking began. Donnie curled into the fetal position to protect himself.

He had just wanted a martini and a ball game. But he got this instead.

What a life!

"I'm puttin' you on the *Highway to Hell*, you snobby asshole," said AC/DC Man, standing over him with the pool cue and giving him another kick.

Bubba watched with amusement and said weakly: "Hey, Stoney, come on. He's down for the count. Let him slither off to his hole."

Thanks, Bubba.

When the drubbing stopped, Rockin' Donnie tried to get up, accompanied by gales of laughter from AC/DC Man and a few Neanderthal goons who enjoyed watching the beating. Bubba turned away, polishing a beer glass and mumbling something about his primate clientele.

After AC/DC Man lost interest in a further beating, Rockin' Donnie managed to hobble home on foot. Once there, he collapsed on his couch and passed out. When he awoke four hours later, he headed to the bathroom to puke. He caught a glimpse of himself in the bathroom mirror. His eyes were black, his bottom lip was cut, and blood was matted in his scraggly black and gray beard.

Donnie's head pounded. The cue shot that probably broke his nose had brought on a waterfall of gore, and his thinning, stringy hair was flat against his head from sweat. He hurt everywhere.

Donnie was a broken man — body, soul, and mind.

He didn't like what he saw in the mirror. In fact, he hated it. He really used to be somebody, at least he thought so, and now here he was, stuck in a town that was miles from the Interstate, a mere dot on the state map. He had sustained two black eyes, a bloody nose, a busted head, and a fatally bruised ego.

That was it.

It was time to put an end to it all.

He went the kitchen table, which doubled as his liquor cabinet, grabbed a bottle of Bushmill's whiskey and poured the warm, welcome booze into a tumbler with the logo of a radio station where he had once worked.

"Life's too short!" the tumbler read. "Rock on, people!"

Yeah, Donnie was ready to rock on, all right.

Straight into oblivion.

He stumbled back to the living room and dropped the needle on a crackling copy of *The Who by Numbers*. He made himself a peanut butter sandwich and walked into the living room, where he collapsed into the worn, cigarette-burned Barcalounger. He lit a joint and gulped the whiskey like a drifter guzzling Sterno.

This is it, he mumbled to himself. I'm done. This town has beat me. Life has destroyed me. Rockin' Donnie has been defeated.

But before he could do anything rash, Donnie drifted in and out of consciousness for the next few minutes, The Who's "Slip Kid" and then "However Much I Booze" blaring in the background. He loosely held the joint in his fingers as hot pot cinders drifted onto the upholstery. He took an occasional hit from the joint but was sailing directly into the abyss of a tormented alcoholic slumber.

Donnie had a few short but tortured, booze-soaked dreams. In one, he appeared on Jerry Most's show in his underwear as Jerry spoke in a language that sounded like Swahili.

He awoke with a start upon realizing he had agreed to be a guest on Jerry's show.

Why? What was the point? To titillate his voracious, contemptuous and contemptible viewers with tales of booze, drugs and debauchery?

Sorry, he thought, that story's been told a million times by guys better than the likes of me.

It was over for Donnie and he knew it. Nowhere left to run to, no radio station that would hire him. He was, he believed, at the end of the line. Fini! Kaput! Kumaliza, as the Swahilis say.

Screw Jerry Most. Donnie wasn't going to open an artery in front of a hooting, live studio audience on a cable TV show. And podcast.

Was it really better to burn out than to fade away?

Donnie had done both.

— 6 —

SUICIDE IN DEERHEAD, OR ACTING OUT A WAKING NIGHTMARE

In the early morning after his *tete-a-tete* with AC/DC Man, Rockin' Donnie was taken to the local nut house by his occasional lover, Liz, who lived nearby. Although she was used to the Rockin' Donnie self-destructive schtick, Liz persisted that he should get some help.

Though Donnie knew Liz was right about getting his head straight, getting some professional help, he mostly ignored her advice.

Liz was Donnie's girlfriend in a loose sense of the word. When Donnie and Liz spent time together, they were usually drinking and smoking pot. They both enjoyed sex while high. She liked sports, especially baseball, and she knew some basic trivia, including the fact that the great Ted Williams was the last man to hit .400 for a season. She loved the Boston Red Sox, but she only watched when they were on television, usually playing the Yankees.

Liz was fiercely independent, but there was a side of her that wanted to be in a relationship, and although Donnie was unstable, she found his quirks entertaining, even alluring. Anyway, she thought he was more interesting than the other Deerhead drones and high school retreads she had dated.

Donnie and Liz didn't like walks in the woods or trips to some tropical island, although they occasionally talked about fleeing to Greece.

Mostly they just hung out and watched TV or went to bars. Like Donnie, Liz knew how to spit beer through her teeth and they sometimes had spit-beer fights. They thought it was hilarious. Many bar patrons who witnessed these juvenile displays did not.

So, Donnie and Liz had a few things in common, things which held together an increasingly tenuous relationship. Liz cared about him in spite of herself. She was fun, and she actually loved Donnie, but Donnie couldn't get serious with her as long as memories of Marie still haunted him. They would haunt him for the rest of his life, and they helped make Donnie a crazy show-off.

In Donnie's mind, no woman ever measured up to Marie, his long-lost paramour. He had spent his life as a big shot trying to impress her and maybe bring her back. They had had some good times, after all.

Those fond, heavily romanticized recollections of his time with Marie was enough for Donnie to keep a certain distance from any woman who dared to be in his life.

But as Donnie had become more and more morose since they had first become lovers, Liz became deeply concerned.

She had a feeling that Donnie was headed for a psychological crash, but she was helpless to do anything as Donnie ignored her pleadings to get some professional assistance in facing whatever demons were tormenting him to an early grave.

"You're losing it," she had said, crying a few days before Donnie's inevitable melt-down. "You're getting help."

So, after a savage beating by a thug at a local bar, Donnie announced to Liz in a phone call that he was going to end his miserable life. His vestigial religious beliefs said that suicide was never an option, that the heavenly gates might be closed to him if he killed himself. But even perdition was better than his current circumstances.

Although Donnie's memory of the incident was hazy, he had apparently phoned Liz at around 4 a.m.-ish Sunday morning, still buzzing and barely coherent from the martinis he drank and the joints he smoked after he limped home from a binge that had resulted in a beating the night before. He announced that he couldn't believe what his life had become, and how he had failed, and how he hated his miserable existence in Deerhead and the tired old music he was forced to play all night, and how he was nothing more than a barnacle on the garbage scow of society and how maybe should just kill himself.

Kill himself?

Whoa.

Donnie was seriously considering putting an end to all the nonsense that were the contents of his otherwise empty life. The drugs, booze, parties, women, rock and roll. They all added up to nothing and Donnie was finally reckoning with the sad facts.

He hadn't wanted to bother Liz with another cry for help, but he didn't know where to turn.

Having sunk into a dark hole, and with thoughts of The End, and with Liz probably sound asleep, Donnie figured it might be a good time to call the local suicide hotline. Every town had one, even jerkwater burgs like Deerhead. He had actually kept a magnet with the suicide hotline number on his refrigerator. Its main function was to support a tattered old poster for a "Booze 'n' Lose" charity gambling night at Milt's Towne Club where he used his talents as a "celebrity" disc jockey as entertainment.

It was right next to a scrap of paper that had Jerry Most's phone number on it.

Dark humor.

A real laugh riot.

But now he had to put the magnet to use. He decided to call the hotline and spill his rancid guts.

Donnie staggered to the kitchen, grabbed the magnet, let the poster fall, and squinted to view the number. He pulled his cell phone out of his pocket and fumbled to make the call.

When he reached the number, he got a recording.

"This is the Deerhead Suicide Hotline," said a metallic and decidedly unempathetic female voice. "If this is a life-threatening emergency, please call 911. Please listen carefully as our menu items have changed. If you are a member of the medical community, please press one. If you are an insurer, please press two. If you are a member of the police department, please press three.

"Otherwise if you would like to speak with a counselor, please hold. Currently there are two other callers ahead of you."

If this is a life-threatening emergency, please call 911? I don't know, Donnie thought, isn't being suicidal a life-threatening emergency? And there were two other people thinking of killing themselves in Deerhead at this hour? Donnie guessed that it wasn't too hard to believe, given the small town's desolate cultural and alcoholic social structure.

He also chuckled to himself over the idea that the hotline's menu items had changed as though he had memorized the old ones. Was there anywhere in the world that didn't have that lame disclaimer?

Donnie tripped over an empty beer bottle on the floor while he paced and waited for the counselor. He made himself a thick peanut butter sandwich and then continued his manic marching as he awaited much-needed help. The suicide counselors were apparently busy advising the two customers ahead of him to put down their guns, that life was indeed worth living.

Really?

Finally, Donnie got a counselor on the line.

"Good evening, this is the Deerhead Suicide Hotline. My name is Sheila. Please tell me your first name and how I might help you."

Sheila sounded more like a cable TV customer service representative than a suicide counselor. Donnie could hear her chewing gum.

Donnie was licking peanut butter off the roof of his mouth when Sheila answered. Sheila heard him smacking his lips before Donnie was finally able to speak.

"Um, yes, I'm very tired, physically tired, tired of life, and I think I'm going to take some pills," Donnie said plaintively. He was beginning to realize this was a serious situation. "Really, I think I might do it."

"I'm sorry to hear that. Again, please tell me your name. I want to get to know you and your crisis."

"Oh, yeah, right. My name is …" Donnie hesitated. He was afraid to use his real name. This was a small town after all.

"Keith," Donnie said. Yeah. Keith, like Keith Moon.

"Hello, Keith, I'm sorry to hear this," Sheila said. She cracked her gum. "Tell me why you want to take pills. And what kind of pills are you thinking of taking?"

What a stupid question.

"What difference does it make, Sheila? I mean really. I'm talking about killing myself and you want to entertain your morbid curiosity by asking for details?"

Sheila breathed a heavy sigh. Clearly this was taking more out of her than Donnie.

"I need to know the type of pills because it will help me determine whether they are the type of pills that would accommodate killing yourself," she said. She sounded irritated.

Donnie took a deep breath, blew air through his nose and shook his head.

"OK, Sheila, you want to know what kind of pills? Ex-lax. I'm going to shit myself to death. OK? Satisfied?"

"Keith, Keith, please calm down," she said. "So how many laxatives have you taken? Have you started cramping yet?"

"I was joking, Sheila," Donnie said. He felt like he was going to cry.

"Joking? I thought you were going to kill yourself. I can assure you this is not a joking matter. Now please tell me what type of pills you're going to swallow."

Bad as things were, Sheila was getting on Donnie's — Keith's — nerves. This wasn't helping him at all.

"Xanax, Sheila, OK? Xanax. I've got hundreds of 'em, but I think 30 will do the trick. As many as I can swallow. Just wash them down with some Bushmill's and it's sayonara, suckers!"

"OK, Keith, what made you feel like taking these pills?"

Donnie decided to go along with the farce.

"I was in a bar. I cracked wise with a local gorilla and he beat the shit out of me. I have two black eyes. A bloody nose. My career's shot. I have no real relationships other than my girlfriend in this fleabag town or anywhere else. Really, what difference would it make if I just beamed out of this world?"

There was momentary silence.

"Sheila?"

"Yes, Keith, I'm still here."

Sheila had apparently spit out her gum. This was getting heavy.

"So, you sound like you've been drinking, Keith? How much did you drink?"

What was this, a coroner's inquest?

"Sheila, I don't know what difference it makes. But I took some lorazepams and I think I had three martinis at the bar, they had horse piss in them, then I had some whiskey here at home, smoked the end of a doobie."

"But you admit you've been drinking."

"Yes, Sheila, I've been drinking," sounding like a little boy waiting to be spanked.

"Well, I think that's the problem," Sheila said sharply. "You're sloppy drunk and depressed because a big bully beat you up after you wise-mouthed him. Boo hoo hoo. Look, Keith, go to bed and sleep it off. You're a drunk. Get some sleep and pick yourself up by your bootstraps."

"I was, uh, thinking I'd get a little empathy here, Sheila. After talking to you maybe now I'll take 40 Xanax. The extra 10 are for you."

"Do you know how many sad drunks call here every night and say they're going to kill themselves? Their girlfriend left them. Mommy never loved them. The car won't start and they got fired from their menial jobs. I've got some people who call here just to spill their guts twice a week. But you're not going to take any pills, Keith. You don't have the guts. This isn't about suicide. It's a drunken pity party and I guess I'm turning down your invitation."

Wow!

Sheila's verbal slap in the face awoke Donnie's fighting reflexes.

"OK, Sheila, maybe you're right. Maybe I'm just a common drunk. Maybe a little shut-eye will do the trick. But before I hang up can I ask you a favor?"

"Sure, Keith, sure," Sheila said, resigned.

"Would you go fuck yourself? It would really give me a reason to live. I would make me feel a lot better."

The line went dead.

Even the Suicide Hotline hung up on him.

Where was that bottle of Xanax again?

Donnie pondered his situation and decided to call Liz. He had reached a point of semi-consciousness, but instinct told him to call her. He was in crisis. She was his girlfriend. Sort of. But she had to listen.

Right?

Donnie sat down on his weathered Barcalounger and called Liz. During his heavily intoxicated, slurred and rambling monolog with her in the pre-dawn hours, he muttered something about playing some Janis, maybe "Ball and Chain" from Big Brother and the Holding Company, and fading out like an old 45 record to the accompaniment of those 30 doses of Xanax, maybe 40, 10 extra for Sheila, to make sure he finished the job.

Maybe he should play Elton John's "I Think I'm Gonna Kill Myself." That would be such a cool song with which to end his life sentence on Earth. And appropriate.

He told Liz that he wanted a clown car and a garbage truck as a funeral procession.

Ha ha.

Liz, naturally alarmed but hardly surprised, spoke slowly to him and firmly instructed him to splash cold water on his face, go to the fridge and grab a beer, sit down, throw on some music of his choice, but not "Ball and Chain," and wait for her to arrive. She said she would arrive in 10 minutes, and she did, since everything in Deerhead was only 10 minutes away.

When Liz arrived, it was close to 6 a.m. and she found Donnie dozing in the ratty Barcalounger. His head was on his chest and the Moosehead beer — Moosehead! — Donnie had grabbed from the fridge was dangling from his hand at a 45-degree angle, ready to drop and spill suds all over the already-sticky hardwood floor. Peanut butter decorated his untrimmed moustache and beard, along with clots of blood. The place reeked like an Amsterdam coffee shop at closing time.

Liz couldn't believe she actually loved this guy, slept with him. Repeatedly.

She walked in and, seeing Donnie's semi-comatose condition, ran to him and slapped his face, fearing he had already gobbled the pills. The beer dropped to the floor and foam dribbled across the warped and stained hardwood.

"Owie!" Donnie said like a naughty child, shaking his head. In his haze he threw up his arms and pressed them against his head rope-a-dope style like the great Muhammed Ali, thinking the AC/DC guy had found him at home.

"That hurt. You spilled my beer. That ... Hey Liz, what are you doing here? Nice to see you. How about a little morning roll in the hay? It is morning, isn't it? Or did I miss another day."

Liz was not amused.

"Look, you stupid shit, you scared the hell out of me with that phone call," she said in an icy tone that made it quite clear that sex was not in the offing.

"Phone call? Was I on the phone? I might have been dialing for dollars, but I don't really remember the chat of which you speak," he said weakly. "Was I making a booty call?"

"Really fucking funny, Donnie," she said, raising her hand as though she was about to hit him again. "You scared the hell out of me with that suicide talk. Goddammit, when are you gonna get your shit together? Now, did you swallow anything? Do I have to get you to the hospital to have your ulcered stomach pumped?"

Donnie looked confused. He scrunched up his blackened eyes as though trying to remember the answer to a difficult trivia question.

"I'm afraid details of our earlier conversation are a bit foggy. I may have said something like that, and could I be blamed? But no, as far as I know I did not swallow any pills after I got home. Yes, I did have a few lorazepams before I hit the bar, and yes, I smoked a joint and had some Bushmill's when I got home," Donnie said. "I even made friends with Sheila at the suicide hotline. But no, I did not consume any other pharmaceuticals. What made you think I would swallow pills for any reason other than recreation?"

"You said you were going to kill yourself, you stupid dickhead! Remember? A little Janis Joplin and 30 Xanax to do the job?"

"First of all, my sometime lover, you needn't identity Janis with her surname. There is only one Janis, now and forever. And as for 30 Xanax? That would knock over Secretariat and Seattle Slew both. I've never had that many Xanax, although I did once try half a horse tranquilizer with Keith Moon. Or did I only read about that? I don't remember. But no, I have ingested no drugs, prescription or otherwise except for a doobie I apparently lit last night after I got home. Look, Liz, it's really nice to see you but if we're not gonna hit the sack together, then I'll have to ask you to leave while I get some much-needed healing sleep."

"Healing sleep? What the hell are you talking about? Look at yourself. Two black eyes, a bloody nose, peanut butter and blood smeared on your face, one suicide threat and I'm supposed to leave you alone? Sorry, idiot, you're coming with me to a special place."

Donnie acted intrigued. "A special place? Like the circus? Will there be animals to pet? Can I feed the goats? Or are you thinking of taking me to bed, which is a very special place when you're in it with me."

"I'm here to take you to that mental hospital," Liz said. "What is it called? Serenity something. Serenity Heights? You know, the local mental hospital."

"Look, this isn't funny, jerk," Liz continued. "You woke me up to tell me you were gonna kill yourself, and I show up to stop you and you're sitting here in your filthy chair in a dope-fueled alcoholic muddle looking like you've been hit by a bus.

"Really? Serenity Heights is what they call the nut cage here? Liz, I didn't know you cared."

"I guess I don't," she said. "But I can't stand by while somebody threatens to take a dirt nap. Whether I care or not, I have to take you in. I'm serious. Get up. Wash your face, get the blood off your lip and beard, and the peanut butter off your face. Then walk with me to my car. I will then deposit you at the local insane asylum."

Somehow, Donnie knew she was right. He needed a change, although he wasn't sure the kooky cookie house was where that transition should take place. But he was resigned. He felt miserable, his head ached and his mouth tasted as though he had been licking the basement floor.

"Ok, Liz, maybe you're right," he said, struggling to his feet. "You won't have to get a net. I'm coming with you, love. But first I have to make a call."

"Who're you calling at this time of day? Nobody's even at work yet."

"I have to call Jerry Most."

"Jerry Most? You mean that bastard with the stupid TV show where people try to kill themselves and he insults everybody, including his wives?"

"Yeah, that's him. But I think he's got a different schtick now, a different type of human spectacle called *Losers on Parade* on a cable access channel. And podcast. I have to let him know whether I want to go on his show when I get out of the squirrel nest. I wasn't going to do it but the more I think about It might be just what I need to cleanse this fetid soul of mine. Kind of a public burning of a dying spirit."

"I have no idea why you need to call him now. Why don't you get in touch with him when you're out of the hospital? Then you can do anything you want. For now, you're coming with me."

"No, really, dear Liz, I have to call Jerry Most. He'll be up. He's out east, so he's an hour ahead and probably already sipping a spicy Bloody Mary. After I call, I'll do anything you want."

"What are you going to do with Jerry Most? Are you gonna tell him you're gonna kill yourself, too?"

"No. Come on, I just want to make sure he doesn't forget me. I thought about it and I think going on his show would be therapeutic. I'm gonna kill the 'Rockin' Donnie' persona, if not my personal being, on live cable TV and a podcast! It'll be a blast. Now where did I put Jerry's number? I think it's on a sticky note on my fridge."

"Wait. Here it is, right behind the condom in my wallet."

"Jesus."

"Hey, the condom is pretty fresh if you're interested. Or maybe you'd prefer bareback!"

"Please, just make your goddamned call and let's go. You've got a date at the local babbling brook."

"OK, hang on," Donnie said as he plucked his cell phone from the cigarette-and-joint-burned coffee table. He walked into the kitchen and stuck Jerry's number to the freezer door. Noticing the phone was sticky, he wiped it off on his beer and blood-stained jeans. Then he placed the call.

"Yell-oh!" the cheerful voice answered almost immediately. "To whom do I have the curse of speaking with at this early hour of this beautiful day?"

This sounded like the ass Jerry Most was supposed to be.

"Is this Jerry? Jerry Most?"

"One and the same, dear boy. What can I do for you at this early hour? I'm not in a money-lending mood if that's what you're calling about. I usually wait till I have my breakfast bagel before I start talking dough. Hey that's not bad. Bagel? Dough? Get it?"

"Uh, yeah, Jer. Hilarious. You're a real card. Jerry, this is Donald Derringer," he said, not sure why he was using his formal name. He'd thought of himself as Rockin' Donnie Derringer for so long he'd almost forgotten his given name.

"Oh yeah, Rockin' Donnie," Jerry said. "Playing all of yesterday's hits today for lonely insomniac small-town rockers! The worst of the '70s comes to life on your show whether they like it or not. Must be a very rewarding gig. You're the future star of my show, no? Are you telling me you're going to bear your soul for the sake of good TV? And maybe some cash and prizes?"

"Yup, that's what I'm calling about. I want to expose the Rockin' Donnie Derringer persona I've carefully cultivated over the years to the ridicule I'm sure you can dish out. I want to kill 'Rockin' Donnie' on your esteemed cable television program and podcast."

"Well, killing is an awfully strong word," said Donnie's would-be tormentor. "How about we say you're going to lay your persona to rest, kind of undertaker talk. That way we don't scare the kiddies and the old ladies, although I do find that the elderly can be quite fixated on the notion of death. I wonder why."

"Well, OK, not kill, but 'lay to rest' my rockin' self. I don't know, maybe I'll become an Orthodox Christian priest. Or a dog walker. Or a shepherd. That would be relaxing."

"Look, Donnie, baby, it's too early in the day to talk business. Why don't you call me Monday when I'm in work mode. Sundays are my day to rest. Call me tomorrow, maybe just before cocktail hour."

"I'm not sure I can call right then," Donnie said. "My friend, my friend Liz, is taking me to the, um, hospital, in a couple minutes. Right after I get off this call, in fact."

"The hospital? What's wrong? A serious case of some gruesome venereal disease? That would also make for an interesting discussion on the show."

"Uh, no, not that kind of hospital. More of a psych ward. I'm having some problems and Liz wants me to get some help. She said I called her and threatened suicide."

"Suicide? Well that's taking things a little far, champ. Liz is probably right. Get to the crazy house and sort things out. But believe me, this will make the show even better. A guy who wants to kill himself? That's compelling television! We might even get picked up by a network and I'll be a household name once again."

"Uh huh, well..."

"Look, Champ, stay in the nut house as long as you need to. We can do the show whenever you're ready. Your story is too good to pass up. But here's a tip: If you want to stay in the loony bin longer, go to the art therapy class and draw pictures of swords piercing bloody giant eyeballs. If you want them to let you out, paint pictures of eagles soaring over mountain tops over a sunrise. Your call, Champ."

"Well, Jerry — uh, Mr. Most — can I call you Jerry? I don't paint, but I wasn't planning to stay in the hospital very long. Just enough to clear my head and figure out what I'm doing with my life."

"Sure, you can call me Mr. Most. Anyhoo, we can have you on the show after you've gone clear. And speaking of going clear, I've already had a lot of coffee and my bladder's ready to bust. Gotta run. Call me!"

"Will do, Jerry. Uh, Mr. Most. Ah, Mr. Most ... I, uh, ..."

But the call had already been dropped.

Just like Sheila from the suicide hotline.

People hung up on him all the time.

The story of Donnie's life these days.

— 7 —

ARRIVAL AT SERENITY HEIGHTS

Serenity Heights, Deerhead's local snake pit, was everything you'd expect of a home for troubled souls and fevered brains.

The waiting room had unobtrusive beige walls broken up by paint-by-numbers portraits of pastoral scenes set in plain brown plastic frames. Behind the admissions desk was an age-old faded poster of a cat dangling by its paws from a rope. The poster said: "Hang in there!"

Inspiring!

Next to the cat poster was a faded drawing of a crudely drawn laughing face that said: "You Want It When?!"

Hilarious.

A tired, sour-faced administrator staffed the front desk as a few other clients in the waiting room twitched and drummed their fingers on the Formica coffee table while they awaited blue-smocked room service helpers to finish preparations for their shelters from the storm.

The axe-faced admitting nurse was not exactly Florence Nightingale. Her sour countenance made it seem as though she had little use for her ill-in-the-head charges. She didn't like her job, but there was little else to do in Deerhead since the tannery went out of business.

She was mean. In fact, she was downright accusatory.

But a small Deerhead workforce and her long tenure at Serenity Heights helped her keep her job in spite of her bad attitude.

"Name?" she barked.

"Donnie … um, Donald Derringer."

"Middle name?"

"Henry. After the baseball player, Henry Aaron. My dad was a big baseball fan, and …"

She glared and rudely interrupted him.

"Why are you here?" she demanded of Rockin' Donnie.

"I came for the spa," Donnie said. "And drinks by the pool. I heard they make a mean martini. You know, gin, extra dry. Shaken, not stirred. At Bubba's, they use horse urine to make them extra dry."

She stared at him and then returned her angry gaze to the admitting sheet. She tapped her pen on the desk.

"So, we have a comedian, do we?" she snarled. "We've got lots of comedians here. The funniest ones are under 24-hour padded lock-up. You want to continue your monologue or should we try to get you acquainted with our nice little booby hatch?"

Booby hatch? That hardly seemed professional. Or nice. Donnie grew apprehensive.

"Um, actually, I feel a lot better. Maybe I should just go home. I need to prepare for my radio show on 'The Rock' Monday night. You know, I've got a Bob Seger six-pack to think about. I'm thinking about leading off with 'Rock and Roll Never Forgets.' Seger at his best!"

Liz elbowed him hard in the ribs.

"He's not going anywhere, nurse," Liz said. "He threatened to kill himself early this morning and I brought him here to get him back among the living."

"Suicidal, eh?" the anti-Nightingale said. "They're pretty easy to deal with. Mostly they just sit around and mope and think deep dark musings about their messed-up lives. Very docile. Now the schizos, they're a blast. Always thinking that we're listening to their thoughts and planning to assassinate the Pope. Lotsa fun."

"I appreciate your sensitive observations," Liz said, "but we've got to get this guy checked in before he self-immolates."

"Hmm, yeah. Well, keep it cool, dearie," the fake Nurse Ratched said. *Cuckoo's Nest* indeed.

Turning to Donnie, she said: "No smoking indoors here, honey," clearly enjoying herself. "No booze. No dope. You get what we throw at you in our cafeteria and nothing else, and we will escort you to our little lunch counter. If you play by the rules, you'll have a tolerable time here. If not, well, we have ways."

She reached for the admissions sheet and placed it on a clipboard. She handed it to Donnie.

"Fill this out and bring it back to me. We're preparing your room as we speak," she said. "Once you bring the paperwork back to me, we'll get you settled in."

Donnie took the paperwork and headed for a cracked brown Naugahyde chair in the corner. Liz sat on the couch next to the chair. He could tell Liz was pissed off at him, but he felt comforted by her presence.

He glanced at the admissions sheet.

"NOK," he said. "What's that again?"

"Next of kin, dipshit," she said. "You do have a relative, right? Or were you hatched?"

"Well, that's an interesting question," Donnie said. "Parents both long dead. No siblings. Haven't talked to my ex-wife in so long I don't even know where she lives. Daughter hasn't spoken to me for years. I think she's at college somewhere. Minnesota, maybe? Or Wisconsin? Or did she graduate?"

"God, you're pathetic," Liz said. "Do you mean you have no one to list as your next of kin?"

"Can I list you, Liz?"

"What? Look, I've gotten drunk and slept with you, but I'm hardly kin. I'm barely your friend."

"Will you marry me then? I'll get down on one knee and ask formally. I need an NOK."

"Piss off, Crazy Man. I guess I love you in some kooky way. But in your condition, I'd sooner marry a carnival barker. This isn't funny. You don't go threatening suicide and then cut up in the mental hospital waiting room."

"Sorry for expressing myself, Elizabeth. I do care for you. Really, I do. Maybe we can make an arrangement for me to express my feelings when I get to my room. We can have some privacy there and I'm sure the cot will be comfortable enough ..."

"Stow it, Lover Boy. Finish filling out the forms so you can get a room and I can get on with my day. And my life."

Was Liz breaking up with him? He sure hoped not. Although they'd been together only a few months, she was the closest thing he'd had to a stable relationship in years. Their ties were flimsy as far as Donnie was concerned. Donnie was no prize, but Liz's small-town wholesome looks and cellulite thighs weren't going to get a lot of second looks, either. She was also loyal as a bulldog and, it seemed, she really cared about him even if she was pissed off at his recent self-destructive behavior.

There was no time to think about breaking up now. He had to list someone who would admit to being related to him. Or even know him.

Donnie decided to list his NOK as The Who's genius guitarist, Pete Townshend. Who would know? Or care?

He returned the admissions sheet and he noticed the admitting nurse's name was Pat. Just Pat. Not Patricia or Patty. Pat. The most androgynous and ugly form of an otherwise beautiful name. He had thought her name was Cruella. The hard-faced Pat grabbed the sheets with one swipe, swiftly picked up the phone like an infielder snatching up a bunted ball and said: "He's ready."

A few minutes later, a large baby-blue-smocked aide walked into the room. He looked like a barrel of laughs with his stern face, caterpillar eyebrows and robotic countenance. He was a formidable character. His arms were as big as Donnie's legs, his square jaw made him look like an ex-Marine. His plus-size body made him appear to be like a man who was not to be trifled with. He had a tattoo on his left forearm that said: "To find yourself, think for yourself." It was accompanied by a crudely drawn caricature of Socrates.

A philosopher!

"Mr. Derringer?" he said with completely flat affect.

"Who, me?"

"Are you Mr. Derringer?"

"Well, I'm Rockin' Donnie if you don't mind," Donnie said nervously. "Are you the one who will take me to my padded room?"

"Yes. My name is Carsten," he said and motioned toward a door with the wooden mannerisms of Frankenstein's monster.

What a stiff.

"Please come with me," Carsten said in an almost ominous tone. "I will escort you to your quarters. Please."

Donnie and Liz stood. Donnie tried to kiss Liz on the mouth. She was having none of it at that moment. She quickly turned her cheek toward his gaping yaw and he wound up with his tongue on her face.

"Down, boy," Liz said. "OK, you go with Carsten and chill out. Get in touch with your thoughts, dangerous as that idea may be. Focus on why you're such a douche. Maybe you'll come out of here a new man. But then again, I doubt it."

As she turned away, she looked over her shoulder and stopped to wiggle her hips as she grinned at Donnie. Then she walked toward the door.

What was that supposed to mean?

"Getting in touch with my thoughts would be ill-advised, Liz," Donnie responded as she headed toward the glass double-doors to exit the fun house. "Getting in touch with my thoughts is what got me here in the first place."

"Whatever. Have fun. I'll see you in a couple days. Maybe."

As she walked away, Donnie got serious.

"Liz," he said quiet and mourningly. "Liz. Darling. Don't leave me here. I don't think I can take this."

"Sorry, Donnie. You created this situation when you called me with a suicide threat. Now you can stay here and get your head screwed on straight."

"But Liz …"

"Bye, Sweetie. Have fun. Call me when you escape."

She walked away, out into the clear blue early day, a day that he would probably have appreciated if he wasn't about to be locked up for his own good.

Donnie sighed.

"OK, let's go, Carsten. I have to go and swat the bats in my belfry."

Donnie followed Carsten through the doorway and apprehensively walked with him down the hall.

He quickly realized that the crazy house was nothing if not amusing. You meet all sorts in the locked wards of a psychiatric hospital, and, truth be told, it can pretty funny if you pay attention and you aren't too zoned out from your own psych meds.

True story: Upon Donnie's arrival at Serenity Heights, a disheveled Jerry Garcia look-alike in blue plaid flannel pajamas and furry blue slippers walked up to him, stopped him and his stoic escort, the ever-taciturn, non-empathetic drone named Carsten, on their way to Donnie's new accommodations.

"Hey, hey, hey, man, hey, hey, hey," the Jerry Garcia guy said with a great deal of agitation and the look of a trapped animal in his eyes. "Do you see that glass over there? The one on the table? With water in it?"

What?

"Uh, yeah, I do. I see a glass of something. What about it?" Donnie asked, in no mood for this kind of interaction.

"OK, OK, OK," flannel Jerry Garcia said maniacally. "Is it half empty or half full? Half empty or half full? Half empty or half full?"

"Look, dude, I don't know what your trip is, but I'm here for depression. I told my girlfriend (was Liz still his girlfriend?) I was gonna kill myself. So, of course it's half empty. Like the rest of my life."

"Oh, man, lighten up," flannel Jerry Garcia said. "It ain't all bad. Not bad. This place'll help ya. By the time they're done with you you'll see the glass is half full. Half full! Half full!"

"Sure, half full of bile."

Wow, wow, wow, wow," Jerry Garcia said. "You're a real downer. A real downer, man."

"Well, yeah. A suicide threat usually means you're a little down, pal. Now beat it, freak."

"Not nice, man, not nice, man, not nice."

"Glad you noticed, *mon ami*."

"Hey, you look terrible! You got black eyes! What happened to you, man? Maybe somebody slugged you cuz you're not nice."

"Yeah, something like that."

So went Donnie's first few moments at Serenity Heights.

This was going to be uproarious fun.

— 8 —

ALONE WITH HIS SCARY THOUGHTS

Carsten dragged Rockin' Donnie to a small dorm room with a bed and a nightstand. A peephole on the door looked in, not out, all the better for staff to check in on their wards. There were no books, no TV, nothing to do but think, which was hazardous in Donnie's condition.

Donnie surveyed his new surroundings as Carsten closed the door. He lay on the bed and assessed his situation.

Savagely hung over. Check.

Depressed. Check.

Suicidal? Check.

Unattached. Well, there was Liz. But that barely counted apparently. Or did it?

Unemployed? Likely. He needed to tell management that he might be unable to play ELO, or even Journey for that matter, until his personal banshees stopped screaming. But saving his job wasn't a priority right now. He had to gather his wits.

Fat, balding, and burned out? Check.

Beaten to a pulp? Check.

Missing Marie? Incessantly. Desperately.

Donnie was worshiping his past, a past of hearts and roses and booze and … and love, with Marie back in their late-20s freewheeling years. It was a past he was always trying to recapture because the present and future seemed so desperately bleak and hopeless.

Those were the days, he pined.

Yet he was left only with fond memories and the torture of knowing his sexual self-indulgence caused their break-up.

His devotion to the past was part of his problem, part of what made him a reckless bastard who cared only for his feelings and his needs. His soul was tortured by his own selfishness, selfishness which related to Marie's having left his life. Donnie was always trying to regain the happiness of that era in his life.

But such pursuits were futile and Donnie knew it. It was the source of two breakdowns and the suicide call to Liz. Liz, who loved him enough to get him help, to be a companion and lover even as his personal arc plunged, crashed to the ground and brought him to a madhouse in Deerhead, Minnesota.

Donnie tried to push the thoughts away as he lay on the cot reminiscing.

He was distracted from daydreaming by wondering if and when a doctor would patch him up. His nose was killing him. It hurt to breathe.

Things weren't exactly looking up. But maybe his stay in Crazy Town would allow him to emerge as a new person, a new Rockin' Donnie. No, a new Donald. Maybe he could even in the process make some good cash and maybe a few prizes — a new Barcalounger? — by starring in the first of Jerry Most's *Losers on Parade* episodes.

Donnie brightened at the thought of baring his damaged soul on TV, even if it was cable access. Oh, and a podcast. How hard could that be? Most people who knew him either personally or by his "Rockin' Donnie" persona already knew his sordid past. He talked about it during his show all the time. Few of his misadventures, both real, imagined and embellished, the ones he remembered anyway, went unreported on any of his radio shows over the years.

He was an open book of malefaction.

Take the time, for example, when he was on stage introducing the Illinois-based band Cheap Trick as "Cheap Joke."

Ha ha!

This was before Cheap Trick made it big, but no one in the band found his joke funny even then. Of course, in the spirit of "Rockin'

Donnie," he had ingested a few unidentified pills and washed them down with a tall glass of Dewar's. As the band stood behind him and he began his intro and correctly named them, Donnie choked on the word "trick" and vomited all over the stage. The crowd was delighted, since few sights are as hilarious as seeing a man puke.

The band, however, was not amused. Nor was the crew.

A burly roadie ran out on stage to wipe up the mess and another kicked Donnie in the butt, knocking him over and into the stinking puddle, nearly taking the first roadie with him. Covered in his own vomit, he staggered off stage and into the arms of the band's massive road manager, who invited Donnie to exit the building post-haste or face the fierce wrath of a monstrous and ornery security guy named Studley.

He related the story on his radio show the next day, telling listeners the whole thing was as funny as any Marx Brothers farce.

Groucho would have died laughing.

Oh, yeah. Puking on stage. A real knee-slapper of a tale.

Donnie was such a card.

Tee, hee, hee.

But as much as he would have liked to, Donnie couldn't escape his past. It was on the public record, and even his fans, and there were probably dozens of them left, knew he was something of a loser. When he thought about it, then, maybe the whole "Rockin' Donnie" thing hadn't been as much fun as all that. Maybe it was even a bit demeaning.

Still, he thought, he may as well go with it. Everything about him was known to the public, to the extent that anyone had been paying attention to him in the first place, and his past was his to keep. Whether he wanted it or not.

He decided that the perfect place to unburden himself of his past misdeeds was to go on Jerry's show and spill his putrid guts. Especially since material gain, and maybe some public notice that would rejuvenate his career, would be involved in revealing his true, mostly true anyway, confessions.

Meanwhile, he slowly realized that he was currently detained in a place he was destined to wind up. The nut house. The loon hatch. The bird cage. The squirrel's nest.

The Cuckoo's Nest! Just like Jack Nicholson!

Cool!

But once the reality of his situation set in Donnie became agitated. The idea of confinement, even for his own good, was daunting. He was a free-range chicken. He couldn't be cooped up, especially in a facility designed for people who were much worse off than he was. Take flannel Jerry Garcia, for example. He seemed like a specimen destined to sleep in bus stations if he were ever released from this bughouse.

At least the Jerry Garcia-looking guy saw the glass half full, though.

Free-range or not, Donnie was going to have to get used to a new routine at Serenity Heights for a few days.

First things first.

It was late Sunday morning and Donnie assumed there was only a skeleton crew at the place. Orderlies, cooks and an on-duty psychiatrist, available for violent incidents only, were the only staff available on this sleepy Sunday.

Donnie figured he would have to have a chat with the admitting psychiatrist Monday morning.

That would be fun.

Then he had to find an infirmary and have a doctor look at his nose and bind his wounds. He couldn't believe there was no one who could have patched him up that day, but it was a sunny Sunday in Deerhead and everyone was out picnicking or boating or whatever else they did on nice days.

Serenity Heights was a booby hatch, not a general hospital. The shrink and general practitioner wouldn't be available until Monday, so Donnie went to the phone-booth-sized bathroom, showered and went back to bed to doze and to suffer from his wounds, physical and psychological, alone, in silence.

Sunday would be a day of restless contemplation and tormented sleep. In any event, Donnie thought, Monday would be more fun than a barrel of mandrill baboons.

With little to do except wander the hallways or doze, Donnie tried to sleep off his hangover and manage his pain as best he could. He did not want to mingle with his maniac cohorts.

But as he lay on the cot, he realized he had not eaten anything since the peanut butter sandwich last night. It was dinnertime and he wanted to eat something, anything, at least to relieve his hunger pangs.

He got up, opened the door, and started looking for Carsten or anyone else who could get him some grub. He stood in the hall looking around like some small-town tourist in New York City. The hall was empty but he heard voices and walked toward them.

He walked to the recreation room and found Carsten talking about Kierkegaard with a ghostly, vacant-eyed patient who simply nodded as Carsten expounded on existentialism.

Donnie walked up to the pair and cleared his throat.

Carsten looked up at Donnie as though Donnie had broken his deeply philosophical train of thought.

"Mr. Derringer," he intoned. "What can I do for you?"

"Um, yes ... ah, Carsten, is it?" Donnie said. "I was wondering if there was someplace where I could get some chow."

"We have a cafeteria, but I will have to escort you there and sit with you as you eat because this is a secure area and you have been deemed a danger to yourself and a likely escapee," Carsten deadpanned.

"OK, Carsten, giddyup! I'm starved," Donnie said. "Let's go get some fine dining."

"Follow me, please," Carsten said, leading Donnie down the hallway toward a security-locked door that was the only barrier between Donnie and food.

Or escape!

But Donnie was too tired to flee and he slowly strolled with Carsten into the cafeteria.

Carsten silently tailed Donnie with every step like a KGB guard in a gulag as Donnie walked to the buffet. He could choose from delicious fare such as fried fish patties, dried-out cheeseburgers, limp French fries, calcified pepperoni pizza, and soggy green beans, just like Mama used to make. Dessert was lime Jell-O complete with embedded marshmallows.

Famished, Donnie grabbed a cheeseburger and a slice of pizza, fries and coffee. It was probably more food than he would eat, but it was all free! Why not gorge?

The spartan dining room was empty and they grabbed a table near the buffet.

Donnie immediately began jamming the cheeseburger into his mouth like a toddler who had just discovered peaches.

Carsten said nothing and Donnie realized the scene was too quiet. He needed some kind of ambient noise. At home he always played music, even if he wasn't paying attention to it.

He couldn't stand silence. It was so boring and it made his ears ring.

Donnie swallowed the remains of the burger, cleared his throat and broke the stillness by asking the reticent Carsten a question.

"What's the deal with the tat?" he asked. "Socrates, is it? Not Aristotle or Zeno?"

Carsten stared at Donnie as though he was a college freshman.

"I am an admirer of the ancient Greek philosophers," he responded. "I love philosophy in general, whether it's Plato or Kant. They help me understand the world of logic, the idea of our very existence. The philosophical paradigm is of great interest to me. It helps to make sense of this chaotic, unruly world. It helps me understand myself. As Socrates said, 'The unexamined life is not worth living.'"

Donnie thought about the perils of examining his own treacherous path of life. Writing the facts of his life in his memoir was hard enough without actually probing its meaningless self-indulgence.

Sorry, Soc, baby, but my life is better without much investigation as to its essence. But Donnie was interested in Carsten's reasons for delving into the metaphysical.

"Pretty deep stuff there, Carst," Donnie said. "Why aren't you teaching somewhere?"

"I am an autodidact," Carsten said. "After a wasted high school career, I found it impossible to gain entrance to any college or university and thus, as a self-educated individual without a degree, I am not as such qualified to instruct at institutions of higher learning. I also believe that trying to teach Wittgenstein to young burnouts and otherwise disinterested youth would be disheartening to say the least."

"So with all that background, you're an orderly at a nut house? Kinda seems beneath you."

"There is nobility in all work, however menial it may seem to those who wish for greater things," Carsten said. "I am content with my job, my books, my home and my life even if it did not or will not reach the heights of your long-established career in radio."

"You know about my career?" Donnie said.

"Yes, I am a regular listener of your late-night show and although I do not always approve of the pedestrian playlist, I enjoy your occasional reminiscences of your wild days. I have always thought I would be a good radio personality. Everyone has a career they dreamed of but never accomplished. Mine is radio. But it has only been a fantasy which I chose not to pursue due to the moronic content of contemporary broadcasting. That would indeed be beneath me."

"Sorry for making a living, Carst," Donnie said sarcastically. "They wouldn't accept me at medical school."

"I do not want to demean you or your profession per se, but as I look at radio it has become, as McLuhan said of television, a vast wasteland. Still, the idea of a radio show with some level of integrity has always appealed to me. I just never thought such a show would be available to me so when I heard there was a job opening here at Serenity Heights for someone of my physical size and stoic demeanor, and since I needed a job that would allow me to sustain my quiet lifestyle of books and music, I availed myself of the opportunity."

Donnie considered all of this for a moment, then, after loudly chomping on the last of the pizza, said: "Hey Carsten, can I take something to eat back to my room in case I get hungry later?"

"Yes, you may," Carsten said, mildly annoyed that Donnie had apparently not been listening. "There is a vending machine in the hall where you might find sustenance."

"Do they have circus peanuts?" Donnie asked brightly. "The orange ones are great but I prefer the colored ones."

"I am not aware of the contents of the machine as I do not eat such garbage," Carsten said.

"Well!" said Donnie huffily. "What are you, one of those freaky vegans? Man, I could never do without a juicy cheeseburger."

Carsten said flatly, "I eat fish and dairy, but not meat. And I don't eat anything from vending machines."

"Suit yourself," Donnie said. "I'm going for the sweets!"

They approached the vending machine and Donnie did not find circus peanuts. After careful consideration he chose one box of Jujubes, one box of Mike and Ikes and a package of peanut butter cups because, well, peanut butter! But when he realized he had no change, or any cash for that matter, he turned to Carsten.

"Hey, Carsten, you got any ..."

"Just push the button for the item you desire," Carsten said. "All food, no matter how wretched, is free at Serenity Heights."

Cool! If only they had free booze and weed, Donnie thought.

Donnie grabbed his candies and Carsten led him to his room without further comment.

"Thanks, Carst," Donnie said as he walked into his austere room. "Maybe later we can talk about Marxian dialectic, but right now I gotta hit the rack for a solid night's sleep. Big day tomorrow and I'm shagged."

Donnie flopped on the creaky bunk as Carsten closed the door.

He grabbed the flat pillow, pulled up the thin and scratchy blanket, and thought about facing the admitting psychiatrist as he dozed off for the night.

The prospect of talking to a shrink made Donnie uneasy.

He had no idea.

— 9 —

ROCKIN' DONNIE VS. DR. SALLY DIXON

Dr. Sally Dixon was one tough shrink.

She was a tall, platinum blonde woman with short, close-cropped hair, and a beautifully angular face that could both launch or sink a thousand ships with just a gaze. She was gorgeous in an icy cold way, and she could cast a devastating, withering glance at any patient — any person, for that matter — who dared to offer her a line of bullshit. She seemed devoid of human emotion, but her disaffected manner actually added to an aura of intense credibility.

Donnie was groggily awakening when Carsten knocked on his door and said it was time for a session with Dr. Dixon. Donnie was instinctively afraid. He hadn't even met Dr. Dixon yet, but he sensed that she was going to force him to face some nasty truths about himself. He also figured she would prescribe some zombifying meds that would take all the "Rockin'" out of Donnie.

Maybe that would be a good thing.

It was Monday morning.

Time for Donnie to face the music.

Donnie and his cheerless companion walked in silence down the scuffed, off-white tiled hallway decorated with art hanging on the beige walls created by previous and current patients. Lots of paintings of Technicolor birds perched on gnarled branches. Sailboats and sunsets, or maybe they were sunrises. Glass half full, Donnie, glass half full. Yes, they were sunrises, the start of a new and better day.

They arrived at Dr. Dixon's office. Carsten, the uber-reserved galoot, knocked lightly on the heavy oak door.

"Enter, please," came a husky female voice from the other side of the door. Dr. Dixon sounded like Lauren Bacall. Mmmmm. Donnie fantasized she would tell him to whistle just like Bacall in *To Have and Have Not*. *"You know how to whistle, don't you, Steve? Just put your lips together and blow."*

Donnie's heart beat like a scared bunny's at the very thought and he felt a lump growing in his pants.

Sexy.

Carsten opened the door and let Donnie in, closing it behind him. It sounded to Donnie like a cell door slamming shut. Dr. Dixon's office was lined with dark-paneled oak walls, burgundy carpeting and small but thick cinder-block glass windows, which Donnie figured were probably hard enough to prevent escape by self-defenestration.

Donnie was now all alone with Dr. Dixon, and he was suddenly terrified. His head and body still ached from his Saturday night bender and subsequent drubbing. His tongue was glued to the top of his dry mouth. His nose throbbed. He had brought the box of Jujubes with him to Dr. Dixon's office because he was starved again.

He hoped she would let him eat the candy while they chatted. But even with the Jujubes Donnie was not ready for Dr. Sally Dixon.

Upon casting his gaze at the doctor, though, Donnie immediately thought she was incredibly sexy. A woman who would be difficult to conquer.

A challenge!

"Sit, please," Dr. Dixon said, standing and pointing to a stiff dark-wood chair on the other side of her intimidating oak desk. The chair had no arms, making Donnie especially uncomfortable and fidgety. He didn't know what to do with his hands.

Dr. Dixon sat perfectly upright and stiffly in the stuffed leather armchair behind her desk. She folded her hands on the surface. Papers were neatly stacked in small piles.

"Don't I get to plop on the couch?" Donnie said, joking feebly and pointing to a soft, dimpled leather sofa at the far end of the room.

Dr. Dixon stood again, slowly, like the Bride of Frankenstein rising from the operating table. Donnie noted that she favored dark pants suits over skirts or dresses. This was a true shame, Donnie thought upon meeting her, because he imagined that she had great legs. Knock it off, Donnie, he immediately thought. This is serious and she isn't going to sleep with you. Or will she? Donnie was always holding out hope when it came to women, even the severe Dr. Dixon.

"You may lie on the couch if you wish, but I suspect that upon your lying down, you will continually have to fight the urge to sleep," she said. "You will not sleep during my sessions. Understood?"

"Yes, ma'am … uh, Doctor?" Donnie said, shifting uncomfortably in the armchair. He nervously loaded his mouth with a handful of candy.

"My name is Sally Dixon," she said. "Doctor Sally Dixon. You may call me Dr. Dixon. And who are you? Please introduce yourself formally."

"I'm, um, Donnie, I mean Donald Derringer," Donnie said, chewing as the Jujubes stuck to his teeth. He smacked his lips and said: "I go by the monicker 'Rockin' Donnie.'"

She gave Donnie the once-over. She stared at him in silence. Donnie felt like a naughty little boy in the principal's office.

"Well, Rockin' Donnie," she said acidly, "welcome to Serenity Heights. I looked at your admission papers and it says you drunkenly called a girlfriend and threatened suicide. That sounds pretty dramatic. Do you like drama, Mr. Derringer? Do you like to scare your friends by telling them you're going to kill yourself? Is that how Rockin' Donnie gets his kicks these days now that his shock jock career has ebbed?

"Are you finally going to act on your suicidal ideations or are you just looking for attention?"

There's that term. "Suicidal ideations."

Donnie shrunk into the chair. As he slouched, he could feel himself blushing with embarrassment. He used his tongue to clean out the remnants of the candy off his teeth and he couldn't choke out a word.

"Donald?"

"Uh, yes, Dr. Dixon," he croaked, pushing his tongue on the roof of his mouth to capture the last Jujube. "I mean no, Dr. Dixon. Liz isn't really my girlfriend. She says she loves me and, I mean, we sleep together sometimes, but…"

She ignored his comment about Liz and continued on like an NKVD interrogator in Stalinist Russia.

"Yes, you do get your kicks that way, or no you don't? You do get your kicks by threatening suicide or you don't? Please spare me your comments about the poor woman whom you've occasionally bedded. It is of no relevance here."

"Um, no, I…"

"No, of course you don't. But the thought of killing yourself has become more dominant in your mind, hasn't it? It's always been there, hasn't it? Maybe you haven't expressed it verbally to anyone else until now, but I suspect the thought of ending it all, although latent for some time, is growing to be a constant companion these days. Is that the case?"

Donnie shifted awkwardly in the chair and meekly said, "I guess."

"You guess?"

"OK, yes, I've thought about thc Big Sleep."

"Your use of colloquialisms like 'Big Sleep' is quite charming and even cinematic but we don't use such terminology here. Suicide is a critical and dangerous issue. It is not to be joked about."

"Um, OK. Look, I just had a bad night. I…"

"Well, may I suggest that that's what happens when you drink yourself into a stupor, smoke gigantic joints and gobble pills by the fistful. You've had many bad nights during your life. Frankly, some might say you're just a miserable alcoholic drug abuser. I don't think you're an alcoholic by the clinical definition, but you do like self-medicating with cheap booze and dope. They help you try to escape something. The question is, what are you running from?"

Donnie knew he was trying to escape his longing for Marie but dared not reveal that to the saturnine doctor.

"I, I'm not quite sure. I don't really think I'm running from anything *per se*. More like avoiding something."

"And what might that be, 'Rockin' Donnie'?"

Sarcasm oozed from her voice as she spat his name. He thought she was being nasty for effect. But she was exercising some much-needed authority over Donnie.

Donnie felt he was under attack and that maybe this psychiatric stuff wasn't going to work. OK, so he screwed up. He shouldn't have called Liz and threatened to die by a Hendrix-like pill overdose. But now he was in a bit of a jam, a jam of his own making, as always, and he didn't know how to get out of this one except by playing along.

"I think I'm trying to avoid thoughts of my failed life and career. Sixty-something years old and my career is shot. And I don't even have an NOK. A next-of-kin. I listed Pete Townshend, the genius guitar player from The Who…"

"I'm familiar with Mr. Townshend and the term NOK, but go on. I saw your admission papers. Tell me why do you think you are a failure?"

"Well, no offense, but a place like Deerhead, Minnesota is not exactly a place where successful people go when their career is soaring. I mean really, it's a dumpy little town in the middle of nowhere. To wind up here is kind of like being in the bardo. Seriously, Purgatory has more to offer than this miserable burg."

Dr. Dixon arched her eyebrows and smiled a reptilian grin. She was moving in for the kill and Donnie was trapped.

"Really," she sneered. "And just what metropolitan area do you find to be Paradise?"

"Well, let's see," he said absently, still calculating whether Dr. Dixon's hard-case attitude was merely posing or whether he actually had a chance with her for a rollicking bed ride. He snapped out of his fantasy and back to reality in time to consider her question.

"Mr. Derringer?"

"Oh. Yes. Ah, the way I look at it, most of Florida is too humid and the cockroaches are bigger than cats. By the way, why do they wear Hawaiian shirts in Florida? Couldn't they have invented Florida shirts? Hey, maybe something with prints of cockroaches on them. Arizona is too hot and you have to check your shoes for scorpions and rattlesnakes. California? Psychopathic killers everywhere. Smog. Earthquakes! And the traffic! Meanwhile the entire Midwest, except maybe for Chicago, is a dead zone of huntin' and fishin' and hams in slow cookers, although Milwaukee is OK and Madison is really cool. But if I'd gone to Madison, without a degree I'd wind up being one of those pathetic aging cab drivers telling passengers about the Brezhnev Doctrine and trying to re-live their glory days in the dumpy bars where they spent their youth. Madison is full of people like that.

"Where does that leave us? I've been to most of these places, so I know them well."

"OK, maybe Portland, Oregon. They kind of leave you alone to be a freak there but they don't have Major League Baseball, so that's out. So, there's Boston. Great town but you can't afford to live there on a DJ's salary. New York is big and scary and rude. Plus, I hate the Yankees. I guess I'm running out of places. I don't know where I'd rather be. I just know it's not in a dead-end burg like Deerhead, Minnesota among the crazies at Serenity Heights."

Dr. Dixon regarded Donnie with silent disdain, then spoke.

"You're a bit of a snob, then. A man who's too good for everybody else and everyplace else. Maybe that's why you submerge yourself in booze and pot and pills. Maybe you're not running from anything at all. You are just easily bored. And you think you're better and smarter than everybody else. I do suspect that you are bipolar and that you are constantly self-medicating with said substances. I will prescribe a medication to treat your symptoms. You will take these medications, possibly for the rest of your life.

"But I also think you've got something of a disassociation syndrome. You've disconnected yourself from all of your misdeeds and human contact. That's why you are such a womanizer. You build walls around yourself because you're afraid of engaging in a real relationship. You believe sex is the only way to make a connection with women.

"In fact, you like to torpedo relationships, sometimes with friends, suicide threats and the like, but especially with women. I'm guessing there are one or two women in your past whom you've hurt and as a result are haunted by the notion of what could have been if only you'd managed to let your guard down and truly let them into your life."

Donnie was getting scared now. He had heard stories about psych meds and how you take them and wind up shuffling and barely conscious. Nope. Not for Rockin' Donnie. But this business about a disassociation disorder?

How did she know?

What a pro!

Throwing up his guard as usual, Donnie rallied a bit. He started behaving like himself, the wise-cracking, mad man who cared not a whit about what people thought of him, least of all some small-town shrink.

"Doc," he said, guessing that she probably hated being called Doc, "ya hit it right on the head. Thank you so much for your insight. I'm cured. I won't be needing drugs after our revealing session. God bless you. Now if you'll excuse me, I have beer in the fridge at home that's calling my name."

He got up to leave.

"Sit down, Mr. Derringer," she commanded. "Do you think this is funny? Maybe like playing 'Gary's Got a Boner' five or six times consecutively during your radio show? Is this funny?"

How did she know about that? he wondered.

"Yes," she snapped. "Your 'rockin' history is well known and only a bit of research unearthed your oeuvre and some of the bizarre acts you've engaged in over the course of your, ah, career."

Donnie ignored her jab and kept up his patter.

"Do I find all of this funny? Do you mean circus-clown funny or Three Stooges funny? I find that most women hate the Stooges. But I'm guessing even you get a chuckle or two when Moe puts Curly's nose on an electric grinder and sparks come shooting out the other side. Come on. That's comedy gold. Nyuk, nyuk.

"Have you ever heard them sing "Swinging the Alphabet"? '*Bee-a-bay,*'" Donnie sang. "Comedy gold, I'm telling you, comedy gold. Educational too! Except now the song is stuck in my head, dammit."

Dr. Dixon grinned slightly but humorlessly.

"I know what you're up to, Mr. Derringer," she said. "You think I'm just some hick med dispenser who can be easily distracted from the real issue at hand. You think that because I chose to practice in Deerhead I'm easily fooled by your big-city posing. You, sir, are an arrogant rock-and-roll poseur with more issues than can be counted in one session."

"Jeez, Doc, you're getting a little defensive. Maybe I should be sitting behind that desk. I can assist you in addressing your own issues. Really. Come on, bare your soul. I'm here to help. Maybe we can get to the bottom of your own inferiority complex."

Donnie was having fun now. Dr. Dixon was not amused.

"Part of your problem is that in addition to a superiority complex, you have insecurities so deep that only alcohol, drugs and sex can mask them," she said. "You feel like a failure. You have the worst of all complexes: You feel like you used to be somebody, and you're haunted by the trail of carnage left with every person you've hurt with your actions and your insensitivity. I wonder how many people have been damaged by their exposure to you and your selfish desire to feed your own ego. In short, Mr. Derringer, you are an ass. A bipolar self-destructive ass who drags everyone around him into your dark and dreary world and can't face your disastrous past and the people, especially women, whom you have hurt."

"Wow," Donnie said. "Now you've really hurt my feelings. I confess. I'm a total jerk. I hang my head in shame. Can I go now?"

"Yes, you may leave our session now," she said. "But I can guarantee our next one will be far more productive. I know you, Rockin' Donnie Derringer. I know you've created a persona you can't escape because your real self is full of insecurities and complete insensitivity to the feelings of others. You live for self-gratification at the expense of other people. You're a borderline sociopath, and as someone who likely had a broken childhood, you think your difficult upbringing is an excuse for your reprehensible behavior. I am right now considering what meds to prescribe you. You're sicker than you know. And I aim to fix that."

"OK, great. I've got something to look forward to," Donnie said with sarcastic enthusiasm. "Our next session should be a barnburner. We can talk about how I secretly was in love with my mother and I wanted to kill my father. Real Freudian stuff.

"But, hey, I've got to get back to my room and gaze at the ceiling while thinking of the many sins I've committed, especially with women. That would ordinarily lead to a terrific whack-off session. It kind of gives me the creeps to have the peephole in the door that looks into my room, not out. I'd hate to think somebody like Carsten would watch me as I conjure memories of the great sex with old girlfriends. On the other hand, it might give me a kinky thrill to think someone, say you, was observing the self-gratification you speak of. Anyhoo, gotta run, Doc."

Dr. Dixon broke his muddled train of thought.

"Mr. Derringer, may I say that you look like you've lost a street fight. Actually, my guess is it was a bar fight. Who was it that didn't think much of your acerbic comedy stylings?"

"It was a lout wearing an AC/DC shirt. Sure, I insulted his crude and juvenile tastes, but he had it coming."

"And so, apparently, did you, at least in the primitive mind of your attacker," she said, raising her eyebrows again. "I will have Carsten escort you to the infirmary where our doctor will examine you for any breaks or internal physical damage you incurred from your drubbing."

"Great, you have your own in-house Dr. Mengele. Terrific."

"I can assure you that our Dr. Rudolph Schwartzhammer is a well-respected, board certified physician. And may I add that your reference to a monstrous Nazi butcher is not witty. It is highly offensive."

"Sorry, Doc. Are you Jewish or something? I didn't mean to offend. Maybe I should have said Dr. Kevorkian."

Dr. Dixon showed uncharacteristic exasperation. Donnie already knew how to push her buttons. He was enjoying this now.

"Please leave now, Mr. Derringer. At once," she hissed.

"Carsten," she shouted, "please take Mr. Derringer to the infirmary."

Donnie thought about a parting shot as he left Dr. Dixon's office, maybe something about having cocktails with her later in the day, but he decided against it. He didn't want to antagonize her any further. She had too much power over his future in the loony bin.

Carsten was waiting outside the door to escort him.

"Carsty, my man," he shouted. "Could you get me a beer?"

Carsten said nothing. He nudged Donnie toward the infirmary with his elbow.

Session over. Like two scorpions in a bottle, the battle with Dr. Dixon was fought to a draw. A lot of stingers, but no real wounds.

So now what?

—10—

THE DOCTOR IS IN

Carsten brought Donnie into Dr. Schwartzhammer's waiting room and told him to sit.

"The doctor will be with you in a moment," he murmured, and left.

Donnie sat on a wooden bench that would have better fit a train station than a doctor's office. He shuffled through the magazines on an end table. *Good Housekeeping. Look Magazine. Look Magazine?* Good Lord, how long had these periodicals been here?

He found a thumb-stained *Sports Illustrated* that must have been several years old judging by the smeared cover. Turns out the Red Sox had won the World Series. In 2004.

As Donnie absently paged through the ancient *Sports Illustrated,* Dr. Schwartzhammer silently entered the room. He was 70-ish, short, nearly bald with a greasy comb-over and he wore horn-rimmed glasses that looked like they came straight out of the 1950s. His mechanical smile revealed yellowing teeth with a gap between his front chompers. He was wearing a frayed white doctor's coat that had his name embroidered over the Serenity Heights logo.

Donnie looked up and stood.

"Mr. Derringer?" he said, with some unidentifiable eastern European accent. Latvian? Lithuanian? German? Who knew? "Are you Mr. Derringer?"

"Yes, I'm Donnie Derringer. You must be Dr. Rudolph Schwartzhammer. I guessed that from the name on your doc's coat."

"Mmm, yes, very well," Schwartzhammer droned, his intensely sour breath filling Donnie's sinuses. "Please follow me to the examination room. I will need to look you over thoroughly, fix your broken *gesicht* and check for any internal damage. From your looks you took a pretty savage beating. Well-deserved, I'd guess."

What? A doctor who thought people deserved beatings?

"Jeez, Doc, I don't think a beating is warranted when you are simply helping someone understand that their music sucks. I mean I was just in a bar when an idiot in an AC/DC T-shirt began…"

Dr. Schwartzhammer interrupted rudely.

"Please don't fill my office with your sordid tales of drinking and fighting," he said sharply. "No one is interested, least of all me. I deal with all kinds here, mostly people who in their haze manage to do stupid things to harm themselves. You are no different, Mr. Derringer. Now, please undress and put on this hospital gown."

Schwartzhammer reached into a drawer and pulled out a paper-thin plain light blue gown and threw it on the examining table. He left the room so Donnie could change, but before he left turned around, looked Donnie in the eye and said: "Make it snappy. I don't want to spend all day examining a drunken depressive."

Donnie widened his eyes in disbelief.

"Are you serious? You think I deserved a beating?"

"Frankly, Mr. Derringer, I don't care what happened," Dr. Schwartzhammer said. "You are here for reasons I cannot even fathom, and I'm supposed to fix your broken body, not your brain. I can only assume that for whatever reason you are here you came because you did something idiotic. That is all. Now put on the gown. I will return promptly in three minutes. Be ready."

"Oh, sure, Doc," Donnie said. "Say, I hope this frock covers my schlong. I don't want to scare anyone."

"You wear the gown with the opening in the back, degenerate. Now, if you please…"

Dr. Schwartzhammer left the room and Donnie disrobed. He had not been offered a change of clothes since he arrived at Serenity Heights, and his blue jeans were spattered with blood from his own nose. They smelled like the beer he had sleepily dumped on himself when Liz found him. His black T-shirt had white lettering on it that said: "Charles Bukowski is Dead. Long Live Hank Chinaski," and it smelled of sweat. He really needed some new garments.

Donnie opened a closet door opposite the examining table, and, ignoring the hooks inside the closet he dropped his clothes on the floor. He put on the gown with the opening in front just to challenge the evil doctor. Donnie laid on his back, stretched and called out: "Come and get it, Doc!"

His average-sized flaccid penis was visible through the gown's opening and it rested on his left inner thigh.

Dr. Schwartzhammer returned and saw Donnie lounging on his back on the examination table, hands behind his head as though he were on a Greek beach. The doctor was incensed as he considered Donnie's impertinence.

"You are quite the comedian, you … you poor excuse for a shock jock," Dr. Schwartzhammer sputtered. "I've heard about you from Dr. Dixon. Do you think you can startle me with your antics? Do you remember where you are and who my criminally insane patients have been? Do you not think I have seen larger phalluses during my career? I can assure you that I have. In fact, I would consider yours to be about average, maybe even on the small side. And the tattoo pointing to your member? A bit jagged. Did you do it yourself?"

"Ouch, Doc! You really know how to play on a guy's deepest insecurities. I'm wondering, though. How many of those large members you speak of have been lodged in your fat ass?" Donnie sassed, grinning. "C'mon, Doc, no shame in that. Come to terms with it. Don't live in your angry closet."

Donnie figured this rigid Teutonic physician was especially homophobic.

Dr. Schwartzhammer took a step toward the examining table and commanded: "Sit up!"

Again, the doctor's breath caused Donnie to cough. He thought he actually saw a housefly drop from the air as Schwartzhammer's acrid exhaust filled the room.

Donnie, realizing that his antagonistic style might once again result in physical pain, slowly arose from his reclining position.

Dr. Schwartzhammer pinched Donnie's chin. He turned Donnie's head with a jerk. Dr. Schwartzhammer was not exactly gentle about it and his bedside manner left something to be desired.

"Your well-deserved black eyes will heal," he said. "There appears to be no injury to the eyes themselves."

Then Dr. Schwartzhammer pinched Donnie's nose and violently shook his head. Donnie nearly blacked out from the pain.

"You diabolical witch doctor!" Donnie screeched. "That fucking hurt and you know it! Fuck!"

"Mmm, yes," Schwartzhammer calmly responded. "I am aware of that in fact. It was just my simple way of determining whether your nose was indeed broken. And yes, your assailant rather effectively smashed your snout. A shame, since it had been such a nice, bulbous, veiny red specimen. Surgery may be required, but as I am not a surgeon it will be up to you to seek further medical help once you are released from this refuge for those with infirm and weak minds.

"I will tape up your nose and send you back down your impertinent, self-destructive and miserable path. I wish you good luck, Mr. Derringer, although since you wound up in this asylum, I believe your luck has already run out.

"By the way, your breath stinks of peanut butter."

Look who's talking!

"Sorry, I forgot the bring Tic Tacs with me," Donnie shot back.

"You should brush your teeth," Schwartzhammer hissed.

"Thanks, Dr. Sunshine. You are a true healer," Donnie said with dripping sarcasm. "From which medieval medical school did you get your training?"

Dr. Schwartzhammer ignored him. He taped up Donnie's nose and asked him to lie back down so he could examine for any possible internal injuries. Donnie giggled as the doctor poked him over various parts of his abdomen.

"Sorry, Doc," he grinned. "I'm a bit ticklish."

There were apparently no internal wounds, but Schwartzhammer couldn't resist a closing argument.

"You have otherwise not been injured, Mr. Derringer," he said. "But may I say that in general you have the body of a withered 90-year-old man. Flabby skin, an idiotic tattoo of an arrow pointing to your prick, and the hair of a simian. Again, did you do the tattoo yourself with a safety pin? Maybe while in jail? The lines are quite jagged and have the look of a kindergartner's first drawing. Still, I'm sure the ladies find you irresistible. Now goodbye. Get out of my office and retreat to your pen."

He stormed out before Donnie could offer a retort. Donnie got up, got dressed and walked out to the waiting room, where Carsten, his constant companion, was waiting.

"Hello, Mr. Derringer. I hope you found medical attention of assistance," he said. "Dr. Dixon has asked that I escort you back to your room, where fresh clothing is laid on the bed."

Donnie didn't respond. He followed Carsten, walking like a condemned man back to his desolate room.

Carsten opened the door and told Donnie to go in and change clothes.

"Dr. Dixon selected the clothing herself," Carsten said grimly. "She said she hoped you would enjoy them."

He walked out, closing the door behind him.

Donnie walked to his bed and saw the clothes. New Levi's. Nice! Clean underwear. Didn't know you cared, Doc!

Underneath the blue jeans and the underwear was a brand-new black T-shirt. Cool. It's my color, Donnie thought.

Donnie picked up the T-shirt and turned it to the front.

It was an AC/DC tour shirt.

Very funny, Dr. Dixon.

Very fucking funny.

— 11 —

ALONE AGAIN WITH HIS SCATTERED THOUGHTS

DONNIE SLIPPED ON THE CLOTHES. The jeans were a little tight but wearable. They pinched his belly. There was no belt. Of course not. You don't give a belt to a man with suicidal ideations.

"Fuck," he spat as he put on the AC/DC T-shirt.

At least the T-shirt fit. At least it covered his navel. At least it was clean.

Donnie hopped into bed. The dorm-room door was not locked but he didn't feel like walking into the recreation room and playing Scrabble with some batshit crazy schizo who might turn on him the minute he used two z's to spell "jazz" and win big points. He also didn't feel like watching *The Price is Right* with the over-medicated, foot -shuffling zombies entranced by the idea of winning a new refrigerator and a trip to Aruba by correctly guessing the cost of such luxury items. In general, he didn't feel like the idea of socializing with the other inmates.

So he lay there again, alone with the thoughts of his life, his misdeeds, his broken past.

Was he really that bad a guy?

Well, yes. He was a total jerk. An asshole by any definition.

But a fun one!

Right?

His thoughts focused on the women he had burned. Especially Marie. Marie was The One, but she became The One Who Got Away because Donnie was too drunk, stoned, and horny to remain faithful.

Dr. Dixon said Donnie was running from something. If so, it was the thought of Marie that Donnie was running from. How he messed up and lost the love of his life.

Donnie thought he never would have ended up in his suicidal state if he and Marie had stayed together. She could have saved him. She was the only woman who drew the idea of marriage out of him. Maybe that was what he was avoiding. He had a wonderful, honest and loving relationship with Marie.

But as was his wont, he had screwed it all up.

Donnie then spent his career showing off for her, hoping that she would track him down and get back together with her fun-loving "wild and crazy guy."

To Donnie, no one compared with Marie, and the guilt he felt over hurting her and losing her was sometimes overwhelming. They had met when Donnie was a hotshot DJ in Rockford, Illinois. Donnie was in his late thirties and he wondered if he would spend the rest of his life entertaining drunks and stoners and X-heads with bad music and crazy capers in increasingly smaller markets. He was beginning to think there must be more to life, he just didn't know what.

Then Marie came along and he knew.

Donnie's itinerant lifestyle had left him unattached to anybody. He had spent time working the big markets, Los Angeles, Dallas, Tampa-St. Petersburg, the Manhattan suburbs of New Jersey but he quickly wore out his welcome in those venues after he engaged in outrageous public misbehavior — he was fond of mooning from the stage at station-sponsored events — occasionally he had to be bailed out of the hoosegow.

Donnie's schtick would become tiresome to his audience and station management, and he was constantly forced to move on to smaller and less metropolitan areas.

Boise, Idaho and Butte, Montana were part of his western-state swing. But there was also Fargo, North Dakota, Wausau, Wisconsin,

Ann Arbor, Michigan and myriad other stops on his decades-long radio life journey through America.

He had been successful in Ann Arbor, especially among the students who thought his sophomoric humor and antics were amusing, but radio station management loves change, and Donnie had become expendable as younger and fresher talent arrived. Donnie was no longer young and fresh at age 36, so after a nation-wide job search involving guys-who-knew-guys he landed in Rockford.

The station even waged a small ad campaign: "Rockin' Rockford, here comes 'Rockin' Donnie Derringer!'"

Rockford turned out to be the last stop on Donnie's career itinerary before he staggered to Deerhead. Rockford was a place where he miraculously lasted for years as the weekday morning drive-time shift.

But radio gigs often end in tears and Donnie was abruptly fired for no good reason he could think of. After his dismissal in Rockford, he stayed in town and started freelancing as a DJ at weddings and local raves in vacant warehouses while he determined his next move. The engagements were sporadic, the money wasn't great and the music was lousy and loud but crowd-pleasing.

It wasn't a great way to make a living but at least it kept him in beer and dope and was sufficient to maintain a scaled-down lifestyle.

Marie had approached him in the DJ booth one night during a wedding reception and requested that he play Tom Waits' "Bad Liver and a Broken Heart," a tasteful request and a song that would accompany him for the rest of his life.

"Um, well, love the song, sweetheart, really I do, but this is a wedding and it's not exactly dance music," he stammered.

"Who cares? They'll just slow dance anyway."

Donnie queued up the beautiful, melancholy song and announced: "We're going to slow things down a bit, ladies and gentlemen, with a little Tom Waits. Enjoy!"

Indeed, they slow-danced.

Donnie had an immediate crush on this woman, this angel, this vision of beauty, so he pounced. He told her his stage name, "Rockin' Donnie Derringer." Then he asked her to dinner. Jumping from coffee to lunch and straight to dinner seemed like quite a romantic leap, but he took a chance.

Incredibly, she agreed.

A few nights later, they met at an upscale Mexican place near Donnie's apartment building that had white tablecloths and tasteful portraits on the walls featuring heroes of the Mexican War of Independence. He arrived first, and as he sat at the table near a painting of Miguel Hidalgo, Donnie got the weird feeling he was being stared at by this Mexican icon. It was probably from the hash he had smoked on the way to the restaurant. He always got a little paranoid when he was high in public places, especially with hash.

Marie arrived and saw him sitting at the table. The hostess escorted her, and Donnie distantly remembered his manners — he didn't want to make any mistakes of decorum. As they approached, he stood and smiled broadly. Marie gave him a quick kiss on the cheek and he pulled out her chair.

So far, so good.

She looked lovely. Absolutely beautiful. Stunning even. Out of her wedding reception gear, Donnie thought she looked really classy. She wore a short blue dress with a medium-cut neckline that beautifully framed her pearl necklace and revealed just a small but tasty hint of cleavage. She was taller than he remembered, and her navy-blue seamed stockings — oh God, were they silk? — highlighted a pair of legs that immediately engendered lustful thoughts in Donnie's stoned brain. He was disappointed that she was wearing flat shoes, but that didn't matter.

Marie's pale blue eyes met Donnie's and his heart stopped. Donnie knew right away that this budding relationship was going to be different from anything he had ever experienced.

Donnie was smitten.

"*Buenos tardes!*" he said, immediately regretting it. It was lame.

She smiled.

"Do you speak Spanish?" she said playfully.

"Um, no, I don't. I'm working on perfecting my Esperanto, though."

"Ah, then *bonan vesperon*."

Shit. Did she actually speak Esperanto?

He stared blankly and panicked for a moment.

"That means 'good evening' in Esperanto, silly," she said. "I thought you were working on your Esperanto skills. And no, I'm not fluent."

"I was joking. I was ..."

"I know you were joking, Donnie," she said. "It wasn't as though I thought you were some United Nations interpreter."

"No, I'm not," he said quietly. He shouldn't have smoked that hash. He was going to have a hard time keeping up with her.

"I'm just a simple disc jockey playing all the hits all the time and trying to make his way through an unforgiving world," he said. "I bring joy to the joyless through the rotten music I'm forced to play."

"That's quite a depressing perspective," she said with a grin. "I thought Rockin' Donnie Derringer would be a wild grab-it-while-you-can kind of guy. I thought maybe you were some kind of maniac. That attracted me to you. I like my men crazy. They're a lot of fun. At least for a while. And the sex is great."

Donnie was gobsmacked. She had already brought up the idea of crazy sex! Stunned, he gazed around the room and pointed toward the ceiling.

"I can swing from that chandelier if you like," he said. "Pants on or pants off. Your choice. I can also howl like a banshee."

"All right, save that for later, wild man. Let's eat."

Donnie was almost hyperventilating. Was this woman, this vision of beauty, really going to sleep with him on their first date? He tried to focus on the matter at hand. Masturbating. Stop it, Donnie! The word is masticating!

They ordered, and in the meantime, Donnie was finally leveling out a little from the deep hash buzz. During the first hour or two, Donnie was a regular Dick Cavett when he was stoned. He became witty and erudite, full of amusing anecdotes. At least he thought so. He was at his best when he was playing the role of stoned talk show host even if he wasn't always as funny as he believed he was.

The happy couple ate and during the meal they drank two bottles of sangria. Suitably buzzed, Donnie asked if they should find a club and go dancing after dinner.

Incredibly again, she said no. She had a better idea.

"Let's go back to your place. We can talk. Hang out. Have some drinks, maybe some bong hits and loosen up. See what happens from there. I have this charming image in my mind of your apartment being a cluttered, tiny hovel with hundreds of books and vinyl records — never CDs — scattered all over and old concert posters spread across the walls. I also imagine there are silverfish, but I'd rather not think of the vermin that likely infest your otherwise messy but delightful domicile. Bugs are kind of a turnoff, really. Bugs and dirty fingernails."

Dumbfounded by his apparent luck, Donnie peered at his fingernails — they were clean — and eagerly agreed to go back to his place. He hadn't cleaned the joint in a week and he hoped there weren't any porno mags in plain sight. Was the toilet clean? Had he left the seat up? He hadn't thought about having a guest, but hell, she seemed game no matter what.

Thusly began a yearlong hearts-and-flowers relationship that made Donnie think of something he had never thought of before. Love. Even marriage. Not kids, of course. But he loved Marie even more than dope and she was practically living with him. The dream of matrimony, foreign though it had previously been in Donnie's booze-and-dope-rattled brain, exploded after Marie found Donnie in the laundry room on top of the hostess at a house party they had attended one snowy Saturday night.

That was that.

Marie left the party in bitter tears. Donnie, being Donnie, figured there was no way out if this mess anyway so he may as well get his money's worth. He stayed the night with the hostess, a woman whose name was Leila or something, he couldn't remember, and when he got home there was no sign of Marie.

There would be no Marie for the rest of his life.

But the night after he betrayed her and got home to a new, Marie-less life, Donnie did what Donnie always did. He sat down on the ratty couch where he and Marie had first made love, lit a joint and sipped the remainder of a bottle of Jim Beam that was sitting on the coffee table. He got up and put "The Who Live at Leeds" on the turntable. He cranked the up sound for "My Generation." Nothing like the heavenly noise and musical chaos of "The Bleedin' Oo" to clear the mind and soothe the violently tortured soul.

Donnie was, of course, filled with intense remorse, an impulse with which he had previously not been acquainted. Even he sometimes felt mild regret for his Don Giovanni-style misdeeds with women. Don Giovanni went to Hell for his philandering, and without Marie, Donnie was in Hades.

He was especially bummed when he figured out that getting laid on a steady basis was no longer a possibility with Marie gone. He and Marie had been highly complementary bed partners. They were often spontaneous and sometimes not careful about using contraception because it was not always convenient in, say, a quiet art museum viewing room.

No matter! They would be together forever whatever might happen.

Ah, no.

Donnie sat on the couch dazed. He sighed deeply, gulped the bourbon, lit his bong and inhaled as though it might be the last time he breathed. Soon the effects of the pot and the liquor took hold of his brain, washing away any feelings of guilt about the laundry room, the hostess and the loss of Marie.

Guilt was a useless impulse, am I right? Donnie thought.

Party on!

Marie will see! Donnie figured becoming a big star would bring her back. He even thought that his crazy capers might be appealing to her. Or maybe she would rescue him from himself.

But as far as Marie was concerned, that was that, Donnie guessed. Every day became just another excuse to drink, smoke, party and maybe get laid. But most of all forget Marie.

Finally, he decided it was time to move on from Marie.

Except he never did.

Donnie could never again listen to Supertramp's "Hide in Your Shell." It was playing while they made love for the first time on his beer-stained and cigarette-burned couch. Van Morrison's "Tupelo Honey" also was off limits because of the painful memories it engendered.

It was their song.

He'd had several other relationships, even with the hostess with whom he had been caught on the pile of dirty laundry at the house party where he lost Marie. Most of the other women he got entangled with were crazoids, but all were meant to compensate for the loss of Marie.

There was Reva, who insisted on being called Rain Child. She was great in the sack, but as most relationships with those types the sex was great, even kinky. With most such affairs, built as they are around screwing, are quite boring for the other 23 and one-half hours in the day.

There was Allie, who had three cats and little time for changing litter boxes. Her house smelled of ammonia and cat shit. But again, the sex was primo and she was even good for few laughs outside the bedroom.

And, of course, there were dozens of one-nighters and a few that were little more than two-week trysts. But none of them were Marie.

Not even close.

Donnie had lost her because he was such a horrible jerk. But that self-awareness only made him worse. Marie wasn't coming back, so he buried himself in the "Rockin' Donnie" persona until he couldn't separate his real self from his wild-man character he had created. He didn't like his real self, Donald Henry Derringer, very much anyway.

From now on, Donnie would immerse himself in his "Rockin' Donnie" persona.

Rock and roll!

That was only part of the reason he was staying at Serenity Heights. The things he was running from, especially memories of Marie and his misdeeds over the years, had finally caught up with him.

And they had cornered him.

— 12 —

GROUP THERAPY

DONNIE WAS THINKING ABOUT MARIE as usual and dozing in his dorm room when Carsten knocked on his door.

"What?" Donnie said sleepily.

"Time for group therapy," Carsten said through the door.

Donnie got up and went to open the door.

"Carsty, baby! Did you bring me that beer I asked for?"

Carsten didn't flinch.

"It's time for group," he said flatly. He was a depressing countenance if there ever was one. God, he must love this job, Donnie thought.

"I take it then that rather than bringing me beer, you're taking me to some fresh hell I must endure in order to escape this snake pit," Donnie said.

Carsten just pointed to a door down the hallway and said: "It's in there. Let's go. Dr. Dixon's orders."

Apparently, Donnie's new nemesis Dr. Dixon was behind this new torture. OK, fine, Donnie thought, wishing he was at home on his couch with his bong and his records, let's do this thing.

As they walked down the sterile hallway, Donnie noticed more art on the walls. Green sheep in a blue pasture with black crows hovering above the pastoral scene. Wonder what that's all about?

Suddenly, Carsten whispered something. Something about beer? No, couldn't be.

"I'm sorry, Carst, did you say something?"

"Beer," Carsten whispered with the subtlety of a hooker trolling for a john on a quiet city street. "I can get you beer."

"I'm sorry, Carsten, but I thought I just heard you say you can get me some beer," Donnie said with a distinct lack of discretion.

"Shhhh," Carsten hissed. Then, again in a breathy whisper, he said: "I can get you anything you want. Except pot. Smoking pot smells and is too easily detected."

"Carsten, I think this is the beginning of a beautiful friendship," Donnie said gleefully. "Beer might make this place bearable. But why would you offer such a token of affection?"

"Shhhh! Look, Donnie, ah, Mr. Derringer, I love your show and I want to be your Sancho Panza. I don't have any meaningful companionship in Deerhead. Anything wrong with that or should I forget about getting you beer?" Carsten was insistent but impassive.

"Right. OK, Mr. Beermeister," Donnie said quietly. "Mum's the word. Just let me know what I need to do to get hold of said potable."

"Don't worry. I'll take care of it," Carsten said quietly. Then, with the persistence of a prison guard: "Now get in there. The group is already assembling."

They arrived at the door to the group therapy. Carsten opened it and Donnie saw the most incredible collection of misfit toys ever collected. Gray metal folding chairs with thinly padded seats were arranged in a semi-circle. Donnie surveyed the scene and at once noticed two beautiful young women with feeding tubes coming out of their noses. Bulimics, as it turned out. The tubes provided them with much-needed nutrition for their emaciated but otherwise gorgeous bodies.

Donnie, of course, wondered if he had a chance for some kinky sex with either or both of them — maybe at the same time! — but he also wondered what he would do with the tubes during a romantic clinch. In any event he was sure he could work something out if the chance arose. God, he was incorrigible. Sex in the mental hospital? Why not? That would be so cool! Thousands of guy points were at stake.

There was also the guy with the Jerry Garcia look of long, bushy graying hair, a beard to match the look. He was quieter now, as though he had determined that the glass was really half-empty after his initial encounter with Donnie. He wore a tie-dyed Grateful Dead T-shirt and tattered blue jeans. A possible partner in crime? It was worth considering. Donnie first wanted to see why the Jerry Garcia was there. Did he strangle his mother with a garden hose? Did he set fire to a library? Donnie wanted to believe Jerry Garcia-guy was a psychotic who wrote his father's name on his bedroom walls in his own blood. It seemed fitting.

Two other guys who looked like any boring suburban pair of neighbors sat next to each other at the far end of the circle. They were fairly nondescript. Both wore dress slacks and button-down patterned cotton shirts, one red and one blue. One wore tortoise-shell glasses. The other wore a vacant stare. Sure, they looked "normal," but that's the thing about being nuts. Most crazies, except for those who shuffle down the street in their pajamas and bare feet, or howl about the end of the world on street corners, don't have any visually identifying characteristics.

There was also a skinny little guy who looked like a near-death Wally Cox sitting next to the guy with the glasses.

Donnie sat in one of the chairs next to the Jerry Garcia guy. He seemed quieter and much less agitated than when he was maniacally asking Donnie about glasses being half full or empty. His head was down and he was breathing softly, muttering to himself.

As the patients sat in silence, suddenly the door opened and a lanky, balding, dark-bearded and John Lennon-style bespectacled man in blue jeans and a denim shirt walked in. He was carrying a notebook and a pen was stuck in his shirt pocket. He introduced himself as Dr. Vincent Betts, but he asked everyone to call him Vince.

"Hello, everyone," he said cheerily.

Only Donnie responded.

"Hello, Vince!" he said with a little too much enthusiasm. He looked around the room. Everyone else was staring at the floor. "Come on, everybody! Say hi to Vince!"

"Oh, boy, tough crowd here, Vince. You've got your work cut out for you with this sack of loons."

"Thank you, mister, um, what was your name?"

"I'm Donnie! Rockin' Donnie Derringer! You've probably heard of me."

"Yes, I have, Donnie, but not because of your professional accomplishments or lack thereof. Dr. Dixon briefed me about you. I guess you're quite the card. But I'd like you to show more respect for your colleagues than to call them a collection of loons."

"Oh, sorry," Donnie said in his usual cavalier fashion. "I was just trying to keep it light."

"Well, this is not a shock-jock radio show or a comedy stage, Mr. Derringer," Vince said sternly. "Everyone here is here because they want to help themselves, not be subject to the ridicule of some erstwhile broadcast wit with a cruel sense of humor."

Other people might have been embarrassed by such an exchange. Donnie just kept it up.

"Jeez, Vinny," he said. "I …"

"Vince, Mr. Derringer. My name is Vince."

"Oh, OK Vinny, I'll call you Vince."

Vince ignored him and turned to the group.

"How's everybody today?"

Again, thick, dead silence.

"Alan, do you want to start?" Vince said to the suburban-looking guy with tortoise-shell glasses.

"Um, not really. But OK," Alan said. "I'm feeling pretty good today. The drugs make me very sleepy but I'm getting control of my thoughts."

"What kind of thoughts are those?" Vince asked. "Are these the same ones you've had before?"

"The thoughts are still there," Alan said, "but I feel less inclined to act on them. Like the time my neighbor mowed my side of the lawn. It drove me nuts. I'm sorry. But it made me very angry when he continually mowed my side of the lawn along our property line. He was on my property. Mowing my lawn. It just wasn't right."

"Why did that make you angry, Alan?"

"Because he had no right to go on my property and mow the lawn. It's my property, not his, and I'll mow the lawn when I feel like it, not when he decides it needs cutting. That's why I bit him. I barely drew blood. But he was on my lawn and he needed to be punished. So, a trespasser invades my yard, I draw a little blood on his cheek and I land here. Doesn't seem right. I was correcting his behavior and defending my castle."

Donnie snickered. Vince swung his head and glared at him.

"Do you think biting him was a good idea, Alan?" Vince asked. "I mean, he was actually doing you a favor when you think about it. Mowing your lawn, that is."

"No favor!" Alan shouted. "He didn't belong in my yard. He needed to be stopped. I wanted to destroy him, I wanted to make him pay. There are boundaries in life. It's part of the social contract. He ignored the boundaries of acceptable behavior. And for all I knew he was part of conspiracy."

"Conspiracy?"

"Don't pretend you don't know about the conspiracy. You're probably part of it yourself."

"Alan, you know there is no conspiracy. We've discussed that in detail."

"I'd expect you to say that, Vincent. Don't think you can fool me. They're everywhere. Even here. One in every four people in this country are Chechen spies."

"If you think I'm in on something, if I'm a possible spy, I wonder if you feel like biting me, too."

Alan bared his teeth and hissed.

"So, you think biting people is within the boundaries of acceptable behavior? Your victim needed quite a bit of surgery to repair the gash in his cheek from your fangs. Despite your characterization of the incident, you hurt him quite badly."

Alan mumbled something and then began growling. Jesus, Donnie thought, this guy thinks like a dog. Biting people?

"Ok, Alan, I think we still need to work on your outlook. When someone cuts your lawn, they're doing you a favor, right? You don't bite the faces of people who are doing you favors, correct? Alan? You don't bite anyone for any reason."

"Yeah, yeah, yeah," Alan growled. "It just pissed me off, that's all."

"It's all right to be pissed off, Alan, although I think you could be pissed off about more important things, but I think you know it's not OK to bite people or do them any other kind of harm. Right?"

"Yeah, I'm working on these anger issues that haunt me. That's why I'm here. But don't try to convince me there isn't a conspiracy."

"I know," Vince said, growing unprofessionally impatient. "We'll go over that more in individual sessions, ok?"

"Yes. But he had it coming, dammit. It was total bullshit!"

"All right, Alan, there's no need for that kind of language. You know that, right?"

"Yeah, right, whatever," he said, then barked.

At this point, Donnie realized he hadn't eaten or showered yet. His thoughts focused on his hunger. That and the idea of sleeping with one of the bulimics. Or both of them.

Cool.

Donnie wanted to leave, get some grub, take a shower, and brush his teeth. God, did he need to brush his teeth. But he figured Vince would not be happy if he abruptly got up and left. He figured it would earn him some kind of crazy house punishment, like hand-cleaning the men's room toilets without a brush or something. So, he sat quietly and tried to be amused.

Vince cast his gaze to another inmate, the other exurban guy with the glassy stare.

"Thomas, how are you today?" Vince said in a syrupy tone designed to keep the agitated nuts calm.

"Fine. I'm fine. Fine, fine, fine," Thomas said. "I feel fine since I seem to be safe in this place."

"Safe from what?"

"The Trilateralists."

"I'm sorry?"

"You know who I'm talking about, The Trilateralists. The One World Conspiracy. Blue helmets. It's what Alan is talking about. He and I have discussed it. The blue helmets. They knew I was onto them. When I started telling people the real truth about what's going on, nobody would listen. I shouted it from the streets, but everyone just looked away. That's why I set fire to the Masonic Hall. They're in on it. The Masons. You know it, I know it, the American people know it. They're listening to us even here, in this very place of insane patients!"

"If everyone knows about it, then why did you need to start the fire?"

Donnie got Billy Joel's "We Didn't Start the Fire" stuck in his head and hummed it quietly.

"Mr. Derringer!" Vince shouted. "Please. Thomas, continue."

"You know why, Vincent. I know you know. Now I'm starting to think you're one of them. Are you here to destroy me for telling the truth?"

Jesus, Mary and Joseph, Donnie thought, rolling his eyes. All I did was make a drunken suicidal phone call I don't even remember to my sometime girlfriend. I'm not going to kill myself, and I'm certainly not as bad off as these people.

Vince calmly looked Thomas in the eye and said sternly: "You know I'm here to help you, don't you, Thomas? You know that the truth you think you're telling is wrong. It's not real. There is no One World Conspiracy, as you tell it. There is just your imagination, right?"

Thomas remained silent, looking at the floor.

"All right, Thomas, thank you."

Just then the Jerry Garcia guy chimed in.

"You know, Vince, I'm thinking that it might be time for me to leave here. Not this room, but Serenity Heights," he said. "I've learned my lesson: Don't eat 'shrooms by the fistful for days at a time because you're going to start seeing things that aren't there. I wound up seeing a little man wearing red sitting on my television who told me to rob a liquor store."

"OK, so did you?"

"Well, I tried but the liquor store owner had a shotgun behind the counter. He told me to stay right there as he called the cops. The little man took off and I was busted but I explained what he had told me, so the police guys brought me here. I still see the little guy. I call him Mel. But he doesn't say much anymore. He just laughs at me now."

"I see," Vince said. "Have the meds helped you deal with 'Mel,' as you call him?"

"Not really," said Jerry Garcia, whose real name was Tony Bates. "He just gets sleepy in between his giggles. But he mocks me and it makes me angry."

Just then someone broke in. It was Wally Cox.

"Maybe you should murder Mel," he said helpfully in a voice not unlike the cartoon character "Underdog." "Maybe crush him to death with your bare hands. Or a pliers! Squeeze the life out of the miserable little bastard. Make his head pop and watch his blood spurt into the ceiling."

"Let's not talk about murdering anyone, even people who don't exist," Vince said. "It's not healthy."

"I was just trying to be of assistance," Wally said.

"Well, why don't we change the subject by talking about why you're here," Vince said, disturbed by the descriptive talk of homicide.

"I'm here because of all of the diseases that are attacking my being…" said Wally, whose real name was Kenneth.

Donnie, upon discovering Kenneth's real name, immediately thought: "What's the frequency, Kenneth?" Sometimes he cracked himself up. Vince saw Donnie smirking but he ignored him.

"And what about the diseases?" Vince said patiently. "Why do you think you have diseases?"

"Because of the symptoms," Kenneth said. "I know I have fibromyalgia because I'm always tired. I have malaria, from the bird-sized mosquitoes in this northern climate. Every night I get rolling sweats as a result. Lyme disease, probably from deer ticks that lurk everywhere in this area. And Q Fever, a little-known condition that often goes undiagnosed. Cattle on the edge of town probably carry that. Infected dust particles in the very air we breathe. There are mold spores everywhere and they trigger my asthma. Those are the diseases that I know of, anyway. Don't worry. I'm not a carrier. I suffer alone."

The guy next to Kenneth moved his chair a few inches away. He didn't want any of Kenneth's diseases, imaginary or not.

"Mm hmm," Vince mumbled quietly. "Have you seen a doctor, Kenneth? Has a doctor given you these diagnoses?"

"I see doctors all the time," Kenneth said plaintively. "I Google these diseases and I even attend medical conferences to get a better sense of treatments. But no one seems to find anything. My last doctor examined me for eight hours. He found nothing. He must not have been a very good doctor. But he sent me here for some reason without curing or otherwise treating me."

One of the young women with the tube in her nose spoke up. Her name was Tiffany. Of course, her name was Tiffany. Everybody in the '80s and '90s named their girls Tiffany or Emily or Kaitlyn. Whatever her name was, Donnie was aroused as soon as she spoke.

Tiffany was interested in helping Thomas and Kenneth with her own talk-therapy.

"Thomas, Vince is your friend," she said nasally. "He's going to, like, help you so you can go home and forget about the tri-whatever you call them. It's not real. Seriously. And Kenneth, you don't look like a sick man. You're, like, imagining all this, you know? You couldn't possibly be that sick and still function."

Kenneth pulled out a handkerchief and let out a loud, dramatic sneeze.

"I'm here because I can't function," he said. "I'm not on vacation or something."

"Jeez, I was just trying to help," Tiffany said, hurt.

Thomas, meanwhile, was no longer on the same level as the rest of the group. He remained sullen, still thinking about the punishment he would mete out to his neighbor if the guy ever cut his lawn again.

"Thank you, Tiffany," Vince said. "How are you today?"

"I'd like to get this goddamned hose out of my face, that's how I am," Tiffany said with no small measure of irritation. "How would you like to have a fucking plastic tube coming out of your face?"

I'll give you a hose in the face, Donnie thought. He never gave up when it came to sex and was both proud and disgusted by his train of thought toward Tiffany. Then he realized he was grinning. He was feeling back to normal, but he was still hungry and itching for a shower. Preferably with Tiffany, hose or no hose.

Vince saw him and glowered.

"You're smirking, Mr. Derringer," Vince said. "Is something funny?"

Uh oh, thought Donnie. He's using my formal name. I must really be pissing him off. Be good, Donnie, be good. Donnie considered saying he was thinking about clowns, but that didn't even work with his temperamental father.

"I was, uh, thinking about chimpanzees. I mean, when people put funny hats on them and make them do tricks, it's pretty funny," Donnie said. "I was at the zoo once and a chimp threw feces at me through the bars. It was repulsive but still kind of funny."

"Are you thinking about chimpanzees because you're trying not to think of a certain late-night phone call you made to a sometime paramour recently?" Vince said. "Maybe you thought that was funny, too. You know, suicide threats are right up there with baby snatchings for their hilarity."

Great. Now he's getting all shrinky on me, Donnie thought.

Vince was a dick.

"No, not really," Donnie said. "I just like chimps. They bring delight to the human race. Is that so wrong? I mean, it's not like I think they're talking to me or something. They're so smart! I just like primates. Did you ever see that old video of a chimp washing a cat? I snicker at the very thought."

"And you think that's an appropriate train of thinking for what we're doing here?"

"Look," Donnie said, catching his stride, "I don't know what's appropriate or inappropriate here in this house of the dead and damned. Biting a guy for mowing his lawn? Burning down buildings? Tubes in the noses of attractive yet emaciated women who think they have a weight problem? A disease-ridden hypochondriac? These people are whack jobs and I'm the one who gets the stink eye because I'm thinking about chimpanzees? Come on, Vinnie, you and I both know I'm sane enough to leave this mad house."

"I'll be the judge of that," Vinnie snapped. "Dr. Dixon and I will be having a chat about you presently. You may return to your room and think about chimps or baboons or whatever animal pops into your head. You are disrupting this session and I will not have it."

"OK, OK, I'm outta here," Donnie said. "But can I think about bears riding tricycles at the circus?"

"Get out."

"All righty then. See you in the funny papers."

Donnie turned and left, but he looked back, squinting and smiling and giving the thumbs up to his fellow patients as he opened the door. He felt like he had scored a victory against the authoritarian atmosphere of the place. He walked back to his room alone singing, "I fought the law and I won."

Carsten apparently was tending to other duties so Donnie walked to his dorm room alone. He sat on the bed, then laid down. There was a lump under the pillow. Two lumps.

Now what?

Donnie lifted the pillow and found two still-cool cans of Milwaukee's Best beer. Swill, yes, but still alcohol. He wished there had been more but he settled for the two.

Carsten, he thought. Dear Carsten had come through. He was a true pal.

Friends forever!

Donnie opened the first can quietly, muffling it with his pillow and hoping to avoid an attention-getting "pfft" from the can. He swallowed the beer with gusto — hey, wasn't that the Schlitz tagline? The beer with gusto? As far as Donnie was concerned, it could have been cat pee. As long as it contained alcohol, he was OK with it. He needed to unwind. This had already been a tough day.

He knew he'd have to dispose of the can, but how? Where?

He looked at the window in the room. It opened, but not enough to get your head through it. Escape prevention, he figured. No matter. The opening was big enough to squeeze a crushed beer can thought it. He finished his brewski and let out a belch. That felt great, he thought. Donnie decided to save the other can for an emergency.

As a minor beer buzz kicked in, empty stomach and all, Donnie crushed the can, lifted the window screen and dropped the can out of the window onto the lawn outside.

Ahhh.

Donnie thought about where to hide the other can. He knew it would be bad news for him and for Carsten if anyone found it. Then he remembered his alcoholic father's solution: Hide it in the toilet tank. The water was clean and would keep the beer cool.

Genius.

Now for another refreshing shower. Donnie opened the toilet tank, placed the precious beer in the water and replaced the lid. It was just then that he noticed there was no shower head. Just a series of small holes in the ceiling of the shower stall. Jeez, they think of everything, he thought. No one's going to hang themselves in the shower at Serenity Heights.

Donnie took off his clothes and stepped into the shower.

The tepid flow of water felt like warm urine. Donnie liked his showers scalding hot, but this would have to do. As he soaped up, he thought about Tiffany and immediately sprang a boner. No, not here, he thought. Someone might walk in on him and get him on some kind of sex addiction rap. He wanted his freedom, not a long-term stay in the happy house.

After a thorough scrubbing, he turned off the water, got out of the stall and toweled himself with a thin cotton towel that didn't dry him so much as it simply smeared the water on his body. Oh well, he thought. I'll air dry.

On the sink was a plastic-wrapped toothbrush and traveler-size tube of Crest. The toothpaste had a whitening formula! He scrubbed his teeth and tongue until his gums bled, set down the brush and walked out into the room and pulled out his new clothes. The clothes he had been wearing had disappeared. He was worried because he loved his Charles Bukowski T-shirt, and he wanted it back.

He slipped on his jeans — he was going commando; no underwear, even though they had given him a new pair — and pulled the AC/DC T-shirt over his head. There now. A beer, a shower and back to bed. All he needed was some tunes but there were no radios or CD players, and certainly no turntables, so he flopped onto his bed and decided to take a nap.

He was only in bed for a few minutes when there was a knock at the door.

It was Dr. Dixon.

Shit.

— 13 —

CHOW TIME!

"Mr. Derringer? May I have a word with you?"

Donnie realized that the stench of beer on his breath had defeated the minty flavor of the Crest. He was exhaling hops so he dashed to the bathroom to brush his teeth again.

"Mr. Derringer," she said more insistently. "Mr. Derringer, may I come in?"

"Hang on, Doc," Donnie responded as he furiously brushed. He swallowed some toothpaste for extra coverage. "I'm taking a real steamer in here, Doc. You may not want to come in right now. There's no fan in here."

"Mr. Derringer, you are testing my frayed patience with you. Please allow me to enter."

Donnie finished brushing his teeth and flushed the toilet for effect. He tried to fart to give reality to his lie about a violent bowel movement but had no success. He walked back into the room and threw the door open. Dr. Dixon, who had been looking into the room through the peep hole, fell forward.

"What is this?" he said incredulously. "Shrink room service?"

"Have you eaten, Mr. Derringer?"

Donnie realized he was really hungry. He hoped they had peanut butter sandwiches in the cafeteria.

"What? Sally! Are you taking me to lunch? I'm not sure I'm ready. I usually go for coffee on the first date," Donnie said, amusing himself. "Jumping straight to lunch is a good sign for my chances, no?"

"No. It is not a date, as you well know, Mr. Derringer," Dr. Dixon said humorlessly. "And you will please address me as Dr. Dixon."

"OK, OK, Doc, don't get all authoritarian with me. Where will we be going for lunch? I could go for something greasy, grease being one of the food groups in my diet."

"I'm taking you to the hospital cafeteria," she said. "I'm sure you will find ample grease there and relieve whatever remnant hangover symptoms you have since your early Sunday morning distress call. By the way, you have night-after breath. You smell like a brewery floor."

His hangover! What great cover! He could hardly wait to get back to the toilet tank.

"I was thinking about eating a little later," Donnie said, sincerely wanting her to go away. "You know, after attending group again. I want to redeem myself to the other kooks. Then I was going to walk over and get some grub."

"First of all, your fellow patients are not called 'kooks' and you will not address them as such," she said. "Second, this is a locked ward. Since you are a danger to yourself, you will need an escort to lunch. I'm sure Carsten told you. Today I will be your escort."

"Wow, they've got an escort service here," Donnie said. "I usually have to spend a couple hundred shekels to get an escort. This will…"

She cut him off.

"Mr. Derringer, please come out of the room and accompany me to the cafeteria. There you may eat anything you want. You will find the offerings typical of most hospitals. Perhaps you can get a slice of dried-out pizza, which I am sure is a staple of your diet. We'll have a little chat and get to know each other better."

"Get to know each other?" Donnie replied. "Is this all leading to something sexy? Mmmm, yummy."

"Mr. Derringer, this will not lead to anything more than your getting better. And, if I may use the vernacular, cut the sex crap. It is not only annoying but it is harassment. I will not have it. Do you understand?"

"Well, I certainly know what would make me feel better, and it's not hospital food, unless they have peanut butter sandwiches. Not peanut butter and jelly — that's disgusting. But perhaps you'd like to come in and close the door behind you. Really, the cot isn't luxurious but it will do for our purposes. We can make do."

"That's enough," Dr. Dixon said, clearly becoming dangerously irritable.

"OK, OK, I'm coming. Do they have Thai food in this cafeteria? I love Thai food. You know what they call Thai food in Thailand? Food!"

Donnie giggled at his ancient joke.

"Come!" Dr. Dixon commanded.

"Mmm, I thought that was the idea behind your visit. Coming. Get it?"

Donnie was on a roll. He was beginning to feel more like himself. Oh yeah, good old Rockin' Donnie was making a comeback, and his first victim would be Dr. Sally Dixon.

"Not only are you not funny, but your statements are a form of unwelcome provocation that I am quite sure you have used on every woman you've ever known," Dr. Dixon said sternly. "We don't tolerate harassment of any kind here, especially on staff. And before you get any ideas about bedding our young bulimic patients — oh, you didn't think I was already on to you about your predatory ways? — please be aware that any inappropriate contact with other patients will result in criminal charges."

"OK, OK, Dr. Mind Reader, let's get some chow," Donnie said, resignedly.

They left Donnie's room and headed for a blue, security-locked door.

Dr. Dixon waved her electronic pass card in front of the small square box and the door popped open. It looked like freedom for just a minute, but with Dr. Dixon marching him down the hall, he knew it was just more confinement in a different venue.

Donnie was stuck like a rat in a drainpipe.

He switched his chain of thought to the idea of bedding Dr. Dixon. He wondered if she'd get all Freudian on him and ask him if he thought about his mother during sex.

Well, only a few times, Donnie thought. By accident.

Ew.

— 14 —

DINING WITH DOCTOR DOOM

The cafeteria was everything you'd expect of a nut house café. About a dozen speckled, aqua-colored Formica tables of two and four seats, one longish table of eight, presumably for group affairs. Since it was nearing 1 p.m. there was no line for food. Just about everybody had eaten already because, well, lunch at the crazy house is one of the best ways to break up the day anyone could think of. Otherwise you were talking to a shrink or lying on your cot, staring at the ceiling thinking of old girlfriends and tragic endings.

Or watching *The Price is Right.*

Donnie and Dr. Dixon walked up to the food buffet. Through the sneeze guard, Donnie spotted a stiff piece of pepperoni pizza and an equally decrepit cheeseburger, its bun wrinkled from so much time under the heat lamps. All the food looked ghastly, but Donnie was not a picky eater and he saw food, or some semblance of it. The grub at Serenity Heights wasn't much different than what he'd eat at home. He grabbed the pizza and tossed it on his Styrofoam plate. Then the cheeseburger.

Nutritious!

Dr. Dixon walked to the salad bar — of course she would have a salad while Donnie ate greasy garbage — filled her plate with iceberg lettuce, tomatoes, some sunflower seeds, and a vinaigrette dressing. She looked over at Donnie.

"Shall we find a quiet table?" she said.

"Yes, with a white taper candle stuck in an old red wine bottle on top of a checkered tablecloth," Donnie said, smirking.

"Your humor, if that's what it is, escapes me, as you may already have guessed, Mr. Derringer. I know it's your coping mechanism but I don't think you realize your situation. You will be here for a few days until we get to the bottom of your self-destructive behavior. In your case it may take longer than just a few days. In the meantime, let's have a casual conversation over lunch."

Oh, gawd, Donnie thought. A casual conversation with Dr. Dixon probably centers on Jungian archetypes and their relationship to Bergman films.

What fun!

They sat at a corner table. Dr. Dixon smoothed a paper napkin on her lap and picked up the plastic fork — there was no metal flatware because a fork could be used as a deadly weapon. Donnie left his flimsy napkin on the table because he knew it would slide to the floor anyway if he put it on his lap.

Dr. Dixon began to speak but Donnie immediately interrupted.

"So, Dr. Spock, how long have you been analyzing mental defectives?" he said, adding, "I really mean Mister Spock, from the old and best *Star Trek* series. Dr. Benjamin Spock was in a different line of gobbledygook to screw up little kids and make their parents feel inadequate. But ..."

"I remind you of Mr. Spock? Please elaborate."

"Well, you seem cool and collected, free from emotional response. Now, I actually admired Mr. Spock when I was a kid. Still do. I guess that means that in some nutty way, sorry, I admire you, too. See, Mr. Spock, he rarely had to grapple with emotions unless he was dealing with some Vulcan fever that made him crazy with lust. And speaking of lust, I..."

"For the last time, I demand that you stop, Mr. Derringer. Again, your feeble attempts at sexual innuendo border on harassment of the punishable sort. But please tell me about your fondness for Mr. Spock."

"Well, for one thing, he had that Vulcan Death Grip thing where he could squeeze a guy's shoulder and make him pass out. He could read minds, even alien minds, by placing his hand on their face. Plus, he had super strength and could kill a guy with his bare hands if he had to. Cool, no? But mostly, he didn't have to deal with his own emotions unless he was haunted by his half-human side. I'd love to be like that, wouldn't you? Come on, Doc, the Vulcan Death Grip? No emotions? Are you telling me…"

"I'm telling you nothing about myself," she said sharply. "Everything you need to know about me is reflected in the many diplomas on my office wall. Now, go on again about Mr. Spock."

"Ok, ok, I guess this will save me a session in your dungeon-like office," Donnie said, sighing hopelessly. "Let me tell you why I like Spock. See, when I was a kid and my old man was on a vodka-infused rampage, he used to clobber anyone in his path. My mom. Me. My sisters. Even the dog wasn't safe. I hated him, and I wanted to fight back, but I was a skinny little shit and fighting back would have just brought on my untimely death. So, I couldn't fight back, and that just brought on a seething resentment that made me hate him more and more every day. I used to be happiest when he was working late or at some bar telling anyone who would listen about how his bosses were idiots and how he'd like to tell them off and quit but he couldn't because he had those miserable kids to take care of. But anything that kept him away from the house was a good thing.

"My old man was a sick bastard. When I was 10 or 12 years old, he used to make me sit with him at night while everyone else was sleeping and he was getting drunk on cheap vodka, the jumbo-sized bottle with a handle. I'd be in my room listening to my albums when I would hear him summon me.

"'Donald, get your head out of those goddamned headphones and come here!'" he would bellow, over the sounds of Alice Cooper.

"Disobedience was not a crime I was willing to commit against this monster, so I'd go to the living room and sit on the floor while he reclined in his lounger, the bottle next to him. If he needed ice for his drink, he'd wave his glass and I would have to go to the freezer and get some.

"He often told me that if I really loved someone, I would have to hurt them because then they loved you more when you were nice to them. I wrote about that in my diary, journal, whatever it is, about how he slugged my dog to prove he loved it."

"I see," Dr. Dixon said. "Go on."

"I didn't want to hate my father, but I did with the intensity of a thousand supernovas. I remember when I was about 12 years old, I became a hockey fan and I forechecked him into the wall as we passed each other in the hallway. He nearly killed me for that one, and I hated him all the more.

"One good thing he did was teach me chess. I would bring the board and set it on the ottoman in front of his chair. We played a lot when he was sober, which wasn't often, and although he always won, I learned from his strategies and tactics. Eventually I picked up some good moves and one day I beat him.

"'Checkmate, old man.'

"He scanned the board, realized that I had indeed defeated him and promptly flipped the board over, sending pieces everywhere. 'You don't beat your father, do you understand, you little bastard?' he said. "Yeah, I understood. And I never played with him again.

"And that's why I wanted to be like Spock. I can't tell you how many times the old *Star Trek* series, the best one, by the way, saved me whenever these damned emotions were getting the best of me. Take the episode "The Corbomite Maneuver." Do you remember that one, where Capt. Kirk bluffed an alien into thinking he would be destroyed if he fired on the *Enterprise*? It was …"

Dr. Dixon cut in again.

"So, you had an abusive father and you wanted to have no emotions so that you wouldn't want to kill him."

"Right on the money, Doc! In fact, I also wanted to be Capt. Kirk, too, 'cause he was smart and cunning and a good fighter. Also, he had such a way with green alien women. But that was another matter. Green, orange, pink, I don't care what color an alien female is if I have the chance to …"

"Mr. Derringer, once again that's quite enough. Your fixation with sex is something we will discuss in your next visit to my office. Tell me, did you and your father play any games together other than chess? Did you play any other father-son type of games? Did you play catch?"

"Sure, we played a form of catch!" Donnie replied brightly. "He used to throw stuff at me all the time. I'd I catch objects with my head or upper body. Ashtrays. Empty vodka bottles. Vases. Whatever was handy. Once he threw a clock at me and missed, embedding the timepiece in the living room wall. I always called that 'the day time flew.'

"The old man would grab something, tell me what a worthless shit I was, and then bean me with whatever was close. It was usually smaller things. Easier to throw and more likely to hit their target, which was me, and pitching lamps at me meant he didn't even have to get out of his chair to hurt me. Convenient, no? Although once he tossed a folding chair across the basement rec room. Hit me smack dab in the forehead. Can you see the little scar?"

Donnie pulled his wet, matted hair off his forehead so she could check out the familial war wound.

"Yes, I see, very nice," Dr. Dixon said. "I guess that one ended your career as an amateur boxer."

Was she joking?

"Um, I never …"

"Yes, I know," she said. "It was a humor joke. You were getting a little upset."

A joke? About getting smashed in the head by a folding chair? When he thought about it, in some ways it did seem funny.

Didn't it?

"In any case, Mr. Derringer, it sounds like the Spock archetype was your hero."

There she goes with the archetypes. Good thing he had taken that semester of psychology. Donnie had been a political science major but he took the psych class because he thought it would teach him how to trick people. No such luck on that count but he had learned some fundamentals. At least that put Donnie on somewhat level ground with Dr. Dixon. He could speak basic shrink language.

"It wasn't just Spock. It was also Jimmy, the 'helpless dancer,' the screwed-up kid in The Who's classic album, 'Quadrophenia.' I am still obsessed with that album. I could relate to Jimmy because like him, my life was pretty fucked up, too. Abusive father, indifferent mother. The heartbreak of that first breakup with your first love. First experiences with pot and speed. But 'Quadrophenia' helped me understand that to be a kid was to be fucked up by the things you can't control. 'Quadrophenia' was loud, angry, angst-filled and noisily beautiful. Just like the noise in my head. Listening to it was so soothing.

"That album got me through my adolescence until I could escape the gulag that was my home. That album and a dozen others like 'The Who Live at Leeds,' and even the mopey Jackson Browne. Jim Croce, too. When he says, *You can keep the dime* in his classic 'Operator,' I still get the chills. Remember when pay phones only charged a dime for a call? Anyway, music kept me in my head, and that's how I became a 'radio personality.'

"I figured by going into radio I could be somebody, a big shot to my family and my old neighborhood. I wanted to impress them all, especially the girls who rejected me when I was young. I wanted to show everyone that I was different from them, better, even. Any other questions, Doc? My shriveled pizza is getting cold."

"Yes, I do have a question," she said archly. "What made you think you were so different? What made you think that 'being somebody,' as you term it, was so important? I'm curious about what made you so ego-centered."

Donnie bit off a chunk of the pizza and chewed noisily. The gross display of open-mouthed chomping gave him time to collect his thoughts. He squinted incredulously at this beautiful but distant shrink.

"Whattya mean?" he said, licking his teeth. "Doesn't everybody want to be somebody? And wasn't it Dean Martin who said, *You're nobody till somebody loves you?* Come on, nobody loves a nobody, especially a self-centered nobody like me. If you're a somebody everyone wants a piece of you. You can be a hotshot and get away with murder if you're a somebody. It's the first rule of celebrity. As they say in Louisiana, the only way for the rich and powerful to get in trouble is to be caught with a live boy or a dead girl.

"But mostly, I wanted to be somebody to prove to the old man I wasn't just another nobody like him."

"I see," Dr. Dixon said, moving in for the kill. "So. You're the little lost boy who grew up in a weird neighborhood and awful family and went on to become 'somebody' and now you think you're just a loser in a small town. Poor baby. You decided that suicide would be an appropriate response to your fallen status. Unfortunately, the 'poor me' stance is not becoming on you at all. You need to come to terms with all this, and I suggest extensive talk therapy. Who have you been showing off for all these years? What have you been trying to prove?"

Uh-oh. She was getting close to his Marie fixation, his showing off for her.

Donnie felt like a squirrel in front of an oncoming car. His mind darted back and forth for an appropriate rejoinder. Indecision could be fatal. He cleared his throat and decided to let silence be his weapon. If he didn't answer she'd be forced to say something else. Most people, even the best shrinks, get uncomfortable with silence.

Donnie just grinned and chewed.

"So, Mr. Hotshot who used to be somebody, you think calling friends and telling them you're going to kill yourself is amusing?" she said, displaying some measure of annoyance that pleased Donnie. He was getting to her.

Fantastic!

"Look, Doc, I've said it was a one-off," he said. "I was pasted and I don't even remember calling Liz. I know blacking out is no excuse for a call like that, but no, I'm not going to off myself. I'm just dying bit-by-bit here in this shithole town. This tired, sorry burg is enough to kill anybody. Isn't it?"

"I have a sense that this wasn't a one-off, Mr. Derringer," she said, spiking the ball into Donnie's court. "I think you've been thinking about offing yourself, as you so elegantly put it, for some time now, and I plan to get to the bottom of this issue. You're going to be at Serenity Heights for a while longer as I determine what is behind these self-destructive urges. The drugs. The booze. The serial womanizing. The desperate need to be a big shot and prove yourself to God-knows-who. It's all part of a larger issue for you, an issue that makes you want to escape something.

"Am I right?" she said.

Hey, that was Donnie's line.

"Look, the only thing I want to escape is boredom," Donnie said. "Ennui is worse than death and there's plenty of it in Deerhead. What I do is put some action in my life, add a little color to an otherwise black and white palette."

"Yes, well, if adding color means threatening to kill yourself, then the only color is black."

The Stones' "Paint It Black" popped into his head. Jesus, Donnie thought, can I go back to my room and stare at the ceiling or think about Dr. Dixon lying naked on her office couch?

Donnie cast his eyes downward, as if chagrined. He thought such an expression would get her off his back. The downcast look was often useful when he was trying to get laid or apologize for sleeping with someone other than his current girlfriend. It was the "little lost boy" look that sometimes engendered sympathy in his audience. With Dr. Dixon, no such luck. She was on to him.

"Your acting abilities are impressive but not the least bit convincing to me," she said. "Believe it or not I've seen your type before. And I've seen far better performances than yours. But I imagine from our short conversation that you have a lot on your mind, and not just sex and controlled substances.

"I have to ask, are you putting your manic thoughts on paper or in a laptop? May I arrange for delivery of a journal to your room so that rather than whiling away your time here wallowing in your self-pity, you could do something productive? I think a journal would help us both get to the bottom of your significant mental illness."

"Funny you should ask, Doc," Donnie said. "I only recently began dumping thoughts of my background, my childhood, my misadventures. I've kept an account of my thoughts in a journal that has traveled with me throughout the years. It mostly consists of random thoughts I scribbled during pot and booze sessions. Lots of drawings of strange animals, space aliens, and don't kid yourself, aliens walk among us. But it wasn't until recently that I got serious about telling my story before, you know, the big sleep I mentioned earlier."

"Excellent," Dr. Dixon nearly exclaimed. "Could you tell me where in your domicile said document is located? I will send Carsten to retrieve it. You will make regular entries and then you will read your entries to me at our sessions, and yes, I do mean sessions with an 's.' We have some work to do together. You should expect to be here for at least a week or two. You will have plenty of time to write and we can discuss your thoughts during our meetings."

"But I have that miserable job," Donnie pleaded, thinking the job might be a suitable excuse to get him sprung from Serenity Heights. "I need to get back to work or they'll can me. I've been axed before, by bigger stations, of course, but I can't afford to lose my gig in this desolate town. It's probably my last one in radio. After this, it's 'Welcome to Walmart.'"

"We will contact your employer and he will find a temporary fill-in," she said. "Believe it or not you are not irreplaceable."

"That's exactly what I'm worried about," Donnie said, dejected.

Donnie told Dr. Dixon that he had left his journal on the rickety desk in the living room. He realized that Liz's rush to get him to Serenity Heights, they had left his door unlocked. He wasn't worried about that. Deerhead was a nice, safe town, after all.

Looks like you'll be doing some more journaling if you're going to get out of here, Donnie thought. Good thing he'd already gotten serious about his memoir.

Yessiree, Donnie was keeping a journal of his memoir and other random thoughts. Why not? It might lead to a book. A bestseller even!

Donald Derringer, memoirist.

Just like Samuel Pepys!

— 15 —

WHERE'S MY BEER?

AFTER THEY FINISHED LUNCH, DR. DIXON escorted Donnie back to his room. Or his cell, as Donnie thought of it. They walked side-by-side in silence. Donnie kept trying to get a peek at Dr. Dixon's ass as she walked.

Nice!

Dr. Dixon interrupted his sick train of thought.

"Writing will help you in your journey out of mental illness," she said gently as she opened the door. "We will provide a ballpoint pen for your use in the journal, but please don't stab yourself in the neck with it. That would create a mess for our unfortunate and over-worked custodial staff. I'm sure Carsten wouldn't appreciate checking in on you and finding that you were lying in a pool of blood. Just write, Mr. Derringer, just write."

The softness of her voice displayed was the first time she showed Donnie any kind of sympathy, if not empathy, even if it was vague.

Naturally Donnie thought of Dr. Dixon's subtle show of tenderness as an opening.

"Care to join me in here, Doc?" he said mischievously. "As I said the cot's kinda small but if we snuggled..."

She cut him off with no small measure of anger.

"Please write," she said sharply. "Again, I trust you are out of danger for the time being. The sooner you begin to get your thoughts on paper the sooner we can discuss them and the sooner you can go back to your normal life, and I do use the term 'normal' advisedly."

"I'll be good," Donnie said. "But can I draw pictures in the journal? I could use some crayons or markers to draw flowers and bowls of fruit. You know, still lifes. I love the beauty of a bowl full of apples. Kurt Vonnegut drew pictures in his books. His rendering of an anus looked like an asterisk."

"You may do as you wish. But markers or crayons won't be necessary. I'm interested in your thoughts, not your artistic capabilities. Now go write. We'll talk tomorrow."

"Yes, Doc. Uh, Dr. Dixon."

Dr. Dixon closed the door, leaving Donnie to his devices. Well, he thought, at least this gives him time to write the life story. He decided Jerry Most would never see its contents, but he was writing for Sally Dixon, not some twisted has-been game show host.

Carsten arrived with Donnie's journal about 30 minutes after Dr. Dixon left Donnie in his cell.

"Your house was unlocked and I was able to easily gain entry," he said. "I locked it as I left. I hope you brought your keys."

"Thanks, Carst," Donnie said. "I left my keys at home somewhere but I can easily break in when I get out of here."

"Very well," Carsten said, and he closed the cell door behind him.

Donnie was alone. He had plenty of time to jot down a few thoughts.

If Donnie was going to write, he would require the kind of inspiration that only alcohol or weed could provide. It was a law of nature. He checked the toilet for the second beer Carsten had left. It was gone. He sloshed around with his hand in the tank to see if the beerski had dropped behind something. But it had disappeared.

Shit.

No hootch. No joints. Nothing.

How the hell was he supposed to write when he was stone-cold sober?

Donnie opened the door to see if Carsten was anywhere to be found. Nope. No sign of his laconic ally. Donnie started to get a little edgy. He needed a beer buzz to stimulate creativity, and this journal would indeed be a mix of imagination and truth. Dr. Dixon could figure out which was which on her own.

He sat on the bed and stared at the journal. Since he had nothing else to do and group sessions were their own form of punishment, he picked up the pen and began to draw a rendering of the first *Starship Enterprise*. He hummed the original *Star Trek* theme as he drew.

"Captain's Log, Star Date, Who Knows? Who cares?

"Day one: I'm being held hostage by aliens in human form who are holding me because they say I'm a danger to myself. What's it to them? Can't an Earth creature live his life, such as it is, as he sees fit? Drink, smoke a doobie, sleep around, catch a ballgame. Play records. Threaten suicide. Who am I hurting? Maybe I've given up on being 'somebody.' Maybe I should stop trying to show off for Marie. Maybe I've thrown in the towel on life itself, and maybe I should keep my self-destructive urges to myself. But hey, as the great Sammy Davis, Jr. said, 'I gotta be me!'

"OK, the suicide threats have got to go. That's what got me here in the first place. I'm not going to do anything rash anyway. I'm just a little frustrated about being stuck in a place like Deerhead. Deerhead, for pity's sake. Americans love to talk about the charm of small towns like Deerhead. But if these microscopic burgs are so great why doesn't anybody live there?

"Is there anything wrong with being a little depressed about living in a place where there are two gas stations; a strip mall that includes three nail salons; dark, dingy bars with names like Nick's Happy Times Saloon, Rollie's Tip Top Tap, Milt's Town Club Inn, and, of course, Bubba's Home Plate. One coffee shop named the Blue Moon Café that serves two types of light-roast bitter swill. A cheap motel with a sign that says "air conditioned." A small bookstore that sells mostly used books and the literary dreck you find at airports, but it at least carries the Sunday edition of *The New York Times*. There was little else in the way of newspapers and magazines other than the *Minneapolis Star Tribune* and the *National Enquirer*. There's a porn shop named Lady Lucy's on the edge of town. And that's it for culture in Deerhead. Why would anyone ever want to leave?

"Ah, yes, Deerhead, I love you so.

"Scottie, one to beam up. The life forms on this planet are hostile."

Exhausted by this deep self-examination, Donnie needed a nap. He began to doze but there was a knock on the door.

Crap. What now?

Bleary eyed, Donnie opened the door slowly as through he was expecting to be hauled off to jail or something.

It was Carsten.

"Carsty, my man!" Donnie whispered. "Thanks for the brewski. But what happened to the second beer?"

Carsten glowered at Donnie and spoke in a low growl.

"Don't ever say anything about that again," he said. "Maintenance found your beer during a routine room check. During inspection, they found your toilet-soaked beer. Staff watches *The Simpsons*, too, so they knew Homer's beer-in-the-toilet trick. They figured it was something you had brought with you. But now I can't risk getting you alcohol again or I'll lose this miserable job, a menial vocation which makes me hate my lonely life. Understand? Shitty or not, I've got to keep this job, just like you have to keep your graveyard shift radio job."

"OK, OK. Jeez, calm down. But to what, then, do I owe the pleasure of your hulking company?"

"You have a visitor," Carsten said. "Someone who wants to see you right away. He says it's urgent."

"He?" Donnie said. "So, it's not Liz? I don't know anybody else in this horrible little town. Except you, pal."

"It's a guy named Mr. Most," Carsten said. "Jerry Most. He says he is the former star of some TV show that I never watched. He wants to see you. I will accompany you to the visitor's area. Let's go."

"Alrighty then," Donnie said. "I sense that adventure awaits. Maybe Jerry Most can bust me outta here."

Little did Donnie know.

Carsten said nothing, nudged Donnie toward the hallway, and they walked toward the false freedom of the Serenity Height mess hall.

As they approached the door to the cafeteria, Donnie stopped and quietly said: "What was with the beer, Carsten, my boy?"

"Be quiet," Carsten shushed. He looked over both shoulders, observed an empty hallway and said: "I like your show. You play cool music. In spite of your crudeness I think we could be buddies. But I need a favor and you owe me one. You've gotta help get me outta here. You think I like listening to the late-night low moans of sex addicts and the ravings of creeps on manic highs?"

"Owe you for what? A can of swill?"

"Whatever you want to call it, it was alcohol, and I knew you needed it. Call it an act of friendship."

"Ok, what can I do for you, my friend?" Donnie said, exasperated.

"I want to have a career in radio," Carsten, deadpanned. "But more important, I want to be your buddy. You know, hang with you, maybe be a regular guest on your radio show."

Donnie almost laughed, but when he realized Carsten was serious, he rolled his eyes so violently they could be heard grinding in the sockets.

"Oh gawd, Carsten. Please. You don't have the personality for radio. What are you gonna do, have a phone-in about Kantian ethics? Look, it's hard enough for me to exist on the weak airwaves of KYJL. I no longer have a career at this age, my friend. I have a job. My status as a 'celebrity' has dropped to 'local personality,' and I'm barely even that. I'm nobody. But least I still have a job if I can get outta here anytime soon. How are you going to get into radio when you barely speak as it is?"

"I've always wanted to have my own radio show and you're going to help me get one. You know people in the business."

"Sure," Donnie said, "I know a lot of people. And I've managed to alienate all of them. I'm not sure I can help."

"You'll find a way," Carston said. "Now let's go see your visitor. He's been waiting. Better call him Mr. Most. He said he doesn't like being called 'Jerry' by androids like me. Nice guy."

"Ok, Captain Carsten. At this point, I'd follow you through the Gates of Hell."

Yet now even more strange things awaited.

Very strange things.

— 16 —

JERRY MOST TO THE RESCUE

Carsten led Donnie down the dreary corridor toward the cafeteria, which doubled as the visitor area. The hallway walls on the way were covered with the art of inmates past and present. There actually was a painting on the wall of a half-opened eye with long, feminine lashes. Blue irises. But severely bloodshot whites. No swords coming out of it or anything but creepy nonetheless. The rest of the canvases were of the requisite pastoral scenes and one portrait of a colorful, beady-eyed fish.

A trout? Donnie guessed.

Whatever.

They entered the nearly empty cafeteria. Empty or not, this guy would be easy to spot at a crowded baseball stadium. He wore a blinding white double-breasted suit, and, in a fashion faux pas of wearing a hat indoors, he sported a snow-white fedora with a blue band. His bow tie was red silk with small black dots, and he looked like an out-of-place Colonel Sanders without the goatee.

He seemed immersed in a magazine, which turned out to be another well-thumbed issue of *Family Circle*.

Great recipes!

As Donnie and Carsten approached, the guy lifted his head and beamed.

"Well, well, well," he said through a wide shit-eating grin and an unctuous tone of voice. "Well, well, well, if it isn't the king of the overnight airwaves, Rockin' Donnie Derringer. In the flesh! I can't tell you what an honor this is. I've heard so much about you. My researchers tell me you once vomited onstage at the feet of a decidedly unhappy Iggy Pop, who then whacked you with his mic. Remember? Lots of other people saw it. Cheap Trick, too, no? You must have quite a weak digestive tract."

Jesus, Donnie thought. Who is this guy? Could this be Jerry Most? He already has researchers looking into my life? This isn't good.

Donnie and Carsten sat down on the plastic chairs across the table from Colonel Sanders.

"Um, yes, I used to drink and do bong hits backstage quite a bit," Donnie sheepishly admitted. "I used to love a good bender before, during and after a show. And even when there wasn't a show."

"Gin and pot being your substances of choice. Am I right?" the man said, with a cloying countenance.

"Yeah, but scotch too and a few lines of coke if I could get my hands on it. Never rode the white horse, though. There's nothing more pathetic than a heroin addict," Donnie said. Might as well go with it, he thought. This guy seems to know everything anyway.

"Wow, you're a regular Keith Richards," the man said with mock fascination. "I'll bet you partied with the best of them."

"If you say so," Donnie said. "Honestly? I don't remember a lot of it."

Actually, Donnie remembered more than he was willing to say. He knew he was a total butthead. He just wasn't ready to face that fact. But it was probably part of what brought him to Serenity Heights in the first place.

"Allow me to FORMALLY introduce myself now that we've gotten acquainted," the man in the blinding white suit said. "My name is Jerry Most, formerly the host of the highly rated and massively lucrative show *Die Trying*. I am now the host of a new and dreary but compelling public access cable TV talk show and podcast called *Losers on Parade*. I'm here to determine whether you'd be a good guest on my show, and I think I already know the answer given our bleak surroundings," Jerry said. "So how long are you stuck with the kooks? In your case my guess is it'll take a week just to detox."

"I'm not sure," Donnie said. "Dr. Dixon said I'll be here for a few days. But they can't hold me longer than that if I don't want to stay. It's against the law."

"Well, use your time wisely," Jerry said. "Are you keeping a journal or something like I asked? We need to get your thoughts on paper so we're ready to question you when you appear on the show. You will, of course, send the journal to us ahead of your appearance. From my point of view, you're a miserable, self-centered snob who wishes he was dead. That makes for great TV. I've said it all along. Americans love other people's misery. Especially people who were once famous but suffered a precipitous public fall. It's a known fact. Polls show it. That's why we're going to have you on my new show."

"Um, well, I think that's a bit of a harsh portrayal, but yes, I'm unhappy I guess," Donnie said. "That's why I'm locked in here."

"Great," Jerry said. "Look, I can't stay long. But you're probably wondering how you'll get to our Berryland, New Jersey studio. Yes, we have a studio there. It's cheap, and since we're initially just a local cable access show and podcast with a limited audience, we can't afford to have a Hollywood or New York studio. We will also do a podcast, though. We already have 34,000 followers lined up who are anticipating carnage from Jerry Most. But it's not like the old days when I was running *Die Trying*. We're on a tight budget for the fledgling *Losers on Parade,* my ex-wife Pinky Lee having taken most but not all of my money in the divorce settlement. But I still get enough royalties from *Die Trying* that she can't get her paws on.

"My show is self-funded, and while I have more than enough to maintain my high-flying lifestyle — even at lower altitude these days — I don't intend to use all of my well-earned money to fund what is essentially a vanity project. Still, I think we have a hit on our hands. Your appearance will help us boost our viewership and maybe even get *Losers on Parade* noticed by the networks."

Jerry reached into the lapel pocket of his white suit coat and pulled out two bus tickets and a big wad of cash. Donnie was incredulous. He couldn't be trusted with cash. It was too easy to buy trouble. Like Keith Richards, Donnie never kept a dollar past sunset.

"What's this?" Donnie asked.

"What does it look like? They're two bus tickets to Berryland and a more-than-generous supply of cash for meals at the truck stops I'm sure you'll enjoy. Maybe you can even stop off at Ohio's Lucky Cat Museum in Cincinnati, or the Mutter Museum in Philly. They have lots of skulls there and, get this, a piece of neck tissue from John Wilkes Booth himself! Stop off at any attractions you want as long as they're on the way to Berryland — I mean Jerryland, New Jersey. Get it?"

"Fucking bus tickets? What, an Amish buggy wasn't available?"

"You bet, Champ," Jerry said. "The bus will get you to our studios in no time. A couple of days, with stops in burgs that make Deerhead look like Lagos, Nigeria. You might even enjoy seeing some open country. And, as a bonus, I have made arrangements for our robotic friend here to accompany you and ensure that you don't wander astray and that you actually make it to Berryland. I like to call the town 'Jerryland,' by the way. It amuses me."

"I've seen plenty of open country," Donnie said. "I spent time in a lot of dinky towns on the way up before I became a big-shot jock. Lotta open country in places like, um, Hammertown. Never been there but I've been to plenty of places like it. Hammertown is from your old show where that fat guy got eaten by baboons, right?"

"The baboons were drunk, actually," Jerry said. "Nobody died. They never did on *Die Trying*. But our viewership was massive because people figured at some point, they'd actually see someone die. It was that sense of anticipation. Our contestants did win some fabulous prizes for courting death or serious injury on TV but they usually came out relatively unharmed.

"Look, that's in the past. I used to be a real asshole, and I tried with limited success to be a real sweetheart. It didn't work, really. I've returned to form. But you, my friend, are a personal project. You'll become a new person when confronted with your many misdeeds on my cable TV show and podcast. It'll be good for your soul. Even better than staying here in Serenity Hills or whatever they call this joint."

"If I thought I had a soul any more I suppose it might be good," Donnie said. "Why should I even do this? What do I get out of it?"

"If redemption isn't enough, how about some of those fabulous prizes I mentioned. Maybe an RV and a Hawaiian vacation and ..." — Jerry paused for the big reveal — "... and a new radio gig in L.A.? I still have connections in the industry there and I'm sure working the night shift in the City of Angels beats sneaking The Buggles onto these small-town airwaves. Always liked that song."

Jerry began singing. "*Video killed the radio star ...*"

"I'll admit a gig in L.A. would be a great way to make a come-back," Donnie said. "But I don't know. Spilling my guts and possibly being confronted by people I screwed or screwed over doesn't sound like the best way to do it."

"OK, sport," Jerry said. "Stay here and play REO Speedwagon or Def Leppard all night in Deerdick. That is, if you still have a job when you get out of this loony bin. Your call."

Carsten spoke up. That Carsten spoke at all was surprising, but he clearly wanted to chime in. He poked Donnie in the ribs.

"Mr. Most is offering you a great opportunity, Donald," Carsten said in a clear deep, stentorian voice that was decidedly different from the near mumbles he issued when escorting patients to and from their rooms and the cafeteria and group therapy. "You could wind up stuck in Deerhead, or maybe even Serenity Heights for the rest of your miserable life if you don't take him up on it."

Donnie was taken aback by Carsten's sudden expression of support. He was surprised by the fact that the normally stoic Carsten said anything at all.

"Carsten speaks!" Donnie said dramatically.

"Now wait, shut up and hear me out," Carsten said, quietly. Was this guy a cyborg?

"This could be good for you, Donnie. It would set you up as a hotshot jock again, and it would get me out of this miserable dive bar of a town, too."

"Wait a minute," Donnie interrupted. "What do you mean you, Carsten?"

"You think I like it here?" Carsten said. "I was born here in Deerhead and I don't want to die here. I smoked too much weed and drank too much lemon-flavored vodka to go to college. I barely made it out of high school, I was cut from the football team for drug-related infractions, and I never cottoned to a vocational career as a spot welder or a turret lathe operator.

"I had other intellectual pursuits in mind that did not involve advanced education. I like to read. But you don't get paid for reading, so I wound up working at Serenity Heights because they figured even if I was a bit dim, which I'm not, I was big enough to restrain even the most agitated patients. My personal life is non-existent. I've never had a girlfriend and I lived with my mother. When she died, I inherited her decrepit old house that will eventually be my coffin when they find my withered, lonesome corpse. No, I am getting out of Deerhead and you're my ticket to a real life, Donnie. You're going to Jersey. And I'm coming with you."

"So that really is why you brought me beer," Donnie said, glaring at Carsten. "You wanted to get on my good side so you could use me as your meal ticket, your trip from hell to a glamorous life. That's kinda low, Carsten, exploiting a man's alcoholic tendencies for personal gain."

Jerry broke in.

"All right, all right, you two lovebirds, don't quarrel," he said. "Sounds like you've got quite a resume there, Carson, or whatever your name is. I can't imagine why you'd want to leave all this. But you're right! You and Donnie make a great pair, and taking a cross-county bus tour from Deerhead to Berryland and then maybe even L.A. would allow you to go on some great escapades together and enter a whole new world of sun, fun and girls who don't look like Tammy Faye Bakker."

"Uh, yeah, well I've had my share of sun, fun and girls," Donnie said. "And booze and dope and cleaning fluid and whatever else I could ingest for a cheap high. I'm thinking maybe landing in the kook house was the best thing that could have happened to me. The food's terrible, there's no booze and my room's a cage, but there's something secure about knowing you'll be taken care of far from the madding crowd, if you will. That's a literary reference, Carsten."

"I applaud your basic knowledge of a book I'm sure you have never read," Carsten said, insulted. "I've read books, too. Yeah, even Thomas Hardy. Hemingway. Vonnegut. Even some of the classics. I'll bet you never made it to page three of the Karamazov Brothers. I made it to page 436. No one ever really finishes that one. But reading is the only thing that gives me pleasure in this shithole town. I've got a hammock under a shade tree in my yard and …"

"Sounds idyllic," Jerry broke in, "but we gotta get you both out of here pronto. I'm showing you the way. Just follow me …"

"Yeah, down the primrose path," Donnie said. "All the way to Gehenna. Sounds like fun!"

"Suit yourself, cowboy," Jerry said. "But if you don't leave now, you'll die in Deershit, Minnesota. You want that miserable fate? Fine by me. I'm just looking for a good episode on my cable TV show and podcast."

"Wow!" Donnie said. "You mean I can find some sort of legacy by being a ratings bonanza for a washed-up game show host? Maybe I deserve to die in Deerhead, anyway instead of being bait for your mouth-breathing audience."

Jerry gritted his teeth and hissed.

"Look, pal, I've chewed up and spit out better than the likes of pissants like you," he said threateningly. "I'm gonna give you a chance to back off the smart-ass act and listen to me. First of all, going on the show will help you get another, better gig and …"

"You mean even better than Deerhead? Jeez, that's quite a proposition," Donnie said, continuing the very smart-ass act that made Jerry so irritable in the first place.

"Fuck you and listen up," Jerry said. "Our little show and podcast may not have the massive audience of *Die Trying*, and yes, it's a public access cable TV show and podcast, but that doesn't make it any less of an opportunity for a has-been disc jockey like you. I'm guessing you haven't been getting any calls from Ronnie Wood to go partying lately, right?"

Ouch. That hurt. But Jerry was right. Not even his cousin Rick Derringer had called him in a dog's life. Donnie had had no rock-and-roll hootchie koo for some time now with his rock and roll "friends."

Just then Carsten stood up.

"I have to take Mr. Derringer back to his room," he said. Turning to Donnie, he spoke.

"Take his offer," Carsten said discreetly, looking to see if anyone was eavesdropping on this lame plot to spring a suicide case.

"Why do you care, Carsten?" Donnie said.

"'I have a vested interest in your success. I'm coming with you," Carsten said. "We're both busting out of here. And just so you know, I'll be joining you on your next radio show. You and Jerry are gonna help me get into the radio business."

"Carsten, you barely speak. How are you going to be on a radio show?" Donnie said.

"Because I know more than I let on," Carsten said. "I'm actually a pretty humorous guy when it all comes down to it. I've got a lot of good jokes. I know a lot of limericks. Do you know how many dirty words rhyme with Nantucket? I've got a million of 'em."

"There you go!" Jerry said enthusiastically. "I can just see you two as L.A.'s newest contribution to the cluttered airwaves. You two will be quite a team! It'll be like a ventriloquist act with you telling Carsten just what to say to make a comedy routine work. New shock jocks, that's what you'll be!"

"But Jerry..."

"Look, cowboy, take the bus tickets and come on my show," Jerry said, nodding toward Carsten. "Just listen to what the man said."

"*He said, 'Do do do, do do do do do,*" Donnie sang.

"Yeah, something like that," Jerry said dismissively, standing and leaving the cash and bus tickets on the table. "Welcome back to the big time, champ!"

"Um, I kinda was there already, the big time, as you call it," Donnie said. "I'm not sure it really did me much good. On the other hand, being trapped in Deerhead does make your offer enticing. But I have one provision before I agree to this."

"Name it, my friend. Jerry Most can make just about anything happen."

"Find Marie," Donnie said. "I want to talk to Marie on your show."

"Marie who?" Jerry said, growing impatient. "Marie Osmond? The one who lost all that weight on those annoying commercials? Marie Antoinette? Oh, God, this isn't some kind of lost-love confessional, is it?"

"Marie Clutter," Donnie said. "And yes, this is a lost love story. I need to speak with her. I'll apologize to her on your show for everything I did to her. But I need to see her. I promise it'll be good TV."

"Clutter?" Jerry responded. "Any relation to that family in that Capote novel that got slaughtered in Nebraska back in the '60s or something?"

"Kansas. And no, she's not related, as far as I know."

"I'll just have to assume you're right about that since Truman isn't here to tell us."

"Whatever," Donnie said. "That's my condition."

"Hookay," Jerry said. "We'll track down this living doll from the past and get her on the show so you can pledge your undying love and maybe get laid. Your call."

"I'm going to be on the radio," Carsten said in his characteristic drone. "I'm. Going. To. Have. A. Show. On the radio."

"Hold your horses, Carsten," Donnie said. "I haven't agreed ..."

"Oh, yes you have," Jerry said. "Take the bus tickets. Here's the cash. I'll talk to the higher-ups of this goofball joint about getting you out of here. Who's the sheriff of this jail house? With whom do I speak to secure your freedom?"

"Dr. Sally Dixon," Donnie said, growing apprehensive at the thought of a Godzilla vs. Mothra-like battle that would happen when Dr. Dixon and Jerry met. "Look, I wouldn't mess with Dr. Dixon. You'll wind up getting me a life sentence."

"No worries, *mon amie,*" Jerry said cheerily. "I'm Jerry Most. I've tamed the wildest of beasts. Just ask my nutty ex-wife Pinky Lee. Let me talk to Dr. Dixon and we'll have you on the air and on the worldwide web in no time."

"Fine," Donnie said, resigned. "Carsten, please take me back to my room. Mr. Most, good day."

"See ya soon, Buckaroo," Jerry said, clicking his heels and walking away in the most gratingly cocky way Donnie could imagine.

So.

Donnie was being offered a trip back to the Big Time. All he had to do was tell a few crazy stories from his wild man days on national TV. Well, public access cable TV anyway. And a podcast. He was going to let America know what a jerk he's been. He'd make them laugh. He'd make them cry. But most of all he'd meet Marie again. He had learned his lesson. Maybe she'd finally take him back. And that would make everything worth it.

Right?

— 17 —

BACK TO REALITY, FOR THE MOMENT

Carsten escorted Donnie back to his room. He was a bit keyed up now. His spirits seemed to rise from automaton to flat affect. He was no longer the taciturn jail guard now that he was more of a pal to Donnie. Donnie still wasn't sure he was prepared for Carsten's undying friendship, but for now Carsten was going to be a partner in cross-country travel and broadcast crime.

Carsten opened the dorm-room door and Donnie hopped into bed. He lay there in silence. He missed the sounds of the city. The clatter and bang. The car horns and the swearing motorists. The beer trucks clanging their half-barrels into the bars.

The only noise he heard was the hum of traffic on the distant Interstate and the occasional screaming in the Serenity Heights hallway.

Donnie was supremely bored. As a result, he began to think, which was always a dangerous activity. And the thoughts always came to the same thing.

Marie.

Donnie was obsessive. Years after he had last seen her, he had romanticized their relationship into an unreality of hearts and flowers and drinking and screwing. He thought about the time they were guzzling swill in some dim gin joint and a cockroach skittered across the bar in front of Marie.

She had smashed the bug with a coaster and called over the bartender.

"Look at this!" she cried in mock horror.

The bartender looked at the flattened creature on the coaster and said: "You bitch. That guy was supposed to race tonight after closing," and he walked away.

Good times.

But in fact, Marie was not perfect. Donnie just never saw any flaws. She was indeed beautiful. But she couldn't have helped him keep his life straight. Or could she? Donnie always thought so.

The possibility of seeing Marie again on Jerry's show, or maybe even — no, don't even think about this — getting back together, overwhelmed him.

With a new L.A.-based radio show, Donnie could even show off for her some more. He realized he'd been showing off for her all these years by becoming a big-time radio celebrity for a while. He would become a star again in L.A. She'd see the new Donnie. He'd take her to movie openings and fancy restaurants. He would woo her. She would see that he really was somebody after all. Then she'd take him back.

Donnie sighed heavily as he lay in bed and then sank into a dreamy sleep in which Carsten was dressed as a St. Bernard who delivered beer in little mugs on his nose. Other than the dream, Donnie slept peacefully that night.

Next morning, a knock at the door woke him with a start.

Now what?

"Donnie, it's me, Carsten," he said in a heavy whisper through the door. "I've got an idea for our radio show. May I enter?"

Donnie got up groggily and stumbled to the door.

"We're going to be a great radio team," Carsten said, sounding characteristically droll but uncharacteristically agitated. "I do impressions. Would you like to hear my Bogart?"

"Uh, no, Buddy, I don't..."

Carsten broke Donnie's train of thought with this: "Louie, this is the start of a beautiful friendship."

Carsten sounded more like a drunken Tom Waits than Bogart. No matter.

"Carsten," Donnie said wearily, "Carsten, Carsten, Carsten. We don't have a radio show. We're probably never going to have a radio show. It's most likely a hollow promise from that huckster Jerry Most.

He just wants me to go on his show and try to redeem myself through self-degradation on cable TV, oh and a podcast, even YouTube, by dangling a chance for me to get back into real radio. Sounds like a lot of fun, but at least some fabulous cash and prizes await.

"Really, Carst, I can't wait to disgorge my rancid inner being for the entertainment of the nation's splintered cable TV and internet audience. It might be good for me, in some distorted way, to air Rockin' Donnie's dirty laundry so I can ditch the character once and for all and live my life with some modicum of dignity. I'm sure Dr. Dixon might think it would be good therapy."

"Come on," Carsten said, his eyebrows furrowing. "Just tell a few of the crazy stories from your rock-and-roll past and you'll be done with it. It might even be fun."

"Fine, Carsten, fine. Why are you here?"

"Oh, yeah. Um, Dr. Dixon wants to see you."

"What? With me in the middle of baking a souffle? Tell her I'm busy."

"Look, Donnie, if you ever want to get out of here you've got to cooperate with Dr. Dixon. Let's go!"

The twosome trudged to Dr. Dixon's office. Donnie followed Carsten down the hall with the usual apprehension associated with a kid waiting for dad to come home from work and beat the hell out of him. They arrived at Dr. Dixon's office. The door was closed, as usual. Carsten knocked softly and opened the door.

Dr. Dixon was seated at her desk looking like the cat who just swallowed the canary.

"Come in, Mr. Derringer," she said dryly. "I've been expecting you. We need to have a chat."

Uh oh.

— 18 —

FLOATS LIKE A BUTTERFLY...

Dr. Sally Dixon frightened him. She represented authority, "The Man," or in her case, "The Woman." Given his hatred for his father, he never did well with authority figures. He despised them, but he treated them with respect even though he held them in deep-seated contempt.

When it came to encounters with Dr. Dixon, Donnie felt like he was about to enter a boxing ring with Muhammed Ali during his prime.

Stings like a bee, indeed.

Donnie entered the tomb-like room and saw that Dr. Dixon had arisen and moved to the front of her desk. Her arms were crossed and she was tapping her foot like a mother waiting up for her son after a prom date.

Carsten closed the door and as Donnie crossed the threshold. The door closing behind him it sounded like a bank vault being slammed shut.

Donnie nervously tried to lighten things up.

"Top o' the morning, Doc! Or is it already afternoon? I never seem to know. What's shakin'?"

Dr. Dixon stood there stone-faced, ready to attack.

"Sit down, Donald," she said icily. It sounded like a command given to a dog who had just crapped on a plush wool carpet.

Donnie sat as she walked back to her desk. She sat, stared at Donnie and tapped a pencil on the desktop. Donnie thought the pencil was making dents in the heavy wood desk.

Dr. Dixon said nothing, adding to the thick silence in the room.

Finally: "So, you've managed to try to secure your release by having an erstwhile TV talk show host lobby me and the administration of this hospital to allow you to go on a bus trip to his cable TV show in Los Angeles or New Jersey or some such place."

"Berryland, New Jersey, actually. Look, I didn't ask Jerry Most to do anything," Donnie stammered. "He approached me. He was the one …"

Dr. Dixon stopped him with a wave of her hand.

"I'm not really concerned with who approached whom," she said with more venom in her voice than usual. "The fact is, Mr. Most offered the administration a substantial amount of money to make improvements on this decrepit facility if I agreed to let you go on a trip to New Jersey to appear on his ridiculous show. I am comforted somewhat by the fact that Carsten, our most stalwart staffer, will be along on this escapade. Hopefully he can babysit you and keep you out of trouble. But why do I see another disaster for you in this … this caper?

"I'll have you know I'm under significant pressure to allow your release. I'm not in the habit of releasing suicidal, likely bipolar, patients who are in crisis. But ..."

Donnie chimed in.

"I'm not in crisis anymore," he pleaded softly as he saw his chance for a ticket out of the nut house hanging on Dr. Dixon's recommendation. "Really, Doc, I certainly feel a lot better than those freaks in group therapy. I mean, sinking your incisors into a neighbor's puss for cutting your lawn? Now that's bizarre. I just got a little toasted, mouthed off to a Cro-Magnon, got beat up, called my girlfriend and dumped an idle suicide threat on her. It could have happened to anyone in that situation."

"Yes, well, be that as it may, I think you're still in crisis and in need of some inpatient therapy," Dr. Dixon said with a sigh. "I recommend meds, perhaps lithium, to settle down that fevered brain of yours. Alas, I doubt that you would take any prescription drug that would help stabilize you. Instead I see you imbibing street drugs you take to make yourself, in your terms, 'blotto,' making your mental condition worse. Self-medication has always been your balm. You are sick, Mr. Derringer.

"Nevertheless, I am going to allow you to take this journey to ... to Berrytown, is it? In hopes that a change of scenery will help you in overcoming your obvious neuroses, bipolarity and various personality disorders. The administration has left me with no choice but to release you although it is against my recommendations.

"So, go. Go with my highly ambivalent blessings, Rockin' Donnie Derringer. May you find the answers to your many questions about life itself. Maybe you will become 'somebody' again on cable TV in New Jersey and the podcast, or whatever. And remember, you will always have a place at Serenity Heights. I predict that after your little vision quest comes to an end we will meet again. For now, you may leave my office and prepare for your sojourn."

Donnie gulped, but managed to thank Dr. Dixon for all she had done for him.

Whatever that was.

She reminded him to write in the journal, though he hadn't had a chance to write much during his stay at the hospital except for his Star Trek riff.

"I'll grab it on my way out," Donnie said. "The journal goes everywhere with me. Writing is kind of 'therapeutic,' as you might say."

"You will not be rid of me, Mr. Derringer," she said. "I will always be in your life at some level even if it's only by remembering our sessions. Yes, I will be there. Suicidal tendencies are not to be mocked or ignored."

Donnie thought it sounded more like a threat than a promise. No matter. Donnie had once again been sprung from yet another jam.

"Thanks! Uh, thanks, Dr. Dixon," Donnie said, sounding like a man who had just been cut down from a rope at the gallows. "Um, Jerry also asked me to keep writing in my journal, or memoir, although he will never see its contents. My life is in the public record and his researchers can find enough material for my appearance on his show. But I will keep writing. Promise!

"As for Most's show, think of it! My deepest thoughts broadcast on a podcast and public access cable TV! But you'll see, Dr. Dixon. I'm OK now. I'll be one of your success stories! Honest! I hope you will watch. Will you?"

"Yes, I will probably find a way to tune in to the podcast if for nothing more than ghoulish interest," she said. "I certainly do not want to watch one of my patients self-immolate on any form of media. My concern is that you are far more fragile than you know. I wish you luck but I predict this is not your last stay with us."

Donnie left the office and fairly skipped down the hall to his room. Carsten was nowhere to be seen.

On the way to his room, Donnie bumped into the Jerry Garcia guy. Donnie had forgotten the guy's name but he was carrying a plastic cup and shuffling zombie-like toward a drinking fountain. Donnie guessed his glass would soon be half-full.

"Hey, man, what's happenin'?" Donnie said. "You look a little more disheveled than usual."

He looked at Donnie and quietly started wheezing the tune of the Bee Gees' "Stayin' Alive."

"Ah, ah, ah, ah, barely alive, barely alive," Tony rasped. He said some new drugs had turned him into a ghost. He filled his glass until it was spilling over the brim and onto the floor, more than half-full. He turned and shuffled off.

Donnie thought that was pretty funny coming out of an addled drudge. But he wanted to say goodbye to whatever his name was.

"Hey, it was good to meet you," Donnie called after him. "I hope Otis or Merv or whatever you call him doesn't bother you anymore. Just wanted to let you know I'm getting outta here. I've been released and I'm going to New Jersey and maybe later California. With Carsten."

The man stopped, pirouetted, and looked at Donnie in horror.

"Do. Not. Go. Out. There," he said onerously. "Do you know what's waiting for you outside these walls? Corruption! Murders! The end times! I'm telling you right now it's all coming apart at the seams out there. You're doomed if you go out there. This is a safe place. It's the devil's world out there. Satan rules the outside world. Stay, stay, stay!"

"Yeah, well, I'd just as soon take my chances," Donnie said. "You know me. Glass half-full now, right? I'll be fine."

He shook his head slowly and turned away. He scuffed his slippers as he shuffled off.

"Goodbye, my bedraggled friend," Donnie said sweetly.

"You've been warned," the guy said darkly. "You'll be back!"

Chilling.

Donnie had been at Serenity Heights for only two and a half days, but it had certainly left an impression on him.

— 18 —

ESCAPE FROM THE PLANET OF THE LOONS

DONNIE WALKED BACK TO HIS ROOM to collect his things before departing. He entered the cage and walked into the bathroom. He looked in the mirror and saw that his black eyes were now more of a faded chartreuse. Donnie's ribs still hurt from the AC/DC beast's kicks, but he was physically on the mend.

Was he on the mend mentally?

Who knew?

He surveyed the room for his belongings. His bloody Bukowski T-shirt and equally bloody jeans had been returned, cleaned. He decided to leave behind the socks and underwear he was wearing upon his admittance.

Yuck.

Donnie hadn't even brought a toothbrush, so he took the one provided by Serenity Heights.

He grabbed his journal and threw it in a nylon laundry bag that had the logo for Merle's Clean 'n' Go dry cleaners. The bag had been provided to carry his things into the free world.

It wasn't long before Carsten came for him.

"Donald," Carsten said in a husky whisper. "I just talked with Dr. Dixon and she said we can leave any time we want. Seriously. Let's go to the bus station right now."

Carsten spoke with all the emotion of a prison guard who just got the day off. Yay.

Carsten had the bus tickets Jerry Most had provided in his hand and he was waving them like winning lottery tickets. Jerry Most had given Carsten the wad of cash for safekeeping. He hadn't trusted Donnie not to escape and go on some maniacal spree.

Carsten handed the cash to Donnie, who stuffed it in his left front pants pocket.

"Hold your horses, Carst," Donnie said. "I've got some business to take care of, not the least of which is quitting my miserable job as a has-been jock at KYJL. I owe them at least a formal goodbye since I missed my shift Monday night. I'm sure management will be devastated. More likely relieved. Then I've got to go to my hovel and pick up a few things. Maybe even a few more pairs of some clean underwear, if I have any, and another T-shirt for the show."

"Very well, Carsten said. "May I come with you to the radio station? I've never been in one and I'd better get used to it if we get a show."

"Ah yes, Carsten, the world awaits your arrival on the airwaves. It'll be the biggest thing since Abbott and Costello."

"Whatever the case may be, I am eager to join you on your trip and I would like to depart posthaste before Dr. Dixon changes her mind and keeps me here."

"Yes, you're coming along," Donnie said. "But you'll have to wait for me in the station's dusty and dark reception area while I talk to my boss, Bobby 'Hooter' Hurd. I don't know how he's going to take the news that the only person willing to work his night shift is leaving for presumably better things."

"OK, great!" Carsten deadpanned. "I'll go get my car and we can drive over to the station, then catch the next bus out of town. I hope we can stop at a Stuckey's on the way to the bus station so I can get a box of Good 'n' Fruity for the ride to New Jersey."

"Uh, I'm not sure they make those anymore," Donnie said. "But maybe you can get a salted nut roll for nourishment during our journey."

They walked out of Donnie's room and just then the admitting nurse, the ever-efficient Pat, shouted down the corridor toward them. She waddled toward the duo, waving several pages of forms.

"Excuse me, excuse me, ex-cu-use me," Pat gasped. She sounded like a winded Steve Martin. "Dr. Dixon says you have to fill out these forms before you're released. Forms are important, you know."

She handed the paperwork to Donnie. He asked for a pen and placed the papers against the wall. He was in no mood to answer inane questions about his stay at Happy Hollow, so one by one, he placed an "x" where his signature was required. Fuck this. On the last one he signed "Keith Moon" as a bit of a tribute to the greatest rock and roll drummer who ever lived. In any case, he was now free to go.

Donnie handed the stack back to Pat.

"Here you go, my love, all the paperwork your sclerotic heart can caress. Now if you don't mind, I'm getting the fuck outta here."

Pat looked sorely aggrieved.

"You don't have to be rude about it, Nut Job," she said, swiping the papers from his hand.

"That's why I love you, Pat. Always thinking in terms of courtesy and the need to make gentle the human condition."

"Piss off, freak. You'll be back."

"We'll see," Donnie said. "In the meantime, sayonara, sucker."

"Just stay away from the medicine jar," she said harshly. "We don't want any accidents, do we, Suicide Boy?"

Pat loved her job.

She turned on her heel and shuffled toward the security locked door at the end of the corridor. She had the electronic pass-key that opened the door and wielded it like a gulag trustee escorting a zek to the firing squad.

"I'm all that stands between you and the free world," she said menacingly, holding open the door. "Unfortunately, Dr. Dixon says you've gotta go."

She glared at Carsten out of the corner of her eye.

"Carsten, you ought to know better than to follow this self-destructive creep into his netherworld of sex and drugs and rock and roll," she said. "You'll be back, too. If Dr. Dixon will have you."

She cackled.

"You two are doomed," she said through peals of laughter. "Looking forward to your return, losers."

"Bye, Pat," Donnie said as he passed through the security-locked doorway into the reception area. "Don't wait up!"

Donnie walked out of Serenity Heights feeling like he'd just been paroled, like he did when he left his parents' internment camp for good. He wanted to call Liz. But she'd clearly had enough of Rockin' Donnie. At least for now. He was a little bewildered dealing with his newfound freedom, but he knew he needed a ride somewhere. The radio station? A bar? The bar sounded good, but again, he had no transportation. And the cash on his person was meant to get him to New Jersey.

Carsten told him to wait right there and Donnie stood in the parking lot blinking in the sunlight, confused about making his next move. He was free to go. But where? A magic feeling this wasn't. He didn't know where Carsten had gone. Donnie was alone and free.

Eek!

Just then Carsten, dear Carsten, walked up on Donnie's blind side. Carsten wasn't wearing his hospital blues. He was clad in tattered blue jeans and, oh God no, a Harry Chapin tour T-shirt. He wore a thick, leather, studded bracelet and looked in general like he'd spent the night in a laundry hamper.

"Hey, Buddy, where to? A bar before we get on the bus?" Carsten said.

"Hmm," Donnie said. "Tempting though that may be, I need to get to the station to tell my boss Mr. Hurd I'm taking a leave of absence. Or that I'm quitting. Whatever he agrees to. Drinking might make the scene more surreal than it needs to be."

"OK. Well, why don't I drive you to the station?" Carsten said. "I will wait in the station lobby while you talk to your boss. I've always thought radio stations were cool. I'd love to hang out while you get dismissed from your late-night responsibilities."

"Your curiosity is a bit sad," Donnie said. "KYJL, 'The Rock,' if you will, a dusty little radio station playing all the dreck the late '70s had to offer. It's not real exciting, Carsten."

"I don't care," Carsten said with a thin smile. "You're my partner now and I'll follow you anywhere. We'll be like Butch and Sundance!"

"Yeah, Sundance. And I'm still not sure about this partner thing. But for now, I'll take your ride, talk to Mr. Hurd and then maybe we'll go to my place and smoke some weed. Maybe even have some beers and then get to the bus station. But I gotta quit or get fired or whatever first."

"OK," Carsten said. "Stay here and I'll walk back home to get my vehicle."

"Great, Carsten. Great," Donnie said. Then: "Hey, Carsten, do you know anything about Mr. Spock? You know, the emotionless Vulcan on the old *Star Trek*?"

"I do," Carsten said. "In my life there has been no real call for emotion. I have no friends, no relationships. I like to think of myself as a sort of a modern-day Marcus Aurelius. He said, 'I have learned to be gentle and meek and to refrain from all anger and passion.' That's me."

Donnie couldn't believe that Carsten, an impassive giant, was quoting an ancient philosopher. But it did explain Carsten's countenance.

Carsten walked home and left Donnie waiting outside the hospital.

As Donnie lingered under the portico of Serenity Heights, a wave of nausea hit him. He forgot to eat that morning but between the greasy pizza and the fact that he was still mildly suffering from his drug-and-alcohol-induced illness, the sun seemed twice as bright and the breeze felt like steel wool on his arms.

He suddenly walked behind the arborvitae trees that flanked the hospital's entrance and puked. It was a real purge, and he felt better immediately.

Donnie looked down at the contents of his gut and observed that he needed to chew his food better. He wiped his mouth on the back of his hand. Bits of food had tucked themselves into the heavy mane of his metacarpus.

Yeah, he needed some beer and pot, but first there was the matter of whether he had a job at KYJL any longer. Or whether he still wanted it when and if he returned to Deerhead.

Jerry Most had promised him a radio show in Los Angeles, which would be terrific if indeed Most still had the influence to make such an arrangement. And to think of silent, philosophical Carsten as his radio partner was a bit daunting.

But appearing on Most's show was even more terrifying. Would Donnie have to confront all of his sins on cable TV? And a podcast. And YouTube. What would they dredge up? There was so much sludge in his past. What kind of interview was Jerry going to conduct? Would they find Marie? There was so much to choose from in terms of the many dreadful or ecstatic fates that would slam into him.

As Donnie fretted, Carsten pulled up. He was driving a rusty white panel van with the shadow of the logo for "Otto's Plunge-it Plumbing Service" and the silhouette of a toilet still visible on the truck's side panels.

Carsten stared forward, then he threw open the creaky passenger door for Donnie.

"Sorry it took me a few minutes," Carsten said. "I had to grab some books and clothes for the trip. But I'm ready to depart. Jump in, my friend. We're off to see the wizard. Get it? Jerry Most is like the wizard because he's going to grant your wish to get a radio show in L.A. And I'm going to be your on-air compadre."

Donnie sighed. Somehow all of it, especially appearing on Jerry Most's show and podcast sounded like a bad idea, but this might be the only way he could see Marie. Donnie had to play the cards he was dealt. He was certainly used to chasing his delusions, so how bad could catching this one be? Donnie had escaped the loony bin, but he had no idea what awaited him on the outside. As grim as Serenity Heights seemed, as restricted as his actions were in the crazy house, there was a certain comfort in knowing he was being taken care of, that the Jujubes were free, that he was being sheltered from the outside world and all the temptations he couldn't resist. That his life could actually change with a little therapy and maybe some psych meds.

Hell no!

Donnie hopped into the Great Unknown as he slid into Carsten's van. He slipped on his safety belt and Carsten reached over, patting him on his knee.

"Giddyup," said Carsten, stone-faced. The muffler-less van rumbled out of the parking lot, belching black exhaust that looked like a James Bond smokescreen.

"Yeah," said Donnie softly. "Giddyup."

Carsten slipped a cassette tape into the stereo and turned up the volume.

"Would you mind playing something other than AC/DC?" Donnie said. "I'm a little AC/DC'ed out."

"No worries," Carsten said. "Here's some nice *Carmen*—the opera, not Eric."

Donnie already wondered what he had gotten himself into.

Maybe he could clear his head with some beer and pot.

Maybe he should have stayed at Serenity Heights.

The again, maybe he should just roll with fate.

But first, he had an appearance before "Hooter" Hurd.

— 20 —

DONNIE REVEALS HIS PLANS TO "HOOTER" HURD

Carsten knew where KYJL was located because it was a Deerhead landmark with its bright rock-damaged marquee and its broadcast tower. He drove his beat-up van apparently shooting for a new land-speed record. As the van belched black ash-colored smoke and careened around Deerhead's curved and tree-lined streets, Donnie found himself clinging to the arm rest for dear life.

Yes, things weren't great, but dying in a crash while riding in a used plumbing van with a mental hospital orderly was not the way he had planned to make his exit from this mortal coil.

"Jeez, Carsten, take it easy," Donnie said. "We don't need to crash into any trees on these lovely arbor-lined lanes. I just need to take care of a few things at home after we go to the station and I give my boss, Mr. Hurd, the glad tidings of my at-least-temporary departure from the nighttime Deerhead airwaves."

"I don't drive much," Carsten said flatly. "There is little reason to use a motor vehicle in Deerhead as many destinations are walking distance. Please excuse my limited skills behind the wheel."

"I'll forgive you as long as you get me to the station in one piece," Donnie replied.

Carsten swerved wide around another corner. He was uncharacteristically enthusiastic about visiting KYJL. It made him think of the possibility of a real live radio gig in L.A. But he was driving as though he had just robbed a convenience store.

"Seriously, Carsten, slow down," Donnie said. "We are not in any hurry. I just have talk to station manager 'Hooter' Hurd and then go home to pick up a change of clothes, my own toothbrush and whatever pot and liquor I have left. Remind me to bring my journal, by the way. Don't let me leave it on the front seat of this luxurious conveyance."

Carsten slowed the van to airliner take-off speed. When they arrived at the station it did not seem as though he would be able to make the turn into the station's parking lot.

Carsten made the turn, stomped on the brake and brought the van to a screeching halt in a parking space right in front of the station's entrance. He cut the ignition and after some knocking sounds the van's engine stopped turning over.

Donnie opened the van door and said: "Welcome to the entertainment and communications heart of Deerhead. What would the kids from Deerhead High School do at the quarry on Saturday nights without 'The Rock' to provide them with a '70s soundtrack to their empty and doomed lives?"

Donnie felt somehow triumphant as he walked toward the glass double doors at the entrance to "The Rock."

He had no job possibilities other than what he suspected was the phantom L.A. gig, but he was about to drop the bomb on his boss and announce his resignation.

How exciting!

When the pair walked in there was no one at the reception desk to greet them. There never was. Mr. Hurd had fired the last receptionist, Amber, in what was ostensibly a cost-cutting measure but also because Amber was known to spend much of her shift in a utility closet with her boyfriend, Billy "Master" Bates, as he was known around town, for reasons Donnie cared not to think about.

As it turned out, one day Mr. Hurd's wife, Sheila, made a surprise visit to the station with a bag lunch for her husband and she noticed Amber's absence from the front desk. She also heard hysterical panting coming out of the closet. When she opened the closet door and found the couple in a naked clinch, that was it for Amber.

It didn't matter. "The Rock" didn't get a lot of walk-in visitors anyway.

The wood-paneled lobby had two well-worn Naugahyde couches arranged in an L-shape that acted as a holding area for anyone who bothered to stop by. Tattered and faded concert bills from bands that had broken up long ago decorated the walls. Taking a glance at the dingy surroundings, a dusty and faded Iron Butterfly poster caught Carsten's eye. How old must that have been?

A noisy squawk box on the wall broadcast the dated rubbish currently playing on KYJL. In this case, it was "Evil Woman." How many times could a person listen to ELO? "The Rock" was proof that at least a few listeners enjoyed the godawful "classic rock" format.

"Grab a piece of couch," Donnie told Carsten. "This'll only take a few minutes."

Carsten sat among the dirty ash trays on the end tables and the other detritus in the lobby. He made himself as comfortable as possible while Donnie headed for Mr. Hurd's office.

"He's probably gonna kick me out, so just give me a minute," Donnie said gleefully. He was used to being fired, so the chance of leaving under his own steam made him a little giddy.

Mr. Hurd's office door was closed. Donnie knocked.

"Mystery guest, please enter," Mr. Hurd said gruffly.

Donnie walked in. Mr. Hurd was surprised to see him.

"Rockin' Donnie in the flesh!" he said. "I thought you were under lock and key at the loony bin!"

How did he know? Donnie guessed that word got around quickly in Deerhead, especially when a radio "personality" was involved.

"Nope," Donnie said. "I'm a free man. Ready to take on the world."

Mr. Hurd was balding but had a long ponytail. He was wearing a brown corduroy sport jacket over a black Crosby, Stills & Nash T-shirt. His gold-rimmed John Lennon-style glasses were meant to make him look hip, but instead they merely framed the crow's feet and tired, haunted eyes that eventually appeared in all aged adolescents.

Hooter Hurd, whose given name was really Howard, was proud of his nickname, a moniker he earned for his constant references to the breasts of women he had no chance of dating or even meeting.

Mr. Hurd eyed Donnie as though he was some sort of alien presence. He didn't often encounter his graveyard shift employee.

"Ah, so what brings you here, Donnie?" Mr. Hurd said. "You know we had to bring in some college kid to fill your late-night shift. He wasn't bad, but he smoked pot out back during long songs and the more he smoked the stranger his playlist got. I mean, Gruppo Sportivo had some fun songs, but they're way off our format."

Hooter Hurd was obsessed with the station's format. He was convinced that even as Boomers got sick of hearing Van Halen, a new generation of listeners would become hooked on the old stuff.

It was that good!

Classic rock was one of the reasons Donnie had to leave "The Rock." He couldn't take the format any longer, and besides, he had a date with Jerry Most on a cable TV show and podcast.

"I'll get right to the point, Mr. Hurd," Donnie stammered. Quitting a paying gig was harder than he thought. "I'm leaving 'The Rock.' Effective today. I'm going to be on Jerry Most's cable TV, YouTube show, and podcast. He said he can get me a radio gig in L.A. No offense to 'The Rock,' but I think I've out-grown the classic rock format anyway, and the night shift wears on a guy my age. Up or out, as they say."

"Jerry Most has a TV show? I thought that dickhead disappeared after that fat guy fought the baboons on his stupid TV show. What channel is this new show on?"

"I'm not even sure if it's a network show," Donnie admitted. "I think it's a local cable access show in New Jersey, but he does have a podcast with some 30,000 followers. And it will be on YouTube. He just wants me to spill my guts on TV for the chance to go back to the Big Time in L.A."

"The Big Time, eh?" Mr. Hurd said. "Seems to me your taste of fame didn't serve you so well. You couldn't even handle it here in our little burg. How are you going to survive in L.A.?"

"I've got to try," Donnie said plaintively. "I never really grew into my role here at 'The Rock.'"

"I'll say. Well, go with my blessing. I'm sure someone else will fill your shoes on the night shift and no one will even know you're gone except those lonely-hearted music dweebs who call at all hours. If … ah, when you do come back, I'll find a slot for you. I can always use big-name talent even if they're has-beens like you. But I'm warning you to stay cool. If you go back to your old ways, you'll wind up serving more time in places like Serenity Heights."

His old ways. Donnie could never escape the escapades that made up his life.

"Thanks for your support, Mr. Hurd. I think," Donnie said. "Look, I've got to go. My partner and I have to grab a bus. We're heading to Berryland, New Jersey, to do the show. I guess this is it. So, thanks for the opportunity."

"Yeah, yeah, whatever," Mr. Hurd said. "Now go. I have to see if that stoner college kid can work your shift. Not easy finding people to work the night shift, ya know. Take off. And close the door behind you. I've got work to do."

Donnie left feeling chagrined, yet hopeful.

He had just left a position he couldn't stand any longer in a town he despised, yet he was uncharacteristically apprehensive, even melancholy. He even thought he might miss his quiet life in Deerhead. But the Big Time was waiting.

The Big Time!

What could be more fun?

The Big Time!

What could be better?

But before Donnie headed cross-country for a chance at tasting fame and glory again, he had to return to his home to gather some belongings for the long bus ride to Berryland.

He walked into the lobby where Carsten was thumbing through an ancient *Creem* magazine with Kiss on the cover.

"I went and did it," he told Carsten. "Now I'm even a has-been in Deerhead. But renown awaits. Let's rock."

They left the building, climbed into Carsten's beater and headed for Donnie's home. Carsten seemed sedate, but then again that was his usual countenance. He drove more carefully this time and said nothing on the way.

After they arrived in a puff of exhaust smoke, they walked in in silence up the porch steps to the front door, which was locked. Using the skill of a drunken cat burglar, Donnie jiggered the old door lock and they entered. Carsten surveyed the house with great interest.

"This is the rock-and-roll world headquarters of the famous Rockin' Donnie Derringer," Carsten said. "It looks humble, what with its crooked stairs and sinking porch, but the inside is really cool. I've seen it before."

"It's headquarters, all right," Donnie said. "Come on in. I can't guarantee the condition of the place, and the toilet makes a Texaco station restroom look like a sterile operating room, but I call it home."

"No worries," Carsten said. "I guess you don't entertain much."

"Well, except for Liz," Donnie said. "And I think she expects my place to be a dump so she doesn't really care, it seems."

Empty liquor bottles littered the floor and Carsten accidentally kicked an Old Grand-Dad across the room.

Carsten gasped at the reek of stale beer and mildew but he enjoyed being in the home of a disc jockey.

"Cool," was all he could say again as he laid eyes on Donnie's massive and well-organized record collection. Tattered concert posters covered the walls, most of them thumb-tacked or taped to the drywall.

The Who. The Jam. The Sex Pistols. The Clash. Johnny Cash flipping the bird.

Public Image Limited?

Excellent.

Carsten thumbed through Donnie's record collection with great admiration.

"The only thing I keep organized is my collection," Donnie said. "Alphabetized by band name and release date. Otherwise I couldn't find The Fabulous Poodles when I really need to listen to them. Or the first, and superior, edition of The Who's "Quadrophenia."

"Excellent."

As Carsten gazed, Donnie noticed a note someone must have slipped under the front door. A note from Liz. It seemed she was mad at Donnie.

Who could blame her?

Donnie picked up the missive and read: "Look, I love you. It's been interesting. But please don't call. At least for a while. You were OK in bed, but it's not worth this."

Ouch.

The thought of losing Liz was one thing, but her insult to his sexual prowess was tough to take. Still, if he ever returned to Deerhead he would make amends with Liz and they could go back to their strained but sex-driven relationship. He could be great at break-ups and reunions with women.

Except with Marie.

Donnie crumpled the note and dropped it on the floor.

"OK, Carsten, I'm going to pick up some T-shirts, a clean pair of jeans, some underwear, whatever liquor I have around here, and my pot stash. Then we can head off into the Great Beyond. You game?"

"Exceptional," Carsten said absently, still marveling at the extent of Donnie's record collection.

Donnie went to his bedroom where he gathered some clothing and stuffed them into a plastic garbage bag. He also found his bag of pot, about a half-ounce left. He grabbed some rolling papers and a dirty pipe. He walked back to the living room. A mostly full bottle of Bushmills sat next to his bong on the coffee table. Donnie picked it up, took a healthy slug, and handed it to Carsten.

"Sorry, Donnie, I gotta drive," Carsten said, pushing away the bottle. "Besides, to the extent I drink at all it is usually a single-malt scotch, if I can afford it. Generally speaking, I find alcohol numbs the senses and I do not need to numb my feelings as I do not have many. I believe in an impassive life, much like Plato, who said, 'The first and greatest victory is to conquer yourself.' I have done so. I have conquered my passions."

"Suit yourself," Donnie said as he glugged from the bottle. "Never too early for an eye-opener. Or too late."

He hadn't been out of Serenity Heights an hour and already he had begun to revert to his old ways.

Oh well.

Carsten was thumbing a copy of Supertramp's *Crime of the Century* album and Donnie was embarrassed.

"I'm not proud of that," Donnie said. "But every album represents a part of my history. That's from high school, obviously. 'Hide in Your Shell' is a pretty good song, but otherwise, well, time passes and things age. And there are also some painful memories attached to that one. Even albums and radio personalities get old. But never too old to rock, right? Let's head out."

— 20 —

BERRYLAND BY BUS

As they left Donnie's rock-and-roll haven, Donnie wondered if he would one day come back to the place, get his things and move to L.A.

Yeah, right.

They boarded Carsten's smoke-belching van and set a course for adventure. Ten minutes later, they arrived at the Deerhead Veterans Memorial Intermodal Transit Station.

Everything in Deerhead was named for veterans. The poor excuse for a town must have disproportionately sent a full battalion off to various wars over the years.

Bravo, Deerhead! Thank you for your service!

The name made the building sound like a grand structure, but in fact it was a dreary, dirty bus station. Carsten parked the van and the unlikely pair walked to the hand-smudged glass doors of the "intermodal" center. It was called intermodal because in addition to the buses, once every few weeks, a train made irregular stops for passenger pickups and drop-offs in Deerhead. Before the railroad nearly went the way of the California condor, the Intermodal was moderately busy with people eager to leave Deerhead.

But for all intents and purposes, without a regular railroad stop, Donnie guessed it was just a "modal" station now.

The station was empty, except for an elderly wino sleeping on one of the wooden benches in the far corner of the lobby. He seemed to be a fixture in the place, as apparently no one had bothered to wake him and send him off on to his next quest for a bottle of Thunderbird wine and a dumpster dive for food behind the local café.

"We've already got the tickets," Carsten said. "But I'll go to the ticket window and find out when the next bus to New Jersey arrives."

"Great, Carsten, just great," Donnie said as he took a seat on the hard bench. "Maybe the ticket taker will even give you one of those bus driver's caps, too."

"I don't think bus drivers wear caps anymore, but there's no harm in asking," Carsten said. He hadn't thought about getting a bus driver hat, but the idea appealed to him.

When Carsten went to the ticket window — there was only one ticket window, of course — he found the ticket-taker fast asleep, leaning back in a wooden chair behind the booth. The guy was a weathered specimen, about 80 years old, and looked like he'd been asleep on the job on a daily basis for years.

At the window was a small sign that said "Tickets" and another indicating the ticket taker's name was "Gus." Of course, his name was Gus. All old men in the transportation and bank security industries are named Gus. It was a law of the universe.

When Carsten noticed that Rip Van Winkle was sleeping, he was afraid to wake him. It just seemed so rude, and Gus seemed so peaceful.

"Hey, Donnie, this guy's asleep. What should I do?" Carsten asked.

"Ah, well, one solution would be to knock on the window and ask him for a schedule," Donnie replied, clearly annoyed. Neither he nor Carsten even knew if there was an eastbound bus that day, so the ticket -taker would be helpful in determining whether the pair should go home and smoke and drink or stay at the station and wait for their bus.

Donnie was already questioning his decision to take Jerry Most up on his offer to appear on *Losers on Parade*. And, bus tickets? Jerry couldn't afford plane tickets? The train? What kind of show was this?

Finally, Carsten tapped on the ticket booth window.

"Gus, um, Mr. Gus?" he said in a loud whisper.

No reply. Carsten knocked on the window a little harder.

Still no sign of life from Gus.

Uh-oh.

Now Carsten was rapping on the window with great urgency.

"Gus? Hey Gus, wake up! Wake up Gus! Gus, are you OK?"

Gus was not OK. Indeed, he had apparently joined the Choir Invisible some hours earlier. He was no longer among the realm of the living.

Gus was dead.

Donnie was trying to get a cat nap on the bench while all the action was taking place. He was still sleep-deprived after the past couple of days. He was awakened by a dead-faced Carsten.

"Donnie. This isn't good, but I believe Gus is dead."

"Gus who?" Donnie snapped. "I don't know any Gus, and to be honest, I really need some uninterrupted sleep before our expedition begins."

"Gus is the ticket taker. The bus guy. I think he's dead."

Just then the wino sat up and rose as though from a long coma.

"Hello friends, what seems to be the matter?" the wino asked. "Your racket is keeping me awake."

As the wino sat up the smell of days, maybe weeks, without a shower filled the room. Donnie gagged. The guy smelled like a dog house in August heat. Donnie turned away to avoid the awful odor, worried that he might puke again. He usually only did that on stage, after all. Or behind the arborvitae bushes at Serenity Heights.

The guy was wearing a dark trench coat with black stains all over it. His face was as cracked as Yogi Berra's catcher's mitt. He was wearing dirty painter pants and his untied black boots showed years of dirt and wear.

"I think your friend Gus here is dead," Carsten said with the calmness of an airline pilot in rough weather.

"Old Gus?" the wino said. "I assure you he is not dead. He's just a sound sleeper. He enjoys his daytime rest. Keeps me awake with his snoring sometimes, though."

The wino stood up and introduced himself with a bow. Donnie felt his throat tighten from the man's pungent aroma.

"I am Randall Guthrey, a citizen of Planet Earth and itinerant counselor to those who need my worldly wisdom," he said in a beautiful, sonorous patois. "Friends across the nation call me Randy. The Incredible Randy, in fact, although I prefer Randall. I am called such because I have been told my perceptive powers of the human condition are indeed incredible. I am at your service. I would sincerely appreciate a little nip if either of you are carrying a potent potable as I currently have a right powerful thirst. In any event, let's check on Gus."

"Sorry, Randy," Donnie said. He did not want to share his Bushmills with Randy.

"No matter," Randy said. "No harm in asking. However, a small donation toward my next drink would be appreciated."

Donnie ignored his request for beer money.

Randy — Randall — walked across the lobby, his trench coat waving like a cape and causing his earthy essence to spread across the lobby. He opened a door near the ticket booth and let himself in. Gus was in his old wooden chair, in repose, still as a house plant. Randy touched Gus's face gently and quietly said, "Gus, hey Gus, old buddy, wake up. These gentlemen need to know when the next bus is arriving."

No response.

"Gus," Randall said in an urgent tone, gently shaking the old man. "Gus, I know you're mostly deaf, but you need to hear me now. Wake up! Gus, arise!"

Gus refused to move despite Randy's efforts.

Randy shook his head and looked at Carsten.

"Oh my, oh my, oh my," he said. "I do believe the angels have come and fetched old Gus and taken him to his glory. Oh, Gus. Poor Gus. My dear old friend Gus."

"You mean he really is dead?" Carsten intoned, suddenly unconcerned about the next bus's arrival. "I would hate to think he has passed, but at least he left this world seated on his favorite perch."

"Indeed, Gus has departed this mortal coil," Randall said. "I think we'd best call Deerhead's most competent undertaker, Mr. Morton K. Morton."

Donnie had mostly been ignoring the ghoulish proceedings as he dozed, but he realized that since a dead guy was involved, he had to jump into the fray.

"Hey, uh, Randall, are you sure that guy is dead? Should we call an ambulance instead?" he said with some irritation over the temporary disruption of his travel plans.

"Oh, yessir," Randy said through the ticket window. "I'm no doctor, but I've seen a lot of dead bodies before. I even woke up next to a dead woman once. And Gus has joined them. He's as dead as Shakespeare. Walter Cronkite, too! Yup, that's the way it is."

Donnie sighed heavily.

"Well, isn't this an auspicious way to start our sojourn to New Jersey?" he said. "A dead guy, a wino, a deadpan hospital orderly and no idea when the bus is coming."

"I object to your characterization of me as a wino," Randy said. "I prefer brown liquor of any kind to wine. I do have some dignity, you know."

"OK, I'm sorry for calling you a wino, Randall. You're not a wino, you're a common drunk, which is a slightly more elevated position on the scale of alcohol abuse. I should know. But though you're not a wino, your friend here is a corpse. Dead as any graveyard resident. I think I'm right in that characterization, correct? Do you, with your incredible powers of perception, agree?"

"Yes, you are, correct, my friend, Gus is deceased. However, may I comment on the rather insensitive attitude you have shown for my pal? Your relative indifference to this situation is abominable. I am offended, sir! Gus was a good man. He outlived his family and was a lonely man, but he was a good person who deserves the dignity of anyone who walked among the living for lo these many years."

"Sorry," Donnie said without the least bit of sympathy. "I'm sure Gus was a good guy and all, but he seems to have been the only one who knew when the bus is coming."

"Never you worry about that," Randall said. "This has been my shelter for many years. Gus never seemed to mind because I kept him company. Usually not many people are to and fro on the bus in Deerhead, as you might imagine, and sometimes the bus doesn't even leave the Interstate to stop here. Gus and I chatted all day once I awoke from my boozy dreams in the mid-morning."

"OK, OK. You guys were lost souls, and I'm sorry he's dead. Really, I am. But how do we get out of here?" Donnie said, growing impatient.

"Well, as luck would have it, I myself know the bus schedule," Randy said. "It has not changed in at least a decade. That means the next bus east will be here at 3:34 p.m."

Donnie looked at his watch. The time was 2:15 p.m. Just over an hour to kill before the bus arrived.

Randall began to weep quietly as he stood next to what was left of Gus.

Depressing!

"Oh my, oh my," Randall sniffled. "Where are we going to bury this good man? I'm sure he had no assets, no life insurance, family gone. He lived off his meager salary from the city for running the Intermodal station. He can't go to the Potters field. He needs to have some dignity. Oh, what are we going to do?"

As Carsten continued to pace absently, Donnie had a thought.

It was a nice thought, a considerate thought, notions otherwise foreign to Donnie's egocentric psyche.

"Look, Randall," Donnie said. He pulled out the wad of cash Jerry Most had given him for travel expenses. Donnie had never counted it but from the size of the roll, the money seemed oddly to be more than they would need to stop at truck stops on the way to Berryland. But Jerry Most's largesse was probably more of a matter of his ego than of generosity and Donnie was more than happy to be the recipient.

What did it matter how much money Donnie had anyway, he thought. He knew he would probably piss all of it away on pot if he could find any and a better brand of booze. It was a thick wad.

But this was a matter of being a decent human being. Donnie, who was not a decent human being, was concerned with no one but himself. Still, he felt sorry for Gus, a man he'd only met as a corpse. Donnie felt he had to act. Donnie awoke to the notion that in this case he had to do something that didn't benefit himself in any way.

Maybe it was something Dr. Dixon had said that got to Donnie. Or maybe he was beginning to mellow and even think of others. Who knew? But he wanted to do something nice, even if it was for a dead guy who couldn't appreciate his kind gesture.

Donnie counted out nine hundred-dollar bills. It depleted his spending money but even after he had plucked the bills out of the green clump, it looked like he would still have plenty for his current needs. In a pinch he could always use his own debit card if Jerry's cash ran out at a greasy spoon on the Pennsylvania Turnpike.

Yes, Donnie was about to do a nice thing, the right thing.

What?

"Randall. Hey, Randall," Donnie in a consoling voice he did not know he had.

Randall snorted into his crusty handkerchief.

"Yessir," Randall said.

"Randy, I've got pretty much," Donnie said. "I don't know what it costs to be buried in this here burg, but I think this will help give old Gus a little send-off, hopefully a hot piece of property with a nice view in the classiest cemetery in town. In fact, here's $50 for your own use. Buy yourself a nice hot meal and some Old Grand-Dad so you can toast Gus on his way out of this lost world."

Randall walked over to Donnie and held out his hand. Randall's face made it look as though he had just changed the oil in an Oldsmobile.

"Kind sir, ah, sir, this is wonderful. I don't even know your name," Randall said through his tears and took the $50.

"Tell everybody in town that Rockin' Donnie Derringer did something nice for Gus. That Rockin' Donnie isn't such a bad guy after all."

No one who ever knew Donnie would believe that, but Donnie was more than willing to help in this case because it was Jerry Most's cash he was throwing away. Still, Donnie felt like he had to get some kind of credit for this uncharacteristic act of kindness if only to assuage his own rotten soul.

"Well, Mr. Rockin' Donnie," Randy said. "Mr. Rockin' Donnie, thank you so much. Without Gus I'm going to be really lonely. He was my only friend, the only one who treated me like a real person. But at least I know he'll get a decent burial, and in Deerhead your money will go a long way toward that end. Thank you so much!"

Just then another idea flashed into Donnie's mind. He always had ideas pop into his head, often at a rapid pace, and he tried hard not to act on the bad ones. Most of his flashes centered on attaining women, pot and booze. But this one seemed kind of cool.

"Randall, where do you live?" Donnie asked.

"It depends, Mr. Rockin' Donnie. I usually sleep here, but with Gus gone I don't know if they'll let me stay. My repose here was kind of a quiet arrangement I had with Gus, and I'm not sure the city leaders even knew about it since few people ever come here. Now that Gus is gone, I'm sure they'll be taking a closer look at operations here, such as they are.

"But as for daytime activities, there are some trees in the park where I nap during the day in summer, and the cook at the local diner often gives me a hamburger if I promise not to hang out there and bother their customers. I do dispense my wisdom on street corners to anyone who will listen, but no, Mr. Rockin' Donnie, I have no permanent domicile. I live hand-to-mouth and rely on the Christian charity of my fellow dwellers of Planet Earth."

"Well," Donnie said, "How's about we make you a partner in our journey to New Jersey? You, me, and Carsten over there. You've got no one or nothing here in Deerhead, why not join us on our journey to the Jersey state?"

Carsten overheard the conversation and interjected.

"Donald, do you think that's a good idea?" he said, showing cool concern at the prospect of having to share Donnie's time. "I mean, the guy smells like someone vomited on a refuse vehicle. And he looks like he fell out of one."

"Now, Carsten, I think you're better than that," Donnie said, chiding his compadre. "This man is simply a bit down on his luck, and we might be able to help him, or at least have some fun together. Randall seems like a good guy. Let's bring him along. And if you're concerned about his personal aroma, we will arrange for him to sit in the front of the bus while you sit in back, out of range of his pungency."

"That would mean I would sit near the restroom. I can't image the germ mutations in that banyo," Carsten complained.

"Ok, buddy, let me explain how it's gonna be," Donnie said. "Randall is coming with us. I have enough of Jerry's money to get us all to Berryland in all the comfort a bus can provide even after we paid for Gus' burial. Are you in or are you out? Are you coming to Jersey or are you going to rot in Deerhead?"

"I'm going with you, Donnie, you know that. The bus is coming soon and I'll be on it with you, Randall or no Randall."

"Great! Now there's the matter of Gus' remains. We can't leave him sitting in that chair to decay. Who knows when the next person is going to enter Grand Central Station here? Randall, what is that undertaker's name and number?"

"It's right here. There's a flier on the bulletin board. Mr. Morton K. Morton, 'The man to call in your time of need.'"

"My time of need? You mean he can get me some more dope? Oh, never mind, I'll call him and send Gus on the first leg of his journey to the Heavenly Gates."

Donnie pulled out his cell phone. Uh oh, it needed a charge. Did he bring the charger? Yup. It was in his garbage bag underneath his journal.

Donnie dialed the number and got a recording. Once again, he was told to pay close attention as the options had changed.

"Press one if you are calling for marketing. Press two for sales. Press three to speak with a representative. Press four to speak directly with Funeral Director Morton K. Morton."

A small-town undertaker has a marketing department? He could only imagine the pitch: "Dead? Call Morton K. Morton. 24-hour service!"

Donnie pressed four to speak directly to Morton. He always wondered about the title "funeral director." What is this guy? What does he mean by director? Is he some kind of Scorsese of carcass disposal?

Morton picked up the call immediately. He spoke softly with the syrupy empathy of a professional who was used to dealing with the bereaved.

"Good afternoon. How may I help you in your time of need?"

"Um, yes, well, it's not exactly my time of need, but Gus here, the intermodal ticket taker, has gone to meet his maker," Donnie said, trying to speak in phony funeral director euphemisms for death. "He apparently joined the Kingdom of Heaven while sitting in his chair at the Intermodal. Can you, ah, pick him up and do whatever you do with the recently deceased?"

"I'm so sorry for your loss, sir," Morton said. "I will arrive presently with the County Coroner. Since Gus apparently died alone, we will need an autopsy to determine cause of death."

"Well, I'm guessing age and atrophy were the culprits," Donnie said. "But you guys go ahead and do what you gotta do. Look, I have to catch a bus in a little while and I'd hate to leave Gus dead in his chair while I'm enjoying a cross-country trip in a squalid transport for transients and other deadbeats who can't afford plane tickets. Um, could you make it snappy?"

"I'm going to ignore your seeming insensitivity toward the deceased as well as your unfair characterization of bus passengers," Morton said. "But yes, we will be there shortly. May I ask how you will fund a dignified departure for your friend?"

"Glad you're focused on the important stuff," Donnie said. "If you must know I have cash I will give you for Gus' planting."

"Splendid," Morton said. "We will arrive in 10 minutes."

Of course, they would be here in 10 minutes. This was Deerhead, Minnesota.

Mortenson and the coroner arrived promptly 10 minutes later. Meanwhile, the bus to Berryland would be arriving in a little while.

Morton was as tall and gaunt as Lincoln. Morton was dressed in the customary uniform of an undertaker. Black suit, white shirt and a red tie for a little splash of color. The coroner, who arrived with Morton, was a stub of a man who wore a tasteful denim jump suit that said "Coroner" stitched on the back in yellow lettering. His name, Dusty Donahue, was stitched in script over his right front pocket.

"Where's the stiff?" the coroner said gruffly. "I've gotta make this quick. They just found the widow Hasselbeck flat on her back at her grubby old Victorian home and I gotta get there before she stinks up the place. Been there a while, apparently. I'm worried the cat might've gotten at her."

Randall, sniffing, pointed to the ticket booth.

Donnie couldn't get the image of the widow Hasselbeck's rotting flesh being consumed by her own unfed cat. Donnie hated cats. This just gave him one more reason.

Dusty walked to Gus's remains and felt for a pulse on his wrist and neck.

"Yup, dead as a doornail," he said, flatly stating the obvious. "Mort, let's load him into the meat wagon. We won't need a stretcher. He's not gonna put up a fight. He's pretty stiff and he's in a reclining position. We can just carry him."

The pair picked up Gus to take him to the coroner's van. Once the old man was securely in the vehicle, Morton returned to the Intermodal lobby as the coroner's van squealed out of the parking lot and headed toward the widow Hasselback's home-turned-coffin.

"Ah, which one of you called me?" he grunted. "Whoever I spoke to said he could fund the burial of our dear old friend. I can't do anything for the departed unless I get some sort of remuneration. We wouldn't want our friend here to wind up in an unmarked potter's field grave. I think we can give him a dignified cremation if not a modest burial for, say, $850. Does anyone have the funding needed for our friend, the dearly departed, uh, what was his name again?"

"He had a name, asshole," said Donnie, who had forgotten Gus' name. "It was, um, Gus. Yeah, Gus was his name."

"Well, then, let's make sure our dearly departed goes to his eternal rest with some kind of dignity," Morton said icily. "I hate to think of the alternative."

Donnie was disgusted by the mortician's inhuman venality but pleased at saving $50 from the $900 he thought Gus' deposit into the wormhole would cost. He counted out $850 and dropped it on the floor in front of the mortician.

"Here's $850 with an extra $25 for flowers," he said. "That's $875 but I'm sure you don't need help with arithmetic since you're used to counting money from the bereft friends and relatives. Take your filthy loot. I might have guessed that you would have been more charitable to a local institution like Gus. But there. There's your lucre. Give him a nice farewell. Now get out of here."

"Sorry for making a living," Morton said testily. "May you find your own good fortunes in whatever endeavor you pursue. I'm sure you will be a great success as a janitor or truck driver or some other menial worker."

Mortenson picked up the bills, stuffed them in his pocket and walked out indignantly but not before slipping Donnie the bird.

"Nice to meet you, fiend," Donnie called back.

— 22 —

OFF TO SEE THE LIZARD

THE BUS ARRIVED SHORTLY AFTER MORTON'S ugly exit. It groaned to a stop.

The crate was everything Donnie expected in cheap cross-country bus transportation.

The vehicle's exterior was spotted by rusty patches. The windows were smeared with grease from the heads of a thousand other voyagers who had boarded in search of their own broken dreams. A black, crudely stenciled logo of the company, "Amerivoyage," had been painted over a faded Greyhound logo.

"I don't know, Donnie. This isn't what I expected," Carsten said apprehensively. "I mean, I've never heard of Amerivoyage."

Donnie snorted.

"What did you expect from the producer of a local access cable TV show and podcast?" he said. "Sure, this is low-budget, and yes, this thing is a junker, a relic of a legion of stories of misery. But he gave us some good cash and the bus will get us to New Jersey. I think."

Meanwhile, Randall was looking at the pair mournfully, still tearful over the loss of his buddy. Now that Gus was gone, Randall was friendless, destitute and without a place to bunk for the night.

"Our carriage has arrived. Randy, are you going to join us?"

Carsten, astonished, muttered something unintelligible, then spoke clearly and firmly.

"I don't think this is a good idea," he said. "This man is a derelict and he smells bad."

"Well, those things are true, but Randall is a human being in need and something of a kindred spirit to boot," Donnie said, almost incredulous about the words he had just spoken. "Let's bring him along for some fun and to help a guy who's down and out. And if we run out of cash, as is a little more likely since I was just shaken down to pay for that dead guy's funeral, Randall can teach us a few lessons in street-level fundraising."

"Do I even know you?" Carsten said. "Aren't you Rockin' Donnie Derringer, the wild man who cares about no one but himself and his need to party and screw strange women?"

"Well, as a matter of fact you don't really know me at all," Donnie said. "We've been together as long as it took for you to escort me around Serenity Heights and we've had a few brief conversations about music and Marcus Aurelius. Oh, and you got me some beer, a favor for which I am grateful. But no, you don't know me."

In fact, Donnie wasn't sure he even knew himself. What was this empathy thing he was expressing? Maybe he should consider it with a joint and some nice, mellow Carpenters. Although Karen and Richard Carpenter were a long way outside of Donnie's rockin' personal playlist, he always loved the sweet sound of Karen's voice. Like most men of his age, he had had a crush on her and always believed he could have saved her from her untimely death.

Or at least get laid by her. That would have been so cool.

In any event, Randall was coming with them. Whether Carsten liked him or not.

Randall looked at Donnie in amazement, as though Donnie had just handed him a good bottle of single-malt scotch. He turned toward Donnie and grabbed Donnie's hands and shook them gently.

"Why, sir, no one has done anything so nice for me since the Schwimmer family invited me to Thanksgiving dinner years ago," Randall said. "Of course, I wasn't able to stay long after Mr. Schwimmer quietly pulled me aside and told me my personal aroma was overwhelming the homey smell of the turkey and stuffing so he asked me to leave, and off I went. But it was a nice thing they did anyway."

"Well, I'm not sure I know much about being nice to people, but the way I look at it, for once I can actually bail someone other than myself out of a jam," Donnie said, smiling.

"Never been to New Jersey. Maybe I could even cross the river and see New York City," Randall said. "I look forward to an adventure with you, my dear new friend. Come on. Let's hop aboard this old beater."

"Indeedy dee," Donnie said, feeling cheerful for reasons he could not understand. This was, after all, a nice thing to do, bringing Randall along on the trek for no good reason other than it was the right thing to do.

Hmm.

Carsten, having boarded the bus, was sitting in the front seat behind the driver, staring out of the window. A worn copy of Plato's *Republic* sat on his lap. He disapproved of bringing the smelly old reprobate along, and he certainly didn't like sharing Donnie's attention.

As Donnie and Randall boarded the bus, Donnie said a stout "Good day, sir!" to the driver, an old stiff named Helmut, who glanced indirectly at him and said, "Yeah, right. Go sit down so we can get out of this hellhole of a town."

Helmut seemed to really be enjoying his job.

Carsten sulked and stared out the window as they passed.

About a dozen anonymous travelers were already on board, having come from God-knows-where and heading into their own personal oblivion. Their hollow eyes gave Donnie the creeps. But then again, Donnie was only recently released from the loon house himself and did not look his best. Accompanied by the grimy Randall the pair did not so much as raise a passenger's eyebrow as they walked to the back of the bus.

Donnie noticed that their rickety transport reeked of cigarettes that had long ago been snuffed out in the tiny ashtrays in the arm rests of the bus's stained seats. Donnie was an on-again/off-again smoker so he didn't mind. Plus, Donnie figured that the stench would cover him if he and Randall sat in the back of the bus. Donnie also figured he might be able to light a spliff without the notice of Helmut.

The bus stank of the body odor of the lost souls who had traveled before them, and no one noticed Randall's essence.

Randall's bouquet was one of a human being who had not washed since the second Bush's administration. It was a combination of vomit, urine and unwashed clothing.

But after getting acclimated to Randy's piquant scent, Donnie found Randall's smell to be kind of homey. It reeked like a stronger version of his own home. It wasn't that bad once he got used to it, pungent though it might have been.

The unlikely pair took their seats in the back row of the bus in front of the rest room. Donnie didn't want to think about the condition of the loo. Meanwhile, Helmut announced "all aboard" over a scratchy-sounding PA system and closed the door.

They were off!

The bus was air-conditioned, barely, but the windows slid open. Perfect for Donnie to discreetly blow pot smoke out of the vehicle's cabin from his one-hitter. It didn't make any sense to be flagrantly open about his pot-smoking lest he antagonize Helmut and get himself kicked off the bus.

The bus pulled out and traversed Deerhead's potholed streets. About one-half mile outside of town Donnie lit up. Mmm. Nice pot eases the pain. He blew the smoke through the open window, reloaded the one-hitter and offered it to Randall.

"No, thank you, kind sir," Randall said. "That's the devil's own product. I am strictly a consumer of liquor, sometimes beer or fine wine, these days. Much better for the soul."

"OK, suit yourself," Donnie said, taking another hit and exhaling it out the window.

Once the THC had settled Donnie's brain, he became curious about Randall. Donnie thought Randall must have an interesting story to tell and that Donnie would actually be able to bear hearing it.

Donnie looked at Randall, who had pushed his seat back in the reclining position, and asked how he became Deerhead's town drunk.

"Well, as with all things, it is a complicated tale," Randall said, eyes closed. "I was once a prominent man, a highly successful, well-dressed and mannerly man, who fell on hard times when I lost my job after having repeatedly been caught at work intoxicated. Back then, I was fond of the juniper berry. That was before I became a connoisseur of the brown liquors. After my last firing, I had no real job skills so I began hopping around the country looking for a place that could use whatever limited services I could offer.

"I found work outside my professional field to be demeaning. Have you ever been a dishwasher after visiting the top of the world? Tough to take, sir, yes indeed, tough to take."

"Really," Donnie said, imagining that Randall had been a corporate executive of some sort. "So, what did you do while visiting the top of the world, as you put it?"

Randall put his head back and smiled, thinking of his glorious past.

"I was a disc jockey, a real celebrity," Randy said. '"Dandy Randy' Randall was my handle."

Donnie got wide-eyed.

He gulped.

— 22 —

RANDALL'S CAUTIONARY TALE

Donnie stammered.

"Wait! You're … you're 'Dandy Randy' Randall? The King of Jazz and *All Tunes Tasty*?"

"One in the same, good sir. I once ruled the airwaves of Chicago, Los Angeles, and all points in between. Yessir, I was once a king before becoming the lowly, alcohol-infused, homeless figure before you. Yes, I was once a hotshot. I knew Miles himself and even met Thelonious Monk and the great Coltrane."

Donnie was almost speechless.

"You knew those guys? You knew Miles Davis?"

"Yessir, I did know Miles. He's the one who dubbed me 'Dandy Randy.' We all had nicknames for each other in those days."

"Holy crap," Donnie marveled. "So, with all the nicknames, what did you call Miles?"

"Miles," Randy said flatly. "You didn't address Miles by anything other than his given name. Strangers had to call him Mr. Davis, but to his friends he was just Miles. The other guys were pretty cool about the names, Coltrane loved being called 'Trane,' for example, but Miles was always just Miles."

"But … but you wound up in Deerhead," Donnie said. "Deerhead, Minnesota, the deadest of dead-end towns. A moribund destination where dead souls congregate and call it a community. How the hell did you wind up in Deerhead?"

"Well, sir, the story is, as I said, like all stories of downfalls. It is complicated and sad, and every bit of it was by my own doing. You see, it all started with a little nip before my shows. Just a trifling little snoot, usually some nice gin, to get me nice and loose and groove to the music I was playing for my highly sophisticated audience. It got me in the mood, if you can understand my meaning.

"Never rode the white horse with those jazz dudes. They all got hooked on it, but to me, heroin wasn't worth the high. It was just too scary. But gin, whiskey, hell, cleaning fluid would do the job if I needed a little mental boost."

Donnie understood all too well the need for alcohol or controlled substances to set the stage for a good show.

"Yeah," Donnie said, "everybody does something like that. It's the nature of our work."

"Indeed," Randy said. "But the nip became a glass. And the glass became a flask, then a whole bottle. Add that to a few hits of the demon weed, which I used to smoke in those days. Next thing I know station management noticed I was slurring my words during my shows. John Coltrane became 'Urp, Dzjohn Coall-trrrane.' Miles Davis became 'Milezh Davish.' Art Pepper became 'Art Pecker.' I sounded like a 45 single at 33 RPM. I spoke in slow motion, slower still as the bottle emptied. Listeners thought it might have been some kind of hip affect but management began to suspect something."

"Hmm. We've had similar paths with station management," Donnie said. "Philistines one and all. Go on. Please."

"Well, as I said, after the nip became a flask, then a flask became a bottle, I started passing out on the air. All the Tic Tacs in the world couldn't cover up the stench of my liquor-infused breath. Each boss I ever had warned about the drinking, of course, but by the time you reach the point I had attained, the sympathetic chats with station managers became stern admonitions. I'd lose gigs and just move on to the next market. It was easy because few had the encyclopedic mind for jazz that I have.

"Of course, as jazz faded from the larger public interest, I found fewer and fewer stations that played anything but rock and pop and other meaningless garbage, the kind of tripe I could just not abide. I finally made it to a station in St. Paul, working the night shift, which I always loved, until my old habits of on-air imbibing returned and I once again lost consciousness during the 3 a.m. hour. It was about five minutes before anyone realized I was out cold because the general manager, my boss, wasn't up at that time of night. My listeners just thought it was some kind of arty dead-air thing meant to challenge them — you know, like that John Cage composition "4'33" — that was simply a record of just plain silence. The musicians on that number just sat onstage with their instruments not playing a note. But no, old Dandy Randy had passed out on the air for the last time.

"I was gone the next morning. I didn't need them to tell me I was finished. I just left. Began drifting. A man with superior musical tastes but no other payable vocation doesn't have much to offer in the job market. It's not as though wedding planners want a jazz DJ running the show. As a result, I did manual labor, bussed tables, that sort of thing just to sustain myself, but it just wasn't for me. I had a cousin, now deceased, God rest his soul, who lived in Deerhead, and I took up with him for a while. When he passed, his daughter sold the house and kicked me out rather unceremoniously. Ever since, I've been sleeping in the bus station, the church or under that tree in the park when the weather was nice. I adapted to my surroundings fairly well and that tree was like an old friend."

"But why didn't you find a place to stay, maybe a homeless shelter or something?" Donnie asked. "I mean, you stayed outside in the Minnesota elements year-round?"

"Well, if things got really nasty, you know, snowstorms or tornadoes and that sort of thing, the aforementioned Presbyterian church let me sleep in a pew," Randy said. "They'd let me use a shower in the restroom to clean up and during the day, the librarian allowed me to hang out and read, an activity I always enjoyed. History and biography were my favorites, but I also picked out various music books to stay sharp in my field.

"I also liked to hang out at the Intermodal and chat with Gus, memory eternal, and sip whatever spirits I could get my hands on. All things considered it wasn't a bad life, but I admit the adventure we are now on has me thinking of a new life. The New York/New Jersey market must still have a place for Dandy Randy, bottle or no bottle."

"Why didn't you contact Hooter Hurd and get an on-air job in Deerhead to make ends meet?" Donnie asked. "By the way, don't you have family of some sort? Sons or daughters? Maybe even a charitable ex-wife?"

"First of all, can you imagine Dandy Randy Randall playing Styx and Kiss for a bunch of small-town burnouts? No sir. Not the Dandyman. I was born to play jazz for a sophisticated audience. And I sure as hell would not have any involvement in playing that so-called smooth jazz bullshit. Pure, unadulterated jazz. I like my music straight. No chaser."

"But family? Don't you have family?"

"Look, my friend, when you live the itinerant life of a radio personality you don't stay anywhere very long. In fact, my years in Deerhead were practically my retirement. Been there two, maybe three years. The offspring that I know of will have nothing to do with an old sod like me. Burned many bridges over the years, yes I did.

"Called one of my daughters once long ago, she lives in Pittsburgh. I asked if she could help me out, maybe give me a place to stay till I got back on my feet. She told me that I should never call her or any member of the family again.

"I am, my friend, an empty man. I have many stories, I have much knowledge, but I have no one to whom I can impart this information. My passing would be noted only by the person who would eventually discover ol' Dandy Randy's remains under my favorite tree in Deerhead."

Donnie was quiet for a moment as he considered Randy's story. Randy was a music snob after Donnie's own heart. A man true to his art. But he was a cautionary tale if there ever was one. Were they part of a breed? A kind of self-destructive archetype that left carnage in its wake? It was something to think about.

After all, it could have been Donnie sleeping under the tree. Or, had he followed through with his suicide threat, sleeping under the cold Deerhead ground.

Eek!

Donnie had run out of questions just as Randall ran out of steam. Randall began to doze.

Meanwhile, Carsten, still mildly annoyed by Randall's presence on their little jaunt, had reached into his duffel bag and pulled out Kant's *Groundwork of the Metaphysics of Morals*, a rollicking bestseller if there ever was one. He was content reading as the bus rolled on.

Donnie sucked on his one-hitter, blew the smoke out the window and gazed at the drab countryside rolling by. He closed his eyes and drifted off, the last thought passing through his head being: "Rockin' in the free world."

Yeah, Donnie was rockin' in the free world on a creaky bus to New Jersey.

Rockin' indeed.

— 24 —

FIRST STOP: TROUBLE IN CIMARRON CITY

Donnie was able to sink into a deep slumber even if he was sitting up in a bus seat with a hole in the upholstery on the back, which caused him to slump uncomfortably.

He woke with a start after a dream in which he was on a plane that made impact with Earth's crust as it headed toward its "final approach" in an oncoming corn field. Donnie, after all of his travels, was terrified of flying. He believed that next to drowning, dying in a plane crash would be the worst way to drop into the Elysium fields of the afterlife. Of course, in his darker moments he wondered if all of his awful misdeeds as a rock 'n' roller would actually earn him admission through the Heavenly Doors. He was afraid that his miserable lifestyle would lead to eternal damnation with demons raking his flesh and *One Day at a Time* being the only thing to watch on TV.

At least Valerie Bertinelli was on that dreadful sitcom.

Yummy.

As Donnie got his bearings, he looked at Randall, who was still asleep and drooling on his ratty coat. Donnie stretched and pulled out his one-hitter. He filled it with a pinch of the ditch-weed pot he had purchased from a 12-year-old kid at a playground in Deerhead, lit it and inhaled deeply.

Meanwhile, for Carsten a trip to New Jersey was about as exotic as any vacation in Tangier. Since he'd never left Deerhead except for a hunting and fishing trip "up nort' der" in Minnesota's wilderness, the idea of traveling anywhere outside of the state line was stimulating beyond his comprehension.

For Donnie, this misadventure was just one in a series. He had no idea what lay ahead, what Jerry Most had concocted for him on his stupid show, but Donnie concentrated on the idea that Marie would be there, that she would finally forgive him and take him back right there on cable access TV. And YouTube. And a podcast. That would make everything right and Rockin' Donnie could become just plain old Donnie, Marie's devoted partner.

What drama!

Donnie thought about Randall and he wondered if his fate was also to wind up lying under a tree and searching for scraps in restaurant garbage cans. Randall was tops, he was one of the best ever, and now he's sleeping next to me on a dingy bus, smelling like a rendering plant and heading for who-knows-what in New Jersey.

Depressing.

But Donnie's train of thought was interrupted by Helmut's voice on the scratchy intercom.

"Next stop, Cimarron City," Helmut's metallicized voice croaked. "Cimarron City, next stop."

Randall awoke and shifted in his seat.

"Slept like a dead man, I did," he said, absently wiping the drool off of his chin. "But now I have to get out and stretch these creaky old legs and maybe urinate. Truth be told, I didn't want to use the bus's restroom. Probably something growing in there with which I do not wish to come into contact."

"I'll follow you out," Donnie said. "I've never seen the Cimarron City bus station and I could use some fresh air and a trip to the can. I can't imagine what this bus' restroom looks and smells like and I'd rather not take my chances except in an emergency."

Randall toddled down the aisle walking like a penguin as he touched the top of each seat to keep his balance. Donnie followed in Randall's fragrant wake. They debarked but could not find Carsten.

Donnie found him dejectedly standing in front of a vending machine.

"Carsten, what's the matter?"

"Darned malfunctioning machine took my quarters and didn't give me the Salted Nut Roll I wanted," Carsten said plainly. "I'm hungry and I want a Salted Nut Roll, that's all. Is that asking too much?"

"In the scheme of things, I suppose not," Donnie said. "Why don't you try the Chuckles? They're seriously sugary. And in fruit flavors. Very satisfying."

"Because, Donald, if I had wanted Chuckles, I would have purchased them," he explained patiently. How could Donnie not understand the need for a Salted Nut Roll?

"Jeez, Carsten, it's a Salted Nut Roll, not an insulin EpiPen," Donnie said.

"Look, it's the principle of the thing," Carsten said. "I paid my money and I should get what I want, darn it all."

Carsten bought the Chuckles anyway and walked back to the bus. Donnie headed for the men's room while Randall was in the middle of the station lobby performing some form of yoga-like stretching. As he limbered up his pungent aroma filled the room. One man nearby gagged. Randall was unconcerned.

"T'ai Chi, my friend," Randall said as Donnie, returning from the rest room, approached curiously. "Helps to balance the body and clear the mind. I am a faithful practitioner of Zhang San Feng's age-old calisthenics. It is also quite handy for developing balance when one is inebriated."

"Jeez, it seems a little weird to do it in a bus station," Donnie said. "I mean, it's bringing stares from other travelers and that makes me uncomfortable. Really. I don't want us to draw any attention."

Randall considered the situation for a Zen moment and said: "Then goest thous and fuckest thyselves."

"Um, OK," Donnie said. "Want anything from the vending machines?"

"No."

"Then I'm going out for a breath of fresh air," Donnie said. "Hey Helmut, do we have time for me to take a little walk around this speck on the map?"

Helmut was slouched against a wall and looked to be sleeping. Not a good sign for someone who was responsible for the safety of a few dozen lost souls on a cross-country trip. He was startled to be addressed by Donnie from across the small terminal.

"You got about 25 minutes, then I leave with or without your dope-smelling carcass," Helmut said. "I have to make a call to HQ to find out our next stop. You may have noticed that we do not exactly operate a large business concern."

Donnie smiled thinly at the old and seemingly embittered Helmut — does anyone really aspire to spend their dotage as a cross-country bus driver? — and announced that he was going to take a walk around downtown Cimarron City. Downtown seemed like a hilarious misnomer for this tiny hamlet, but what kind of trouble could be foisted upon him in the scene of deserted streets, empty hardware stores and souvenir shops?

As usual, trouble found Donnie.

Donnie sauntered out of the bus station toward the business district and lit his one-hitter. He looked for an open bar and down the main street he found a little dump called Molly's Pub and Restaurant. He thought of a nice cold martini that would combine with the pot to take the edge off of traveling hundreds more miles in Helmut's squeaky, filthy bus.

Donnie would never find out what the inside of Molly's looked like. As he blissfully inhaled the dope, he left behind him a cloud of smoke that did not escape the attention of a young police officer who had been walking his beat down the desolate street.

The gendarme hurriedly walked up behind Donnie and tapped him on the shoulder.

Donnie turned around and blew out pot exhaust.

"Ah, Mr. Citizen," the cop said.

Mr. Citizen?

"Are you smoking marijuana?" said the lawman. He began sneezing.

"Well, sir, I am indeed finishing the end of a one-hitter I found on the sidewalk," Donnie said. Then he indignantly added: "What kind of place would have such devices on the street? I'm shocked. I was simply trying to keep this substance out of the hands of some local junior high dropout. Is that so wrong?"

As the pot smoke lingered, the cop sneezed again. His name was Officer Bobby Booker. It said so on his shirt pocket. Nasally, he said Donnie was breaking the law by possessing a banned substance.

"I could arrest," he sneezed, "I could arrest you for this infraction. This is serious business."

"Really," Donnie said with mock incredulity. "Your streets are littered with marijuana paraphernalia and I am to be arrested for merely picking up what I thought was clutter from your otherwise clean avenues. I should be commended for keeping your city clean."

"Well," the cop sneezed. "Your story stinks like that pot. I think you are someone from out of town who has no respect for the law. We don't smoke marijuana in our fair city."

"Really?" Donnie asked acidly. "Have you ever set foot on the high school grounds of your, ahem, fair city?"

"We're not talking about the high school we're talking about you openly smoking pot on Main Street. I oughta haul you in."

"Technically speaking, Officer, I am not in possession of marijuana since all I have here is a pinch remaining in this one-hitter," Donnie said. "Are you going to arrest me for such a minor infraction? Do you think that would hold up in Judge Crater's court, or whoever your judge is here?"

"OK, smart guy," the cop said, holding back another sneeze. "Here's the deal. You're going to get back on your bus or whatever brought you here and never come back. Understand?"

"*Alles klar, Herr Kommissar.*"

"Then get outta here, you dope-smoking vagrant," Officer Booker commanded while trying to hold back another sneeze.

Booker walked past Donnie and as he walked away, he shouted over his shoulder, "I don't see you moving! I said move on."

Donnie walked back toward the bus station and found a liquor store. While the selection wasn't great, he spied a quart bottle of gin called The River Jordan, which sounded almost holy, grabbed it, and walked to the counter.

"Hello there," said the man behind the counter. "Name's Stash. What's yours?"

"Bond. James Bond."

"Oh, a funny guy," Stash said. "Yer name ain't Bond."

"Nah, you're right," Donnie said, looking at the Old Style clock on the wall behind the bar. He had about 12 minutes to get back to the bus station. "My name is," he thought for a split second about his favorite rocker name, "Moon. Keith Moon."

"Funny name, there, Moon," Stash said. "I once knew a guy named …"

"Thanks, Stash, but I gotta run to the bus station. I'm headed to New Jersey to be on a cable TV program and podcast and I can't miss the bus."

"Well, well, well, a TV star, eh? What channel will you be on? Maybe I'll watch. Famous people don't often walk in here. Mostly town drunks and unemployed mill workers. Well, Mr. TV star, your money is no good here. Take the bottle and have a good trip."

If nothing else, this was a friendly town.

Free booze!

"Thanks, Stash. You have a great day!" Donnie said brightly. "I gotta run."

Donnie guzzled a portion of the bottle and walked briskly to the bus station. When he arrived, Helmut was standing in front of the bus, arms crossed, tapping his right foot.

"Had enough sight-seeing, pothead?" Helmut snarled. "You're two minutes late. I've got a schedule to keep. Now I'm going to have to speed in this crate to make up time. I don't know why, but I waited for you. Get onboard."

"Yessir!" Donnie said, standing straight as a soldier at attention. *"Heil!"*

"Funny. Very funny, *Scheisskopf.*"

Donnie boarded the bus and saw Carsten with a dozen candy bars on the seat next to him. He had returned to the machine and came back with a cache of Chunky bars, Nestle Crunch bars, Chuckles, all the best bounty a vending machine could offer. Except a Salted Nut Roll. Carsten saw Donnie climb aboard and said flatly: "I couldn't get those nut rolls to fall. But I'll settle for these."

"Then you're good to go, my soon-to-be diabetic friend," Donnie said, heading toward the back of the bus. Randall was already in back, but he moved to the window seat across from where he and Donnie had been sitting on the first leg of the trip.

"Lotsa land to see," Randall said. "Lots of beautiful, pastoral scenery."

"Yeah, beautiful scenery," Donnie replied. "Can't wait to see the Ohio Turnpike."

He sat down and used the sleeve of his jacket to wipe the grease from the window. Might as well see the Great American landscape clearly as he killed time on the way to New Jersey. He pulled the gin bottle out of his coat and took a swig, then fell into a sweet pot- and booze-infused series of dreams.

Jersey, here we come!

— 25 —

HIGHWAY TO HELL

As the bus headed east, Randall slept while Carsten stared out the window at the dreary landscape. A few hills punctuated the otherwise flat land that made up that part of the American panorama.

Donnie opened the window and lit his little pipe. He filled his lungs. He had no idea of how dull traveling was on the Interstate. Lots of billboards for attractions like "Al's Alligator Farm" and various waterparks as well as one for the "Dick Schickler Chevrolet" car dealership just outside of a dump called Antioch.

Donnie was amused at the name "Dick Schickler" and wondered why he didn't go by the name "Richard," but he decided that with a last name like Schickler there wasn't much he could have done to make the name less comical.

He pulled out his journal and duly noted the attractions.

The American Interstate system is incredibly boring, he concluded.

There was nothing to see from the dirty bus window as Helmut guided them down the highway. Donnie saw a huge seagull circling a landfill and wondered when Americans would eventually fill the Grand Canyon with plastic water bottles and Styrofoam cups.

The dope helped, though, as the otherwise drab colors of the scenery seemed brighter and deeper.

Donnie put the journal back in his bag and climbed out of his seat. He toddled to Carsten's perch in the front of the bus. The seat next to him was empty so Donnie sat down.

"Hey, Carsten, buddy, how're they hanging."

"Fine," Carsten said, without looking at Donnie. He was deep into Kant.

"You don't talk a whole lot, do ya, Carsten?" Donnie said.

"Don't have much to say," Carsten said. "I live in the house my mother left me in a small town where I have no friends. I drive a junker van that doesn't take me much farther than the county line, so I don't get out much. I wish I could write but I can't. But I read a lot. Read and drink. In Deerhead that's about all you do, unless you have a sex partner, which I do not. I don't like to hang in bars, so I have little interaction with people except for my fellow employees at Serenity Heights, and believe me that is not a crowd I would hang out with. Shrinks like Dr. Dixon and the other docs won't give me the time of day. They wouldn't spit in my face if my nose was on fire.

"Other orderlies like me don't have much to talk about except the weather and football. Can't really talk to the patients. By the way, I hate football. I'm more of a baseball guy myself, because I appreciate nuance, not head-smashing…"

"Wait a minute Carsten, you sound like a man who's got a lot to say," Donnie said.

"Yeah, I just don't have anybody to say it to," Carsten said laconically. "I'd love to discuss Russian history and literature or the hard-edged writing of Norman Mailer or Raymond Chandler. I have a few opera albums at home that I like to listen to, although I do like Styx or Tull or The Who. But I don't have anyone to discuss *Aida* or *Don Giovanni* with. I have learned to live the life of a loner, a man who isn't quite lonely but would love to have someone around to talk to. But I don't and I have come to accept that. You, Donnie, are the closest thing I've had to a friend in that miserable town, and I hope I can rock on for a while with you. You know, rock on!"

Carsten saying "rock on" sounded like an English teacher about to read *Moby Dick* to a class of sixth graders.

"I'm honored, Carsten, but you must know that many of my friendships have been a bit short-lived, not just with women but really with people in general," Donnie said sheepishly, taking a swig from the bottle of River Jordan gin. "I try to be a good and reliable friend, but

I'm a terrible user of other human beings. I know it but it's just a part of my nature to be an ass. I'm glad you feel that way about me and I hope I can live up to the minimum standards of friendship. Is all this why you put those beers in my room at Serenity Heights?"

"I knew who you were. I listened to your show at night. Great — for classic rock, anyway — but I wasn't a regular caller. Too shy, I guess. But I thought if I could be a pal of yours it was worth the risk. I knew that being cooped up without any alcohol in that joint would probably make you nuttier than when you were admitted. In fact, I regret that it wasn't a full sixer."

"That, my friend, would have gotten us both in a heap of trouble, but I appreciate the sentiment. Thank you. Thanks for being my friend for however long this relationship will last. Really, it means a lot."

The conversation ended abruptly as Carsten turned back to the window.

"I don't know if I could talk about *Aida* with you, Carsten, but I have a pretty good idea what *Don Giovanni* was all about. A man after my own heart, really, although doesn't he wind up in Hell?"

"Yes, he did," Carsten said absently. "Maybe Deerhead was your personal hell, Donnie, after all you'd done. Think about it."

Donnie didn't want to think about it. He left Carsten, returned to his seat in back of the bus and plopped down. He took a long pull of The River Jordan.

He put the bottle back in his bag and leaned back. He looked over at Randall, who was himself in the arms of Morpheus. He thought about Randall's story and got a chill. Could Randall's story wind up to be Donnie's too? He shuddered again and began to drift into a dream-laden sleep.

Within minutes, he had his first nightmare. Or something like that.

It involved Dr. Sally Dixon. She had invaded his brain.

Dr. Dixon appeared to him dressed in a red, sequined evening gown that slinked down her statuesque figure. She was wearing a tiara. All of it was quite fetching.

He was sitting on a wooden chair in an empty room with red walls that matched Dr. Dixon's dress. She was staring at him.

Before Donnie could get the word "hello" out of his mouth, the stern voice of Dr. Dixon said: "Good afternoon, Donald. I'll ask a silly question but are you up?"

"Oh, man, Dr. Dixon, am I ever," Donnie said. "I was having this dream and you were in it and…"

"Enough!" she shouted, loud enough to rattle Donnie's head. "Spare me your perverted thoughts and please keep me out of them."

"But Doctor, it's a dream," Donnie pleaded. "I can't control that."

"There are many things you can't seem to control," she said. "Mostly your penchant for drunken sex, marijuana and anything else you can swallow. I'd appreciate it if you left me out of your thoughts except for the clinical advice I can provide."

But this was Donnie's dream, so of course the vision of Dr. Dixon shimmied over to him and sat on his lap. Donnie was immediately aroused. He hadn't had a wet dream since high school but it looked like he was headed for a moist mess in his pants. The bleachy odor would help to offset Randall's rank smell.

She leaned into him and whispered sensually in his ear.

"Rock and roll is dead," she said. "Long live Rockin' Donnie Derringer."

What?

Donnie awoke with a start. *Dreamus interruptus.* He had been sleeping so deeply that upon waking he had to get his bearings. Where am I, he thought. Oh. Yes. A bus. To Berryland, New Jersey. There's Randall. Carsten up ahead near Helmut the bus driver.

All good.

His dream about Dr. Dixon fell short of him having uncomfortably damp underwear, which was a good thing since he had a lot of road to travel until he'd get a chance to change. But he pondered the meaning of the dream. Was he becoming infatuated with his shrink? Patients fell for their mental health professionals all the time. For one thing psych doctors had to listen to people talk about themselves endlessly. They always expressed some form of empathy unless said patient was engaged in something criminal or self-destructive. Then they got intense.

Otherwise, they listened quietly with only the occasional gentle questions about their patient's madness. They were kind. They were nice. They were understanding. And in Dr. Sally Dixon's case, totally hot. Donnie knew she was unattainable. But that made her all the more sexy. She was the ultimate challenge for Donnie's supercharged libido.

"I must not think bad thoughts," Donnie said to himself while still mulling the remote possibility of sleeping with Dr. Dixon.

Donnie snapped out of his sex-infused Dr. Dixon fantasy and pulled out his one-hitter again. He had enough pot to get him to New Jersey, but after that, obtaining more would have to be a priority. He lit up and inhaled deeply, blowing the smoke out of the window. It seemed he didn't need to be so discreet. Helmut didn't seem to care about anything as long as everyone behaved and didn't talk in a loud voice.

Donnie then reached for the bottle of River Jordan. He saw that Randall was awakening from his own road-trip-induced slumber and Donnie offered him the bottle.

"Why thank you, kind sir," Randall said, taking it and gulping the alcohol. "Mmm. River Jordan. Holy water, really. This potable and I have become well-acquainted over the years. It hits the spot, yes it does. I thank you!"

Donnie pulled out the one-hitter and waved it at Randall, but Randall refused the offer.

"Makes me too hazy," Randall said. "I've got to keep my edge."

Sure, Randall, your edge must be quite dull with all that booze you've been swilling for most of your adult life. Donnie kept that thought to himself. He didn't want to challenge Randall's self-control on at least one intoxicating substance.

Donnie leaned his head against the window and tried to take in the countryside. Stimulating though his conversations with Randall and Carsten had been, he was bored out of his mind.

He walked up the aisle to Helmut's seat at the helm of the bus.

"How long until we get to Jersey?" he asked.

"If you come back here and ask that question again, I'll take the long way," he said. "What are you a fricking nine-year old? Are we there yet? Are we there yet?"

"I'm sorry, Herr Helmut," Donnie said. "I'm just going crazy staring at this drab landscape."

"Yeah, well, why don't you go back there and take a few more tokes on your one-hitter," he said. "If you think this is dull, wait till you see the Indiana Turnpike. We'll be stopping soon in Dudleyville, Indiana. I'll fill up the tank, you can get out and stretch your legs, and maybe find another liquor store while you ponder what kind of excruciating torpor the residents of that dead city must live in."

"Well, I live in Deerhead, so I know a little about that."

"But at least Deerhead is in proximity to civilization in the Twin Cities. Indiana is a whole different level of tedium," Helmut snarled. "Now go back there and sit down. Leave me alone while I'm driving."

"So much to look forward to on this trip," said Donnie, who turned around and sat next to Carsten, who was himself dazed with boredom.

"Is this it? Is this America?" Carsten asked. "It's not even that pretty. It looks like a lot of places like Deerhead. I'm really disappointed."

"OK, Carsten, there aren't a lot of visual topographical challenges in these parts, but the mountains, the ocean, the Grand Canyon, even the Great Plains are all gorgeous in their own right. Before long we'll be sprung from cages on Highway 9 in New Jersey. Yes, this is mind-numbing but it turns out that our region is one of the most scenery-challenged areas of the United States."

"Yes, well, I wish we were going to those other places, Yosemite and such," Carsten said, dejected. He grabbed the book on his lap, *The Last Days of Socrates*, opened it and stared into it.

"Don't worry, Carst," Donnie said. "We're going to stop in Dudleyville, Indiana soon. We can get out and find a place to get a decent drink. That will improve your outlook."

"Fine."

"Have it your way. Be bored."

"Look, Donnie, I just thought this was going to be some kind of adventure with you. I love hanging with you, but not like this." Then he brightened. "Hey, you want to talk about *Madame Butterfly*?"

"'Fraid I don't know much about it, pal," Donnie said. "I can talk about 'Tommy' but I don't know much about history, don't know much about geometry, and *Tommy* is the only opera I can really discuss, but that often requires more drinks and drugs to really explain."

Carsten became sullen again. He turned back to the window without saying anything.

"Kinda moody, aren't you, buddy? I assure you, my good friend, adventure awaits. You're with Rockin' Donnie Derringer. Let's see how we can generate some excitement at our next stop."

Just then there was a loud buzz on the loudspeaker.

"Next stop, Dudleyville, Indiana. After a stop there you will no longer fear hell, ladies and gentlemen."

"See, Carst! Dudleyville! How can we avoid a memorable experience in a place like Dudleyville?"

"Yeah, I'm sure their library even has racy stuff like Henry Miller."

The bus pulled into Davy's All Night One-Stop. The sign also said "Eat." Beer signs in the window indicated they served alcohol as well. Good thing America's truckers had a place like Davy's to loosen up with a drink and slow them down from their amphetamine high before they careened down the highway with 30,000 pounds of bananas.

"Dudleyville," Helmut buzzed. "Exit at your own peril."

Donnie grabbed Carsten and pulled him toward the door.

"Let's grab some grub and get a drink," Donnie said. "That will cheer you up. You've been eating candy this whole trip."

They left the bus and stood outside waiting for Randall. He emerged looking ragged, as though he had been sleeping under his tree in Deerhead.

"Randall, my man," Donnie said, and hoping Randall would take his suggestion he said: "Hey, Randall, I think they have showers here if you want to freshen up. I'll buy you some soap and shampoo."

"Why, I think that is a capital idea," Randall said. "May I have a few dollars to pay for said shower accompaniments?"

Donnie pulled Jerry Most's wad of cash from his blue jeans pocket and handed Randall a $50 bill.

"Get yourself a shower, maybe a T-shirt and jeans or some new clothing of some kind," Donnie said. "Your stuff is ready for a Dumpster."

"Yes, but I cannot leave my coat behind. It contains all of my earthly possessions."

"OK, maybe give it a rinse or something. It smells rank."

"As you wish," Randall said. "Now I will go into this fine establishment and clean my body for the first time in weeks."

"Ah, get some toothpaste and a toothbrush, too."

"Mr. Derringer, even in my current state I know the value of brushing and flossing even if I don't always do it."

Donnie and Carsten followed Randall to the truck stop. Randall opened the first of the glass double-doors for them, Carsten grabbed the interior door, and as they lurched toward the bar Randall went off to buy soap and shampoo and find the showers.

They sat down in the middle of the bar, open seats on either side of them and the bartender, a monster of a man named Gil, approached them.

"*What'll you have, old time flavor*?" he said, singing the old Pabst Blue Ribbon jingle. He grinned. Gil's lineman size and the likelihood of a shotgun behind the bar ensured that Davy's would be a safe place to sup and drink.

Donnie looked at the menus placed behind the napkin holders on the bar. He saw they served peanut butter and jelly sandwiches. He thought about the luscious peanut butter but he didn't like to accompany it with jelly.

Ick.

He chose another culinary path.

"I'd like a Bloody Mary, spicy, and a cheeseburger, with fries, for myself. My partner here — I don't mean partner in that sense, if you know what I'm saying — I mean my compadre, can order anything he wants."

Carsten said he'd never had a Bloody Mary so he ordered one, but not spicy, along with a chicken breast sandwich and chips.

"Well, here we are, on the road. Just like Kerouac. Except on a bus," Donnie said.

"Yeah, Kerouac," Carsten mumbled. "The only thing that would make this scene better is music on the jukebox."

"Um, look around, buddy. Do you really think they have anything other than modern country dreck?"

"Good point."

Just then two women came to the bar and sat on either side of the two travelers.

Donnie shifted uncomfortably in his seat. He wasn't looking to spend any of Jerry's money on drinks for strange women.

The women were road-tested. They were fading beauties with deep creases in their faces but a homey attractiveness. Donnie thought, sure, it's been a while. A few days. I could do either of these two. Any port in a storm.

The woman who sat on Donnie's right introduced herself as "Candy." One Carsten's left was named "Dolly."

"Uh, yeah, nice to meet you Candy, Dolly," Donnie said. "But my friend and I are just taking a break from a long journey to Berryland, New Jersey. We weren't looking for company, but since you're here ..."

"I have a cousin in Jersey," Candy said. "Sherleen. Haven't seen her in years."

"Well, if I bump into her, I'll say hi from you," Donnie said.

"You're funny," Candy said. "I bet you're a lot of fun!"

"You don't know the half of it, uh, Candy."

Carsten, meanwhile, was making small talk with Dolly but he was clearly not interested in dining with her. He wanted his time with Donnie to be uninterrupted. Ironically, now that he had someone to talk to, he had nothing to say, not that he thought Dolly would want to discuss Marxian dialectic.

Conversation between Donnie and Candy was becoming animated. Giggles. Chortles. Outright hand-slapping laughter.

"I like you," Candy said, gently placing her hand on the inside of Donnie's thigh. Then, whispering, said: "Let's go someplace private. Wanna meet me in the women's room in about three minutes?"

Donnie thought about it. Well, she wasn't bad. And he always craved sex. That was nothing new but he thought it would be kinky to get laid in a truck stop women's room. Guy points!

She got up and disappeared into the bathroom.

Gil brought the Bloody Marys and placed them on the bar. Dolly and Carsten were chit-chatting idly; it was clear that the conversation wasn't going to lead to a discussion of *La Traviata*.

As Donnie got up to go to the women's room, Gil leaned over and quietly told Donnie that Candy was a real nice, pretty girl.

"She's not a prostitute or anything," Gil said. "But she's got kids, so if you're doing anything with her, don't worry, I won't let anyone in the ladies' room until you get back. But if you could give her a few bucks, that would be nice."

Donnie thought about the idea of paying for sex. But this wasn't really paying for it, he rationalized. It's more like helping out a single mom.

Yeah, that's it.

Donnie went off to meet with Candy.

"Where you going?" Carsten asked.

"Sorry, pal, gotta take a major dump," Donnie said. "I'll be back in a few minutes."

"Oh, OK," Carsten said.

Gil looked at Donnie and smirked.

"Cleanest restrooms of any truck stop in Indiana. Don't forget to clean up after yourself. Food will be here soon!"

Donnie walked into the women's room and saw Candy beckoning him into a stall. She had stripped to her underwear and Donnie was surprised to see she had a great body.

Excellent!

Donnie and Candy entered one of two stalls. Gil was right. Everything was pretty clean.

The stall was tiny, of course, so they decided to keep the door open for a little room. Gil was watching the door, so nobody would come in and disturb them. He was that kind of guy.

Upon entering the stall, Donnie dropped his pants. Candy handed him a condom.

Damn! I hate these things, Donnie thought. But it was too late to object. He was ready for action with Candy.

Carsten was gazing at his Bloody Mary like a chimp examining a flea picked off his fur. He wasn't sure he liked it. Too much tomato juice, not enough booze.

Dolly was trying to make conversation.

"How's your drink, sweetie?" she said.

Carsten did not like her familiar tone.

"Oh, it's fine, honey," he said. His sarcasm sent Dolly a clear message and she was shortly off to find more pleasant companionship.

Gil walked over and brought the food. He turned to the back bar and began polishing cocktail glasses. Carsten wolfed down the food and hoped Donnie would come back before his burger and fries got cold.

Just then a bus pulled up and about two dozen people got off, including three Catholic nuns. Gil ignored them all as they stared at the surroundings and looked for a place to sit.

"Sit anywhere you want," he said, glancing briefly. He was surprised to see nuns in the place, but at a truck stop, you see all kinds.

One of the nuns asked Gil for directions to the women's restroom.

"Ah, it's closed for cleaning right now, but if you wait a few minutes, it'll be ready for you," he said, wondering if Donnie and Candy had finished up.

"But I really must use the restroom now," she said tensely. "I've been traveling for some time and I don't like the restroom in the bus."

"Just wait a second, Sister. You'll be fine."

"But I can't," the nun said, and hurried off to the restroom. She pulled open the door and the randy couple were in their clinch. Candy's back was against the wall and Donnie was lifting her up and down, hands around her waist.

The nun shrieked. Candy screamed. Donnie said, "Shit, I was almost there."

Candy hurriedly began putting her clothes back on.

"A nun saw me screwing," she cried. "In a truck-stop restroom. Now I know I'm going to hell."

Donnie pulled up his pants and said: "Sorry, Sister! Nature was calling."

Candy was sobbing as the shocked nun ran to the vacant stall.

Donnie, now fully clothed, called to Candy, who emerged disheveled but dressed.

"I'm so sorry, honey," she said. She threw her arms around Donnie and suggested they go to her car to finish what they had started. The nun was moaning in the stall.

"I'm sorry, Candy," he said. "But I've never been busted by a nun before. That's kind of creepy, don't you think? An omen maybe? I don't think I could pull it off for the rest of the day. Yuck."

"Aw, honey, come on."

"No, really," Donnie said. "I haven't felt like this since my mother caught me pleasuring myself with a *National Geographic*."

Just then Donnie remembered what Gil had said about Candy needing money for her kids.

Donnie was going to give Candy $100, but since Donnie hadn't finished when the nun walked in, he figured he was due a discount. The nun was in the stall, making noises that made it seem as though she might have food poisoning.

"Oh, God," she said, and then Donnie heard a loud splash.

Donnie's stomach turned and he removed Candy's hands from around his neck.

"Look, I know you've got kids and everything," he said. "I'd like to give you a little something to help you get by."

He reached into his pocket for the wad of Jerry Most's cash. Then he reached deeper and began to panic.

The money was gone.

— 25 —

CANDY SCREECHES INTO THE SUNSET

CANDY LOOKED AT DONNIE WITH CONTEMPT.

"You mean you don't have any money?" she scoffed. "What a loser. I take my pants down for you and I get nothing. I got kids. You're a deadbeat."

"Um, do you take debit cards?" Donnie asked sheepishly.

Candy turned away and stalked out of the building. She did not wait for Dolly. Candy drove away with squealing tires. Donnie was unfazed by Candy's diatribe. He'd heard all of it before.

But where was the money? He'd given a fifty to Randall for his shower. OK, did he pay for the drinks? Not yet. Did he give it to Carsten? He should have, but he hadn't. Donnie ran back to the stall. Maybe he dropped the cash when he took off his pants. He checked.

No dice.

By now the nun had emerged from the stall. She was startled to see that Donnie was still there.

"I'm so sorry to have interrupted, believe me," she said. "I can never forget the sight of you and that trollop copulating against the wall. It was repellant. But I've never had such cramps. I was doubled over. I thought I was going to mess my pants."

"Yeah, thanks for the report, Sister," Donnie said. "Did you happen to see a wad of cash around here?"

"I'm afraid not," she said, vigorously scrubbing her hands. "I was a little distracted by the sight of you and your paramour and the searing pain in my abdomen, so I wasn't really able to inspect the room before I entered. Did you check all of your pockets?"

Why do people ask that question when something is missing? Of course, he had checked his pockets. He found his wallet in his back pocket, but the cash was nowhere to be found.

And then: Candy!

Candy had stolen Jerry Most's cash. How else could he have lost it?

She was a professional, all right, and this kind of heist was probably part of her daily routine. Now she was gone. So was the money.

Donnie smiled when he thought of Candy buying herself some expensive cosmetics, shopping for toys for the kids. Maybe buying some quality hootch and pot for herself. He appreciated the irony of a cheap hooker stealing Jerry Most's money.

He held the door for the nun as she left the restroom and he walked to Carsten, who had been joined at the bar by Randall. He looked like a new man. He and Carsten were talking about the greatest left fielders in baseball history.

Ted Williams, of course.

They looked up at Donnie.

Randall smirked at him.

"I understand you had a rendezvous in the ladies' restroom. I'm sure you found the accommodations suitable for such a sordid act," he said. He broke into laughter.

Then Helmut walked into the truck stop and announced that the Amerivoyage to New Jersey would be leaving in five minutes.

Donnie looked at the pair and said: "Do you guys have any cash? Credit cards?"

Carsten instantly knew Jerry Most's cash was missing. By now, Carsten almost expected this from Donnie. Donnie was his newfound friend, but Donnie did not seem like a responsible keeper of any money, least of all a clump of cash from Jerry Most. Carsten regretted not taking it from Donnie and giving it to him as needed. Now Donnie had managed to piss it away.

That Donnie!

Randall spoke first.

"Well, Mr. Derringer, as you might imagine, a debit card does not fit my hand-to-mouth lifestyle, so no, I don't have one. I'll bet Carsten does."

"I do," Carsten said, indignant. "I'll cover the bill here but after that we're going to have to figure out how to split expenses, Donnie. I'm not draining my checking account so you can be massacred on TV. This is your vision quest, not mine, friend."

Donnie was a little hurt by Carsten's attitude. Friends helped friends, right?

Well, Donnie usually didn't. But that was beside the point.

Donnie didn't know how much he had in his checking account. He never did. He always figured if there was a problem it would be rejected so he remained blissfully unaware of his assets. For all he knew as long as a card worked, he was still rich. It was better not to check. The potential for depression and anxiety was too great if he found out that he was stone broke.

"I think I've got enough in my checking account to pay 'til we get to Jersey," Carsten said, "but then I'll have to get more funds from Jerry Most to get us to Los Angeles or wherever we wind up."

As they left, Gil looked up at Donnie and winked.

"Hope you enjoyed the service here," he said. He guffawed as he turned away to attend to a drunk at the end of the bar whose nose was touching the Formica surface.

Donnie stuffed the burger in his empty pocket and grabbed a few fries. The trio walked out of the double doors to the bus, Carsten grumbling to himself all the way. Carsten and Randall climbed into the bus, Carsten taking his seat in front and Randall moving to the back. Helmut looked at Randall and said: "What's with you? I thought you were some homeless bum traveling with these losers."

Randall smiled.

"Yessir, I am indeed a man of the world, someone without a permanent address. The type of traveler I am sure you are well-acquainted with. Homeless. Down and out. But I am not a bum. And I clean up well. Right, Carsten?"

"Yes, of course," Carsten said of his rival for Donnie's attention. "Yeah, right, cleans up well. Whatever."

Helmut turned to Donnie.

"Did we have fun?" Helmut asked Donnie as he climbed aboard.

"Ficken sie dich," Donnie said. He thought he had said, "Fuck yourself" in German, but Helmut just told him to sit down.

Whether Donnie had said it correctly or whether Helmut understood if he did, Helmut burst into laughter.

"Got rolled, eh?" Helmut said. "Who would have thought as fine an establishment as this would be a den of thieves?"

Donnie flipped him off and stumbled to the back of the bus.

He'd only had a sip of the Bloody Mary and the cheeseburger, which arrived during Donnie's assignation in the restroom, was now mush in his pocket. He would eat it anyway.

Donnie was relatively sober. He did not like to be in that condition so he reached for the last of the Jordan River. He drank the remaining contents, sat back and belched.

Helmut crackled on the PA system.

"Ah, ladies and gentlemen, we've had a change in schedule," he said. "For those of you who are traveling to our stops in Hunter, Pennsylvania and beyond, we'd like to ask you to disembark from this pleasure boat and wait for the next bus, which will take you to such sad places.

"This is now an express bus to New York City. Yes, that means we'll be skipping any stops in New Jersey, for those swamp dwellers who want to return to their reedy home. Sorry about that. Can't stand Jersey myself, so it's just as well.

"We will arrive at Grand Central Station in Manhattan, where this bus will reach its terminus. If you are traveling beyond New York, and really why would you want to ever leave The City That Never Sleeps, buses and trains to your final destination will be available at the station."

A few grumbling people grabbed their things and got off. One young man nudged Helmut with his back pack as he left the bus.

"This really sucks," he shouted.

"Yes, it does," Helmut said. "Thank you for traveling Ameri-voyage."

"Never again," the kid shouted.

"We'll miss you," Helmut said.

"All aboard for Grand Central Station in Manhattan, New York City," Helmut crackled over the loudspeaker.

Donnie strode up to Helmut and explained that he and his two traveling companions needed to get to Berryland, New Jersey and that he thought the Amerivoyage bus was going to take his threesome there.

"Company orders," Helmut hissed with the authority of a German *Obergruppenfuhrer*. "We need to get this crate to New York for some repairs, and plus the government said we could ditch the Jersey stops. The towns there are too small for us to make any marks, uh, dollars. But as it turns out, there are many modes of transportation to The Garden State available at Grand Central. Personally, I don't care if you get there or not. Now go to your seat and enjoy the ride. By the way, please continue to blow your pot smoke out the window. I'm allergic."

Donnie went to his seat in the back of the bus, leaned back in his seat, and looked at Randall. He knew they could figure out how to get to Berryland from Manhattan, but he began to realize he was about to put himself through a terrible ordeal at the hands of Jerry Most.

"What the hell am I doing?" he said, rhetorically.

"Donald, does anybody know what they're doing? Ever?" Randall replied breezily.

Donnie reached for his one-hitter, stuffed it with ganja and inhaled.

Donnie was voluntarily heading for his own doom on *Losers on Parade*.

He was beginning to have heavy doubts about the whole thing. Maybe being on a show like that wouldn't impress Marie after all. Maybe she wouldn't show up. Maybe he just should go back to Deerhead and make do with what was left of his life, listen to his records, drink and smoke dope with his new friend Carsten and just hang out until the bitter end. He didn't have to get a gig in Los Angeles to do that.

But still…

The prospect of seeing Marie on Jerry Most's show would make it all worth the degradation of Rockin' Donnie Derringer. She would finally take him back, right? Maybe with *Losers on Parade,* Donnie could bury the "Rockin'" part of Donnie Derringer on the show and prove to Marie that deep down he was a decent, even trustworthy guy after all. Maybe Dr. Dixon was right, that he could no longer separate Donald Henry Derringer from the "Rockin'" persona he created years ago.

Maybe he did need the meds she suggested.

In any event, Donnie's fate was sealed. He would go on the show, purge himself and begin a new life.

What could possibly go wrong?

— 27 —

CARSTEN SEES GRAND CENTRAL

TIME PASSED. HOURS SLIPPED AWAY. Nothing happened. Donnie thought he would never leave the bus but in spite of his boredom, he made no journal entries except for one.

> What if Marie doesn't show up? What if I put myself through the pain of Jerry Most's show and he hasn't found her? My entire life would be meaningless. Of course, it isn't the most purposeful existence now. But still...

He chose to avoid writing further on the topic of Marie, but Marie was all he could think about. It would do no good to obsess about her further on the written page. He put the journal in his bag and closed his eyes.

From the front of the bus, Carsten felt cooped up but he read and slept for the rest of the trip. It wasn't much different from his home life in Deerhead. Randall spent the trip down for the count. Even a lumpy bus seat was more comfortable than sleeping in a church pew or under a tree, and Randall was able to get some quality sleep.

Finally, as the bus pulled into Grand Central's terminal, Carsten's mouth was agape at such a large and majestic space. In his mind he might as well have been at the Taj Mahal.

"Last stop, Grand Central," Helmut hissed over the bus's PA system as he pulled into the dark bus terminal. "Please debark in an orderly fashion and remember to bring your pathetic belongings."

Carsten was first off the bus and, making a New York tourist's first mistake, he looked up to see the sheer size and scale of his New York surroundings. His starry-eyed gaze was immediately interrupted when a man in a dirty Mets jacket and cap walked up to him.

"Hello, brother," he said. "Hey, I'm looking for some cash for a bite to eat and maybe catch a ballgame in the cheap seats. No really, I'm just looking for food money."

Carsten thought about Donnie having lost their dough.

"Um, I'm sorry, but all I have is a debit card," he said.

The Mets fan suddenly turned surly.

"You'll never make it in this town, you bum," he said and walked away.

As always, Carsten was nonplussed by his encounter. He waited for Donnie and Randall as he continued to scan the high ceiling and steel girders above the track.

Donnie and Randall exited and Donnie said to Helmut, "Nice driving."

"Yeah, driving," Helmut said, disgusted. "That's what I do. Drive. All day. All night. I drive."

Donnie and Randall debarked and headed to the Rotunda. Donnie grabbed Carsten by the arm and said: "Stay close. I know a guy who was taking a dump in the restroom here and someone kicked in the stall door and robbed him."

"But it looks so nice," Carsten said dreamily.

The three made their way through the main concourse and Carsten, still amazed, kept Donnie's arm as they traversed the crowd and looked for the gate for the New Jersey bus. Randall walked a few steps behind them looking straight ahead. He had never seen the place before and did not himself want to be bait for a con man among the gaggle of commuters.

"Don't make any eye contact," Randall warned Carsten.

"All of Deerhead could fit inside this building," Carsten muttered.

They made their way to the gate and the bus to New Jersey was already boarding. They got on the crowded bus and Carsten found a window seat while Donnie and Randall split up in aisle seats. As the bus made its way out of the city and hit New Jersey, Carsten marveled at black swamps and towering pylons.

Donnie and Randall slept.

After a short ride with stops in Newark and a few other New Jersey burgs Carsten had never heard of, they made the Berryland stop.

Donnie and Randall awoke when the driver called Berryland and Carsten disembarked and waited for them outside the bus.

"Here we are," Donnie said with mock cheer.

"Yes, here we are," said Carsten, still agog at his new surroundings. "In Berryland. It … ah … isn't as pretty as I thought it would be."

"I'm not sure what you expected, but New Jersey is known for swamps of Jersey," Donnie said. He laughed and said: "They don't call it the Garden State for nothing."

Donnie pulled out his cellphone and called Jerry Most.

"Yell-o!" Jerry shouted. "Could this be Rockin' Donnie Derringer? I've been expecting your call."

"Yeah, it's me," Donnie said. "And I have two compadres with me, Carsten and Randall."

"Well, well, well, welcome to New Jersey," Jerry said. "I'm sure you'll enjoy your stay. Just watch out for the swamp mosquitoes. They're vicious."

Donnie began to itch at the thought of the biting insects.

"OK, Jerry, so we're here. Now what?" Donnie said.

"I'll arrange for my intern Haley to pick you up and take you to your motel," Jerry said. "She'll be there soon and will take you to your accommodations at the beautiful Bedside Inn. The locals call it the 'Bedbug Inn,' but I wasn't going to put you up in a Hilton or something. All you need is a good night's sleep to prepare for the show tomorrow. A bed is all you need, but they may even have a swimming pool!"

"I'm sure our stay will be enjoyable, Jer," Donnie said, slapping a mosquito that had landed on his arm. "Can we get three rooms?"

"Ha ha," Jerry said. "What do you think this is, *The Merv Griffin Show*? No, you will have to stay in the same room. See if you can get two beds and a cot but if you have to sleep in the same bed I don't really care. I'm not paying for your pals to have their own rooms. Make it work with what we've arranged. It will be like a little overnight play date.

"Just be here on time tomorrow. Stop by around noonish. We'll prepare you for the show as your buddies find a way to while away the hours until the show starts. It will take some time to round up our special guests, but we hope to start the show at some point late afternoon, early evening. Maybe you'll even bump into some of your old cohorts before we start the program and you can introduce them to your new pals."

Donnie felt the hair on the back of his neck stand up. This was real. He was going to be on a TV program and podcast recounting his misdeeds. He was afraid to ask if Marie would be there because he didn't want to know the answer. What if she didn't show and he appeared on Most's show simply to be confronted by long-forgotten transgressions? The whole thing would be pointless without Marie.

But Donnie assured Jerry Most he would be at the studio at the appointed time.

"Excellent!" Jerry said. "We've gathered some real characters from your squalid past. Should have a good crowd, too."

"Can't wait," Donnie said, increasingly terrified.

Just then an ancient, battered Lincoln Continental pulled up and a young woman leapt out.

"Hey there! I'm Haley! Jerry Most sent me. You looking for a ride?"

"Yeah, we're going to the Bedside Inn or something," Donnie sighed. "Me and my two friends here."

"Well, hop aboard," Haley bubbled. "I'll getcha there to the Bedside Inn in no time."

Donnie called to Carsten and Randall, who had been across the parking lot discussing God-knows-what, and Donnie crawled into the back seat with Randall. Carsten sat uncomfortably in the front passenger seat with Haley. He was shy and he had no idea how to begin a conversation with a young, attractive woman.

Donnie and Randall rode in silence to the motel but Carsten felt he had to break the dead silence.

"Um, ah, Haley, have, have you ever read Jean-Paul Sartre?" he stammered.

"No, Sir," Haley said. "I majored in journalism in college. We didn't talk about him. Whoever he was."

Fortunately for all involved, the conversation ended when Haley pulled the Lincoln into the Bedside Inn parking lot.

"Here we are, boys!" she cried. "This is the place! I'll be back to pick you up around 11 tomorrow. They have a nice continental breakfast here so eat your fill of long johns and crullers and bagels. You don't want to be hungry for the show!"

Donnie's nerves were so rattled and he was so bone tired from riding for hours on the bus that eating at any point was a low priority. He didn't know if he could keep food down at this point.

They got out of the old beater and headed for the front desk of the motel. The clerk looked like he was 12 years old. He knew Donnie was coming, but hadn't expected Randall and Carsten. No matter. He assigned them a room with a queen-sized bed and said he would bring a cot to the room.

Donnie would have slept on the floor, he was that weary. The cot arrived and Randall volunteered to sleep on it because he was used to more rugged bedding outdoors. Carsten climbed into bed with Donnie. Carsten was wearing gym shorts and a Superman T-shirt.

"Superman, Carst? You a big fan?" Donnie asked.

"More like *Ubermensch*," Carsten said. "You know, the Nietzsche idea of a superior man."

"Ah, so you're superior," Donnie said. "You and your books have made you a super being."

"Not in the least," Carsten said, picking up his copy of George Bernard Shaw's *Man and Superman*. "It is what I strive for, to be above the fray of the human condition. You should read this play, Donnie. It might interest you. It's got a section on Don Juan in hell."

Donnie quivered at the thought of hell. Would his myriad misdeeds carry him there after he he smoked his last doobie?

Nah.

He rolled over in bed to go to sleep. Randall, comfortable in the portable bed, was humming something.

"Randall, please," Donnie rasped. "I want to sleep. Desperately."

"I'm sorry, my friend," Randall said. "I like to hum the opening bars to Miles' great 'So What'," Randall said. "It soothes my soul and helps me to rest."

"Fine," Donnie said. "Just don't go through the entire piece. I'm tired."

Just as Donnie dozed off, Carsten said: "Do you mind if I keep the desk light on, fellas? I'm a light sleeper and I like to read when I awaken in the middle of the night."

"Sure, Carsten," Donnie said. "A light will keep the monsters away, too."

But a light could not keep Donnie's personal monsters at bay.

Nothing could.

— 28 —

LOSERS ON PARADE

MORNING CAME AND THEY WALKED sleepily to the continental breakfast area. Carsten piled scrambled eggs with cheese, a muffin, and some strawberry yogurt on a plate. Randall marveled at the bounty laid out before them, but he only ate a stale bagel with strawberry cream cheese and some fruit salad.

Donnie was too nervous to eat. He sat at a Formica table with his compadres and tapped his foot incessantly as he thought about the fate that lay before him. No one said anything. After they finished eating, Carsten shoved a bagel, an apple and two granola bars in his pocket because he wasn't sure when he'd eat again that day.

They walked to the lobby of the motel and Carsten thumbed through the brochures in a rack beside the door. He picked one up and wondered why anyone would want to visit the burial site of Elsie the cow.

As Carsten considered the various attractions in the brochures, Haley pulled up. She got out of the car and walked into the lobby.

"It's showtime, gentlemen!" she said, genuinely excited.

Haley's call woke Donnie out of a sleepy stupor and felt like a shot to his cerebral cortex. He wondered if he could go through with his coming ordeal. But it was too late. He knew he had to face the music, if only to see Marie.

Donnie thought about having a drink. Or smoking from his one-hitter. But no. He figured he'd have to be mentally sharp for this nightmare. He looked at the stained carpet in the motel lobby and swore he saw a silhouette of the Virgin Mary. Great. Now he was seeing things.

Or was he?

They left the lobby and piled into the Lincoln in silence. Donnie was scared, Carsten was just too shy to say anything in Haley's presence and Randall just quietly took it all in. Haley drove as though she was taking her driving test.

When they arrived at Jerry Most's studio, they found that it was merely a warehouse that Most was using to house his show. And podcast. Donnie didn't care what the building was, he just wanted to get the whole thing over with.

When they entered the "studio" another young woman, Sara, told them Jerry Most had not yet arrived.

"He said he's really busy," Sara said. "Something about waiting for the pool cleaner to come to his house."

And so it went for the next several hours as Donnie anxiously stewed, Carsten read contentedly and Randall played solitaire with a deck of cards he always carried.

Finally, the warehouse door flew open and Jerry Most walked in with a flourish.

"*Mi amigos!*" he shouted. "Are you ready for some compelling television? And a podcast? We've gathered a cast of reprobates not usually seen on this side of a prison wall."

Donnie gasped.

"Shit," he said. "What have you done?"

"What have we done? We brought everybody we could find from your checkered past."

Jerry grinned deviously and added: "Sad to say we found out that some of your old associates are dead. But still, we have enough characters here to make this show a regular *Dean Martin Celebrity Roast*!"

Jerry called to Haley, who was waiting eagerly for him to issue commands.

"Haley, take Mr. Derringer to our humble green room where you can apply make-up to Rockin' Donnie's withered face. We want him to look his best. Sara, take these other ruffians to our makeshift auditorium where they can pick the best seats in the house before our gang of wrongdoers arrives."

Donnie followed Haley as she led him to the green room. He was in a daze. As Haley haphazardly applied make-up she hummed a song. The tune was familiar to Donnie but he couldn't quite place it.

Then it clicked.

"Are you humming the godawful ditty known as 'Seasons in the Sun', Haley?" he asked.

"Yuppers," she replied. "It was in my dad's CD collection, *Sounds of the '70s* or something. It became my instant favorite. You're all set, by the way."

"Seasons in the Sun." It was one of the most dreadful earworms ever performed and as it rolled around in Donnie's brain, he thought there would be no joy, no fun during the coming trial.

But his fate was sealed.

This was going to be awful, but he'd pay any price to see Marie.

— 29 —

SHOWTIME!

As the cameras set up, Jerry and Donnie were seated in worn, red crushed velvet armchairs facing one another. A fern was set behind them for tasteful décor.

Jerry glowered at Donnie. He said nothing as Donnie began to sweat.

The camera guy told Jerry they were ready, and Haley cued up the Beatles' "I'm a Loser."

And thusly began Donnie's trauma.

Jerry smirked while he introduced Donnie as the first guest on the first airing of *Losers on Parade.*

"He's the first loser to lead our dismal procession!"

The disheveled mass of humanity booed.

Some welcome.

Donnie sat like a stone figure as Jerry Most began prowling around the stage. Jerry silenced the crowd and Donnie buckled in for a rough ride.

But he was going to see Marie! He could handle Most's barbs and the crowd's hostility was the price he had to pay for seeing her.

But the cost of seeing her was savage.

Most brought out a series of misfits who related Donnie's wild tales, including the time he climbed up on the stadium roof at a spring training game "to get a better view of the proceedings on the field and beyond."

The gendarmerie later insisted that he climb down and they simply issued a warning not to go up there again.

Amazing.

But for the most part, excepting Most's audience-baiting, the show was unspectacular. Lots of stories about him throwing up in inappropriate places, pissing on friends' couches and the like.

No new ground was broken in revealing Donnie's exploits. They were already on the public record. Donnie had put them there by boasting and joking about them on his radio shows.

As the show began to wear down, Donnie realized he had met all types of friends and associates, courtesy of Jerry Most. Without Jerry's efforts, or the work of his staff, Donnie would never again have encountered his friends "Rancid," "Elephant Boy," and his long-lost pal "Nervous Trevor," a man with whom he'd shared airtime during a two -year spell in Las Vegas when he and Trevor ruled the airwaves with stunts like "What Are You Wearing, Baby?," in which random women were called and asked to remove their intimates to titillate their largely adolescent radio audience.

Sexy!

By removing their bras and panties while remaining on the phone and describing their actions to Donnie and a blushing Trevor, the women could win small amounts of cash and tickets to tractor pulls and, if they simulated a screeching orgasm, the grand prize: a raffle for a chance to see Mariah Carey in concert.

Donnie could never understand how tickets to a Mariah Carey concert could be considered a reward of any kind. But he was often aroused as strange unseen women peeled off undergarments and provided low moans to the listening audience while he and Trevor encouraged more and more outrageous acts. Simulating oral sex with a cucumber was always a big hit.

But like most such tired routines, comedy bits that others before him in other cities had already pulled off, both management and the audience grew weary of the stunts and moved on to other stations that played all the rockin' hits the people were begging for: Led Zeppelin's "Black Dog," Tom Petty's "Don't Do Me Like That," and, of course, Donnie's least favorite song by The Who, "Behind Blue Eyes."

Now Donnie's escapades were coming back to haunt him on Jerry Most's TV show and podcast. He never really thought of himself as a disgusting loser, but the carnival of drunken tales confronted Donnie like a slap from a betrayed lover. Again, it would all be worth it once Jerry brought Marie onstage.

That would be Donnie's grand prize.

Donnie assumed Marie would appear at the end of the show, the "surprise guest" Jerry had promised, and he even planned to get down on one knee, beg forgiveness, and ask Marie to marry him. Finally. He had even brought the crummy ring that he bought years ago in the event he had ever bumped into her.

But before the ultimate meeting with Marie, Donnie had to sit through the TV reunions with a cast of characters that he barely remembered.

One by one, Jerry brought any number of miscreants on stage to relive some of Donnie's greatest hits.

It was all coming back to him, bit by bit as long-forgotten cohorts such as Stiv and Shakey related tales such as the time he ate four Quaaludes before a tailgate at a Milwaukee Brewers game and he climbed up to the roof of a parked Greyhound, proclaiming it to be the *Magic Bus* as his then-girlfriend Sheena nervously screamed at him to come down lest he fall off and kill himself. Back then killing himself didn't seem like such a bad fate, but Donnie climbed down after he determined there was no magic in the bus but there was in the massive electrical tower he had tried to climb in the parking lot near the bus.

After screechily proclaiming himself to be "Spiderman" as he ascended, he realized that no one, not even Sheena, was paying attention any longer. He came down sheepishly and re-joined the party by guzzling Olympia beer from a beer bong. By the third inning of that baseball contest Donnie was head-down and only occasionally regaining consciousness to scream, "He was safe!" on plays where there were no baserunners, or, "You're blind, Ump!" and again, to the umps, "Hey, Cyclops! Open your eye! You're missing a good game!"

Play ball!

As the hour-long show dragged on, Donnie was forced to listen to more dusty tales he had long since forgotten, and for good reason. Muggsy told of the time Donnie guzzled wapatuli, a mixture of every cheap liquor known to mankind mixed with powdered fruit punch and water to cut the taste, and puked on the living room wall at a house party where he was a guest and did not know the hosts.

Hardy har har.

Sure, it had been great reliving the glory days with old compadres.

Or was it?

Donnie's old and long-forgotten buddies looked shaggy and burnt-out, so much so that Donnie didn't recognize some of his old partners in crime. Of course, were they not themselves appearing on a show with Donnie as the guest, they probably would not have recognized Donnie's grizzled countenance, either.

So OK, this was going to be a trip down a drug-and-alcohol-muddled memory lane. Stay focused, Donnie, Marie will eventually come out as the guest star. Listen to the addled and embellished takes of debauchery and wait for Jerry to introduce her, supposedly as a surprise. But it would be no surprise to Donnie. If anyone could find his long-lost love, it was Jerry Most. Or his young staffer Haley, anyway.

Finally, a guy calling himself "Stevey B" recounted Donnie's legendary on-stage performance drunkenly ripping the guitar off a musician playing in a local Rockford band named Crossfire and attempting to perform Pete Townshend windmill guitar chords, missing the instrument altogether as the guitarist struggled with him to regain control of his axe. The guitarist retook the instrument and promptly swatted Donnie on the ass with it, sending the would-be Townshend to his knees. As Stevey B recounted it, Donnie then crawled off the stage to gales of laughter from the audience.

Jerry Most's audience was in stitches, too.

While each of these incidents reflected the "Rockin' Donnie" persona, and though he found them hilarious, nearly each and every public indiscretion led to his firing at whatever station that had seen and heard enough of his antics.

As the stories continued, Donnie realized it was some kind of miracle that he was never arrested. He always used "celebrity" status to escape prosecution. A guy named "Toots" told the audience about the story that got him fired at his last decent gig in St. Paul.

As Toots related the tale, he and Donnie were in a dive bar in Minneapolis when someone played Frank Sinatra on the jukebox. Donnie hated Frank. He walked over to the jukebox to play some Sex Pistols, but he found nothing but '50s crooners on the selection list.

"And then," Toots said, trying to control his laughter, "... And then Donnie picked up a bar stool and shattered the glass on the music machine screaming, 'No future for you!' I'm telling you we never ran so fast. We even left our money on the bar 'cuz we had to scram."

Toots broke down in guffaws and walked back to his seat.

No future. Never had Donnie felt more like that line. But Toots's yarn had the audience in stitches.

Were they laughing with him or at him? At that point Donnie no longer cared as long as his antics made for hilarity and broadened his image as a mythical mad-man party boy.

Good times!

Donnie subtlety checked his watch as Jerry began a monologue about the strange days that made up Donnie's squalid life.

"Well, folks," he preached directly into the camera. "What we have here in Donnie Derringer, excuse me, 'Rockin' Donnie Derringer,' is an object lesson of debauchery, lunacy and a complete disregard for the feelings of other people, whether they were friends or lovers for whom he promised undying love if they provided him with kinky sex on demand.

"This man, Rockin' Donnie Derringer, is not a decent specimen of humanity. He's a jerk. A seemingly irredeemable asshole, if you will. I ask you, my loyal audience, what do you think of this piece of human flotsam?"

The audience, several hundred strong, booed lustily.

Donnie sat stiffly on his lumpy studio chair only a bit chagrined as Jerry delivered his monologue. Donnie had tried hard not to laugh when some of his old mates recalled their antics together. Occasionally, he had to stifle a snicker as one by one, friends, relatives and lovers told stories about his party boy image that was more reflective of the behavior of an insecure adolescent than of a decent human being. His infidelities, his indifference to human feelings, his drug and alcohol abuse and general self-absorption painted a portrait of a troubled soul trying to find peace through sex, drugs and rock 'n' roll.

He wondered if there would be any more mystery guests who would shame him with some sort of peccadillo Donnie had left in his past. In some ways, Donnie was embarrassed by all of the storytelling. Yet he also thought it would solidify his legend. His legion of listeners in his heyday and the dozens of viewers of Jerry's show would certainly look at him as a latter-day Keith Moon.

Donnie was actually amused by the whole experience and thought maybe he shouldn't kill his rockin' persona after all.

But a surprise awaited and Donnie was holding his breath.

Meanwhile, Jerry continued. As he spoke about Donnie, Jerry sounded more like the awful, judgmental wanker from *Die Trying* than the guy who turned himself around with his subsequent show, *Try Living*, a program so filled with unctuous sweetness that viewers eventually abandoned it for other fare such as the ever-popular *Robot Fights* or *Couples at War*, a show in which soon-to-be divorced spouses aired their soiled laundry to a slathering public.

"Seriously, folks, I wonder if this piece of human rubbish has any qualities that would allow him to create meaningful relationships, if he could look at himself long enough to make the changes necessary to become a respectable member of society, a dependable mate, a devoted friend, someone who can avoid climbing on rooftops and settle down to a normal life. What say you, Rockin' Donnie Derringer?

Jerry hawked up the adjective "rockin'" as though expectorating a hair from his throat.

Donnie sat silently for a moment, stunned. What was this, anyway? A Stalin-era Soviet show trial where he admits his sins publicly before he is declared guilty and shot by a firing squad? Donnie might have preferred that to this debacle. But he soon returned to form. Gathering himself, he began his defense.

"Look, Jerry, first of all, have there ever been any people who have entered a relationship with me and not known what they were getting into? Have I ever engaged in false advertising? Maybe my life should have included a warning that said, 'Use caution while entering,' but in any instance, has anyone ever thought they could tame a wild man? Did they not sense the danger of being with a guy who calls himself 'Rockin' Donnie Derringer,' a man who lived his life as a disc jockey, for heaven's sake? Did they think they were getting involved with an accountant, or, or an insurance agent? How could they think they were anything but deluded characters in my own tragicomic play? Did I commit random acts of self-destruction and maybe take a few people with me on my twisted path? Sure. But nobody could have been fooled into thinking they were going to make me a better person, although many women tried.

"Did any station manager who hired me, fresh from one headline-grabbing on-air incident after another, believe they could maintain a tight leash on a guy who claimed to be masturbating to a picture of The Pretenders' Chrissie Hynde while moaning into the mic? A lot of those stunts got me gigs at big radio stations until I ultimately disgusted station ownership.

"You, Jerry Most, former jerk-off host of a mean-spirited death-defying game show, know better than anyone else that you are what you are. You, Jerry, are still a big ass, but you've managed to cover it up for a while with a nice-guy shtick designed to get you new TV shows. Well, Jerry, you're not fooling anyone, either. Why else would you host a show called *Losers on Parade,* you phony.

"I had a miserable childhood and decided to spend the rest of my life doing whatever struck me as fun, humorous or entertaining. Is that a crime? Have I hurt anybody? Well, maybe on some emotional level I have left carnage in my wake, but you can go to hell if you want to judge me on your … your stupid cable TV show and podcast. Really, Jerry, is this how far you yourself have fallen? Sorry, but your disdain means nothing to me.

"Now, where can I get some gin? I've had my bellyful of this and could use a stiff drink. Better yet, a joint."

The small audience screamed approvingly. But Jerry was not finished with Donnie. He had one final surprise in store, one that would make Donnie squirm.

"That's all very nice, Mr. Party Animal," Jerry said. "You were a poor, little abused boy who grew up to heap that very same corrupt maltreatment on everyone you met. Poor little Donnie. Come on everyone. Give him some applause. His bruised ego needs a little public lovin'."

The audience booed. Thumbs were pointed down. Middle fingers rose.

Donnie thought to himself that this was a browbeating, not entertainment. On the other hand, this was America, a place where schadenfreude made for great viewing and high ratings. But really, what was Jerry's problem?

Meanwhile, Jerry paused dramatically as he strutted around the tiny stage. Then he smiled grimly like a medieval executioner just before that guillotine blade dropped on some hapless innocent's neck.

"Donnie, we told you before the show that we'd bring out some surprise guests, people whom you've known throughout the years. But now we're going to bring out a new friend with whom you've only recently become acquainted."

What the hell, Donnie thought. Carsten and Randall are in the audience. Who could Jerry be talking about? And then it occurred to him, an awful thought, one that terrified him more than appearing on this stupid show to face his misdeeds. Then Jerry said…

"Let's bring out Donnie's new shrink, excuse me, doctor of psychiatry, Dr. Sally Dixon. Welcome, Dr. Dixon!"

The audience hooted while it applauded. This was going to be good. The producer cued up Warren Zevon's "The Sin."

God, no, not this, Donnie thought. This is absolutely cruel.

But there she was. Dr. Sally Dixon, someone whose clutches Donnie thought he had escaped. She was wearing an off-white pants suit with white stilettos, her blindingly blonde hair trimmed short against her head, blue eyes wide and blazing as if she were ready for a fight. Donnie thought she looked dangerously gorgeous and he couldn't suppress his usual thoughts of having sex with her. But this was no time for daydreaming. Donnie had to be at his best.

This wasn't the jolt of seeing Marie, he thought helplessly as he anticipated his public torture at the hands of Dr. Dixon.

Sally Dixon elegantly strode on stage like Meryl Streep at the Oscars, her white countenance shimmering under the stage lights.

Even in white, Sally Dixon was scary. She sat in a dirty blue swivel chair that looked as though it had been brought over from Jerry's office. She faced Donnie from the other side of the set and gave him a snaky smile.

Donnie braced himself.

"Dr. Dixon," Jerry said jovially. "You saw Donnie at a mental hospital called Serenity Heights back in Minnesota when he wasn't so rockin', when he had threatened to join Ricky Nelson's heavenly "Garden Party," am I correct?

Turning to Donnie, Jerry glared. "Pills and liquor, wasn't it, Judy Garland? Too chicken to use a Magnum?"

Donnie was astonished at Jerry's cruelty. Wasn't he the guy who created *Try Living* under the guise of being a sweetheart? Apparently, he had returned to form, back to the *Die Trying* days. This was the real Jerry Most, a bitter, mean and blisteringly sarcastic shithead who lived for the torment of others, especially sorry specimens like Donnie.

Donnie mumbled something unintelligible and Dr. Dixon spoke up.

"I am prohibited by law from discussing details of Mr. Derringer's hospitalization. Indeed, I will probably be in some professional trouble just for being here. But I am here because Donnie is a danger to himself and I cannot let him destroy himself. However, I can confirm, as he already did to Mr. Most, who visited him, he did for a fact make some threats about curtailing his existence. That is why we met at Serenity Heights. As his doctor I recommended that he remained hospitalized until he was able to regain his existential balance. But when you, Mr. Most, appealed to our administration with a promise of improvements to the facilities, Mr. Derringer embarked on an expedition to this studio in, what do you call it, Berryland?"

"You're right in the heart of our fair city, Doctor," Jerry said, "our dirty, fetid, little town in the Jersey swamp. Now, Doctor, tell us a little about your experience with our friend Donnie. Come on, spill it!"

The crowd began to bay again.

Donnie squirmed in his perch, nervously picking at its stuffing where the chair was torn. Guilty as charged, he thought.

So what?

As Dr. Dixon continued, Donnie realized he was bored. Digging up all the detritus from his past was a bit tiresome after a while. His glance at Dr. Dixon turned into a deep gaze. Man, she is hot, he thought.

By now Donnie wanted to get out of there. He thought of an abrupt departure, stage left, but he was hooked on the notion that at any minute Jerry Most would bring out Marie.

It would be worth the wait. And the public flogging.

Jerry piped in.

"So, Dr. Sally Dixon, do you think Rockin' Donnie Derringer is a loser? Someone worthy of being a *Loser on Parade*?"

She paused while the hyenas in the audience chanted, "Loser, loser, loser."

"While I understand that the primary mission of this program is to publicly humiliate your guests, in that regard, you have succeeded with Mr. Derringer," she said. "That is all I can say."

"But is he a loser?" Jerry insisted.

"He's a bum, he's a loser, he's a loser on parade!" shouted one wit.

Someone else picked up a folding chair, waved it menacingly and shouted, "He's a loser! Let's get him!"

Haley and Sara rushed to restrain him before he caused real damage. Though the tough guy wriggled out of their grasps, he put the chair down and walked out of the studio.

Jerry laughed and resumed.

"Well, well, well," he said, smiling broadly at Donnie, "you seem to engender some real hostility. Your mother must be so proud."

"Um, I think my mom is dead," Donnie said innocently.

"You think? You think?" Jerry said, facing the crowd, the camera tight on his face.

"Loser, loser, loser!" the crowd chanted.

By this point, Donnie had long had enough of the public abuse. He was suffering the tortures of the damned. Only the demons raking his flesh were missing.

He wanted to walk out, but he stayed, he stayed because there were about ten minutes left in the show and Jerry had yet to produce Marie.

Meanwhile, Jerry was pacing across the stage toward his guest star. He stuck his face directly into Donnie's and said: "I pronounce Rockin' Donnie Derringer to be a loser! A loser!

"Am I right?"

Jerry was using Donnie's line, "Am I right?" to further energize the mob. It somehow seemed unfair, yet Donnie appreciated the irony of his own line being used against him. Of course, the phrase was not exactly copyrighted.

But then Jerry announced that he had one more surprise guest, and Donnie nearly melted. It would be Marie. He just knew it. He would be reunited with Marie and they would move to Los Angeles where he would have a radio show and a new life.

Little did he know.

"Ladies and gentlemen, my gathered multitude, we have one more guest to join us, one more person who can tell us what a loser we have on our hands," Jerry said excitedly. "And here she is!"

Donnie was ready to pee in his blue jeans as the mystery guest walked on stage. He nervously tugged at his Springsteen *The Rising* tour T-shirt as he waited in nervous anticipation.

Then from backstage out she came.

It was Marie!

She looked exactly as she had when he met her all those years ago. Incredibly, she hadn't aged a day. She looked like she was still about 30 and she was as beautiful beyond Donnie's limited vocabulary to describe. Just to look at her made Donnie's eyes fill with tears.

She wore a long, blue, patterned peasant dress, just like the old days. Incredibly, her long raven hair had no gray, and her eyes were the same baby blue that made him feel as though she could see right through him.

Marie! Oh, God, it's Marie. Donnie's hands were trembling.

"Donnie!"

Jerry snapped Donnie out of his misty melancholic haze.

Donnie was staring at Marie but he finally managed to blurt, "Huh?" as the savages giggled.

"You seem gobsmacked, Mr. Derringer," Jerry chortled, "but here she is, our special guest, the one you've been waiting for! Rockin' Donnie Derringer, meet your daughter, Angel! Angel, this is the father you've never met. I'll let Angel tell you all about herself."

Daughter? What the fuck? Donnie was crestfallen. He wanted to cry. He wanted to see Marie so badly and his expectations were crushed. On the other hand, he was apparently meeting the daughter he never knew he had, so he was experiencing some real mixed emotions. He should have been happier than he was to meet his beautiful daughter.

Where was Marie?

The audience whistled and hooted while Donnie pressed his memory to figure out when Angel had been conceived. He quickly realized the obvious. Donnie never used protection and Marie allowed it because she thought they would spend their lives together. It must have been just before the laundry room incident.

And now here was Angel, his daughter.

Donnie recovered from the shock enough to offer a meek "Hello, Angel," as he tried to get his bearings. He got up to hug her but she would have none of the syrupy and bogus sentimentality of such a gesture. She shrugged him off, staring at Donnie and saying with a sneer, "Hello, Dad. Nice to finally meet you, dad. I've heard so much about you, dad."

His daughter's snotty tone seared Donnie's rancid soul.

"None of it good, I take it," he mumbled.

"What's that?" Angel said.

"I said, none of it good."

"No, indeed, none of it was good, not a bit of it," she said. "I'm not even sure why I showed up here, although Mr. Most offered me a generous and much-needed honorarium for me to complete your public disgrace."

The congregation of barbarians gave her a standing ovation and a boisterous cheer.

Donnie began to speak but they shouted him down.

"Sit down and shut up, loser!" was only one of the catcalls that arose from the audience.

"Meet the daughter you never knew you had, asshole," screeched a woman wearing a sweater with an American flag on it.

They began to chant, "Loser, loser, loser" again until Jerry's amplified and distorted voice rose above the cacophony.

"OK, OK, quiet down and let's listen in on what promises to be a scintillating conversation," he shouted. The crowd hushed in anticipation of a real blood-letting.

"Angel, Angel, I am so sorry," Donnie said, on the verge of unusual tears — unusual for the no-regrets Donnie.

"Sorry doesn't cut it, buster. Apology not accepted," she scoffed. "Because of you I had to grow up as a virtual orphan."

Orphan?

Wait a minute. Oh God, no, Donnie thought.

"Yes, you heard me," she rasped. "An orphan. You know, a kid without parents. My teenage years were especially lively as I was shuttled between autocratic aunts and indifferent grandparents. Oh, it was entertaining, all right. Really amusing. You should be proud of yourself."

"But Angel," Donnie said, voice shaking. "Where's your mother? Where's Marie?"

"I hate to break it to you, cowboy, but my mother died when I was ten years old. Breast cancer. And just so you know, it wasn't much fun watching your only parent die. I was alone while you were out rockin', Donnie. And I am alone now, you sick bastard."

The crowed went "Oooooh!" as Angel spoke. But they were transfixed by this revelation.

Donnie had thought all along that showing up on Jerry Most's show would be an agonizing and miserable experience. But now Marie was dead and his daughter was berating him on cable TV and a podcast.

Shit!

Meanwhile, the crowd of Huns moved to riot mode until Jerry raised his hand to quiet them and spoke.

They hushed, slavering over Donnie's torment.

"Angel," he pleaded. "Please, let's talk. Out of public view. Can I take you out to dinner?"

Angel glared at Donnie with all the seething resentment she could muster.

"No," she said.

And that was it. She turned on her heel and stormed out to wild applause.

Jerry was elated. This was going to go viral. Rockin' Donnie Derringer going down in flames like a shot-down P38 under anti-aircraft attack.

Jerry shouted over the din: "Thanks, everyone, our audience, our viewers and our podcast fans. I want to thank our sponsors, Speedy Al's Brushless Car Wash, where scratches on your paint job are a thing of the past, Tony B's Famous Steaks, where you can witness a mob hit on any given night, and Buddy Budzinki's Funeral Home and Mortuary, where the dead are treated better than when they were living.

"Thanks, and good night to all of you boors at home!"

Donnie sat, stunned.

He had spent his adult life trying to impress Marie, trying to woo her back by showing off his fun side. To win her back.

But Marie had been in the grave for years. And she brought a spitting-image daughter into the world without even telling him. The daughter, once found, was now lost forever because of the very antics that were designed to impress Marie. She wanted nothing to do with her erstwhile father.

That he found out about his daughter on cable television and a podcast, his shock and humiliation, were there to see forever for anyone who had internet access. He would be immortalized as a loser, a *Loser on Parade*.

Loser.

Randall walked toward the stage to scrape up the remains of Rockin' Donnie Derringer. Meanwhile, Jerry walked off stage, indifferent to Donnie's plight. Jerry was an entertainer, after all, and he loved to grind his guests into dust.

Rockin' Donnie Derringer had finally gotten his comeuppance.

Donnie mouthed Jerry's name, trying to bring him back so they could talk about the radio gig Jerry promised in LA.

"Come on, my friend, it's over," Randall said gently. "Let's go."

"But ..."

"I know, I know. The gig in L.A. I have my doubts about Mr. Most's ability or willingness to keep that pledge," Randall said.

Carsten joined Randall and said: "I'm sorry for your pain."

Donnie stood and took a few wobbly steps like a newborn colt.

Donnie's astonishment at his treatment by Jerry Most — what happened to the reformed "nice guy" image he had cultivated after *Die Trying*? What was with the abuse?

As Donnie stumbled off the stage, with a helpful arm from Randall and Carsten right behind, he called out for Jerry.

"What about the radio gig in L.A.?" he shouted. "You promised, you bastard. Come out and let's talk business, asshole. I can't go back to Deerhead, Minnesota. I can't."

Jerry had retreated to his backstage office. The door was closed. And locked.

Donnie rattled the doorknob and beat on the door, screaming.

"You ... you dickhead, you promised to get me out of Deerhead and send me to L.A.," he screamed, near tears.

Randall patted Donnie's shoulder to try to calm him.

"You said it yourself, Donald," Randall said. "He's a dickhead and he either can't or won't live up to his obligation. Nobody is getting a gig in L.A. Let's go, my friend. It's over."

Donnie hung his head. He was crestfallen. He was even ashamed, which was a new feeling for him. Maybe Randall was right. It was indeed over. "Rockin' Donnie" was dead. Now all that was left was for Donnie to pick up the shards of his wretched life and piece together something that made living at least bearable.

But where?

All signs pointed to Deerhead.

Donnie had been worried that any psych meds Dr. Dixon prescribed would take the rockin' out of Donnie.

But it was Jerry Most who had reduced Donnie to a zombie.

Donnie felt dazed and hopeless. He'd been had by a mean-spirited cable TV has-been.

Son of a bitch.

Randall put his hand on the small of Donnie's back and guided him away from Jerry's door.

"Seriously, Donald, let's not engage in more humiliation," Randall said quietly. "Let's go."

Just then Jerry's office door swung open. Angel emerged just ahead of Jerry. They were laughing.

They stopped in their tracks and stopped giggling when they saw Donnie and his last remaining pals.

Jerry strode to Donnie and grabbed his limp hand. He was grinning. Angel was glaring.

"Great show, Donnie, great show," he said, smiling broadly. "This one's gonna help us take off. We took down Rockin' Donnie Derringer on TV and on a podcast. Fantastic. Just fantastic."

Jerry was rubbing his hands. He was elated about what he had just inflicted on Donnie. He had taken down a once-prominent radio "personality."

Excellent!

Donnie always knew he was a ne'er-do-well, a self-centered stinker.

But really, did he deserve all this, to be a televised victim of public abuse?

Well, yes.

At least in Jerry's mind. And maybe in Donnie's, too.

"Well, Hotshot, what did you think of the show?" Jerry said. "Pretty cool, no? You got to share some crazy memories with your old buddies and their boring tales of debauchery, glory days and all that, but you also got to meet your daughter. Sorry about Marie, by the way. But here's your daughter, the one you didn't know you had! Standing right before you! Angel, your thoughts?"

Angel looked at Donnie as though she hated him with the brilliance of a thousand suns.

Donnie braced himself, but no amount of preparation could have saved him from the bloody diatribe that followed.

There was a thick silence as Angel prepared to verbally projectile-vomit bitter bile on Donnie.

"You weren't even there when she died. I watched her waste away in agony as you were partying in God-knows-where. Oh yeah, you're rockin', Donnie, really rockin'. Maybe you were somewhere squiring some drug-addled bimbo while the so-called love of your life lay dying in a desolate hospice. Oh yes, dad, I knew all about you and your antics. She often talked about how much she loved you and how you broke her heart in a laundry room at some party, how she could never trust men again, especially you.

"She never married because she thought no one could measure up to you. But oh, she did love you. And you weren't there when she died. She asked me to try to find you, but why would I do that? I didn't want her to see you and I'm glad she never got to lay eyes on your deceitful, druggy puss. It would have broken her heart again just to lay eyes on you, you miserable bastard.

"I hope you die alone and screaming. And I hope you wind up in hell. And by the way, you must be so proud of me, a daughter you never even knew until I showed up on Jerry's miserable show.

"Those are my thoughts, Jerry. Those are my musings about my erstwhile father. Go fuck yourself, Rockin' Donnie Derringer. Go smoke some weed and drink yourself blind, you irredeemable son of a bitch. But know for the rest of your life that people hate you, most of all your daughter, a daughter you will never see again. And all the booze and dope and fucking in the world won't change that."

She began to cry hysterically as she turned and walked out of the building.

Donnie figured nothing could be worse than this. But it seemed that whenever he asked himself what could possibly be worse, he always found out right away.

And he did.

"Well, that was enlightening, no?" Jerry asked snidely. "A daughter you never knew who you thought was your long-lost but now dead lover, but wait. There's more!"

Oh, God, no, Donnie thought. Now what?

"We wanted to bring another guest to the show, but she didn't want to see you. Now the list of people who never want to see you again is a massive group, I suppose, but this one would have been a real catch for our little piece of guilty entertainment."

"What are you talking about?" Donnie was getting desperate for Jerry to let up.

But no.

"We also found your daughter from your short-lived, long-ago marriage to your first wife," Jerry chirped. "Yes! Our researchers are great, and they managed to find someone you haven't seen in years! It was your daughter, Jenny. And while she didn't want to join the fun here, she did send a brief letter for you. It goes:

"'Dear Dad,'" Jerry read. "Dad is in italics, by the way. A nice method of indicating sarcasm. I love it. But I'll continue: 'Dear Dad, How are you? Me? I'm miserable and I blame you for my despondency. I never had a dad to talk to when things got rough, and Mom could only handle so much.

"As the years went on, bereft of fatherly advice and companionship, I began a self-destructive path that led me to teen pregnancy and the requisite abortion. Yeah, Dad, I slept around a lot looking for the love I never got from you. Of course, that's a shitty way to live, but that was my life. There were drugs. Pot. Coke. And finally, a meth addiction that led to my hospitalization.'"

Donnie was, for once, speechless. No witty rejoinder could lighten the situation before him. He felt as though he would vomit. But she was right. He had truly screwed up and there was nothing he could do about it now.

Donnie needed his pipe and some cheap liquor. Those were his only coping mechanisms.

Just then Jerry piled on.

"Couldn't have said it better myself, Angel and Jenny. This dude's a real scumbag. That's why I brought him on my show. Watching him be crucified on TV and my podcast made for great viewing and maybe, just maybe, this show will get me back on a network, which would be fantastic."

Donnie thought about the radio gig in L.A., and he realized it was a false promise, a hollow gesture designed to lure him to Jerry's show. In Donnie's twisted mind, he should at least have been rewarded for this public beating. Nonetheless, he asked Jerry about it.

"So, OK, there's no L.A. radio job? You conned me into showing up on this podcast or whatever to humiliate me in front of hundreds of people? You're worse than I am. You're a snake!"

"And this comes as a surprise, *mon ami*? You really thought I could get you a job in radio after all the bridges you've burned? Look, friend, I gave it a shot but there are ten-foot-pole marks on you from people who won't touch you. An-y-where. You're done, pal. May as well go back to Buckhead or whatever that little career graveyard is called.

"Oh, and you thought I had become a sweetheart since I put down my idiotic but highly rated network show, *Die Trying*? You know, the one in which I insulted everyone from my wives to contestants and, if I recall, even the Pope? The show where people performed insane acts to defy death and collect cash and prizes? No, Donnie, I'm the same dick I always was. I tried the nice guy thing but it just wasn't me. As Yogi Berra supposedly said, 'You can't get a leopard to change its stripes.' It cost me my third marriage to the lovely Pinky Lee.

"I can't help myself. I am what I am, and by the way, I've destroyed better than the likes of guys like you. I will admit you're a big catch, but in the end you're just another wad of filet mignon I've ejected from this smart mouth of mine.

"You won't go away empty-handed, though, cowboy. We've got some gift certificates to Applebee's, tickets for two for a raft ride on the East River, two passes to the Bronx Zoo, two tickets to a Trenton

Thunder minor-league baseball game and, of course, train tickets back to Deer Ass, or wherever you came from, for you and your loser compadres. I noticed you added one to your party, so I'll give you three of everything.

"Now fare-thee-well, my dickish pal. I gotta go. Reservations for a nice dinner in the city, you know. I'd take you to dinner with me but I don't like you. So, it's good night and good luck to you, Rockin' Donnie Derringer, you jerk."

Donnie hadn't suffered this kind of abuse since he lived with his father. He thought that as a result of his dysfunctional upbringing he could withstand any verbal or even physical blows. But this was on a wholly different scale and level. Meeting Angel, who hated him, losing Marie to breast cancer, listening to vitriol from Jenny, and now taking shit from Jerry Most was more than he could bear, and he thought he had borne it all.

He called out to Jerry as he walked away. Jerry stopped and turned around with military precision.

"What?!" he said, growing impatient.

"Why?" Donnie asked. "Why did I have to walk into this trap, an ambush where public shaming is part of the show? Why did you do this to me? Am I that bad a guy? I spent my life trying to impress Marie with my silly antics. I thought she would come to miss me when she heard about the greased pig I let loose at an Ariana Grande show. Wouldn't she miss my puckish sense of humor?

"And you confront me with a daughter I've never met, someone who hates me with a seething rage and who looks just like Marie? You hit me with the fact that Marie is dead and that my showing-off was futile? I mean seriously, why did you do all this to me?"

Jerry laughed derisively.

"I did it for the ratings, pal. This will go viral, I'm sure of it. The public beheading of a known and once-famous bastard makes for great TV. And, I hope, it will get me back on a major television network where I belong. Unlike you, Donnie, I still am a Somebody, although currently on a lesser scale, and I have a chance to make it big again. This was kind of an audition. And when the network execs get their eyes on this, I'll be riding high again.

"But if you ask why would I do this to you other than for the ratings, then I guess you are completely unfamiliar with my oeuvre. Look, pal, I tried to redeem myself after *Die Trying* with *Try Living*. I tried to be a nice guy and make people happy. But then I realized that I hate people. Really, I consider the human race to be a bunch of me-first selfish sons-of-bitches who would sell their own mothers if it meant receiving in return a nice gas grill or patio set in the bargain. America is a mean-spirited agglomeration of materialistic and spiritually vacant drones who believe the almighty dollar is king and they have constitutional rights to screw their neighbors. They don't want to be around people who aren't like them — people of color, for instance — but they covet the possessions and even the spouses of the very people whom they believe are like them.

"We have low-brow tastes, which explains the popularity of your various idiot radio routines. If you want to hide a C-note from the average American, you could put it in a book and they'd never find it, assuming they had any books at all that they hadn't purchased at an airport newsstand.

"We drive like maniacs and cut each other off on the freeway at 80 miles an hour in order to be the first one to the next exit. Pathetic smokers who can't give it up use the streets as ashtrays. We roar our motorcycles at 3 a.m. I could go on and on, but the fact is I am a product of the very society I despise. Yes, me! Jerry Most is the same kind of flea-ridden rat who cuts in line at the grocery store and aspires to some level of wealth that is unattainable for most people but remains their focus.

"I am Rockin' Donnie Derringer, a true American. Green-blooded and selfish as the next guy. And you, Donald, are the same kind of detritus that is spewed by our I-got-mine-so-fuck-you lumpen proletariat society. So, I chose you, as one of the smallest but most self-centered assholes on the planet, to publicly taunt into abject depression. In a way we are much the same person. Except in my book, you are a minnow and I am the shark who feeds on chum like you. Does that make sense to your ego-driven mind?"

Donnie had no smart-aleck answer. He stood there like an opossum in the porch light. Not moving, and unlike the opossum simply playing dead, he wished he were just plain dead. Road kill rolled over by a steaming dump truck full of filth and driven by Jerry Most.

Jerry had defeated him. Defrocked him as the high priest of rock-and-roll sleaze. Gave him his well-deserved comeuppance. Yes, Rockin' Donnie was dead, but it was homicide, not suicide.

Donnie struggled for a response. "I … I'm sorry," he muttered.

"Yeah, well that and four bucks gets you a large coffee," Jerry sneered. "So glad you're sorry, but I'm not the one to whom you should apologize. Why don't you say that to all of the people, especially women, whose spirits you have broken over the years while you were rockin', Donnie."

With that Jerry Most abruptly disappeared out the stage door.

Donnie was running the proceedings through his head like the replay of a car accident.

Daughters hate me? Check.

Made a fool of myself on TV? Check.

Podcast? Check.

Marie dead? Oh, God, check.

Just then Donnie felt a hand on his shoulder. Too light to be Randall or Carsten. No, it was the gentle touch of the otherwise decidedly ungentle Dr. Sally Dixon. Donnie turned and was almost glad to see his former tormentor.

"Doc," he breathed. "Doctor Dixon. I never thought I'd see the day when you were a bright spot. But as it turns out I could really use a warm chat and maybe some of those mind-numbing meds you have the power to prescribe. I am, as they say in your world, in crisis. Seriously, I need to atone or talk or something. Help!"

Dr. Dixon lifted her hand from Donnie's shoulder and offered a thin, yet seemingly empathetic smile.

"I was worried about you, Donald. I knew all this would happen the minute you left Serenity Heights for this dreadful exhibition," she said. "That's part of the reason I came out here, to swampy New Jersey, in the middle of hundreds of desolate warehouses and empty potato chip bags rolling down streets like tumbleweeds.

"Yes, Donald, I see you as someone who could really use my help, someone who actually took a first step toward healing by appearing on this ... what, podcast? TV program? Whatever. I think tonight we saw the decimation of 'Rockin' Donnie Derringer,' the complete destruction of an ego-based persona that you could no longer separate from your real being. Indeed, I cannot even fathom what the 'real' Donald Derringer would look or behave like. Can you?"

"Um," was the only response Donnie could gin up.

"No need for a reply right now," Dr. Dixon said. "You are far too dazed to come up with any kind of cogent response. That is quite all right. But right now, it appears you are jobless with no real prospects. But you should think about extensive therapy.

"In the meantime, I implore you to return to Serenity Heights to get a grip on your life and discover the 'real' Donald Derringer."

The "real" Donald Derringer. Hmm. Immediately, Donnie went to his mental sound library. The Who's "The Real Me" came to mind.

But unlike the song, it wasn't so much that Donnie wanted to ask whether people could see the real him. It was whether he could see himself. That would prove to be problematic and Donnie would be forced to get in touch with the real Donald.

Oh, man.

— 30 —

DR. DIXON TO THE RESCUE

In spite of himself, as Donnie stood in the backstage area of Jerry Most's torture chamber, he knew Sally Dixon was right. He needed to retreat to a place where there was no judgment, only psychic healing. He would no longer go to Serenity Heights and laugh at men who have imaginary diseases or hostile intentions toward lawn-mowing neighbors.

Donnie was willing to consider having an open mind about Serenity Heights, about Deerhead. Maybe he could at least reach a state of contentment in Deerhead, if not happiness. His experiences in the bigger metro markets did not do him any good, as he well knew.

Dr. Dixon placed her hand back on Donnie's shoulder and Donnie resisted his automatic impulse to make an inappropriate move, maybe place his hand on hers or pull her close. She was his doctor and that's all she would ever be, he realized.

Damn!

"Can I trust that you'll be back?" she said. "I must leave shortly to catch a plane back to Minnesota so I can resume my duties tomorrow. In terms that you can understand, do we have a date?"

Ordinarily, Donnie would have translated the word "date" into dinner and a roll in the hay. But although Donnie had lusted after Dr. Dixon, he pushed such thoughts from his mind.

"Yes," he said, quietly as a hooker's whisper on a quiet backstreet. "I'll come back, Dr. Dixon."

Sally Dixon clapped her hands together, snapping Donnie out of his haze.

"Excellent," she said. "I will see you upon your return to Deerhead."

Return to Deerhead.

Oh, God, what a thought.

Still, anyplace was better than Jerry Most's warehouse studio.

Dr. Dixon had one more thing to say.

"Donald, I'm sure you know that Rockin' Donnie Derringer is dead, that you must change your life in order to survive. I'm guessing that your job at the Deerhead radio station has reached an end. You cannot get your job back due to your absence and your antics here on the stage.

"But let me offer an incentive to your return to Serenity Heights. Indeed, I could talk to the administration about getting you a position as a counselor. You would still be an outpatient remaining under my care, and although I am aware that you have no credentials for advising patients, I believe your life experience could serve as an abject lesson on what one should not do in in order to cope with their mental illness."

Donnie was shocked by Dr. Dixon's offer, especially under the circumstances. But he managed to mutter a weak, "OK."

Dr. Sally Dixon walked away triumphantly, gracefully, like a ballerina walking offstage to a standing ovation and shouts of "Brava!" She had finally won over Donnie to her way of thinking about his manic condition.

Randall and Carsten, who had been watching helplessly from a safe distance on the other side of the room, both walked up to Donnie. Randall tried to hug him but Donnie shoved him away. He was processing the whole experience and he just didn't feel like any demonstrations of goopy sentimentality right then.

"Come on, my friend," Randall said. "Let's get outta here. This place is no good for you."

"Yes," Carsten said with no emotion in his voice. "Yes, Donald. Let's go."

Randall put his arm around Donnie, a gesture Donnie now accepted, and Randall led him out to the stage door and out of the building. Carsten was right behind them.

The trio stood outside in the parking lot. Crows cawed from the high-tension wires and electrical pylons that decorated the skyline in this section of New Jersey. Donnie thought that even the filthy ravens were laughing at him.

They were more or less stranded and needed to get to the train station, but Haley came out of the studio and offered them a ride.

Donnie felt wounded beyond repair.

But at least he now had hope, an emotion that he had never experienced. He might have steady work when he returned to Deerhead, thanks to Dr. Dixon. Maybe there would be a happy ending after all. A job, intensive therapy. Maybe a nice girlfriend if Liz could be convinced he had changed his ways. His appearance on *Losers on Parade* was certainly life-altering.

Haley opened the doors of the Lincoln and Donnie threw himself in the back seat.

He needed to get out of Berryland.

Now.

Haley started to head for the train station as the Lincoln's springs squeaked like a teenage boy's bed at midnight. Donnie, bereft of cash since his encounter with Candy, asked Carsten and Randall if they had any cash for the trip home.

"Excuse me, Mr. Derringer, are you actually asking if I have any money?" Randall said with a grin.

"Uh, I was actually talking to Carsten," Donnie said. "I mean, I didn't think you could bankroll a trip back to Deerhead, Randall."

Carsten's mother told him he should always have cash in his pocket "just in case," so he kept some dough in a money clip in his pocket. He hadn't intended to spend it, but this was just the sort of emergency Mom had warned him about.

"I have cash," Carsten said, nonplussed by Donnie's request. "I thought perhaps it might come to that."

The car fell silent and Carsten attempted to lighten the mood.

"I have some Chuckles if you want one some," he deadpanned. "They're fruity and chewy. Mmm."

Donnie threw visual darts at Carsten and his feeble attempt at humor.

"Do you really think Chuckles are going to pull me out of this emotional pit?" Donnie spat. "Thanks, but no thanks, Carsten."

"I was merely attempting to cheer you," Carsten said, a little insulted.

Donnie didn't respond, his glazed eyes staring straight ahead.

Haley announced that they were near the train station.

"It's been nice meeting you all," she said. "Good luck, Rockin' Donnie. Good to see you other guys as well."

The train station was actually located in the heart of a dingy town called Hamilton, not Berryland. Donnie assumed the town was named for Alexander Hamilton.

Donnie walked ahead of Carsten and Randall into the fairly well-appointed train station, still stunned from their collective experience on *Losers on Parade*. It hurt Carsten to see his new best friend attacked on Jerry Most's show.

Randall just sighed heavily.

"It was nice of Mr. Most to provide us with train tickets to Deerhead, as I could not have put up with another long-haul bus ride," Carsten said, pulling three train ducats from his duffel bag. "Even he seemed to understand the grueling nature of riding the bus. At least we can travel in some comfort."

"Yeah," Donnie said dryly. "Jerry Most is a helluva guy."

— 31 —

LAST TRAIN TO DEERHEAD

Hamilton, they discovered from a monument in the middle of the train station lobby, was not named for Alexander Hamilton. It was named for a wealthy local early-20th-century gunrunner and heroin kingpin, Robert "Booby" Hamilton, who donated chunks of money — in cash — to the town for improvements to the public library, construction of a small convention center and, of course, the train station. Booby's public donations kept the local cops off of his case because he was regarded as a civic leader, a real stand-up guy even considering how he obtained his lucre.

The boys walked through the revolving door and Carsten stopped suddenly as he tried to open the Chuckles wrapper as he walked. Carsten's sudden halt caused Donnie to smash his nose against the glass.

Perfect!

They stood in the station's ornate rotunda and stared at the arrival and departure boards.

National Train, the line which would carry them back to Deerhead, apparently had routes to various and sundry hellish burgs where Donnie imagined the populace was as eager to flee as he had been from Deerhead.

Doggsville, Pennsylvania. Head, Ohio. Donnie chuckled at the notion of living in a place named Head. Was there a Fontaine, Ohio? Then Fillington, Indiana before they pulled into Chicago. Then it was Elk, Wisconsin and, further north, Bear, Wisconsin. It took a while to find Deerhead, on the board but after a thorough search, there it was — Deerhead, Minnesota.

It was 25 minutes until the train's departure to Deerhead and several dull points in between.

They wandered to the gate and dropped themselves three abreast on the plastic chairs at the gate.

No one spoke. Then Carsten said: "Well, that was quite an experience, for me at least. I'll bet it will make for interesting conversation at the coffee shop."

Donnie swung his head and said to Carsten: "Yes, Carsten, please debrief the fine people of Deerhead, my last stop in life whether I like it or not, so that my humiliation may be complete," he hissed.

"Well, you have to admit that this was an indescribable occurrence," Randall said. "But think of it this way: Being on a TV show for any reason makes people respect you more. It is a known fact that television elevates any person who appears on it, whether it's a game show or a torture chamber like the one that just consumed your entire life in a fire of degradation.

"In fact, when they stream the show on Jerry's podcast, I think you should encourage all of Deerhead to witness your appearance. I think it will bring you some notoriety of the sort that makes people say hello to you and smile as you walk down Main Street."

"Thanks for your support, Randall. I'm not so sure your efforts will bring said notoriety. But that will be great," Donnie said in high dudgeon.

Randall was taken aback by Donnie's reaction to his harmlessly encouraging comment.

"Frankly, Donald, I am not accustomed to being spoken to that way," he said indignantly. "I know you're in a miserable condition but I am your friend, and I'm only trying to put the best face on the situation."

"Sorry, Randall," he said. "My brain is frying right now." He wished he could light his one-hitter but decided such an act could lead to an arrest, as pot was probably not legal in Hamilton. Apprehension by local authorities would be just what Donnie needed.

After his harsh reaction to Randall, Donnie sulked in silence.

The train arrived and the conductor called out: "All aboard the train to Sioux Falls. That's in South Dakota for those unfamiliar with the Great Plains states. Stops in Segersville, New York; Head, Ohio; Fillington, Indiana; Hammertown, Wisconsin; and dozens of other map dots in between. All aboard. Last car is the quiet car for those of you who would like to spend a cross-country trip contemplating how your life led you to going to any of these places."

Wow, Donnie thought. That wasn't very nice. I'm sure these small towns had their good points.

Or did they? After his experience in Deerhead, Donnie didn't know any more.

As they got in line to board the train, Randall stopped suddenly and spoke to Donnie.

"Donald, and, ah, Carsten, too ... I've decided not to return to Deerhead," he said. "I'm an old man, but I still think there is something better out there for me. Where better to seek a future than in the New York metropolitan area? I was fine in Deerhead, but I was going nowhere. The worst thing that can happen to me in the city is that I will be homeless. But I have already attained that status and I'd like a change of venue, maybe get a sense of the excitement from new surroundings.

"My life is not an easy one, but I am prepared to attempt to make it better. If nothing else, those from whom I am begging money will be more affluent than the ones who offer charity in Deerhead. Who knows? Perhaps I could try my hand at getting another radio job. New Yorkers love their jazz, after all, and I still have my voice.

"In any case, gentlemen, this is the end of the line for me.

"Donald, I hope this experience will lead to better things for you, a life change, maybe. You need to remember how I ended up sleeping under trees and in bus stations. You have been following my path of self-destruction and without change you, too, might wind up slumbering in a church pew. Take heed, my friend, and remember me well, Donald.

"And Carsten, it wouldn't hurt you to loosen up a bit, maybe show some emotion, laugh, cry and rid yourself of the flat-affect automaton that you have become. Try living, my friend. Now that you have seen other environs you might be inspired to travel or even consider a change of residence yourself. Some fun is what I prescribe for you, Carsten. Be human. Deerhead may have deadened your spirit, but I assure you that you have a happy life to live if you come out of your non-emotive shell.

"And now, my friends, return to Deerhead with my blessings. Make the best of it. Make it home safely, and I will make every effort to stay in touch, but with my lifestyle, that will not be easy. This is not goodbye, but I will say, 'Until we meet again.' And please let me walk away without further adieus. No hugs, no handshakes. Just let me go."

Carsten watched Randall with no emotion as Randall walked away. Donnie became melancholy. He liked Randall, but Donnie did indeed look at Randall as a life lesson. Donnie did not think he would do well sleeping under a tree. Lightning would strike if he entered a church to sleep on a pew.

But now Donnie had a vague reason to be optimistic. He no longer had to live up to the "rockin'" persona he had created for himself. Dr. Dixon had offered him the possibility of a job and help for his mental health.

Donnie realized he had a place to live where all of his records were at his fingertips, and really, Deerhead was nice and quiet. Maybe quiet was just what Donnie needed.

Maybe he could be happy.

Nah.

But still…

Meanwhile, Carsten gently pushed Donnie toward the train just as he had nudged him into Dr. Dixon's office.

The two boarded and looked for seats in the quiet car. Neither of them had the use for cell-phone chats by people talking about last night or their children's soccer games or big business deals.

They found two seats next to each other on the train and Donnie let Carsten have the window seat. Carsten stared out the window as the train pulled out. He marveled at the distant Manhattan skyline and thought he would like to return some day.

Donnie sighed and closed his eyes. He knew lighting up on a train would be verboten, so he decided to ride home sober.

"Rockin'" Donnie Derringer.

Sober!

Donnie loved traveling by train. It was relaxing. It always lulled him to sleep. You see the best and worst of America from the point of view of the train tracks. Carsten, fascinated, leaned his head on the window and just stared like a child with a ViewMaster staring at the pyramids of Giza.

Donnie slept for a good part of the peaceful, uneventful trip. In fact, rocking along the train tracks was an experience that was — serene!

The last few days had worn him out. He was roused from his slumber only occasionally at stops or when a new passenger used Donnie's aisle seat as a support while finding a place to sit.

At a few spots, Carsten nudged Donnie to show him a point of interest.

"Look at the size of those salt piles," Carsten said at one point. "They must get a lot of snow here."

"Carsten," Donnie said, "please leave me alone unless we pass some spectacular incident like a car fire. I have a lot to process and I need to sleep."

As Donnie drifted in and out of sleep his brain was alternating between frightening dreams involving worms crawling in his beard and thoughts of what had happened to him in the past week.

He thought about Dr. Dixon. He thought about being a victim of Jerry Most on *Losers on Parade*. He thought about Deerhead. Liz. He thought about the greatest left fielders ever to play the game and although he loved Carl Yastrzemski, no one could beat Ted Williams as the best of all time.

Donnie was wasted, and not from drugs and alcohol.

His life was wasted.

— 31 —

PARTYING TO THE END

WHEN THEY FINALLY ARRIVED IN DEERHEAD, Carsten drove Donnie to his house. Donnie invited him in for some serious drinking and dope-smoking. They wound up sitting and yakking for the better part of the evening. At this point, it was clear that Carsten loved Donnie. He enjoyed his tales of adventure. They disagreed on the '70s music that Donnie had long ago grown weary of, but for which Carsten still had a soft spot, his interest in opera notwithstanding.

Carsten even thought he could convince Donnie of the artistic value of old rockers like Tull and Styx as emblematic of the '70s' musical sensibilities.

"I mean, come on, Donnie, how can you ever get sick of 'Come Sail Away'?" Carsten said. "OK, I realize 'Lorelei' is a bit goopy, but I still like it. And what about Journey? 'Don't Stop Believin' is killer!"

Donnie reached for a nearby Old Grand-Dad bottle and took a long and deep slug. He was beginning to feel the effects of the alcohol. That's when he usually began waxing philosophical and his musical lectures began.

"Look, Carsten," he said, plunging into an inebriated monolog about music. "I know you like opera, right? Symphony? Jazz? Now, as opposed to rock, which one of those genres has already and will likely continue to endure for another century? My point is that, with the exception of music by bands like the Beatles, The Who, the Stones, Dylan, even the likes of the Beach Boys or the Clash or Elvis Costello, most music, especially pop music, has become disposable. Do you really think that even in twenty, thirty years people will relish the music of Celine Dion? Or, God help us, rap. Seriously, will the Beastie Boys have the same staying power of Springsteen?

"Now take the blues, which I adore. The blues have become a relic of the past, even though the music will endure, at least in some part because it not only speaks to the human condition, but is an important part of American culture and history. My point is that most of music, especially that of artists like John Mellencamp and, yes, your Styx, is headed for the dustbin of history."

Carsten yawned.

"Jeez, Donald, that's awfully pessimistic," he said. "Not everything is awful. I'll be listening to a lot of that '70s stuff for the rest of my life. If you can't get sick of it, it does indeed withstand the test of time."

Donnie's mind was wandering as he was still processing the events of the past few days through the alcoholic swirl, and he wasn't sure he liked the result.

A return to Deerhead. Serenity Heights.

Really?

But he quickly snapped out of it and responded to Carsten: "Me? A pessimist? Who would have thought? Add cynic, boozehound, and pothead and you have the complete package of good old 'Rockin' Donnie Derringer.' I mean, my hopes and dreams did not lead me to taking a job as a counselor at a crazy house in Deerhead, Minnesota. Throughout my life, I always knew something bad was going to happen, and throughout my life, it did, although admittedly my behavior may have played a hand in that."

"You've moved off topic a bit, Donald," Carsten replied with a little more emphasis than was customary for his philosophical countenance. "But if I can follow your careening train of thought, I have to say that Deerhead, Serenity Heights and a quiet life aren't so bad. I've lived most of my life in Thoreau's state of quiet desperation, thinking I might be missing something, but I find solace in my books, my music and an appreciation for the stillness of small-town life. I think if you gave it a chance this sort of life might actually suit you. The Big City certainly didn't do you much good."

"You might have a point there, Mr. Sho-crates," Donnie said. He was slurring his words, shit-faced. "Maybe I could settle down with Lizh and learn to live the peash-ful life. But in the meantime, I will take a huge hit from my red elephant-head bong. Then I will drink more whish-key. I'll consider what you have said in my normal druggy haze and maybe I can recon-shile myself to thish town."

Donnie could see two Carstens, two bongs, two coffee tables, and he watched as the room slowly revolved.

It was about 1:30 in the morning when Carsten finished his beer and recognized that Donnie, at the moment, was in another world.

Carsten, who probably could have made a Breathalyzer explode himself, stumbled across the room to Donnie and poked his shoulder.

"Hey, Donnie. Donnie, pal," he said. "I think I'm gonna go. It's late and I'm pretty buzzed. I need to sleep this off."

Donnie awoke and looked at Carsten as though he had never seen him before. Once he got his bearings he said: "Carsht, please shtay. I need company tonight. Seriously, you could shleep on the couch and we could find a nice shaloon tomorrow and do some day drinking."

"No, Donnie, I can't," Carsten said. "For one thing, your couch is probably crawling with microbes from who-knows-what, and since tomorrow is Sunday, I'm just going to sleep in. Maybe read a Russian novel or something on the porch in the afternoon."

"Really?" Donnie said, trying to focus. "You're going to read a book? How did you manage to find one you haven't already colored in?"

"Funny, Donnie, funny. But I'm taking off," Carsten said, and did.

Donnie was left alone, sitting in his living room, contemplating the deeper meaning of everything that had happed to him up to this point. In and out of good jobs, in and out of relationships and public humiliation. Donnie guessed that his life added up to nothing. But at least he had a good time, or so he thought.

But they can't take away the memories.

Somehow, Donnie was comforted by those memories, even if not all of them were good. They were what made Donnie "Rockin' Donnie."

Wild man!

Donnie got up and grabbed the garbage bag he had stuffed his things into when he left for Berryland. He dug out his journal and went to his desk to make an intoxicated entry into his journal.

He picked up his pen and began to write. His handwriting was shaky but he wasn't writing for anyone but himself now. It didn't matter if it was legible to anyone else.

This is what he wrote:

> So this is where it all ends. Deerhead, Minnesota. Serenity Heights. I'll probably die here now. This is the end of the road. I'll just have to try to adjust to where I have wound up. Maybe that's OK. It certainly wasn't what I had planned, but then, I don't remember exactly what I had planned in the first place. They say the best way to make God smile is to make plans. But I guess this is it. Maybe I can...

Donnie fell asleep at the desk without finishing the sentence. He awoke with his head on the desk a few hours later, pen still in hand. He straightened up and sleepily walked to his bedroom, falling into bed.

Donnie spent the next day catnapping and watching a 1 p.m. Minnesota Twins-Boston Red Sox game. He loved baseball. It grounded him and made him feel comfortable because, along with music, baseball got him through his childhood. After the game, he watched a noir classic, *The Killers*, on TV, but because of his constant dozing he couldn't remember the ending.

He ate stale cornflakes and drank beer that day while he waited for night to fall. Donnie thought Carsten said something the night before about coming over and even his stuck-in-the-'70s, dispassionate presence would be a welcome interruption of Donnie's boredom.

Carsten startled Donnie when he walked in. Since he had figured that Donnie expected him, he entered Donnie's place through the unlocked screen door without knocking. They were pals, right? Pals don't knock when they come over.

He had brought a cheese and sausage pizza and a few vinyl records with him. The B-52s, the Cars, the Clash, the Jam, Yes, Journey, of course, and, for some reason, a double album of Bizet's "Carmen" that would not be played that night.

Carsten knew Donnie would never countenance opera in this house, but he thought he could prove to Donnie that his interest in such a magnum opus was evidence of his intellect and diverse musical tastes.

Carsten had also brought a 12-pack of a local micro-brew called "Deerhead's Finest" and a bottle of a cheap whiskey called Drunken Sailor. Along with the pizza, he also brought a bag with store-brand potato chips and pretzels. Perfect accompaniments to another bender.

Let's rock!

Donnie, bong and whiskey bottle on the table next to his Barcalounger, was already into his cups. Miles Davis's "Birth of the Cool" was on the turntable and Donnie seemed to be in some kind of trance.

"Oh, hey, Carsty, how's it going?" Donnie was already slurring a bit. Donnie's cocktail hour seemed to have started early that day. He was still emotionally swimming in everything that had happened to him.

It was OK with Donnie that Carsten had just walked in. Carsten was there to party with his new and only friend.

"Rockin' Donnie Derringer in the flesh," Carsten said stiffly like a first grader reading his first words. "Let's, um, par-tay!"

"Yeah," Donnie said, yawning. "Par-tay."

Carsten showed Donnie what he had brought. Donnie approved but he asked if Carsten had brought dope, too.

"I'm not sure where to get pot, Donnie," he said. "But I brought you ample potables."

"That's great, Carsten, thanks. But you could have gone to the grade school to get some pot. Everybody knows that. Keep that in mind for next time."

Donnie lit the bong and offered it to Carsten. Donnie had enough pot to get them through the night as they dissected Coltrane's riffs, and later, during *The Who Live at Leeds*, John Entwistle's ability to anchor the band as Keith Moon and Pete Townshend bashed away.

Carsten took the bong from Donnie, lighted it and inhaled deeply. He quickly felt the warm, euphoric effect of the THC swimming in his brain. The feeling was new to him and he found it not altogether unpleasant.

He sat down on the sofa and felt Miles' trumpet make sounds that seemed like they came from Heaven itself.

"That's great pot," Carsten said.

"Ditchweed, but it'll do for now," Donnie said.

They stared at each other.

Carsten broke the quiet by beginning another paean to old-time rock.

"Come on, Donnie, how can you ever get sick of Bob Seger's 'Rock and Roll Never Forgets'? And 'Main Street' practically makes me weep to this day," he said. "And Seger is right. Once a rocker, always a rocker! Rock and roll never forgets, Donnie. Never. And what about Yes? OK, their album 'Tales from Topographic Oceans' is incomprehensible, but 'Roundabout' is a classic. And so are deep cuts like 'Yours is No Disgrace' and 'Starship Trooper.' I could go on and on."

"Carsten, I must have played those ditties on my shows hundreds of times since the '70s. It's time to put some of this stuff to bed for good. Smother them. Put them in the archives and forget them.

"And by the way, if constant repetition of '70s music hasn't already made you brain dead, the '80s were awful. Name one album other than 'Born in the USA' that has survived the test of time. Even the singles suck. 'Come On, Eileen'? Or 'Do You Really Want to Hurt Me'? And God-help-us '99 Red Balloons.' Dreck! Dreck, I say. Eighties music should be buried deep in some government vault where they will do no more harm to the minds of those who thought those were great songs. And don't get me started on the 1990s, the advent of hip-hop and rap. Music is going down the tubes. And speaking of the Tubes, White Punks on Dope — the live version — should be in the Smithsonian or something. At least it should be in the Rock and Roll Hall of Fame.

"My point is, my dear friend Carsten, that musically, we're finished. All the great songs have been written and played to death on banal shows like mine. There is nothing left but the dregs of a bereft collective human imagination. It's all derivative or inferior covers of great songs by the best bands. Just about everything, with a few exceptions, worth hearing has been written. It's over, Carsten, except for fond memories of our high school and college years ... I'm sorry, Carsten. I know you didn't attend college."

Donnie reached for the whiskey bottle and took another gulp. The booze could be soothing or it could make him irritable. A discussion of old music put him in the latter category. He was in no mood for a debate.

"Look, whatever people like is fine by me," he continued. "Music is in the ear of the beholder. I'm just saying it's all over, at least for what's left of rock music. Now it's just variations on themes from bands long gone."

Donnie loved having a partner to get drunk and high with, but after his monolog Carsten went silent again, no talking and no music. Donnie was barely intelligible as he spoke.

Miles had played the last note of the record side and that's when Donnie suggested they play "the greatest live album ever," The Who Live at Leeds.

"Perfect," said Carsten, who would have accepted anything Donnie played.

Donnie set the bottle down and wobbled across the sticky floor to the turntable.

"Vinyl, buddy, always vinyl," Donnie said. "I have an original pressing with a note on the label that says 'Crackling Noises OK. Do Not Correct' or something like that. Makes the whole thing more real if you ask me."

Carsten chimed in. "And that particular version of 'My Generation' is the greatest live performance of any band anywhere," he said. "But this is old music. How come you don't hate it? Why aren't you sick of this, too?"

Donnie explained that certain '70s artists were exempt from contempt, starting with The Who. Bowie. Neil Young.

"Indeed," Donnie added, "I agree with you, my friend, that 'My Generation' may have been the greatest rock anthem of them all. When I die, I hope it's playing in the background. I can't think of a better way to go. *Hope I die before I get old*. That's been my mantra for years, but here I am, old and in the way. I'm done, Carsten. I don't have anything left. I got old."

"Don't talk like that, Donnie. You've got some gas left in the tank. You've got a new life in Deerhead. Let's just party and enjoy the music!"

Donnie placed the needle onto the record and as Pete Townshend ripped into the first chord, Carsten leaned back in quiet, dope-fueled ecstasy.

"This is so cool," he said, stone-faced. "I'm cranking tunes, getting pasted, doing bong hits, and listening to The Who with my new buddy. What could be better?"

"I suppose getting laid is better," Carsten said, although he didn't know.

"But getting laid with The Who in the background while stoned with a bottle on the nightstand is better," Donnie responded. "In fact, I should call Liz. She always was open to a spontaneous booty call. She's really pissed at me, but I think I can work my wiles on her."

"Ah, do you want me to leave?"

"No, Carsten, I'm not suggesting anything right now. We're having too much fun. I can tell by your red eyes." Donnie rose and flipped the record over. "OK, wait, here comes 'My Generation.' Let's shut up and listen."

Carsten leaned his head back and closed his eyes. Not only was the music perfect for the moment, he was getting body rushes from the pot.

"OK, here it comes," Donnie said.

And then the guitar kicked in: *Bom bom bom bom, bom bom bom bom...*

Then Roger Daltrey kicked in: "*People try*..."

Donnie, back in his Barcalounger, sat with his elbows on his knees.

"Listen to Entwistle's bass line," he said. "And there was never a better drummer than Keith Moon, rest his shattered soul."

"Some say Neil Peart was better. Or Carl Palmer," Carsten said dreamily.

Such talk was blasphemy in Donnie's house.

"Screw Peart and Rush and Emerson, Lake and Palmer," Donnie said ominously. "I will brook no argument about Moonie being the best. And please don't talk to me about Zeppelin's 'Bonzo' Bonham. Not even close."

With that, Donnie began to pass out, bottle in hand.

But he rallied, as he always did.

Rockin' Donnie could party with anyone, anywhere, all night.

Donnie was still absorbing The Who, but it wasn't enough to keep him from contemplating the deeper meaning of everything that had happened to him up to this point. In and out of jobs, shitty and otherwise, in and out of relationships and public humiliation. Donnie guessed that his life added up to nothing.

But at least I had a good time, he thought.

Or did he?

They continued their musical soiree until the wee hours. It was just before the roosters at the farms just outside of town began crowing when Carsten woke up. He finished his beer and recognized that Donnie was in another world. Passed out cold.

Carsten called to Donnie from across the room. The record on the turntable, 'Blonde on Blonde,' was making a scratching noise. Carsten picked up the needle and called out to Donnie.

"Hey, Donnie-pal, I think I'm gonna go," he said. "It's really late, I'm pretty intoxicated and the birds are singing. I need to get to my bed."

Carsten took the whiskey bottle out of Donnie's hand before more liquid spilled on the tacky floor. He set it on the table next to Donnie's chair and quietly said: "Good night, sweet prince."

Carsten was in terrible shape from liquor and pot, and probably should have stayed on Donnie's couch. But he wanted to wake up in his own bed and he dreaded the idea of what lived on and in Donnie's sofa.

He slipped quietly out of Donnie's house and stumbled to his van. As high as he was, he was in the mood for Yes. He slipped 'Tales from Topographic Oceans' into the cassette deck. He had listened to the album dozens of times before in a vain attempt to figure it out. But in his current condition it was the only way to make sense of that cryptic album.

The sky was beginning to brighten as Carsten drove home, always traveling at the speed limit and making sure not to swerve over the double yellow line separating the right lane from the left. Because Deerhead itself was so tiny, he made it home with no incident in about seven minutes.

Donnie, meanwhile, was snoring and sleeping fitfully.

He awoke with a start and although he should have gone straight to bed, Donnie was hungry. He had eaten some pizza, but otherwise his diet had consisted of alcohol and pot that day.

He took a swig from the whiskey bottle, arose from his chair, bottle still in hand, and walked like a man on stilts to the kitchen. Donnie hadn't been grocery shopping in weeks, but he decided there must be something to eat that the roaches hadn't gotten at. Blackened bananas in a bowl on the kitchen counter were swarmed by fruit flies.

Screw it. Donnie considered disposing of the bananas but really didn't feel like walking to the garbage can and, hell, fruit flies have to eat, too.

Donnie placed the whiskey bottle on the filthy kitchen table and checked the refrigerator. In it was a loaf of stale bread. Donnie found out putting most food in the fridge was the only way to keep the vermin from dining on his victuals. He pulled out the bread and closed the graffiti and magnet-bedecked refrigerator door.

Donnie hoped to find something in the barren kitchen cabinets that could accompany the bread.

And sure enough, there it was.

Peanut butter! His constant dietary companion. Two jars! Always two jars because he never wanted to run out of this staple. Donnie had been eating peanut butter since he was a first-grader, nearly every day for his entire life. He joked that if researchers wanted to conduct a study on the longitudinal effects of consumption of massive amounts of peanut butter, he should be the first subject. If he got paid for it, of course.

Donnie found a clean plate, his only plate, placed the bread on it and spread a thick layer of peanut butter on both pieces.

That ought to hold him.

Grabbing bottle and plate, Donnie hazily maneuvered himself back to the living room and nearly tripped on a stack of records he'd left out as he and Carsten partied. He would have to file them later. When it came to his music, Donnie did not like disorganization. It was the only part of his life that wasn't chaos.

Donnie made it to the Barcalounger, set the plate on a nearby coffee table and took another swig of unneeded whiskey. He sat, placed the bottle on the table and lifted the plate. There was more peanut butter than bread on his sandwich, but that's how he liked it. Thick.

Mmm. Peanut butter.

Donnie grabbed the TV remote and started channel surfing. As usual, there was nothing interesting to watch. Springsteen was right: 57 channels, nothing on.

As he channel-surfed, he found a non-denominational preacher with a lilting Southern accent telling lost souls that they could save themselves and maybe even get rich if they called his switchboard to donate money to his church.

"You only get what you give," he shouted. "God wants you to be happy, and a contribution will show him that you are indeed giving to get. It's as simple as that. Now please call and get yourself on the right track with God. Give, give and give and He will take care of you."

Donnie settled on the preacher channel. He always loved watching hucksters use Jesus as a pitch man to sell the gullible on the notion that by making the preacher rich, they would become rich themselves.

He picked up the plate with the delicious peanut butter sandwich and took a bite. The bread was stale and tough to swallow and, combined with the peanut butter, booze, and pot, made him feel nauseated. Still, he took a second bite as the faux minister implored people not to condemn themselves to an eternity of suffering in the Lake of Fire by ignoring his plea for contributions.

Suddenly Donnie realized that he had followed the first bite with the second a little too soon.

"Jai-sus wants you to be a good Christian through giving," the preacher shouted as Donnie began to feel a heavy lump in his peanut-butter-laden throat. He tried to swallow but could not. He took a swig of whiskey to try to wash down the bolus, but that only made matters worse and he began to gag.

Donnie tried to breathe but could not. He was struggling, clutching his throat, but the sandwich was lodged in his trachea. He tried the Heimlich maneuver on himself with no success. Donnie was choking.

To death.

The TV was blaring.

"Jesus wants to help you, but you have to help me and my church first!"

Donnie's brain was in chaos. He was afraid death was approaching.

It was.

Donnie collapsed as the preacher called out, "Only your contribution will get you right with God! Jesus wants to save you!"

Donnie was pissed that if this was it, he was not listening to "My Generation." But as he struggled for breath, he hoped the preacher was right, that Jesus wanted to save him.

The legendary "Rockin' Donnie Derringer" did not die a rock-and-roll death in a bed with hookers and booze and drugs. His demise, like most people's, was prosaic. Nothing legendary about Donnie's demise at all.

Death by peanut butter.

Donnie collapsed and hit his head on the hard-wood floor. The blow hardly mattered.

Donnie was already dead.

Peanut butter had betrayed him after all these years.

Figures.

— 33 —

"THIS IS THE END, BEAUTIFUL FRIEND"

CARSTEN CAME TO DONNIE'S HOUSE TO check in on him the next day. He didn't know what to do when he discovered Donnie's corpse lying twisted on the floor. He called an ambulance, but Donnie had been dead for hours. The attendants, two hefty millennials named Max and Ryan, asked Carsten if he wanted to say anything before they put Donnie in a black vinyl bag and hauled him away.

"Good-bye, my friend, the best friend I ever had. Rock on, Donnie!" Carsten intoned.

"Cool," Max said. "Let's go."

They placed Donnie in the bag, then they lifted him like a side of beef, hefted him out the door, and dropped him in the back of the ambulance.

Max walked back in and asked Carsten where they should take Donnie.

"I don't know," Carsten said. "Maybe to Morton Morton's funeral place?"

"Will do," Max said. "But since he died alone, the coroner's gonna want to have a look-see at him first, then they'll send him to Morton's."

"Fine," Carsten said.

A stunned and confused Carsten did not know what to do, so he used Donnie's cell phone to call Hooter Hurd at KYJL to say Donnie wouldn't be coming to get his job back — that he died.

"Wow, I knew he was off the deep end but I didn't things would go this far so soon," Hooter said. He was almost excited to hear about Donnie's entry into Rock and Roll Heaven. It was real news in Deerhead that a guy like Rockin' Donnie Derringer was dead. Usually whatever news they broadcast had to do with downtown fender-benders and the occasional stabbing at the local biker bar, Rosie's Roadside Bar and Grille.

"That dude Donnie had 100 lives and I guess he finally spent 101 of them," Hooter said. "But I'll break into our Genesis triple-shot to make the announcement to the world. Thanks for calling. I gotta go."

After the call ended, Carsten realized he had to give Dr. Dixon the sad news. He did not have her personal number so he called Serenity Heights.

To speak with Dr. Dixon, Carsten had first to go through Pat, the nurse whose sheer spite made her seem as though she had apparently had an internship at a maximum-security prison before joining the Serenity Heights full-time staff.

Carsten called the hospital switchboard and, of course, Pat answered.

"Serenity Heights," she said dourly. "If you're suicidal please call the hotline and whine to them. I don't need that crying and mewling and puking that is part of the repertoire of weak people like yourself. Otherwise, whattya want?"

Pat really enjoyed her job.

Carsten was almost afraid to identify himself to Pat, but he needed to talk to Dr. Dixon.

"Hi, Pat, it's Carsten," he said, voice shaking just a little.

"Carsten!" she shouted into the phone sarcastically. "How nice to hear from you! I thought maybe you'd gone driven off a cliff with your friend Derringer. But here you are, calling, no doubt with the news I heard on KYJL just now. They interrupted Genesis' 'Invisible Touch' to break the news. Your friend is dead, so they say, although I'd have to see it to believe it. Did someone drive a stake thought that black heart of his? He was a mess, but he was a survivor."

"Um, yes … well, yeah, Donnie's dead, and I need to speak with Dr. Dixon."

"I'm sure she's been waiting by the phone just for your call," Pat said. "Hang on, loser, I'll connect you."

Carsten was placed on hold while Pat tracked down Dr. Dixon. He listened to some unidentifiable violin music on the line. Finally, Dr. Dixon picked up.

"Hello, Dr. Dixon?" Carsten said in a whisper. "Dr. Dixon, this is Carsten."

"Yes, Carsten, I assume you are calling me to tell me your friend had passed into the afterlife," she said. "I heard about it on the radio. And if you're wondering I, too, listen to the sounds of the 'The Rock' between patient sessions. They take me back to better days."

"Yes … ah, yes, Doctor, Donnie's dead," Carsten said. "He was blue when I saw him and he was clutching his throat. There was a half-eaten peanut butter sandwich on his coffee table. The coroner is investigating but I think he choked on the sandwich. I wish I could have been here to save him."

"Mmm, most unfortunate," Dr. Dixon said dryly. "He might have made a good counselor, someone who could show patients what not to do with their lives. Carsten, you had to know he was going down the path of destruction that led to his ultimate demise. And he was going to take you with him. But choking to death on a peanut butter sandwich? How utterly ridiculous.

"Carsten, I know you two had become dear friends, and I have been long concerned that by associating with Donald you would have suffered the same sort of drug-induced downfall. You can now use Donald's passing as a lesson on what not to do with your life. You have my condolences with the hopes that you will learn from this sad situation."

Carsten thought for some reason that Jerry Most needed to hear about Donnie's death. He walked through the apartment in search of Most's contact information and saw it on the kitchen counter where Donnie had left it after he took it out of his wallet next to the condom.

Carsten called the number and Jerry answered immediately with a cheery "Yell-ow."

"Yes, Mr. Most? This is Donnie Derringer's friend, Carsten," he said, voice trembling.

"Ah yes, Carsten!" Jerry said as though speaking to a long-lost friend. "You were the large henchman who accompanied Rockin' Donnie to my show. What can I do ya for?"

Carsten was pleased Jerry had remembered him but unhappy with himself for displaying any emotion. He was no Marcus Aurelius after all.

"Don't tell me. A super-sized human beast such as yourself must be thinking of going into professional wrestling, no? And you want me to be your promoter, is that it?"

"Mr. Most. I just wanted to call you and tell you that Donnie died."

"Oh, dear," Jerry said. "And just what method did he choose to join all the other dead disc jockeys? Sorry, I meant radio personalities. Celebrities, whatever. But anyway, what did he overdose on? Did he have a heart attack while screwing some bar hag he picked up during a bender? I can't wait to hear!"

A little shocked by Jerry's insensitivity even under these circumstances, Carsten said dully: "He was my best friend. And now he's dead."

Carsten's Spock-like deadpan demeanor was cracking, but he held himself together as he described Donnie's ultimate downfall.

"I think he choked on a peanut butter sandwich," Carsten said. "He was alone. No hookers or anything. He just plain died."

"Whoa!" Jerry shouted into the phone. "You mean to tell me that he choked on peanut butter? If you'll forgive me, within the context of Donnie's miserable life, that is hilarious."

Carsten said nothing.

Jerry broke the heavy silence.

"OK, cowboy, are you holding it together?" Jerry said. "I'm sorry your friend croaked, but how does this involve me? What effect does it have on my glorious life? Why are you interrupting my session with a spicy bloody Mary?"

Carsten thought an extended conversation with Jerry would only get worse as time wore on. He got right to the point.

"Mr. Most, none of us has much money. The cash you gave Donnie was stolen during the trip. I earn a meager salary, but I want to give Donnie a dignified funeral."

"Why am I not surprised that he pissed away the cash?" Jerry said, slightly amused.

"Donnie lost the remainder of whatever you gave him while he was copulating with some strange woman at a truck stop. I could use some help for his funeral and burial."

"No offense, but it seems ironic that the word 'dignified' would apply to anything related to Rockin' Donnie Derringer. Let's face it. He wasn't exactly someone who would get a state funeral."

"Yes, but …"

"I know, I know, he was your friend. So … what would it cost to put your friend in his grave? I guess I can help to pay for his funeral. I guess I owe him something given that I ruined his life on TV, YouTube, and in my podcast for the sake of getting a lucrative network gig. And by the way, my show did get picked up. The network execs loved the segment with Donnie and want me to find other degenerates to degrade. I won't have to look hard. After the show with Rockin' Donnie you'd think people wouldn't want to undergo the 'Jerry Most Treatment' — or mistreatment, as the case may be. But people will do anything to get on television. It's a known fact. Actually, his death will help to promote the show. Nice!

"As for the funeral, tell you what, have whatever undertaker who will handle the sad proceedings send me an invoice. I'll take care of it. I suppose it's the least I can do, and since it is really the very least, I'm willing to participate. Funeral costs are a drop in the bucket since my new network contract. They're droplets of spittle in the ocean."

"I really appreciate it," Carsten said. "I'll have Mr. Morton, the funeral director, send you the bill."

"Great," Jerry said and gave him the address where Carsten could send the damages.

"Thank you, Mr. Most," Carsten said. But the connection was dead. Jerry Most had hung up on him.

Then he called Liz with the news. He knew she and Donnie had been on the outs, but her number was in the Deerhead directory so she was easy to find.

Carsten's hand trembled a bit as he hit the buttons on the phone. She picked up immediately.

"Liz … ah … Hi, Liz," Carsten said awkwardly. "This is Donnie's friend Carsten. I work at Serenity Heights. That's where I met him. Um, Liz, I don't know how to tell you this but I have some bad news. Donnie's dead."

Liz gasped.

"What?" she shouted. "Jesus. I was pissed at the shithead but I didn't want him dead. Shit, shit, shit. What happened?"

"He choked on peanut butter, I think," Carsten said. "He's gone."

"I could have listed any number of ways I thought that dickhead would die, but peanut butter? Not a heart attack from watching porn and masturbating? Wow. Did he not have jelly? That might have helped slide it down."

Liz caught herself with that remark. It was inconsiderate given Carsten's feelings and the fact that she used to sleep with Donnie.

"OK, Carsten, where are we gonna get the money to plant him?" she said. "And I do mean 'we.' I feel partially responsible for making sure he doesn't wind up dumped in the landfill."

"Actually, that's covered," Carsten said, numbed to the point of detachment. "Jerry Most is going to pay for it."

"Who?"

"Jerry Most, the talk show host who makes people laugh by tormenting his guests."

"OK, whatever," Liz said. "Let's get down to that funeral home and talk to what's-his-name, Morton or something. I'm not saying I'm going to cry over that selfish bastard's death, but I am kind of sad and I'd like to help you, Carsten," she said softly.

She hung up.

— 34 —

A VISIT WITH MORTON MORTON, UNDERTAKER

SINCE MORT MORTON'S FUNERAL "PARLOR" was the only such place in Deerhead, they had to deal with Morton himself, an amoral man Carsten knew did not like Donnie from their encounter at the Deerhead Intermodal Station.

Liz and Carsten arrived and walked up the weedy, cracked sidewalk to the entrance. The place looked eerie. It was an old Victorian brothel that Morton had converted when he started the business of dealing in death. The building's dark brown brick, covered in places by overgrown ivy, its twin belfries standing like two otherworldly guards, looked like a place where Death itself reigned.

The building had a chimney in the back that rose bleakly into the gray Deerhead sky. The stack was connected to the crematorium oven, which was one way of disposing of a body that Carsten imagined Donnie would have liked.

Down in flames.

A blazing fire as a way out of this veil of tears.

But Carsten didn't like the idea. Not for his pal Donnie.

As Carsten and Liz approached the wide, windowed redwood doors, Morton himself came out to greet them.

"A good day to both of you," Morton said, feigning a mortician's sadness. "Please come in."

Liz was so creeped out by the surroundings that she took Carsten's arm as they walked past the undertaker and into the foyer. She looked around at the red and black walls, the high, beamed ceiling and paint-by-number landscape portraits punctuating the gloom and said: "Is this place a whorehouse?"

Morton overheard Liz and was deeply offended.

"Madam, I can assure you that this is not a place of ill-repute," he said stiffly. "In fact, it is one of the finest of funeral homes in northern Minnesota. Yes, it has a bit of a history, if you will, but that history is long past.

"Oh, OK," Liz said. "I didn't mean anything. It was a joke."

Morton ignored her.

"Now to the matter at hand, the passing of Mr. Derringer," Morton said. "On a personal note I only met him once, but that exposure caused me to personally dislike him almost immediately. He struck me as a real scallywag, if you'll pardon that characterization. Yet as a chronic insomniac I often listened to his late-night show on KYJL. Indeed, I used to call him with requests or just to chat. He was always accommodating. My handle was 'Rocky the Rocker.' Amusing, no?

"But the hard fact was that your friend was a bit of a … how shall I put it … a dislikeable shitheel. Pardon my French, but I'm sure you would not disagree. Still, it is my duty to bury him, and you will excuse me if I take some pleasure in that."

Carsten and Liz were silent. That was a little rough. They both knew Donnie was not the greatest guy in the world, but they both had a connection to him. To Carsten, he was the coolest, the best friend he ever had. Liz, well Liz and Donnie had something, although she was never sure quite what.

Morton interrupted them as they were engaged in their deep existential thought process.

"Nevertheless," Morton said, "nevertheless, I will provide for the best possible funerary proceedings your budget will allow. If I may ask, what is your budget? The larger the better, of course, if you want to send off your friend with all appropriate dignity."

"Well, the expenses are going to be paid by Jerry Most," Carsten said. "You know, the former game-show host and now talk-show host."

"'Most, the host you want to roast,' or something like that," Morton said. "I had thought he faded into merciful obscurity after his inane death-by-misadventure TV show was finally canceled. What is he doing now, that he could afford to pay for this undertaking?"

Undertaking. Morten loved that double entendre.

"I guess he signed some kind of mega-contract with a network that wanted to broadcast his new show, *Losers on Parade*," Carsten said. "Donnie was on that show a little while ago."

Morton burst into laughter.

"*Losers on Parade*?" he chortled. "I'm sure he made a buffoon of himself on a show like that."

"Yes, in any event, Mr. Most will pay for everything. Funeral. Burial. Incidental costs," Carsten said. "He said you should send him the invoice."

Carsten handed Morton a piece of paper with Jerry Most's contact information.

"I don't think Mr. Most wants to spend a lot of money on this — 'the very least,' he said. But he'll cover expenses."

"Excellent," Morton said. "Now what should we do to give Mr. Derringer an appropriate send-off to the Netherworld? Any ideas?"

Since neither Carsten nor Liz had ever planned such an event, Carsten thought out loud.

"Well, first, I don't think he would have liked cremation," Carsten said. "Donnie needs his fans to say goodbye to him one last time."

"Oh yes, I agree," Morton said sarcastically. "We'll put out an extra three chairs for his legion of devotees."

"One more thing," Liz said. "When he was depressed, he told me he wanted a garbage truck and a clown car to lead the procession when he bit the Big One, as he said. I think we owe him that much. It would be pretty cool."

"Cool indeed, and appropriate," Morton said. "I shall call the city to arrange for the refuse truck, and the Shriners probably have a clown car available. We will have the burial at Deerhead's finest cemetery, a place where local dignitaries are buried. It will cost more, as it is a beautiful site to celebrate life, get it? Celebrate life in a graveyard?"

Neither Carsten nor Liz found any humor in Morton's feeble attempt at humor.

"Anything else?" Morton said. "Perhaps a fireworks display?"

At that point, Carsten and Liz decided to leave. They'd had enough of Morton Morton and his inconsiderate remarks. But they figured he knew what he was doing.

"No, we're good," Carsten said. "Thanks. I think."

Morton remained sitting at his desk as they left.

Morton then called out: "Do you have a preference for a casket? I can select one that looks like a racing car."

Carsten turned around and told Morton he wanted the nicest coffin available. Jerry Most was paying for it anyway.

Liz took Carsten's arm again and they walked out of the dead house to the van.

"What a dick," Liz said.

"Compared to Morton, Donnie looked like a saint," Carsten said.

— 35 —

A CLOWN CAR AND GARBAGE TRUCK FUNERAL

On the day of the service, Carsten and Liz walked into the funeral home together, Liz once again taking Carsten's arm. The gesture gave Carsten inappropriate thoughts, but he pushed them away.

There were three separate rooms for viewing those who had recently joined the march of the dead. Donnie was in room 1A, the Forest Room. The room's motif was indeed that of a pine forest, the floor -to-ceiling bubbled wallpaper looking much like the woods that surrounded Deerhead.

Upon entering, Liz, wearing a black dress that aroused even the dispassionate Carsten, gasped as she got her first view of Donnie from across the room.

Liz began to sob heavily and initiated her act as bereaved widow, although her relationship with Donnie had been so tenuous. Death has a way of magnifying even the smallest of feelings.

She threw her arms around Carsten and said: "This is so awful! I can't believe he's gone. What am I going to do?"

Carsten was confused.

"What are you going to do?" he said. "What do you mean, what are you going to do? Were you two that close? I would think you'd just go back to the life you had before you met Donnie. I thought you dumped him after you took him to Serenity Heights."

"I don't know," she said. "I feel so alone. Donnie was the closest thing I've had to a relationship in years, and the sex was crazy, although I would never admit it to him. I guess I liked him more than I thought."

Carsten shushed Liz.

"You shouldn't talk about sex in a place like this," he said. "It's kind of sacred, isn't it?"

Carsten tried to ignore Liz's inappropriate sex comments as they walked up to view the dearly departed.

Donnie lay in his beautiful sliver casket. It appeared to be made of steel. Donnie's head was unnaturally positioned on the pillow, with his hands positioned in a thumbs up gesture. Someone, probably Morton, had placed a jar of chunky peanut butter next to the corpse.

Ha ha.

Carsten wasn't sure if it was some kind of sick joke, but on second thought, Donnie would have laughed at the idea being buried with a jar of peanut butter.

One thing, though. Donnie hated chunky peanut butter.

That didn't matter now.

The thumbs-up gesture, meanwhile, was Carsten's idea.

Thumbs up, Rockin' Donnie!

As is the case with most lifeless human bodies, Donnie looked like a wax figure of himself. Except that the funeral director, Morton Morton himself, had done Donnie's make-up in a strange way that made him look like a drag queen. Mascara, eye liner, the whole bit.

It was the mortician's final insult to Donnie to make him look ridiculous in state.

Being dead, Donnie didn't care, of course, but Carsten was quite annoyed and he decided to confront the funeral director, who was standing behind them.

Liz was bawling over Donnie's body as Carsten told Morton: "That make-up you slapped on his face makes him look like he should be wearing an evening gown. My friend looks ridiculous. I don't want this to be my final memory of my pal. I mean, he looks like some kind of sick harlequin."

Morton glanced at the reclining Donnie and said: "Hmm, so it does. Most unfortunate. I did what I could to make him look natural, but his face bloated as he choked, making heavy makeup a necessity."

"But this?" Carsten said incredulously.

Morton, insulted, said: "This was not an easy situation. He looked like a dead man even alive, and choking did not help his appearance. I just thought Mr. Derringer would enjoy looking … ah, shall we say, like a glam-rock star."

Morton walked away as Carsten stood at the bier and said, "I'm sorry, buddy, I'm so sorry. I felt like you were really a friend. We had an adventure, didn't we? It wasn't fun but now you're past the awful Jerry Most and all the people who have tortured you during your too-short life. You're in a better place now. I hope."

Carsten, who prided himself in his flat stoicism and the fact that "I don't think too much about anything," stiffly said, "Goodbye, *amica*. I wish I had met you long ago."

That was it.

Liz, meanwhile, kneeled and said a few prayers while blubbering like a newlywed wife before her dead spouse.

"Liz, are you OK?" Carsten asked, handing her his handkerchief. "Can I get you some water?"

"No, Carsten, thanks, I just need to process all of this," she said, standing. "I am really going to miss this guy's giant …"

"Liz, please stop!" Carsten pleaded. "This isn't the place."

"Sorry," she said. "I just haven't had it since I dropped him at the nuthouse and dumped him. Dumped him when he was most in need! I've been in need myself since then, by the way. In a different way. But how can I ever forgive myself?"

Carsten was getting frustrated, although somewhat excited, by Liz's repeated sexual innuendos. He turned to walk away, only to see Dr. Sally Dixon standing behind them, waiting for her chance to bid adieu to all that was left of Rockin' Donnie Derringer.

Carsten was startled to see his boss as he led Liz away, but Dr. Dixon gently put her hand on Carsten's free shoulder.

"Carsten, I'm so sorry," she said. "I believe he had become a good friend to you and you will miss him. But I am sure he is in some magical place in Heaven, although he may have needed to do some explaining before he rose to those majestic heights."

"Thanks, Dr. Dixon," Carsten said. "He wasn't such a bad guy, really."

"I know," she said. "He certainly had many and varied faults, but he was no worse than any politician."

Just then Liz began wailing.

"I can't believe he's gone," she wept. "I think maybe I loved him or something. But I sure am going to miss ..."

Carsten cut her off.

"OK, Liz, that's enough," he said firmly. "Let's let Dr. Dixon have her moment with Donnie."

As Carsten escorted Liz to the back of the room, Dr. Dixon approached the funerary box. She didn't use the kneeler, but she spoke softly, as though Donnie might hear her.

"Well, Donald, you've finally done it," she said. "I might have thought you might have gone in some kind of blaze of glory. Being shot by a jealous lover, say, or maybe strangled by a radio station manager who was tired of your juvenile antics. Even passing out and dying on the floor at a party with your hosts simply believing you were passed out. But a peanut butter sandwich? How very plain. It seems like a distinctly unfair way of going for a character like you.

"I tried to save you from yourself. But I couldn't have saved you from gooey peanut butter. I think you were beginning to turn your life around. You would have been an asset to Serenity Heights. Apparently, your friend Liz had deeper feelings for you that might have led to a stable relationship. I might have given you a job that, while new to you as a helper of others, would have given you reason to get up in the morning, a reason to hope for better days ahead. I would have made you a counselor, given your deep understanding of and experience with drug and alcohol abuse, but you weren't quite ready for that as your consumption continued notwithstanding my vain attempts to get you to quit.

"Alas, Mr. Derringer, I thought I could save you from yourself, but I failed and for that I am sorry. And so, it's goodbye Rockin' Donnie. I truly hope your rockin' soul is at rest."

Dr. Dixon's train of thought was interrupted by a woman's voice behind her.

"Hey, um, are you almost finished?" said the woman, dressed in black with a black head scarf. "There's other people who'd like to say goodbye."

Dr. Dixon turned, smiled tightly, and walked away. The mourner, a true burnout if there ever was one, did not know Donnie personally during his spectacularly action-packed life. But she felt she needed to explain herself. She had listened to Donnie faithfully when he was jocking at a Los Angeles station.

"I was his biggest fan," she said, sniffling. "When I heard he had died I wanted to be here. One time I called in and he asked me to take off my sweater and bra, and I did. Kind of turned me on, but …"

"Yes, I'm sure that was one of the high points of your life," Dr. Dixon said. "I'm going to find a place to sit. Nice to meet you, and my sympathies at the passing of your radio hero. I'm sure he would have appreciated your presence here, and by your rustic but pretty looks I'm guessing he would have tried to bed you. But alas …"

"You think so?" said the mourner, who identified herself as "Cindy from Burbank," a moniker she had adopted for her repeated calls to Donnie's show. "Really, I would have done him for sure, but we never had the chance to meet face to face."

"I guess he will simply have to live in your fantasies for the rest of your life," Dr. Dixon said. "By the way, your current bra-less look would, I'm sure, be a subject of great interest to Donnie and almost seems appropriate at the moment. Now if you'll excuse me…"

Morton Morton then walked toward them and suggested they find seats, that the service was about to start.

Sally Dixon sat in a padded folding chair in the back of the room as Cindy from Burbank found a spot in the front row.

Cindy was Donnie's biggest fan.

A few strangers had also joined the mourners. That was Deerhead. A place where funerals were thought of as entertainment for the lonely, bored souls who occupied the little town.

Standing at the door was Hooter Hurd, the station manager from KYJL. He looked awkward, as though he had no idea why he was there or what he should do.

Morton walked to him and suggested to Hurd that if he wanted to pay his last respects to Donnie, now was the time.

"No, really. Look, he worked for me, so I thought I'd stop by, but frankly I'm afraid of stiffs," Hooter said. "I figure I owed him this much, to show up for his funeral service. If it's OK by you, I'm just going to stand in the back here."

"As you wish," Morton said. "We're about to begin."

Morton strode to the front and took his place behind a makeshift, weathered pulpit that appeared to have been constructed at the high school woodshop. It consisted of pine and plywood spray-painted black.

Classy!

Morton, dressed in a black poly/cotton all-weather suit and a starched white shirt with red tie, took his place as the room went silent except for the sobbing and sniffing of Cindy from Burbank, who felt the need to apologize.

"I'm sorry," she said, snorting into a Kleenex. "He was my hero."

"No need to apologize, madam," Morton said. "This is indeed a sad occasion, at least for some people, especially yourself."

Cindy snorted and leaned back her head. She was getting a nosebleed and went quiet as a result.

Carsten and Liz sat in the front row opposite Cindy. Carsten was holding Liz's hand in his lap to comfort her. Instead of solace, Liz could feel Carsten becoming erect. She left her hand there because she knew dead Donnie wouldn't be jealous and, well, she thought Carsten was kind of cute in an austere way.

Carsten thought Donnie would have been proud of him for getting aroused by his own sometime girlfriend at his own funeral.

I'm rockin' on, Donnie, Carsten mused.

Morton had been pushed into service for Donnie's funeral because local clergy thought Donnie to be abhorrent after he characterized clergy in general as lunatics and swindlers during one of his shows. He called them witch doctors dressed in black, charlatans selling the gullible the hope of a better times when they left this world.

Ministers and priests who had made Donnie the subject of sermons and lectures about what hell would be like for degenerates like him, had had it with Donnie and refused to officiate at his funeral.

How nice.

Morton walked up to the lectern and cleared his throat noisily, signaling the beginning of what was more a monolog than a sermon.

"Dear brothers and sisters," he rasped, taking a drink of water that was hidden on a shelf under the makeshift pulpit. "I did not know Donald Henry Derringer personally, but I had a brief encounter with him at the Intermodal station and, of course, listened to his occasionally amusing radio show on KYJL during bouts of insomnia.

"Frankly, my brush with Mr. Derringer was highly offensive. Indeed, I am guessing that there are only a few people who have not suffered from the scourges of Donald's whip-smart tongue. He did awful, sexist, profane radio shows that, although accompanied by great music from the '60s and '70s, were designed to offend. It was his nature to use his sarcastic wit to destroy his human targets for the amusement of his listeners.

"From what I knew about Rockin' Donnie Derringer, he was a total ass. Anyone who has viewed his appearance on Jerry Most's recently released podcast knows what a self-centered jerk he was. Indeed, he seemed to be an irredeemable, selfish, oversexed drug and alcohol abuser who believed the world owed him something and, whatever that something was, he searched for it and destroyed it upon its discovery. He didn't know what he really wanted, but he didn't think he was getting it, so he took what he could. Women, drugs, alcohol-infused parties and self-abuse.

"According to Dr. Sally Dixon, as well as his friends Carsten and Liz, who were kind enough to provide some insights into Donald, he grew up in an abusive home, and he decided to take it out on the rest of the world as an adult. He reached a point where he could not separate his real self from the overblown radio personality that apparently amused others who aided and abetted his escapades. These people, his listeners, his abettors, became fodder for Donald's insatiable ego. He fed off of their approval, their laughter.

"Yet I personally believe that no one, even Rockin' Donnie Derringer, is so irredeemable as to be turned away at the Gates of Heaven. He had some good traits, I'm sure, although those characteristics were known only to those who could get close to him, and I have heard that he was generous to those of his friends who were in need, holding their hand during bad acid trips and the like.

"Yes, I believe that even a lowlife like Donald was escorted by an exhausted guardian angel to Heaven itself. He is indeed in that better place, perhaps chatting with Jimi and Janis and drinking to his own memory. Rest assured that Donald Derringer is sleeping with the angels, although only a gracious and forgiving God Himself knows why.

"Godspeed, Rockin' Donnie Derringer. Rest in peace. And rock on."

At that, Cindy began howling with deep sorrow. Liz was crying on Carsten's shoulder. Dr. Dixon sat stiffly as though she was listening to one of her own dull post-grad lecturers. Although her own beliefs were vaguely spiritual, she was happy with the thought that Donnie had once and for all bailed himself out of a life full of self-made conundrums.

Morton closed Donnie's casket as Cindy shouted, "Goodbye, Donnie!" a Kleenex stuffed into her right nostril to stop the bleeding. "I was your biggest fan and I loved you!"

She pulled down the front of her dress and displayed her ample bosom. Morton, snapped at her.

"Madam, please," he said, shocked as Cindy wailed and pulled up her top.

Morton announced that since there were too few people in attendance to be pallbearers, he and a young woman assistant, along with any volunteers, would wheel the casket on a cart to the hearse — or meat wagon, as Donnie would have called it.

Liz touched the casket as Morton wheeled it down the chapel aisle, and Cindy stopped it to embrace the coffin as it passed her, weeping uncontrollably. Her bra-less but now covered breasts spilled over the casket and Carsten thought Donnie would have appreciated that.

Carsten, who had assigned himself to being a pallbearer, helped Morton slide the casket into the hearse as the small group followed out the door. Carsten and Liz boarded Carsten's smoke-belching van as Cindy climbed into her Prius. Hooter Hurd had already gone back to his KYJL office. A garbage truck, full and stinking, was parked in front of the hearse, just as Liz had asked and as Morton had arranged. The driver, a palooka named Buzz whose boxing career left him with significant brain damage, said he was honored to be part of the proceedings, but he added that the trip to the cemetery was on his route anyway and his boss didn't mind.

Buzz was one of Donnie's occasional late-night callers. He went by the handle "Busy Buzzy." He was a fan of the dreadful John Mellencamp and Donnie never played the former "Cougar" despite Busy Buzzy's repeated requests for "I Need a Lover."

Meanwhile, Dr. Dixon told Carsten she wasn't going to join the mourners at the cemetery.

"I have said everything I had to say and done everything I could to help Mr. Derringer," she said. "I honestly believe he was putting his life together. I tried to protect him from himself. But I could not have protected him from a thick peanut butter sandwich. Life can be very strange."

She thanked Carsten for all the work he and Liz did in setting up Donnie's funeral. And then Dr. Sally Dixon turned and sauntered off. Her presence was required at Serenity Heights.

Just then Carsten remembered an item he needed to give her.

"Wait, Dr. Dixon. Dr. Dixon I have something for you," Carsten called out.

As she returned, Carsten pulled Donnie's journal out from between the driver and passenger seats. Carsten knew from many hazy conversations that Donnie had been keeping a journal. He had even showed it to Carsten one night as they were talking about the meaning of life.

"Maybe this memoir will help explain my existence here on the planet," he had told Carsten. "Who knows? Maybe I could get it published. It could be a best-seller! I'd be famous again! I'd go on a book tour and do wild interviews!"

Whether or not the journal had that kind of value, Carsten had the good sense to grab it from Donnie's desk after they hauled his cadaver away. Carsten figured that even if Donnie's life had been a public mess, prying eyes had no business snooping into Donnie's deepest and darkest private thoughts.

But Carsten had no compunction about giving the book to Dr. Dixon.

Carsten passed the journal to Dr. Dixon through the driver window. She looked at it carefully, then said: "Thank you, Carsten. I had instructed Donald to keep a journal. I knew he was working on it and I wondered what would happen to this document. I'm glad to have it. Perhaps it will serve as a Rosetta Stone to decipher how the events in Donnie's life affected him. But then again, I doubt it."

"I did not read anything in it," Carsten blurted out needlessly. "It would not have been right. But I thought that as his doctor, you might have some use for it."

"I know you did not open Donald's journal," said Dr. Dixon. "You are a good man for that. You are too honest to so much as glanced at it. But I do indeed have use for this. It may help me in my understanding of other patients who have Donald's self-destructive tendencies. In any case, thank you again."

Carsten thought about everything Dr. Dixon had told him about Donnie just then. He sat in the van for a moment and mused. He took a deep breath and then he looked at Liz, gripped the steering wheel with his left hand and said: "I need some appropriate music."

Carsten slid Jethro Tull's "Aqualung" into the cassette tape deck on the dashboard. He turned the volume up to 10. This was no time to play an opera. Donnie would have wanted an old classic, one that he once told Carsten he could still tolerate, even enjoy for all of its pretentious seventies flourishes.

"*Duh, dun, dadda da dun,*" thudded Martin Barre's guitar.

"How old is this van?" Liz shouted over the Ian Anderson's sneering vocals. "I mean, you have a cassette player in the dash. How long ago did those disappear?"

"Liz, honey," he said. Did he just call her "honey?" Uh oh. He blushed and cleared his throat.

"I mean Liz," he said, "this vehicle has been with me since high school, class of '81. The odometer broke long ago so I don't even know how many miles I've traveled in it. But it continues to serve me well as long as I commit to occasional fixes. Also, I have a massive cassette tape collection. Why let these classics go to waste by buying the same albums or tapes on CD?"

"Have you ever heard of streaming services?" Liz asked innocently.

Carsten, slightly offended, said: "These are classic tapes. These are fine."

Meanwhile, a clown showed up to lead the procession to the cemetery. He poked his head through the van's open window on Liz's side.

"Hi, I'm Biscuit the Clown," the buffoon said. "Are you the one who asked me to walk ahead of the procession?"

"Um, yes," Liz said. "Did you bring a clown car?"

"Well, no, and I'm sorry about that," the jester said. "It's locked in the Shriners' garage and I don't have a key. I couldn't find any other clowns who were willing to join me anyway. Uh, Mr. Derringer was not exactly popular with us clowns. He often made fun of us merrymakers on his show. Child molesters in creepy make-up, he called us. But everybody should have their last wishes honored, so I agreed to be here."

"Thanks for coming anyway," Liz said. "We're about to go to the cemetery."

"That's fine," Biscuit said. "It's only a few blocks away so we won't be blocking traffic as we travel at a walking pace."

Liz thought the idea of blocking traffic in Deerhead was funny. Generally speaking, traffic consisted of elderly women traveling in their cars at walking speed to the post office or grocery store. If the procession blocked their path they could wait, Liz thought. What else have they got to do anyway?

Biscuit walked to the head of the procession and waved Buzz and the hearse ahead. Carsten and Liz followed with Cindy from Burbank bringing up the rear. It was boiling outside and Carsten's van did not have air conditioning. The sun was beating down on the black asphalt pavement, making the soles of Biscuit's floppy clown shoes hot and he fairly hopped all the way to the cemetery like a man walking across smoldering embers.

They arrived at the little cemetery, named for St. Adalbert, patron saint of Poland, by Polish Catholic parishioners who had migrated to Deerhead from the Chicago area. Morton had received permission for the burial there from the empathetic cemetery administrator, Louis

Stratten. Stratten hoped Donnie's remains would rest comfortably among Deerhead's elite and maybe even attract distraught visitors.

Donnie was a Deerhead celebrity after all.

The tree-lined lane offered a cathedral-like covering and provided modest shelter from the oppressive heat. The cortege moved slowly through the cemetery, past the graves of Deerhead's town fathers and mothers and other local dignitaries.

Donnie, whose religious beliefs were certainly strained if they existed at all, would have appreciated the irony of being buried in a Catholic cemetery along with Deerhead's honored dead.

Donnie also would have enjoyed the notion that upon finally settling down and coming to terms with the charms of small-town living he would give up the ghost. He had decided to be content, to accept his life in northern Minnesota.

Then death by peanut butter.

C'est la vie!

In a few short minutes, they reached the gravesite. The funeral party climbed out of their respective vehicles to form a semi-circle around the six-feet-deep hole. Donnie would take his final rest beneath a dying maple tree. Morton took his place at the edge of the grave and muttered the 23rd Psalm, "The Lord is my shepherd, I shall not want …" as they lowered the casket. Cindy was howling, "No, no, don't go, Donnie! I'm your biggest fan!"

Buzzy pulled away, honking. He had to get back to his trash pickups. Biscuit honked his big red clown nose and then he quietly dropped a fake flower from his red hat onto the descending casket. He flopped away saying, "It's not gonna be much fun getting back to my car in these duds. Man, the street is hot on my soles!"

Liz gripped Carsten's hand as he stared at the ground. He was having a hard time maintaining his phlegmatic composure but as always, he managed to keep his cool demeanor.

Cindy, who had purchased a bouquet of roses at a gas station on her way to the funeral, threw the flowers onto the casket as it sank to its final destination deep beneath the rich Minnesota Lester Loam.

Each of the mourners threw a fist-full of dirt into the hole and walked away, Cindy still crying while Carsten and Liz held hands on the way to Carsten's van. Morton simply disappeared without so much as a kind word.

It was all over.

Rockin' Donnie Derringer was rocking no more. He was now enjoying his eternal rest even if rest had never been one of his favorite activities. Donnie had at last freed himself from every jam he'd ever worked himself into, so there was that.

Carsten and Liz walked toward the van and Carsten suddenly stopped. He slipped his hand out of Liz's, turned, and walked back to the grave alone for one last farewell.

Carsten looked at the marble grave marker and saw the words he had composed himself in Donnie's honor.

The wide marble stone said simply: "Derringer. What the hell was that all about?"

Carsten let a tear roll down his cheek and he smiled.

THE END

About the Author

Bill Zaferos has been a newspaper political reporter, a political consultant and public relations and advertising executive who became a first-time author in his sixties with the publication of his first book, the rollicking ***Poison Pen***. He grew up an asthmatic kid who watched a lot of '60s and '70s television shows, and he especially loved the original *Star Trek, The Outer Limits, The Twilight Zone,* and the Watergate hearings. He wrote ***Poison Pen***, during a manic high and left it on the shelf for 15 years before it was published.

Zaferos, a Milwaukee native who lives in Dunedin, Florida, has since come to terms with his mental illness, and he wrote *Serenity Heights* in his well-medicated "right mind." The result is the darkly humorous tale of burnt-out disc jockey "Rockin'" Donnie Derringer and his misadventures as he tries to impress his long-lost sweetheart with crazy and sometimes inane antics that eventually land him in Serenity Heights, the local mental hospital where he lives in Deerhead, Minnesota.

Zaferos is a diehard baseball fan with split loyalties to the Milwaukee Brewers and Boston Red Sox. He is also a music devotee, especially to the music of The Who and Bruce Springsteen, and his musical snobbery is reflected in "Rockin'" Donnie's personality.

He is a journalism and political science graduate of the University of Wisconsin-Madison and received his M.A. at Marquette University.

Bill's email, should you wish to send a comment:
billzaferos58@gmail.com

CPSIA information can be obtained
at www.ICGtesting.com
Printed in the USA
LVHW082308160622
721508LV00012B/665

9 781595 988911